The Gold Coast

By Kim Stanley Robinson from Tom Doherty Associates

The Blind Geometer
Escape from Kathmandu
Future Primitive: The New Ecotopias (Editor)
The Gold Coast
Green Mars
Icehenge
The Memory of Whiteness
Pacific Edge
The Planet on the Table
Remaking History
A Short, Sharp Shock
The Wild Shore

The Gold Coast

KIM STANLEY ROBINSON

A TOM DOHERTY ASSOCIATES BOOK
NEW YORK

THE GOLD COAST

Copyright © 1988 by Kim Stanley Robinson

This book was originally published as a Tor hardcover in February 1988.

This book is printed on acid-free paper.

Cover art by Tony Roberts

An Orb Edition
Published by Tom Doherty Associates, Inc.
175 Fifth Avenue
New York, N.Y. 10010

Library of Congress Cataloging-in-Publication Data

Robinson, Kim Stanley.
    The Gold Coast / Kim Stanley Robinson.
        p.   cm. — (Three Californias)
    "A Tom Doherty Associates book."
    ISBN 0-312-89037-0 (pbk.)
    1. Orange County (Calif.)—Fiction.   I. Title.   II. Series:
Robinson, Kim Stanley. Three Californias.
PS3568.O2893G65   1995]
813'.54—dc20   95-4272
                                                                                CIP

First Orb edition: June 1995

Printed in the United States of America

0 9 8 7 6 5 4 3

The Gold Coast

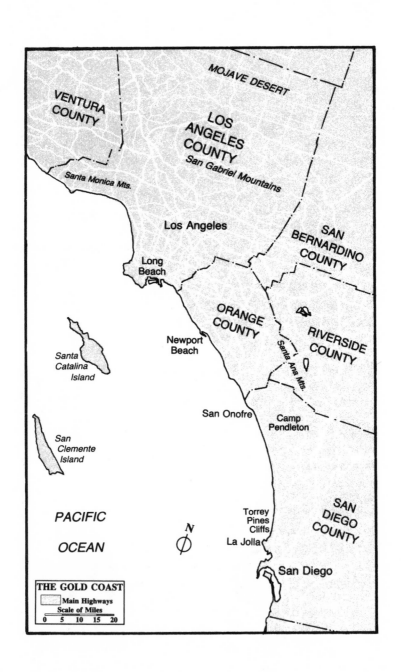

PACIFIC

OCEAN

MOJAVE DESERT

VENTURA
COUNTY

LOS
ANGELES
COUNTY

San Gabriel Mountains

Santa Monica Mts.

Los Angeles

Long
Beach

SAN
BERNARDINO
COUNTY

ORANGE
COUNTY

RIVERSIDE
COUNTY

Santa Ana Mts.

Santa
Catalina
Island

Newport
Beach

San Onofre

Camp
Pendleton

San
Clemente
Island

Torrey
Pines
Cliffs

La Jolla

SAN
DIEGO
COUNTY

N

San Diego

THE GOLD COAST
Main Highways
Scale of Miles
0   5   10   15   20

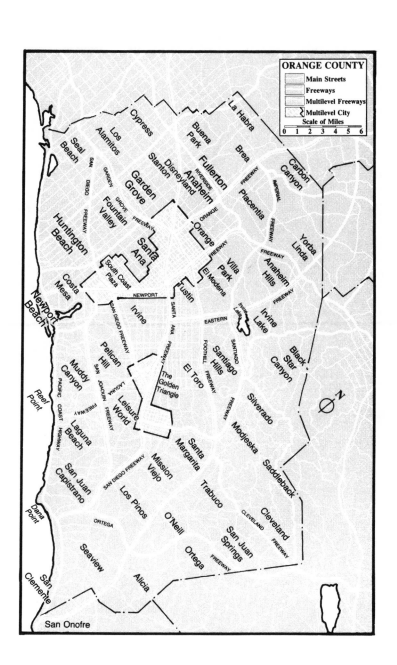

ORANGE COUNTY

- Main Streets
- Freeways
- Multilevel Freeways
- Multilevel City

Scale of Miles
0 1 2 3 4 5 6

1

Beep beep!

Honk honk.

Jim McPherson sticks his head out the window of his car, shouts at a Minihonda whose program has just automatically slotted it onto the onramp ahead of him. "You cut me off!" The man in the Minihonda stares back at him, looking puzzled. Jim's ancient Volvo swerves sharply up the curving track and suddenly Jim's hanging halfway out the window and teetering, face inches from the concrete of the freeway. Abe Bernard grabs his belt and pulls him back in, whew!

Night in Orange County, here, and the four friends are cruising in autopia. Stars of their high school state championship wrestling team, ten years past that glory, they roll over the seats of the Volvo and try to pin Tashi Nakamura, to keep him away from the eye-dropper of Sandy Chapman's latest concoction. Tash was their heavyweight and the only one still in good shape, and they can't do it; Tash surges up through their arms and seizes the eyedropper, all the while singing along with one of Jim's old CDs: "*Some*body give me a *cheese*burger!" The onramp bends up, curves more sharply, the contacts squeak over the power-and-guidance electromagnetic track in the center of the lane, they're all thrown into a heap on the backseat. "Uh-oh, I think I dropped the dropper." "Say, we're on the freeway now, aren't we? Shouldn't someone be watching?"

Instantly Abe squirms into the driver's seat. He has a look around. Everything's on track. Cars, following their programs north, hum over the eight brassy bands marking the center of

1

each lane. River of red taillights ahead, white headlights behind, some cars rolling over the S-curved lane-change tracks, left to right, right to left, their yellow turnsignal indicators blinking the rhythm of the great plunge forward, click click click, click click click. All's well on the Newport Freeway tonight. "Find that eyedropper?" says Abe, a certain edge in his voice.

"Yeah, here."

The northbound lanes swoop up as they cross the great sprawl of the intersection with the San Diego, Del Mar, Costa Mesa, and San Joaquin freeways. Twenty-four monster concrete ribbons pretzel together in a Gordian knot three hundred feet high and a mile in diameter—a monument to autopia—and they go right through the middle of it, like bugs through the heart of a giant. Then Jim's old buzzbox hums up a grade and suddenly it's like they're in a landing pattern for John Wayne International Airport over to their right, because the northbound Newport is on the highest of the stacked freeway levels, and they are a hundred feet above mother Earth. Nighttime OC, for miles in every direction. Imagine.

The great gridwork of light.
Tungsten, neon, sodium, mercury, halogen, xenon.
At groundlevel, square grids of orange sodium streetlights.
All kinds of things burn.
Mercury vapor lamps: blue crystals over the freeways, the
    condos, the parking lots.
Eyezapping xenon, glaring on the malls, the stadium,
    Disneyland.
Great halogen lighthouse beams from the airport, snapping
    around the night sky.
An ambulance light, pulsing red below.
Ceaseless succession, redgreenyellow, redgreenyellow.
Headlights and taillights, red and white blood cells, pushed
    through a leukemic body of light.
There's a brake light in your brain.
A billion lights. (Ten million people.) How many kilowatts
    per hour?
Grid laid over grid, from the mountains to the sea. A
    billion lights.
Ah yes: Orange County.

Jim blinks a big wash of Sandy's latest out of his eye, watches patterns pulse. All at once, in a satori illumination, he can see the pattern all the other patterns make: the layers of OC's lighting, decade on decade, generation on generation. In fact certain grids are lifting off and pivoting ninety degrees, to match the metapattern of the perceived whole. "I'd call this one Pattern Perception."

"Okay," Sandy says. "I can see that."

"You could take aspirin and see that from up here," Abe objects.

"That's true. I can see that too."

"Ought to call it Agreeability," says Tashi.

"That's true. I can see that."

"We're at the center of the world," Jim announces. Abe and Tashi start looking around like they missed the marker—should be a plaque or something, right? "Orange County is the end of history, its purest product. Civilization kept moving west for thousands of years, in a sunset tropism, until they came to the edge here on the Pacific and they couldn't go any farther. And so they stopped here and *did it*. And by that time they were in the great late surge of corporate capitalism, so that everything here is purely organized, to buy and sell, buy and sell, every little piece of us."

"Fucking Marxist Commie."

"They must have liked lights."

Jim shakes them off, waxes nostalgic. Mentioning history reminds him of the night's mission. "It didn't used to be this way!"

"You're kidding," says Tashi. He and Abe share grins: Jim can be funnier than the video.

"No, I'm not kidding. This whole basin was covered with orange groves, over two hundred square miles of them. There were more oranges then than there are lights now."

"Hard To Believe," his friends chorus together.

"But true! OC was one big orchard." Jim sighs.

Abe and Tash and Sandy eye each other. "That's a lot of trees," Abe says solemnly, and Tash stifles a laugh. Sandy doesn't bother; he goes into the famous Chapman laughing fit: "*Ah,* hahahahahaha— *Ah,* hahahahahaha."

"Say, don't you want to get off here?" Tash asks.

"Oh yeah!" Jim cries.

Abe ticks over the lane-change switch and they swerve into the right lane, then spiral down the offramp two levels to Chapman Avenue, eastbound. Sandy's street. Only two levels here, and eastbound is the upper. In El Modena even that ends and they're back on ground level, in two-way traffic. "What now, Professor?"

"Park in the mall," Jim says.

Abe parks them. Jim consults his map for the last time. He is tense with excitement; this is a new idea, this mission, a sort of personal archaeology. Years of reading his local history books have given him an uncontrollable urge to recover something—to see, to touch, to *fondle* some relic of the past. And tonight's the night.

They are parked in front of the El Torito restaurant at the end of the Hewes Mall. "This El Terriblo incorporates the oldest building in the area," Jim explains. "It was a Quaker church, built in 1887. They put a big bell in the tower, but it was too heavy and during the next Santa Ana wind the whole building fell over. So they built it again. Anyway, you can't tell now, the restaurant is built over it and they use the old room as a casino. But it gives me a coordinate point, see, on the old maps. And exactly a hundred and forty yards west of here, on the other side of the street, is the site of El Modena Elementary School, built in 1905."

"I missed that," says Tash.

"It's gone now. Razed in the 1960s. But my mom's great-uncle went there as a child, and he told me about it. And I looked it all up. There were two wooden buildings with a dirt yard in between. When they demolished the buildings they filled the cellars below with the debris, then covered it all in concrete. I've got the location of those buildings pegged exactly, and the west one is directly under the Fluffy Donuts Video Palace and its parking lot."

"You mean," says Abe, "we can just bust through the parking lot surface there—"

"Yeah, that's why I wanted you to bring some of your tools—"

"Bust through the concrete surface there, and dig through three or four feet of fill, and get down to the—get down to the *debris* of El Modena Elementary School, 1905 to 1960 A. D.?"

"That's right!"

"Well, shoot," Abe says. "What're we *waiting* for?"

"*Ahhh*, hahahahahahahaha . . ."

Out of the car, grab up packs of equipment, walk down Chapman. Faces stare from passing cars at the sight of people walking. Jim is getting excited. "There was a foundation stone, too, with the date carved on it. If we could find that . . ."

At Fluffy's people dressed in the bright spectrum-bend primaries fashionable this year are downing incandescent green and purple and yellow donuts, then setting out into the holo reality of what appears to be African savanna. The four friends skirt the building and enter a small dark parking lot, bounded by Fluffy's, a supermarket wall on one side, a movie complex wall on the other, and an apartment complex wall at the back. The glow of OC, reflected off low clouds, gives them all the light they need. Jim points out the chalkmarks he made during his reconnaissance trip, there on oil-splotched old concrete just behind the wall of Fluffy's. "Should be right under here."

Abe and Tash take off the backpacks and get out Abe's freeway rescue tools. Abe shakes his head at the sight of them. "I really shouldn't have taken these, we always have spares but you never know. . . ." He picks up an oscilloscopic saw, Tash a needlejack, and they crack the surface and chop a hole fairly quickly. It's noisy work, but the ambient white noise of the city covers most of the sound. They put on work gloves and start pulling up broken blocks of concrete. The blocks are only about four inches thick, so there isn't much problem. Stuck to the undersides of the pieces are inch-thick crusts of old asphalt. "They just poured it right over the old surface," Jim says. "Great stratification at this site."

Soon there's a square hole about four feet on a side, there in the parking lot. "They're going to think someone was trying to break in and steal the secret donut formulas," says Tash. He and Sandy sing the Fluffy advertisement in a soft falsetto:

All sugar lovers in the know
Love what we leave in that round hole. . . .

"Well, Jim?" Tash inquires. "I don't see any El Modena Elementary School. Looks like dirt to me."

"Of course. That's the fill. We've got to clear it out."

Sandy hands Jim a short-handled aluminum shovel. "Your turn."

So Jim goes to work.

He is not strong; he was the flyweight on their wrestling team, in the 123-pound class despite medium height, and he relied more on speed than brute force, even when Coach "Mad Dog" Beagle had them lifting weights four hours every day.

Nor is he skillful; every stab and scoop of the shovel yields only a handful of dirt. Disgusted with these results, he puts one foot forward, takes the shovel in both hands, raises it far overhead, brings it down in a vicious strike—only to be jerked to a halt by Tashi's big hand grabbing the stock in midair. "Goddamn, Jim, you were just about to amputate your own foot! Watch what you're doing, will you?"

"*Ahh*, hahahahahahaha . . ."

But he is enthusiastic. And eventually the hole is about two feet deep, and Jim is having serious trouble keeping dirt from his side walls from sliding down to the bottom of the hole. Abe takes over and makes better progress. An hour or so after the start of the operation, he drives the shovel down and there is a wooden *thunk*. "Oh ho! Yo ho ho, in fact! Buried treasure."

Abe clears dirt away from a big beam of wood. It's solid hardwood, dry and unrotted. Next to it they find a dressed stone block, one side beveled and fluted.

"All right!" Jim exclaims. "This is it! This is the kind of foundation stone that's supposed to have the date on it."

Abe scrapes the stone's side clear of dirt. No date. "Might be on the other side. . . ."

"Gee, Abe," says Tash, nudging Sandy with an elbow. "How much do you think that stone weighs?"

Abe gives it a kick. "I don't know. Maybe a ton."

"Ah, come on!" says Jim.

"Yeah, okay . . . maybe only seven, eight hundred pounds."

"*Ah*, hahahahahahaha."

"How about a piece of this beam for a souvenir," Abe suggests to Jim. "Just a starter, of course." He takes the oscilloscopic saw and neatly slices off a triangular section that looks like a wooden prism, or an antique ruler. He hands it up to Jim. "Don't touch the black side for a minute or two."

Jim regards it dubiously. So this is the past. . . .

"Whoops!" says Sandy, who has ESP in these matters. He looks around the corner and out to the street. "Police." He has an escape route already planned, and without a pause he is gone down an alley between the supermarket and the ap wall, into the applex. Sandy can't afford even casual conversations with the police, much less an arrest for violating a parking lot surface.

The others snatch up Abe's tools and follow Sandy, just as a cosmic white light xenon beam snaps into existence and torches the parking lot with its glare. Amped-up voices of authority command them to stop, but they're already into the warren of the applex, as safe as roaches under the refrigerator. Except this time the police are in after them, can't let these hoodlums be tearing up the parking lots of OC, and it's chase time, the four friends dodging in irregular dispersal from the closetlike courtyards to second- and third-story walkways, dumpster nooks, doorway niches . . . The applex is typical L-5 architecture, dominant form of the twenty-first century, but it's smaller than most OC applex mazes, and there just aren't as many good spots to scurry into. Crossing one twelve-by-twelve courtyard Jim stumbles over a kid's robot and drops his archaeological find, it clatters away and he's hopping around trying to locate it when Sandy runs into him and drags him off into a nearby elevator nook. Just in time, because a policeman wearing a helmet with an IRHUD happens by and well, who knows but what he can see the heat of their footprints right there on the ground!

Maybe so. He's paused in the courtyard. Sandy and Jim, praying that their shoe soles have been thick enough, crouch in the dark elevator doorway and watch the policeman's headlamps swing around the minicourtyard.

For a moment the beam of light illuminates the fragment of wood, there under a dead bush.

"Now, that's a piece of wood," Sandy whispers in Jim's ear. "And that"—gesturing after the departing policeman—"is a night in jail. You have to weigh your priorities, Jim. You've got to *think* before you act. . . ."

They recover the piece of wood and sneak off in the other direction. By this time Jim is hopelessly disoriented, but part of Sandy's ESP is a perfect internal compass, and he leads them east,

then back down through the applex's laundry/recreation/adminis-
tration building, with its wall of five hundred mailboxes, and out
to Chapman Avenue again.

The copcar is still parked in front of Fluffy's. Ah ha, there's
Abe and Tash, up ahead of them. After them and across the street
to Jim's car. "What happened to you guys?" Tash asks.

"I dropped the piece of wood," Jim says. "Had some trouble
finding it."

"I hope you were successful," Abe chides him, "or we're
sending you back for it!"

"No, here it is! See?"

His friends laugh loud and long. All's well that ends well.
They jump in the car, click on the motor, slide back onto the track
and roll out onto Chapman. Abe says, "Let's get this precious
fragment to the museum and track down to Sandy's to see how
the party's going."

"*Ah*, hahaha. No party tonight, boys."

"That's what you think."

2

The next morning Dennis McPherson, Jim's father, takes United's
commuter flight from LAX to National Airport in Washington,
D.C. He wakes as the Boeing 7X7 drops back into the atmosphere,
shuffles the papers on his lap back into his briefcase. They haven't
helped him. Of course he's napped for most of the short flight,
but even if he had been reading them they wouldn't have helped.
He's here, first, to meet with Air Force Colonel T. D. Eaton, to
confer on the progress of the Ball Lightning program, one of the
big contracts currently in development at McPherson's company,
Laguna Space Research. It's not McPherson's program, however,
and he doesn't know how to explain the delays that have plagued

it. His old friend Dan Houston should be fielding this one, but
Houston is down at White Sands, trying to get a successful trial
out of Ball Lightning's acquisition/pointing/tracking satellite. And
McPherson has other errands to run in Washington, so he's been
stuck with this one too. Great.

The other purpose for this visit is a conference with Major
Tom Feldkirk, from the Air Force's Electronic Systems Division.
Feldkirk requested the conference without giving a reason for it,
which is worrying. LSR has several contracts with the Electronic
Systems Division, and the problem to be discussed could be in
one of a number of areas.

Because the truth of the matter is, LSR is struggling these
days. Too many proposals have been lost, and too many of the
contracts won have gone into delays and overruns. The Air Force
is coming down on such problems harder than ever, and whatever
Feldkirk wants to discuss, it isn't likely to be good.

The plane floats down the Potomac River basin and lands.
Time to get to his hotel.

He goes onto automatic pilot. So many repetitions. . . . He's
become chief errand boy at LSR for this kind of thing, sent to
Washington about twenty times a year to put out one fire after
another. (Off the plane, into the terminal. He's refined his luggage
to a single flight bag, and goes straight out to the taxi line.) From
all these more-or-less diplomatic assignments you might guess he
was a hail-fellow-well-met kind of guy, someone who could pal
around with the flyboys and drink away their objections. Not so:
Dennis McPherson is a reserved man, with a contained manner
that can make people nervous. (Into a taxi, off to the Crystal City
Hyatt Regency. Traffic bumpertobumper on George Washington
Parkway lower level.) He can handle his end of dinner talk as well
as the next man; he just isn't into a bonhomie that in this context
has to be transparent and false always, and therefore offputting.
This is big business, after all, the biggest business: defense. Why
even pretend that your favorite buddy is some Air Force jock you
have to deal with?

Into the Crystal City Hyatt Regency, a big irregular space
filled with mirrors, escalators, cascading fountains of water and
light, walls of glossy greenery, hanging elevators, overhanging
balconies. He threads the maze without a thought and checks in,

goes up to his room. Into the chrome-and-white-tile bathroom, to stare into the darkened mirror, perhaps clean up a bit before the day's work.

Pink freckled skin. He needs a shave. Strawberry-blond hair, as Lucy always calls it, receding from a round Irish forehead. Cold blue eyes and deep vertical creases between his eyebrows; he's a stocky stubborn figure, one of those smoldering Irish who don't say much, and now he looks harried, tired, annoyed. It's going to be a tough day.

Strange how it's come to this. McPherson began as an engineer—damn it, he *is* an engineer. He has a degree in aerospace engineering from Cal Tech, and even though he's hopelessly off the edge these days, he can still follow it when his design people describe things. And McPherson can see the larger patterns, where engineering touches both invention and administration. But management itself? . . . Other program managers got there on leadership, they know how to coax or bully extra results out of their teams. McPherson's boss Stewart Lemon is a perfect example of this type, the Dynamic Leader of the business schools. McPherson leaves that kind of Napoleonic style to others, and in fact he despises it in Lemon. For his part, he just figures out what has to be done, and lays it out. Low-keyed approach. (Shower, shave.) No, it's not leadership that got him out of engineering and into administration.

How did it happen, then? He's never been too sure. (Into the day's clothes: colorless conservative dress, appropriate for Pentagon dealings.) He can explain technical matters to people who don't know enough to fully understand them. Administrators in LSR's parent company, Pentagon people, congressional aides . . . people who need to have a clear idea of technical problems before they can make their own decisions. McPherson can do that. He's not sure why, but it happens. He tries to explain, and they usually get it. Strange. His wife Lucy would laugh, perhaps angrily; she considers him awful at "communicating." But that's what's gotten him where he is, and really it's not funny; it means that he has somehow strayed out of the line of work where he might have enjoyed himself, been comfortable.

Half an hour to kill. He turns on the video wall's news program. The war in Arabia is heating up; Bahrain is embroiled now, with U.S. Marines fighting the insurgents, which shows it's serious. They're finding the Hewlett-Packard IRHUD helmets are giving them a big advantage in night fighting, but the insurgents have some old Norwegian Kongsberg Vaapenfabrikk Penguin missiles that are wreaking havoc on the U.S. fleet offshore, all the aluminum in those old destroyers melting like plastic. And some Hughes Mavericks left over from the war in Thailand, still doing yeoman service in the desert hills . . . seems like most of the forty odd wars currently being fought are employing obsolete equipment, and the results, for democratic forces, are a real mess.

McPherson wanders past the bold rainbow of the immense bedspread to the window of his room. There before him stands the Hughes Tower, a hotel/restaurant/office complex, one of Crystal City's newest. Crystal City is getting bigger every year, the defense industry towers looking like an architectural rendering of their business, steel and glass ICBMs densepacked and pointed at the sky. All the money that leaves the Pentagon is funneled through these towers, through the crystal city of weapons procurement.

It's time to get over to the Pentagon. McPherson feels himself coming out of automatic pilot. Tuesday morning, Crystal City, USA: time to go offtrack, onto manual, into action.

Short taxi ride to the Pentagon. Into the security complex, out with his lapel badge. A lieutenant picks him up and they drive down the endless giant white corridors in a cart, dodging all the motor and foot traffic. They might as well be on a street. McPherson always gets a kick out of this blatant attempt to impress people. And it works, too, sure. The Pentagon may be old, but it's still immense. Seems to him that the latest reorganization has taken notice of current fashion; service and division markers are painted in bright spectrum-bend colors that pulsate under the xenon bulbs, against all the white walls.

He meets Colonel Eaton at the Air Force's SD Battle Management Division office, and Eaton takes him into one of the center courtyard commissaries. They talk over a lunch of croissants and salad. McPherson outlines some of the problems that Houston's team is having with the boost-phase interceptor.

Ball Lightning: the job is to detect and track as many as ten thousand Soviet ICBMs, launched simultaneously; then aim ground-based free-electron laser beams, bounce them off mirrors in space, and destroy the ICBMs while they're still in boost phase. It's a tough job, and McPherson is glad it isn't exactly his. But now he has to take Colonel Eaton's grilling about it, which is informed and relentless. The test results in your proposal, Eaton says, indicated that you could solve the problems you're telling me about. That's why you have the contract. Get it together, and soon. Or it's a Big Hacksaw for you.

McPherson cringes at the reference to the Hacksaw disaster, a gun program axed by the DOD for incompetence; it was the beginning of the end for Danforth Aerospace, which is now just a name in the corporate history books. That kind of thing could still happen; a big program could go bad so disastrously that it got the axe and brought its whole company down. . . .

So. Great lunch. McPherson tries to remember what he ate as he makes notes of the conversation, in the LSR offices on the top floor they rent in the Aerojet Tower. Apparently it didn't agree with him. Salad? No matter. He spends the rest of the afternoon on the phone to OC, and then to White Sands, to tell Dan Houston that the heat is on. Dan knows that already, and in an anxious, almost frightened voice, he asks for help. McPherson agrees to do what he can. "But it's not my program, Dan. Lemon may not give me the time to do anything. Besides, I'm not sure what I can do."

That evening Major Tom Feldkirk comes by and picks him up, and they track over the river into Georgetown.

Feldkirk is around forty-five, ex-flyer, wears his black hair longer than they'd like it back on base, in a swoop over his forehead and well down his back. He's dressed casually, sport shirt, slacks, loafers. McPherson has dealt with him twice before, likes him all right. They park in an underground lot, walk up onto a brick sidewalk and into the usual Georgetown crowd. They could be two lawyers, two congressmen, two of any part of Washington's success structure. They discuss Georgetown, the fashionable bars, the crowds. McPherson is familiar with the area by this time, and can mention favorite restaurants and the like.

"Have you been to Buddha In The Refrigerator?" Feldkirk asks.

McPherson laughs. "No."

"Let's try it, then. It's not nearly so bad as it sounds."

He leads them down M Street, then up one of the little sidestreets, where it looks like it could be 1880, if you ignored the tracks out on the cobblestone street. Or thought of them as streetcar tracks. McPherson has a brief vision of monorailed antique street cars, then reins in his thoughts. This is business, here. . . .

Inside, the restaurant looks Indian. Cloth prints of Buddha and various Hindu deities hang on the walls: six-armed, elephant-headed, outlandish stuff. McPherson's a bit worried, he prefers not to eat food he doesn't recognize, but then the menu turns out to have twenty pages, and you can order anything you can think of, but with every meal you'll get some fine Buddhist vegetables. That's okay. He orders salmon fillet. Feldkirk orders some kind of Asian soup. He was stationed on Guam for several years, and developed a taste for the food. They discuss the Pacific situation for a bit. "The Soviets have got the choke points," says Feldkirk, "but now we're stationed outside them all, so it doesn't really matter."

"Leaves Japan and Korea kind of hanging."

"True. But with the Japanese arming themselves so well, they can take the front line of their own defense. We can cover them from behind. It's not a bad situation."

"And Korea?"

"Well! . . ."

Their meals are served, and as they eat they discuss the Redskins and the Rams, then technical aspects of the war in Burma. McPherson begins to enjoy himself a bit. He likes this man, he can get along with him, he's sort of a kindred spirit. Feldkirk talks ruefully about his two sons, both now at Annapolis. "I took them sailing a lot when we were on Guam, but I never thought it would lead to this." McPherson laughs at his expression. Still, Annapolis is awfully hard to get into. "And your kids?" Feldkirk asks.

"Just one. He's still hanging out in Orange County, teaching night classes and working in a real estate office part-time." McPherson shakes his head. "He's a strange one. A brain without a program." And Feldkirk laughs.

Then the meals are done, they're lingering over drinks and cheesecake, watching Washington's finest chattering around them. Feldkirk leans back in his chair. "You're probably wondering what I've got in mind for tonight."

McPherson lifts his eyebrows: here it comes. "Sure," he says with a smile.

"Well, we have an idea for a system that I want to discuss with you. You see, the RX-16 is almost operational now."

"Is it?" The RX-16 is Northrop's RPV, a remotely piloted vehicle, which in certain quarters of the Electronic Systems Division is all the rage now: a robot jet craft with classified speeds, perhaps up to Mach 7, and capable of turns and rolls that would kill a pilot. Made of kevlar and other lightweight stealth materials, it has the radar signature of a bee. It's one of Northrop's most successful recent contracts, and McPherson was in fact aware it is about to go into production, but he didn't want to say so.

"Yeah. Great plane." Feldkirk looks wistful. "I bet it would be a real kick to fly one. But the time for manned fighter planes has passed, it looks like. Anyway, we've got some ideas for the use of this RX-16 in the European theater."

Use against the threat of the Warsaw Pact invasion, then, the Big Contingency that has stimulated so much of the conventional weapons upgrade spiral between the superpowers. McPherson nods. "Yeah?"

"Well, here's what we're thinking. The RX is ready, and for some time to come we think it'll be a good deal faster and more maneuverable than anything that the Soviets will have. Now if the tanks ever roll, we'd like to be able to use the RXs against them, because if we can do that, it might turn into a shooting gallery situation. We have in mind flying the RXs straight down at full speed from sixty thousand feet to terrain-following level, having them make covert runs down there, finding a dozen tanks and clotheslining the Harris Stalker Nine missiles to them, then popping out and up. And turning around for other runs, until the missiles and fuel run out."

"Stuka pilots would recognize the flight pattern," McPherson remarks, thinking about it. "So you need a navigation system for the terrain following." Tree-top contouring at a mile a second or more. . . .

"That's right."

"And covert, you say." Which means they don't want the plane sending out investigating signals that can be picked up by enemy detection systems. This contradicts the desire for tight navigation and makes things tough.

"That's right." The standard device for locating targets, Feldkirk goes on, a YAG laser operating at the 1.06 micron wavelength, won't do anymore. The new window for targeting lasers is from about eight to fourteen microns, which fits between the upper and lower ends of the Soviets' latest radar systems. "This means a CO-two laser, probably."

But CO_2 lasers don't penetrate cloud anywhere near as well as those using yttrium/aluminum/garnet. "You want it all-weather?" McPherson asks.

"No, just under the weather, day and night."

So they weren't concerned about fog, for instance. McPherson suddenly imagines the Soviet tanks waiting for fog to start World War Three. . . .

"How much weight?"

"We'd like it under five hundred pounds, if you've got it in a single pod. Maybe seven fifty if you put it in two wing pods. We can work that out later."

McPherson lets out a breath. That's a constraint for you. "And how much power can the plane give the system?"

"Maybe ten KVA. Ten point five, tops."

Another constraint. McPherson thinks about it, putting all the factors together in his mind. The components of such a system exist; it's a matter of putting them together, making them work on this new robot jet.

"Sounds interesting," he says at last. "I think we could make a proposal, given that my boss likes the idea, of course."

Feldkirk is shaking his head; a small smile makes him look boyish. "We aren't going to put out an RFP on this one."

"Ah!"

The meeting suddenly makes sense.

Legally, the Pentagon is obliged to offer all their programs for open bidding by contractors. This means publishing a Request For Proposal in *Commerce Business Daily*, which outlines the specifications for what they want. The problem with the system, of course, is that Soviet intelligence can buy *Commerce Business Daily* and get an excellent idea of the capabilities of the American military. In this case, they would know to close the window in their radar systems. "And," Feldkirk says, "if they know they have to speed up their antiaircraft response, and can do it, then we're no longer in the air. So we've decided to go superblack with this one, and deal with the company we judge would do the job best."

Illegal, of course. Technically. But the Pentagon is also charged with defending the country. Even Congress recognizes that some programs have to be kept secret. In fact, black programs are an acknowledged part of the system, and a few members of the Armed Services Committees hear about them regularly. A superblack program, however . . . that's between the Pentagon and the chosen contractor only.

So, LSR has a contract. Other defense contractors won't complain about it even if they do hear rumors, because they've all got secret programs of their own.

Feldkirk continues justifying the decision to make the program superblack. "We figure we've got other ways to keep the Soviets from rolling, for now. We don't need to make this public, to scare them. So while they're ignorant of it, we've got a safeguard—if the tanks do roll, they're goners. Ducks on the pond, as obsolete as aircraft carriers. Meanwhile, the government can get serious about the negotiations to get battlefield nukes off the front line. That should help reconcile the Soviets to our space installations, and it eases the use-'em-or-lose-'em situation with the artillery nukes in Turkey, Saudi Arabia, Thailand, all the rest. Nobody's ever liked those, but we're still living with them. This way, we might be able to end that risk—we just won't need battlefield nukes anymore to do the job, and that's the bottom line."

McPherson nods. "That would be good all right." He doesn't like to reflect on how fully American strategy is entangled in nuclear weapons; the situation repels him. It just isn't smart defense. "I'll have to consult back at the office, you know."

"Of course."

"But, truthfully, I can't imagine we'll turn it down."

"No."

So Feldkirk raises his glass, and they toast the deal.

And the next day McPherson gives Stewart Lemon a call, first thing.

"Yeah, Mac?"

"It's about my conference with Major Feldkirk at ESD."

"Yeah? What'd he want?"

"We've been offered a superblack."

3

McPherson's boss, Stewart Lemon, stands in his office before his big seaside window, looking out at the Pacific. It's near the end of the day, and the low sun turns Catalina apricot, gilds the sails of the boats as they glide back in to Dana Point and Newport Beach harbors. His office is on the top floor of LSR's tower, on the coastal cliff between Corona del Mar and Laguna, overlooking Reef Point. Lemon often calls his window view the finest in Orange County, and since it includes no land but the distant bulk of Catalina, it may well be true.

Dennis McPherson is on his way up to give him the details of the meeting with Feldkirk, and Lemon, considering the meeting, sighs. Getting one's employees to put their maximum effort into the work is an art form; one has to alter one's methods for every personality under one's command. McPherson has been working for Lemon for a long time, and Lemon has found that the man works best when driven. Make him angry, fill him with resentment, and he flies into his work with a furious energy that is fairly productive, no doubt about it. But how tiresome the relationship has become! The mutual dislike has really become quite real. Lemon watches the contained insolence, the arrogance of this uncultured engineer, with an irritation that barely holds on to its amusement. Really, the man is too much. It's gotten to be almost a pleasure to bully him.

Ramona buzzes to tell him McPherson is there. Lemon begins to pace back and forth before the window, nine steps turn, nine steps turn. In McPherson comes, looking tired.

"So, Mac!" He gestures him to a chair, continues to pace in a leisurely way, staring out the window as much as he can. "You got us a superblack program, eh?"

"I was told to pass along the offer, that's right."

"Fine, fine. Tell me about it."

McPherson describes the system Feldkirk has requested. "Most of the components of the system are fairly straightforward, it'll only be a matter of linking them in a management program and fitting them into a small enough package. But the sensing systems, covert terrain ranger and target detector both—there could be some dangers there. The CO-two laser Feldkirk has suggested is only lab-tested so far. So—"

"But it's a superblack, right? It's only between the Air Force and us."

"That's right. But—"

"Every method has its drawbacks. That doesn't mean we don't go for it. In fact, we can't very well refuse the offer of a superblack—we might never get another one. And the Pentagon knows it's a high-risk program, that's why they've done it this way. And it's always the high-risk projects that bring in the highest profits. What's your schedule looking like, Mac?"

"Well—"

"You're clear enough. I'll assign the Canadair contract to Bailey, and you'll be clear to go at this thing. Listen here, Mac." Time to stick in a needle or two. "Twice in a row now you've been manager of proposals that lost. They were too expensive, too elaborate, and you almost missed the deadline for turning them in, both times. It's important to beat the schedule deadline by a couple of weeks, to show the Air Force we're on top of things. Now here you've got a superblack program, and there isn't a schedule per se. But with something outside normal channels like this, the trick is to get it done fast, while all conditions still obtain. You get me?"

McPherson is staring out the window, not looking at Lemon. The corners of his mouth are tight. Lemon almost smiles. McPherson no doubt still believes his losing proposals were the best made, but the truth is you can't afford to be a perfectionist in this business. Projects have to be cost-effective, and that requires a certain realism. Well, that's Lemon's contribution. That's what's gotten him where he is. And this time he's going to have to ride herd a little more closely than before.

He stops his pacing and points at McPherson, surprising him. "You're in charge of this one because I think the Pentagon people want it that way. But I want this done *quickly*. Do you understand?"

"Yes."

The clamming up does absolutely nothing to hide the anger and contempt in McPherson's eyes; he's as easy to read as a freeway exit sign. TURN OFF HERE, OVER THIS CLIFF. Now he will go back down there and work himself sick to get the program done quickly, to jam it back down Lemon's throat. Fine. It's that kind of work that makes Lemon's division one of the most productive at LSR, despite the myriad technical difficulties they encounter. The job gets done.

"Let me know when you've got a preliminary proposal worked up. You'll fly out and present it to them as soon as it's done."

"The targeting system and the management program may take a while—"

"Fine. I'm not denying there are problems to be solved, there always are, aren't there? I just want them dealt with as soon as possible." A bit of dictatorial irritation: "No more getting bogged down! No more excuses and delays! I'm tired of that kind of thing!"

McPherson leaves with his jaw clamped so hard that he can barely mumble his good-byes. Lemon can't help but laugh, though there is a part of him that is genuinely angry as well. Arrogant bastard. It's funny what it takes to get some men to give it their all.

Next comes Dan Houston, the last conference of Lemon's day. They do this a lot. Dan is a completely different situation from McPherson: more limited technically, but infinitely better with people. He and Lemon have been friends since they both began working for Martin Marietta, years before. The same head-hunter lured them to LSR, bringing Lemon in at the higher position, a distance Lemon has only extended through the years. But

Houston doesn't begrudge it, he isn't envious. Lemon can charm him. In fact, if Lemon were to come down hard on Dan it would only hurt his feelings, make him sullen and slow him down. It's necessary to coddle him a bit, to pull rather than push. And the truth is, Lemon likes the man. Houston admires him, they have a good time together sailing, playing racketball, going out with their allies Dawn and Elsa. They're friends.

So he sits down when Houston comes in, and they look out the window and critique the tacking of the boats clawing back from the south toward Newport. They laugh at some really bad luffs. Then Lemon asks him what the latest is with the Ball Lightning project. Houston starts bitching about it again.

It's one of their three biggest contracts, and inwardly Lemon seethes; they can't afford for it to get bogged down too much. But he nods sympathetically. "No one's solved the dwell time problem," he says, thinking aloud to himself. "The power requirements are just too much. The Air Force can't expect magic."

"The problem is, they thought we had it solved when they gave us the contract."

"I know." Of course he knows. Who better? It was Lemon who okayed the inclusion of those Huntsville test results. Dan can be kind of a fool. . . . "Listen, have you gotten McPherson's input on this?"

"Well, I've asked him for it. He doesn't like it much."

"I know." Lemon shakes his head. "But Dennis is kind of a prima donna." Got to play this carefully, as Dan and McPherson are also friends. "A little bit, anyway. Get him to talk to your design team, and the programmers. See what he can suggest. He'll be busy with a new proposal of his own, but I'll tell him to take time for this. You can't spend the whole of every day working on one project, after all."

"No, that's true. Lot of waiting to be done." Dan sounds satisfied; he'd like the help. And McPherson has a certain flair for the technical problems, no doubt about it.

Not only that, but this way Lemon can begin to tie McPherson into the Ball Lightning program, and all its troubles. Lemon is just annoyed enough with McPherson to enjoy the idea of this move. He'll really have the man under some screws, and who knows, McPherson might just troubleshoot Ball Lightning as well, even if he does dislike the program. Excellent.

They chat a bit longer, discussing in great detail the rigging of a ketch running down to Dana Point. Beautiful yacht. Then Lemon wants to go home. "I'm doing *navarin du mouton* tonight, and it's a slow cooker." Houston dismissed, Lemon's off to his car in the executives' lot. The Mercedes-Benz door slams with a heavy, satisfying *clunk*. He clicks in a CD of Schumann's Rhenish Symphony, lights a cigar of Cuban tobacco lightly laced with a mild dose of MDMA, and tracks south on the coast highway toward Laguna Beach.

It's been a good day, and they've needed one. LSR is a division of Argo AG/Blessman Enterprises, one of the world's corporate giants; Lemon's boss, Donald Hereford, president of LSR, is based in New York because he is also a vice-president at A/BE as well. Fascinating man, but he hasn't been pleased with LSR's record in the past year or two. News of this new superblack should take some heat off concerning the Ball Lightning problems and the recent string of lost bids. And that's good. Lemon shifts over to the fast track, lets the Mercedes out.

He decides to dice two cloves of garlic rather than one into the *navarin du mouton*, and maybe throw in a basil leaf or two. It was a little bland the last time he made it. He hopes Elsa managed to find some good lamb. If she bothered to leave the house at all.

4

Dennis McPherson leaves LSR some time after Lemon and tracks home. Up Muddy Canyon Parkway past Signal Hill, through the Irvine condos to Jeffrey, turn left on Irvine, right on Eveningside, left on Morningside, up to the last house on the left, now a duplex;

the McPhersons own the street half of the house, along with the carport and garage. As he tracks into the driveway and under the carport Dennis sees Jim's shabby little Volvo out on the street. Here for another free meal. Dennis isn't in the mood for any more irritants at the end of this long day, and he sighs.

He enters the house to find Jim and Lucy arguing over something, as usual. "But Mom, the World Bank only lends them money if they grow cash crops that the bank approves of, and so then they don't do subsistence farming and they can't feed themselves, and then the cash crops market disappears, and so they have to buy their food from the World Bank, or beg for it, and they end up owned by the bank!" "Well, I don't know," Lucy says, "don't you think they're just trying to help? It's a generous thing to give." "But Mom, don't you see the principle of the thing?" "Well, I don't know. The bank lends that money with hardly any interest at all—it really is almost like giving, don't you think?" "Of course not!"

Dennis goes back to the bedroom to change clothes. He doesn't even want to have the day's debate clarified. Jim and Lucy argue like that constantly, Lucy from the Christian viewpoint and Jim from the pseudo-socialist, both mixing large matters of philosophy with questions of daily life, and making a mash of everything. Lord. It's just theoretical for the two of them, like debaters going at it to keep in practice; just one more part of their constant talk. But Dennis hates arguments, to him they're no more than verbal fights that can make you furious and upset you for days after. He gets his fill of that kind of thing at work.

They're still at it when Dennis comes back out to read the daily news on the video wall. WAR IN BURMA SPILLS INTO BANGLADESH. "Stop that," he says to them.

They eye each other, Jim amused, Lucy frustrated. "Dennis," she complains, "we're just talking."

"Talk, then. No bickering."

"But we weren't!" Still, Lucy gives up on it and goes to prepare dinner, telling Jim about members of her church, with Jim asking highly informed questions about people he hasn't seen in ten years. Dennis scans the news and turns the wall off; tomorrow the headlines'll say the same thing, artfully altered to appear original. WAR SPILLS INTO (pick country)—

They sit down to dinner, Lucy says grace, they eat. Afterward Jim says, "Dad, um, sorry to mention it, but the old car is tending to shift lanes to the right whether I want it to or not. I've done what I could to check the program, but . . . I didn't find anything."

"The problem won't be in the program."

"Oh. Ah. Well, um . . . could you take a look at it?"

The visit is explained. Irritated, Dennis gets up and goes outside without a word. The thing is, he's over a barrel; the freeways are in fact dangerous, and if he refuses to fix Jim's car and tries to make him learn to do a little work of his own, then next thing he knows he'll get a call from the CHP to tell him the fool's car has failed and he's dead inside, and then Dennis will have to wish that he'd done the damn repair. So he drives the thing into the garage and goes at it, unscrewing the box over the switcher mechanism by the light of a big lamp set next to him on the floor.

Jim follows him into the garage and sits on the floor to watch. Dennis slides back and forth on the floor-sled, putting all the screws in one spot, testing the magnetic function of all the points in the switcher . . . ah. Two are dead, two more barely functional, and commands are being transferred right on through to the right-turn points, which explains the problem. Small moment of satisfaction as he solves the little mystery, which wasn't, after all, so mysterious. Anyone could have found it. Which returns him to his irritation with Jim. There he sits, spaced out in his own thoughts, not learning a thing about the machine he relies on utterly to be able to lead his life. Dennis sighs heavily. As he replaces the points with spares of his own (and they're expensive) he says, "Are you doing anything about getting a full-time job?"

"Yeah, I've been looking."

Sure. Besides, what kind of job is he fit to apply for? Here he's been going to college for years, and so far as Dennis can tell, he isn't qualified to do anything. Clerk work, a little marginal night school teaching . . . can that really be it? Dennis gives a screw a hard twist. What can Jim do? Well . . . he can read books. Yes, he can read books like nobody's business. But Dennis can read a book too, and he didn't go to college for six years to learn how. And meanwhile, here he is out on his back after an eleven-hour day, fixing the kid's car!

Time to make him help. "Look here, take that point and reach down from above and insert it into this slot here,'' pointing up with the screwdriver.

"Sure, Dad." And Jim moves around the motor compartment, blocking the floor lamp's light, and leans down into it, the point between his fingers. "There we go—oops!"

"What'd you do?"

"Dropped it. But I can see where it went—down between the motor and the distributor—just a sec—" And he's leaning down, stretched out over the motor, blocking Dennis's light.

"What're you doing?"

"Just about—uh-oh—"

Jim falls into the motor compartment. His weight sinks the front end of the car abruptly and Dennis, flat on his back underneath it, is almost crushed by the underbody.

"Hey! For God's sake!"

It's a good thing the car has decent shocks—put in by Dennis himself last year—otherwise he would have been pancaked. Very carefully he tries to roll from beneath the car, but the edge of the body hits his ribs and . . . well, he can't scrape under it. "Get your feet back on the ground and take your weight off the car!"

"I, um, I can't. Seem to have my hand—stuck under this thing here."

"What *thing here*."

"I guess it's the distributor. I've got the point, but—"

"If you drop the point, can you get your hand free?"

"Um . . . no. Won't go either way."

Dennis sighs, shifts sideways until he tilts off the floor-sled, it bangs up against the car bottom and he slides down onto the garage floor, smacking the back of his head. A slow, awkward shimmy past the track pickups, which are pressed against the ground, and he's out from under the car.

He stands, rubs the back of his head, looks at the waving legs emerging from under the hood of the car. It looks like the kid just up and dived headfirst into the thing. In fact that's probably pretty close to what he did. Dennis takes a flashlight and directs its beam into the motor compartment; Jim's head is twisted down and sideways against his chest.

"Hi," Jim says.

Dennis points the flashlight at the end of Jim's arm, where it disappears under the distributor. "You say you've let go of the point?"

"Yeah."

Sounds like he's had a clamp put on his throat. Dennis leans in, reaches down to the distributor, pulls the clips away and lifts the distributor cap. "Try now."

Jim gives a sudden jerk up, his hand comes free and his head snaps back up into the hood of the car, knocking it off its cheap metal stand so that the hood comes down with a clang, just missing Dennis's fingers and Jim's neck. "Ow! Oops."

Dennis looks over the frames of his garage glasses at Jim. He reopens the hood. He replaces the distributor cap. "Where did you say that point was?"

"I've got it," Jim says, rubbing his head with one hand. With the other he holds the point out proudly.

Dennis finishes the job himself. As he screws the box back on he gives all the screws a really hard final twist; if Jim ever tries to get them loose (fat chance) he'll know who screwed them in last.

"So how's your work going?" Jim asks brightly, to fill the silence.

"Okay."

Dennis finishes, closes up. "I'm going to have to be in Washington most of next week," he tells his son. "Might be good if you came up an evening or two and had dinner here."

"Okay, I'll do that."

Dennis puts the tools back in the tool chest.

"Well, I'm off now, I guess."

"Say good-bye to your mom, first."

"Oh yeah."

Dennis follows him back in the house, shaking his head a little. Legs waving about in the air . . . kind of like a bug turned on its back.

Inside Jim says his farewells to Lucy.

"How come we haven't seen Sheila lately?" Lucy asks him.

"Oh, I don't know. We haven't been going out that much, these last weeks."

"That's too bad. I like her."

"Me too. We've just both been busy."

"Well, you should call her."

"Yeah, I will."

"And you should give your uncle Tom a call too. Have you done that lately?"

"No, but I will, I promise. Okay, I'm off. Thanks for the help, Dad."

Dennis can see him forgetting the promises to call even as he walks out of the door. "See you. Be careful," he says. Try not to get stuck in your car's motor compartment. As the door slams shut Dennis laughs, very shortly.

5

Jim tracks away angry. He forgets instantly about calling Sheila, about calling Uncle Tom; he's too absorbed in his own feelings. Long minutes alone on the freeway, so much of life spent this way; thinking angrily, sifting and rearranging events until it's all his father's fault, until he's angry only at Dennis and not at himself. That look over the glasses, after he managed to extricate himself from his damned car! Humiliating.

He parks in South Coast Plaza's subterranean garage, takes the elevator up to the top of the mall, south end; some of the most expensive apartments in OC are up here. Through one sound-proofed door comes the thump of percussion and a tiny wash of voices. In Jim goes.

Sandy and Angela's ap consists of six big rooms, set like boxcars one after the next. Window walls in each face southwest; it's a heliotropic home. Outside these windows a balcony extends the whole length of the ap. The balcony and all the rooms but the bedroom are filled with people, maybe sixty of them. It's the nightly party, no one is too excited. Sandy's not there yet. Jim walks into the kitchen, the first room. There are houseplants everywhere, giant ones in giant glazed pots. They look so healthy they might be plastic; people say Angela has a polymer thumb.

Jim sees no one he particularly wants to talk to, and continues through the kitchen to the balcony. He leans on the chest-high railing and looks down at the lightshow of coastal OC, pulsing at the speed of a rapid heartbeat. That's his town.

Jim's depressed. He's a part-time word processor for a title and real estate company, a part-time night school teacher at Trabuco Junior College. His father thinks he's a failure; his friends think he's a fool. This last has been his angle, of course, he's cultivated it because laughs are at a premium among his friends, and they're all comedians; the fool routine keeps Jim from being nothing more than part of the laughtrack. But it can get old, old, old. How much nicer it would be to be . . . well, something else.

Sandy shows up, three hours late to his own party. SOP. "Hell*ooo!*" he shouts, and Angela Mendez his ally comes over to give him a kiss. He moves on, his pale freckled skin flushed with excitement. "Hey, hello! Why are you just *sitting* there?" He goes to the music wall, cranks the volume up to say a hundred thirty decibels, Laura's Big Tits singing "Want Becomes Need" over thick percussion that sounds like twenty spastics in a room full of snare drums. *"Yeah!"* Sandy pulls some girls off the long beige couch in the video room, starts them dancing around the screens hanging from the ceiling, he won't be satisfied until everyone is dancing for at least one number, this is understood and everyone gets up and starts to bounce, happy at the action. Sandy flies from dancer to dancer, shoves his face right in theirs, psycho grin pulsating, pale blue eyes popping like they might fall out and bob at the end of springs any second now: "You look too *normal!* Try *this!*" And they're holding eyedroppers full of Sandy's latest, Social Affability, Apprehension of Beauty, Get Wired, who knows what the little label will say this time, but it's sure to be fun. Sandy's the best drug designer in OC—famous, really. And he doesn't disdain the old-fashioned highs either. Angela is mixing pitchers of margaritas in the kitchen, Sandy is stopping at certain broad-leafed houseplants and pulling giant spliffs from hiding places, lighting them with a magnum blowtorch, throwing them at people, shouting, *"Smoke this!"* Jim, looking in from the balcony, can only laugh. There is a Sandy who is subtle, thoughtful, quick-witted, a culturevulture in Jim's own league; but that isn't him in there, putting the jumper cables to his own party. Time for a different act: Wired Host. Is there an eyedropper with that on the label?

Jim goes to work on an eyedropper called Pattern Perception (so his name has been chosen!), with a couple whose names he can almost remember. Blink, blink. Are those stars or streetlights? "I'm fourth-generation OC," he tells them apropos of nothing. "I have it in my genes, this place, I have a race memory of what it used to be like when the orange groves were here."

"Uh-huh."

"Nowadays we'd have a hard time living that slowly though, don't you think?"

"Uh-huh."

There's something lacking in this conversation. Jim is about to ask his companions if they have brains at home they can plug in but forgot to bring, or if they have to pretend like this *all* the time, when Tashi interrupts. "Hey McPherson," he says from the French doors to the game room. "Come take up the paddle."

Of course this is Jim the Fool they're requesting. His ping-pong style is a bit unorthodox, call it clumsy in fact; but that's okay. Any request is better than none.

Arthur Bastanchury is just finishing off Humphrey Riggs, and Humphrey, Jim's boss at the real estate office, hands over the sweaty paddle to Jim with a muttered curse. Jim's up against the Ping-Pong King.

Arthur Bastanchury, the Ping-Pong King, is about six feet two, eyes of blue, dark-haired and wide-shouldered. Women like him. He's also a dedicated antiwar activist and underground newspaper publisher, which Jim admires, as Jim has socialist ideas himself. And an all-round Good Guy. Yes, Arthur, in Jim's opinion, is someone to reckon with.

They take a long warm-up, and Jim discovers he has blinked the wrong amount of Pattern Perception. He can see the cat's cradle in time that he and Arthur are creating, but only well after the fact, and the contrail-like after-images of the white ball are distracting. It looks like trouble for McPherson.

They start and it turns out to be even worse than he expected.

Jim's got quick hands, but he is awkward, there's no denying it. And his fine-tuning is badly out of order. Giving up, more or less, he decides to go recklessly on the attack, thinking Let's get this fucking pinko, which is funny since he actually agrees completely with what he knows of Arthur's political views. But now it's useful to go into a redkiller mindset.

Also useful not to care about appearances; Arthur is a power player with a monster slam, and Jim has to make some, well, funny moves—twists and contortions, dives into the walls and such. . . . In fact, Angela hears he's playing and comes in to move her plants out of danger. Fine, more room to maneuver.

Still, Jim is losing badly when he tries a vicious topspin and smacks himself right in the forehead with the edge of his paddle. General laughter accompanies this move; but actually, after the pain recedes and the black lights leave his vision, the blow seems to have stimulated something inside Jim's brain. Synapses are knocked into new arrangements, new axons sprout immediately, the whole game suddenly becomes *very clear*. He can see two or three hits ahead of time where the ball is *destined* to go.

Jim rises to a new level, a pure overcompetency, his backhand slam begins to work, any opportunity on that side and a snap of the wrist sends over a crosscourt shot angled so sharply that people sitting right at netside take it in the face. Alternate those with down-the-line backhands, tailing away. These slaps plus the bold, not to say idiotic, dives into the wall to retrieve slams when on defense, reverse the game's momentum. He takes his last serves and wins going away, 21–17.

"Two out of three," Arthur says, not amused.

But it's a mistake to go for a rematch when Jim is on like this. So much of ping-pong is just the confidence to hit the thing as hard as possible, after all. Second game Jim feels the power flow through him, and there's nothing Arthur can do about it.

Jim can even take the luxury of noticing that the video room next door is filling up with spectators. Sandy has turned on the game room cameras, and the watchers are treated to eight shots of live action, all played out on the big screenwall and the various free screens hanging from silver springs that extend down from the ceiling: Jim and Arthur, flying around from every angle. The game room clears out, in fact, as people go into the video room to observe the spectacle, and the two players have room to really go at it.

But Arthur's out of luck tonight, Jim's getting a sort of . . . *uncanny* ability here, premonitions so strong that he has to hold back on his swing to allow Arthur time to hit it to the preordained spots. What a joy, this silly table game.

Second game, 21–13. Arthur tosses his paddle on the table. "Whew!" He grins, gracious in defeat: "You're hot tonight, Jim Dandy. Time for those margaritas."

Jim starts to wind down. He looks around; Tashi and Abe weren't even in the game room or the video room. Too bad they missed it, Jim likes his friends to see him being more than just The Fool. Oh well. The act is its own reward, right?

Sometimes Jim has a hard time convincing himself of this.

"Nice game," says a voice behind him. He turns; it's Virginia Novello.

Adrenaline makes a little comeback. Virginia, Arthur Bastanchury's ally until just a couple months ago, is Jim's idea of female perfection. Standing right there in front of him.

Long straight thick blond hair,
Bleached by sun but still full of red and yellow.
Yes, they sell that hair color, and call it California Gold.
She's a touch under medium height.
It's the body women go to the spa to work for.
Virginia goes there herself.
Sleeveless blouse, embroidered white on white, scoop
    neck.
Muscular biceps, little toy triceps,
Perfectly defined under smooth tanned skin. Whoah.
Aesthetic standards change over time, but why?
The California Model's features: small fine nose, curvy
    mouth, wide-set blue eyes.
This is the Look, in the society of the Look:
Freckles on cheeks, under a sunburn that might start
    peeling right now.
That brake light in your brain. . . .

Well, it's worth a little adrenaline, Jim thinks. Of course everyone is beautiful these days, we're in California after all, but for Jim, Virginia Novello is *it*. And here she is talking to him. She has before, of course, a bit remotely perhaps, and in the context of Arthurness, but now . . . Jim offers her his new margarita and she takes a sip. Arm muscles slide and bunch under tan skin, silky hairs on forearm gleam in the light. Her white blouse is a nice change from all the spectrum-slide primaries in the room. These are fabrics that are colored in a very narrow band of the spectrum, say fifteen hertz, so that you can, for instance, just begin to see a blue blouse shade into violet, or yellow into green, across the whole of the piece of cloth. It's a great look, and very popular because of that, but still, a change is nice. Kind of bold.

"Ping-pong is funny," Jim says. "It really varies from day to day how much you can count on your game working. You know?"

"I think most sports are like that. The edge comes rarely. Maybe it goes beyond sports, eh?"

Jim nods, regarding her. Her smile, seldom seen, small and controlled, is actually quite nice. He doesn't know much about her, despite the admiration from a distance. Business executive of some sort? Funny match with Arthur's political activism. Maybe that's why they broke up. Let's not worry about it.

They go out on the balcony, and Jim asks her about her work. She helps to administer Fashion Island, the old mall above Newport Beach. So she's working for the management company hired by the Irvine Corporation, which owns the land. The old rancho dismemberment wealth, extending two hundred years into time . . . although Irvine's only a name now, the family long out of it. Jim talks about this aspect of the land ownership of OC, and Virginia listens, interested and inquisitive. "It's funny, you never think about how things got this way," she says brightly.

Well. Jim does. But he passes on that. He tells her about the recent archaeological dig under Fluffy Donuts, making himself the butt of the jokes, and she laughs. The Fool, after all, can be a useful role, as he already knows. Especially after a show of competence at the ping-pong table; then it can be mistaken for modesty. They watch cars track over the freeways. Leaning over the red geraniums that line the balcony's top, their arms brush together. It's accidental and means nothing, sure.

"Do you surf?" Virginia asks.

"No. Tash tried to teach me, but the moment I stand the board flies away and I fall down."

She laughs. "You've got to just commit and jump up without thinking about balance. I bet I could teach you."

"Really? I'd love it." No lie. Virginia at the beach? What an image. "Tash just always says, like I've done it on purpose, 'Don't *fall*, Jim.' "

She laughs again.

Now, at this time Jim is in alliance with Sheila Mayer. As his mom would be quick to point out. They've been allied for almost four months now, and it's been a pretty good four months, too. But Jim has been taking it for granted for some time; the thrill is gone, and Sheila is a Lagunatic and doesn't get up to central OC more than twice a week, and Jim has been entertaining himself pretty frequently with other women he's met at Sandy's. All his friends therefore know about it, and he's come to consider himself a free man, though Sheila might be surprised to hear it. But there's not been a really comfortable time to discuss it with her, yet. He will soon. Meanwhile he fancies that his infidelities make him a little less The Fool in the eyes of his friends, a little more The Man of the World.

And at the moment he isn't thinking about any of that anyway. He's forgotten Sheila, in fact, and if he's thinking about friends, it's only a vague underfeeling that he would be *really* impressive if allied with Virginia Novello.

They talk for quite some time about the relative values of surfing and bodysurfing, and other philosophical issues of that sort. They go in and sit down on one of the long beige couches and drink more margaritas. They talk about Jim's work, people they know in common, music groups they like. The party is getting emptier, only the old regulars left, Sandy and Angela's actual friends. Sandy drops by and crouches at their feet to chat for a while. "Did Jim tell you about our attack on the parking lot?"

"Yeah, I want to see this piece of ancient wood you liberated."

"Did you bring it, Jim?"

"I'm having it made into the handle of my ping-pong paddle."

They laugh; he made a joke, apparently! This must really be his night.

Tashi's ally Erica stands over Sandy, grabs him by his long red ponytail and pulls. "Sandy, are you going to open the sauna and jacuzzi tonight?"

"Yeah, haven't I already? Man, what time is it? One?" The psycho grin grows impossibly wide, Sandy goggles at Erica with his lecher leer. "Come on along while I turn on the heat, you can test it out for me."

"Test what out for you?"

Arms around each other they walk toward the sauna and jacuzzi room at the end of the ap, calling for Tash and Angela.

"Want to jacuzzi?" Virginia asks Jim.

"Sure," he says coolly.

They follow Sandy and Erica and Tash and Angela and Rose and Gabriela and Humphrey and one or two others down the hall and into the Jacuzzi room. Sandy snaps on light, water heater, sauna heater, water jets. The room is hot, humid, filled with Angela's most tropical houseplants, hanging in a network of macramé. Redwood decking, redwood walls, domed skylight, big blue ceramic tile Jacuzzi bath: yes, Sandy and Angela live a good life. They go into the changing rooms and strip.

Of course they do this often at Sandy's place, social nudity is casual and no big deal at all. That's why Jim's left eye has gotten stuck looking straight into his nose, from trying to watch both Virginia and Erica undress at the same time. Surreptitious knuckle in there to free the poor thing, for more looking you bet; video saturation has trained Jim, like everyone else, to a fine appreciation of the female image. Now when arms are crossed and those blouses come over those heads in a single fluid motion, breasts falling free, hair shaken out all over shoulders, the men exhale a happy connoisseur's sigh. No doubt the women get a little peak in the readout too, moment of pseudotaboo exhibitionism here, quite a thrill just to Take It All Off in Front of Everybody, whoah, besides here's all these wrestler/surfer muscles everywhere. . . . But it's a casual scene, sure, of course, obviously.

Naked, they go out into the Jacuzzi room and step into the

bath. Rose and Gabriela, long-time allies, duck each other under the hot water. Steam and laughter fill the room. Debbie Riggs, Humphrey's sister, comes in to find out what the noise is all about. The water's too hot for Virginia and she sits dripping on the decking beside Jim. They all talk.

> Bodies. Wet skin over muscles. We all know the shapes.
> Ruddy light breaks in wet curls of hair.
> Wrestlers' bodies, swimmers' bodies, surfers' bodies, spa
> bodies.
> Tall breasts, full from the collarbones down.
> Cocks float in the bubbles, snaking here and there, hello?
> hello?
> Hello?
> Curled pubic hair: equilateral eye magnets.
> Blink blink, blink blink, blink blink (in the brain).

Virginia leans forward over powerful thighs to check one manicured and painted toenail. She's gone for the muscly look, especially in arms and legs, although her lats show a lot of rowing and her abdominals a lot of sit-ups. It's a nicely balanced look, refreshing after some of the other women's extremism: Rose, for instance, who has left her upper body childlike while her bottom and legs are immensely strong, or Gabriela, who has bench presser's pecs and campily big breasts over boyish hips and long slim legs . . . both just going with their original forms, both bizarrely attractive in their own ways; but there's something to be said for moderation, the standard proportions taken to their perfect end point.

Virginia gets back in the water, she and Jim are pressed together flank to flank. Bubbles cover the scene below. Passing an eyedropper their fingers touch and it seems to complete a circuit of some sort. Slick bodies are everywhere, sliding together like a pod of dolphins. Across from them Angela, who has an angelic body, hormonic aid making it lusher than standard but who's complaining, stands, legs apart, arms overhead to hold the eyedropper to upturned face: a vision. The *image*. . . .

A breast shoves into his arm. "I live in SCP north," Virginia says suddenly, under the crowd noise. "Want to come over?"

Jim, master of wit as always, says "Twist my arm."

6

Their wet hair cools in the breeze blowing scrap paper around the parking garage. A two-minute drive to the north side of South Coast Plaza, where there is a set of condos that match the aps Sandy and Angela live in. Up to Virginia's place, inside, a laughing race to the bedroom.

Virginia flips on the lights, turns on the video system. Eight little cameras mounted high on the walls track them with IR sensors, and two big sets of screens on the side walls show Virginia undressing, from both front and back. Jim finds the images arousing indeed, and by the time he gets his pants off half the screens show him with a hard-on waving about wandlike; Virginia cracks up and pulls him by it onto the bed. They maneuver into positions where they can both see a wall of screens. Images of Virginia—

> Smooth curve of thigh; it's spent a lot of time on the bike machines.
> Blond wash of hair above.
> Black pubic hair below, shaved to an arrow pointing down and in.
> Blink! Blink!
> Swinging breasts (the Image).
> Lats, standing out from rib cage—

—pierce him utterly. She straddles him, slides onto him. Ah: the vital connection. She's on top and she plays at holding down his wrists, so that her biceps bulge and her face is in exquisite profile as she looks to the screens to her left, and her breasts . . . well, it's almost enough to distract Jim from the screens, but on the wall he's looking at there is a view from above his head, so he can still see breasts falling from taut pectorals, while the screen next to it has the reverse angle, and shows the obscene, porno-graphic, not to say anatomically improbable image of his cock sliding in and out of her: concealed by the big muscles of her bottom, revealed pink and wet, concealed—

The screens flicker and go blank. Glassy gray-green nothing-ness.

Virginia jumps off Jim. "What the fuck!" Angrily she punches the buttons of the control panel over by the light switches. "It's *on!*" But no pictures. The cameras are not following her as she moves, either. "Well, what the hell!" She's flushed with exertion, exasperation, she tries the buttons again, hitting them hard. "The damn thing must be broken!" Something in her tone of voice makes Jim start to go limp, despite the way she looks standing there. Besides, he's distracted himself. What happened to them? "Can you fix it?" she asks.

"Well . . ." Dubiously Jim rolls off the gel bed and looks at the control panel. Everything appears to be in order there. . . . He looks up at all the cameras; cables still extend from them into the walls. "I don't *think* so. . . ."

"Shit." She sits on the bed, bounces beautifully.

"Well, but . . ." Jim gestures at the bed. "We've still got the major piece of equipment."

Her mouth purses into a moue of irritation. She glances up, flips his deflated cock against his leg. "Oh yeah?" She laughs.

Now Jim, who is beginning to get a bit concerned, cannot afford a decent bedroom video system himself, and his little set is always breaking down. So he's used to ad-libbing in difficult situations like these. He takes a look in the bathroom. "Ah ha!" There's a free-standing full-length mirror in the great skylighted expanse of the bathroom, and full of hope he pulls it out into the bedroom. Virginia is draped out on the bed like a centerfold, looking for eyedroppers in the bedside table drawer. "Here we have it," says Jim. "Early version of the system."

She laughs, gives him directions as he positions the mirror. "Down a little. There, that's good." Quickly they are back at it, across the bed so they can both look to the side and see the mirror, where their twins thrash away. It's disconcerting to have the twins looking back at them, but interesting too, and Jim can't help grinning lasciviously at himself. The image itself is different also, the video's softness and depth of field replaced by a hard, silvered, glossy materiality, as if they've got a window here and are spying on a couple in some more glassy world.

When they're done, Jim drawls "Pret-ty kink-y." And can't help laughing.

Virginia isn't amused. "I'll have to get the repairmen by to fix it, and I hate that. It's always, 'Excuse me, ma'am, but we need a test of some kind to see if the system's working.' "

Jim laughs. "You should tell them to fuck themselves, make that the test."

Virginia scowls. "They probably would, the perverts."

Well, okay. Now that they're done, Virginia gets restless. Appears she still wants to party some more. Jim's agreeable, whatever this beautiful new friend likes is fine by him. He likes to party too. So soon they're up, dressed, back to Sandy's.

7

On the way up to Sandy's they run into Arthur Bastanchury, who is returning to the party's end carrying a big over-the-shoulder bag. Jim is uncomfortable, here he's just gone to bed with Arthur's ex-ally and who knows what's still going on between them, really. But both Virginia and Arthur are cool, and after they go inside and sit in the video room and chat for a while about what's on the screens, Jim relaxes too. We're in the postmodern world, he reminds himself, alliances are no more than that: every person is a sovereign entity, free to do what they want. No reason to feel any unease.

Sandy and Angela, Tashi and Erica come out of the jacuzzi room wrapped in big thick white towels, steaming faintly. They go on into the kitchen to rustle up a late-night snack. Arthur puts his bag on the floor and opens it, begins to arrange things inside. "So are you coming with me?" he shouts into the kitchen.

"Not tonight," Sandy calls back in. "I'm beat." No word from the others. Arthur makes a face. "Ginny?"

Virginia shakes her head. " 'Fraid not, Art. I told you before, I think it's a waste of time."

Arthur looks disgusted with her, and abruptly she gets up and walks into the kitchen, where their friends are laughing over something Sandy has done or said. Ruefully Arthur shakes his head: he's going to have to go it alone again, the expression says.

"What's a waste of time?" Jim asks.

Arthur pins him with a challenging stare. "Trying to make a difference in this world. Virginia thinks that trying to make a difference is a waste of time. I suppose you think the same. You all do. A lot of talk about how bad things are, how we have to change things—but when it comes to a question of action, it turns out to be nothing but talk."

"Don't be so sure!"

"No?" Arthur's tone is careless, his grin sardonic; he looks down to arrange the papers in his bag. Offended, Jim rises to it. "No! Why don't you tell me what you have in mind?"

"I've got some posters in here. I'm going to do an information blitz in the mall. Here—" He pulls one out, hands it up to Jim without looking at him.

From one angle it's a holo of a wave at the Pipeline, a perfect tube about to eat some ecstatic goofy-footed surfer. Shift the poster just a bit, though, and it becomes a holo of a dead American soldier, perhaps taken in Indonesia. The legs are gone. Under this apparition bold letters proclaim:

DO YOU WANT TO DIE?
Open Wars in Indonesia, Egypt, Bahrain, and Thailand.
Covert Wars in Pakistan, Turkey, South Korea, and
Belgium.
There Are American Soldiers in Every One.
350 of Them Die EVERY DAY.
THE DRAFT IS BACK. YOU COULD BE NEXT.

Jim rubs his chin. Arthur laughs at him. "So?" he taunts. "Want to come with me and put these up?"

"Sure," Jim says, just to shut off that contemptuous look. "Why not?"

"It could land you in jail, that's why not."

"Freedom of speech, right?"

"They have ways around that. Littering. Defacement. These things have to be lased off, they have molecular-ceramics bonds on the back."

"Hmph. Well, so what? Are you planning to get caught?"

Arthur laughs. "No." He stares at Jim, a curious look in his eye. Despite the events of the night—Jim's ping-pong victory, his jump in bed with Arthur's ex-ally . . . or perhaps because of them, somehow . . . Arthur seems to have some curious kind of moral high ground, from which he speaks down to Jim. Jim doesn't understand this; he only feels it.

"Come on, then." Arthur's up and off to the door. Jim follows him out and just has time to register the scowl on Virginia's face, there in the kitchen. Oops.

"Let's start at the north end and work our way back here," says Arthur as they descend to the ground floor of the mall. They get on the empty people mover and track through the complex to South Coast Village, buried under the northward expansion of the mall proper. "Good enough. Let's keep it fast, say twenty minutes total. But casual. Watch out for the mall police."

They start down the wide concourse of the mall. Escalators in mirrors branch off to a score of other floors, some real, some not. "Put the posters up then rub this rod over them. That activates the bond."

Jim puts one small poster up, on the window of a Pizza City. This one's a holo of a naked girl standing in knee-deep tropical surf; the shift of angle and it's another blood-soaked fallen soldier, with the words "THE DEFENSE DEPT. RUNS THIS COUNTRY—RESIST" underneath. "Whoah. This might spoil a few dinners."

By now it's nearly four A.M., although it's impossible to tell inside the mall, which is as timeless as a casino. The big department stores are closed, but everywhere else the windows and mirrors and tile walls gleam with a jumpy neon insistence:

Lights! Camera! Action!
Long central atrium, five stories tall.
Plastic trees, colored light fountains. Reflected
Images. Game parlors, snack bars, video bars: all open, all
    pulsing.
Hey, guess what! I'm hungry.
The South Coast carousel is spinning. All its animals have
    riders.
Glazed eye. Clashing music spheres. Blinks.
Gangs in the restroom niches, in closed shop entries.
Into an expresso bar. Hanging out.
Shopping.
On Main Street.
You live here.

Jim and Arthur slap their posters on walls, windows, doors. "The mortuary is really hopping tonight," Arthur says.

Jim laughs. He hates malls himself, though he spends as much time in them as anyone. "So why do you poster a place like this? Isn't it a waste of molecular ceramics?"

"Mostly, sure. But the draft has gotten teeth since the Gingrich Act was reenacted, and a lot of people in here are bait. They don't know it because they don't read newsheets. In fact when you get right down to it they don't know a fucking thing."

"The sleepwalkers."

"Yeah." Arthur gestures at a group lidded almost beyond the point of walking. "Sleepwalkers, exactly. How do you reach people like that? I published a newsheet for a while."

"I know. I liked it."

"Yeah, but you *read*. You're in a tiny minority. Especially in OC. So I decided to move into media where I can reach more people. We make videos that do really well, because they're sex comedies for the most part. The newsheet equipment has been converted to poster work."

"I've seen the ones on Indonesia that Sandy has in his study. They're beautiful."

Arthur waves a hand, annoyed. "That's irrelevant. You culture-vultures are all alike. It's all aesthetics for you. I don't suppose you really believe in anything at all. It's just whatever attracts the eye."

Without replying Jim goes into the McDonald's, puts up a

poster over the menu. On the one hand he feels a little put upon, it's a bit unfair to attack him while he's right here risking jail to put up these stupid posters, isn't it? At the same time, there's a part of him that feels Arthur is probably right. It's true, isn't it? Jim has despised the ruling forces in America for as long as he has been aware of them; but he's never done anything about it, except complain. His efforts have all gone to creating an aesthetic life, one concentrating on the past. King of the culturevultures. Yes, Arthur has a certain point.

When they rendezvous outside Jack-in-the-Box, where Arthur has been at work, Jim says, "So why do you do all this, Arthur?"

"Well just look at it!" Arthur bursts out. "Look at these sleepwalkers, zombieing around in some kind of L-5 toybox. . . . I mean, this is our country! This is it, from sea to shining sea, some kind of brain mortuary! While the rest of the world is a real mortuary. The world is falling apart and we devote ourselves to making weapons so we can take more of it over!"

"I know."

"That's right, you know! So why do you ask?"

"Well, I guess I meant, do you really think this kind of thing"—swinging his poster bag—"will make any difference?"

Arthur shrugs, grimaces. "How do I know? I feel like I have to do something. Maybe it just helps me. But you have to do *something*. I mean, what the hell do you do? You type a word-cruncher for a real estate office, you teach technoprose to tech-nocrats. Isn't that right?"

Almost against his will, Jim nods. It's true.

"You don't give a shit about your jobs. So you drift along being ace culturevulture and wondering what it's all about." The grimace intensifies. "Don't you believe in *anything*?"

"Yeah!" Feeble show of defiance. Actually, he's always thought he should be more political. It would be more consistent with his hatred for the wars being waged, for the weapons being made (his father's work, yes!)—for the way things are.

"I've heard you talk about the way OC used to be," Arthur says. They spot a mall cop and stand watching the keno results appear in the Las Vegas window, green numbers embedded in glass. When the cop has passed Arthur covers the numbers with another dead soldier. "Some of what you say is important. The attempts to make collective existences out here, Anaheim, Fountain Valley, Lancaster—it's important to remember those, even if they did fail. But most of that citrus utopia bit is bullshit. It was always agribiz in California, the Spanish land grants were grabbed up in parcels so big that it was a perfect location for corporate agriculture, it was practically the start of it. Those groves you lament were picked by migrant laborers who worked like dogs, and lived like it was the worst part of the Middle Ages.''

"I never denied it," Jim protests. "I know all about that."

"So what's with this nostalgia?" Arthur demands. "Aren't you just wishing you could have been one of the privileged land-owners, back in the good old days? Shit, you sound like some White Russian in Paris!"

"No, no," Jim says weakly. They plaster restroom doors and walls with posters, approach the May Company at the south end of the mall. "There were some serious attempts to make cooperative agricultural communities, here. A lot of them had to do with the orange groves. We have to remember them, or, or their efforts were wasted!"

"Their efforts *were* wasted." Arthur slaps up a poster. "We'd better get out of here, the cops are bound to have seen some of these by now." He pokes Jim in the arm with a hard finger. "Their efforts were wasted because no one followed up on them. Even this kind of thing is trivial, it's preaching to the deaf, making faces at the blind. What's needed is something more active, some kind of *real resistance*. Do you understand?"

"Well, yeah. I do." Although actually Jim isn't too clear on what Arthur means. But he is convinced that Arthur is right, whatever he means. Jim's an agreeable guy, his friends convince him of things all the time. And Arthur's arguments have a particular force for him, because they express what Jim has always felt he should believe. He knows better than anyone that there is something vital missing from his life, he wants some kind of larger purpose. And he would love to fight back against the mass culture he finds himself in; he knows it wasn't always like this.

"So you mean you *are* doing something more active?" he asks.

Arthur glances at him mysteriously. "That's right. Me and the people I work with."

"So what the hell!" Jim cries, irritated at Arthur's dismissals, his secretive righteousness. "I *want* to resist, but what can I do? I mean, I might be interested in helping you, but how can I tell when all you're doing is spouting off! What do you *do*?"

Arthur gives him the eye, looks at him hard and long. "We sabotage weapons manufacturers."

8

The bones of whales lie scattered in the hills.

For millions of years it was a shallow ocean. Water creatures lived in forests of seaweed, and when the creatures and the forests died their bodies settled to the bottom and turned to mud, then stone. We stand on them.

Overhead the sun coursed, hundreds of millions of times. Underneath tectonic plates floated on the mantle, bumped together: pieces of a jigsaw puzzle, trying to find their proper places, always failing.

Where two pieces rubbed edges, the earth twisted, folded, buckled over. That happened here five million years ago. Mountains reared up, spewing lava and ash. Rain washed dirt into the shallow sea, filling it. Eventually it came to look like what we know: a chain of sandstone mountains, a broad coastal plain, a big estuary, an endless sandy beach.

And so a hundred thousand years ago, on a continent free of human beings, this land became home to fantastic creatures. The Imperial mammoth, fifteen feet tall at the shoulder; the American mastodon, almost that tall; giant camels and giant bison; an early horse; ground sloths eighteen feet high; tapirs; bears, lions, saber-toothed tigers, dire wolves; a vulture with a twelve-foot wingspan. Their skeletons too can be found in the hills, and the bluffs above the estuary.

But time passed, and species died. It rained less and less. The plain was crossed by one river, our Santa Ana River, which was older even than the mountains, cutting through them as they rose. This river fell out of the mountains to the estuary of our Newport Bay.

Around this big salt marsh grew the salt-tolerant plants, arrowgrass, pickleweed, sea lavender, salt grass. Upstream, along the fresh river, trees grew: cottonwood, willow, sycamore, elderberry, toyon, mulefat; and up in the hills, white alder and maple. Out on the plains grew perennial bunchgrasses, needlegrass, and wildflowers; also sagebrush and mustard; and up in the hills, chaparral and manzanita. In low spots on the plain there were freshwater marshes, home to cattails, sedges, duckweed, and water hemlock; and there were vernal pools, drying every spring to become flower-filled meadows. The foothills and the slopes of the mountains were covered by live oak forests, the oaks protecting grassy understories, and mixing with walnut, coffeeberry, redberry, and bush lupines; and above them, higher on the mountains, were knobcone pines and Tecate cypress. All these plants grew wildly, constrained only by their genes, their neighbors, the weather. . . . Evolving to fill every niche in conditions, they grew and died and grew.

Offshore, among the myriad fish, our cousins lived: whales, dolphins, porpoises, sea lions, sea otters, seals. Around the marshes, in the reeds, our brothers lived: coyotes, weasels, raccoons, badgers, rats. On the plains our sisters lived: deer, elk, foxes, wildcats, jackrabbits, mice. In the hills our parents lived: mountain lions, grizzly bears, black bears, gray wolves, bighorn sheep. . . . There were a hundred and fifty different species of mammals living here, once upon a time; and snakes, lizards, insects, spiders—all of them were here.

This warm dry basin, between the sea and sky, was—and not so long ago!—crawling with life. Teeming with all manner of life, saturated with the vigor of a complete ecology. Animals everywhere—in the grasslands, and the tidal marshes, and the sagebrush flats, and the oak forests of the foothills—animals everywhere. Animals everywhere! Animals everywhere. Animals . . . everywhere.

And the birds! In the skies there were birds of every kind.

Gulls, pelicans, cranes, herons, egrets, ducks, geese, swans, starlings, pheasants, partridge, quail, finches, grouse, blackbirds, roadrunners, jays, swallows, doves, larks, falcons, hawks, eagles, and condors, the biggest birds in the world. Birds beyond counting, birds such that even as late as the 1920s, a man in Orange County could say this: "They came by the thousands, I am a little reluctant about saying how many, but I can only say we measured them by acres and not by numbers. In the fall of the year the ground would be white with wild geese."

I can only say we measured them by acres and not by numbers.

The ground white with wild geese.

9

Abe Bernard guns his GM freeway rescue truck down the fast track, scattering the cars ahead with the power of the truck's sound and light show. ''Get out of the way!'' he shouts, his swarthy hatchet face twisted with anger. He and his partner Xavier have just been tapped out a few moments before, and he is still a bit jacked on the initial adrenaline surge. The driver of a passing car flips them off; Xavier says ''Fuck you too, buddy,'' and Abe laughs shortly. Stupid fools, when they've crashed he hopes they lie there in the metal remembering how often they obstructed rescue teams, realizing that other fools are doing it that very moment as the trucks try to get to them. . . . Another recalcitrant driver ahead, Abe turns up the siren to its full howl, the music of his work: ''Get—out—of the *way!*''

They're into the permanent traffic snarl where Laguna Canyon Highway meets the Coast Highway, pretty beach park to the right, century-long volleyball games still going, sun glancing off the sea in a million spearpoints. Abe keeps the siren on and they push cautiously through a red light, up the Canyon Highway. Beside him Xavier is on the box trying to get some more information on the accident, but Abe can't hear much through the siren and the radio crackle.

The oceanbound lanes across from them are bumpertobumper and crawling, and without a doubt it's worse on the far side of the accident, everyone overriding their carbrains to slow down and stare over into the other lane, bloodlust curiosity surging. . . . But going upcanyon they can still move; they haven't reached the accident's backup yet.

"Indications seem to be that the track has once again been left behind, causing two cars to occupy the same space at the same time," Xavier says in his rapid on-the-job patter. "We suspect lane changing is perhaps the culprit. My, look at the traffic ahead."

"I know." They've reached the backup. Ahead of them the brake light symphony is blinking, redred, redred, redred redred redred. Overrides everywhere, nowhere for people to go, impossible for the computers to clear things up when the lanes clog this badly, it's time to take the old Chevy supertruck offtrack, yes this baby has an *internal combustion engine* under its big hood. "Independent lo-comotion," Xavier sings as Abe turns the key and revs the engine, 1056 horsepower, atavistic Formula One adrenaline rush here as he steers them off the magnetic track into the narrow gap between fast-track cars and the center divider, roaring along in vibratory petrol power, let the poor saps breathe a bit of that carbon monoxide ambrosia, nostalgic whiff of last century's power smog as they zroom by almost taking off door handles, sideview mirrors, sure why not clip a few to give them a story to tell about this ten-millionth traffic jam of their OC condo lives? Abe still gets a bit buzzed putting the antique skills to work, firing by all the cars; he's just short of his first anniversary on the job. He cools it, drives closer to the center divider, still just manages to squeeze the gap left by some Cadillac monster, fiberglass body a replica of the 1992 cow, "Sure buddy, *I'm* the one in a *car*, here, a big fucking *truck* in fact and I'll shave your whole plastic side off if you don't get *over*."

They barrel up the curves of the canyon road past traffic stopped dead on the tracks, past the condos covering the hills on both sides, ersatz Mediterranean minivillas in standard OC style

—these carefully named Seaview Clifftops because they're the first homes upcanyon without the slightest chance of a glimpse of the ocean. Vroom, vroom, vroom, past the complex's too-small-to-be-used park, where as Jim tells it a hippo that escaped from Lion Country Safari settled down to establish a little hippo's empire in a pond, until they darted him to crane him out and killed him with too much tranquilizer, the idiots. And just past that heraldic fragment of OC natural history they accelerate over chewed asphalt covered with trash and chips of broken headlight plastic, around a corner and into the *sota*, the scene of the accident. One Chippiemobile there off the tracks, its rooflight doing a strobe over the scene, red eye winking over and over.

Abe puts the truck in neutral and turns on the exterior power system, and they jump out and run to the scene. CHP are out on the tracks doing what they do best, setting out flares. Fast lane is a mess. As they approach Abe feels the sick horror and helplessness that anyone would feel, *oh my God no*, then he passes through the membrane as always and the professional takes over, the structural analyst trying to comprehend a certain configuration, and the best way to extricate the organic components of it from the inorganic. . . . And the horrified helpless witness is left up in a back corner of the mind, staring over the shoulder of the other guy, storing up images for dreams.

This time one of the lane-changing tracks appears to have malfunctioned. It's rare, but it happens. Working correctly, the computer controlling the magnetic track takes a request from an approaching car, slows cars in the adjacent lane to make a gap, slots the car onto the lane-change track and into a quick S-curve onto the track of the desired lane, fitting it neatly into the flow of traffic. No room for human error, and really it's thousands of times safer than letting drivers do it. But the one in ten million has come up once again, and the cause of accident is *sits*, something in the silicon; a car in the middle lane was tracked directly into the side of another in the fast lane, knocking it off its guidance system and into the center divider, while the first car spun and was plowed into by a follow-up car. All at around sixty-five mph. One more follow-up crunched mildly into the mess. The driver of that one, saved by the power of electromagnetic brakes, is out and babbling to the Chippies with the usual edge of hysteria. Abe and Xavier hop around the three main participants. The car against the center divider has a single occupant, crushed between dash, door, and divider. Chest cavity caved and blood-soaked, neck apparently broken. On to the impacting car, a couple in the front seat, driver unconscious and bleeding from the head, woman trapped underneath him and dash, bleeding heavily from the neck but apparently still conscious, eyes fluttering. Main follow-up with heavily starred windshield, not wearing those seat belts were you, two people already dragged out and on the ground, heads bloody.

"Those two in the middle car," Xavier pants as they run for the truck. "Yeah," says Abe. "The one on the divider is dots." Meaning dead on the spot. Xavier grabs his medic pack and hauls back to the car, Abe brings the truck down the shoulder as close to the middle car as he can get. Then he's out and pulling the cutters from the truckside, yanking on the power cord, hands shoved down into the sleeves, it's waldo time here and novice expert cutter Abe Bernard now has all the power of modern robotics in his hands. He starts snipping the flimsy steel of the car's sidewall as if it were chocolate. There's no resistance to the sheers at all. Water streams out over the metal under the cutters, spraying over Xavier who is crawling around just beyond the reach of Abe's work, squeezing into the new hole to do his medic routine. Xavier did two tours on Java with the Army and is very good indeed. At this point they could sure use another man or two, but budgets are tight everywhere, lot of rescue trucks to be kept manned and ready for tap-out, and budgets are tight, budgets are tight!

The horrified witness in the back of Abe's mind watches him snip steel as if he is cutting origami, with Xavier and the woman passenger just beyond the end of the blades, and wonders if he really knows how to do this. But the thought never reaches the part of Abe's mind that's at work. A Chippie comes over to help, pulls the wet steel back with his gloved hands, Abe keeps cutting, they make a good new door approximately where the old one used to be, and Xavier's got some compress kits plastered on the woman and is busy injecting her with various antishock superdrugs and a lot of new plasma/blood. Then it's time to get her into the inflatable conformable braces, neck and spine held firm and they reach in and everyone takes a hold, carefully here, breath held, warm flesh squeezed between the fingers, blood trickling over the back of the hand, they lift her out, oops her hand is caught, Abe snips the folded section of dash and she's free. Onto a stretcher, off to the ambulance room in the back of the truck. They run back and extricate the man, who may or may not be living, his head looks bad indeed but they stretcher him and run him into the gutbucket, lay him next to the woman. "Shit I've got to confirm the guy in the lead car," Abe remembers, grabs Xavier's steth and runs back. He has to break a window and lean in to get the steth on the driver's neck. Readout shows flat and he's back to the truck. A private gutbucket has showed to pick up the two from the follow-up car, Abe gives them a quick thumbs-up and guides the cutters as they're reeled back on board and jumps in the driver's seat, seat belt on yes, off they go. These old gasoline hogs can really accelerate.

Xavier sticks his head out the window that connects the cab to their rolling ER. "Going to the Lagunatic Asylum?"

"No, the canyon is so fucked up, I figure UCI is faster."

Xavier nods.

"How are they?"

"The guy's dead. He was dots, I imagine. The woman's still going, but she's lost a lot of blood and her heart's hurting. I got her patched and plugged in and she's drinking plasma, but her pulse be weak still. She could use a proper heart machine." Xavier's black face is shiny with sweat, he's looking uptrack anxiously, he wants them to go faster. Abe guns it, they rocket around the last curve onto the Laguna Freeway link between 405 and 5, left on 405 onramp and up the San Diego Freeway, not ontrack but on the shoulder beside it, flying past the tracked cars on their left, pushing 100, 105, quickly to the University Drive offramp and onto the meandering boulevard, here's where the driving gets tricky, don't want to pull a Fred Spaulding here, Fred who put a rescue truck into an overpass pylon and killed everyone aboard except the crash victim in back, who died two days later in the hospital.

Headlights, taillights, don't you dare make that left turn in front of me there isn't time *screech*, he puts the siren on full volume and the howl fills everything, throat sinuses cranium, they reach the campus and go down to California Avenue, hang a mean left and fire up the hill to the ER driveway and up to the ambulance doors. By the time he's out and to the back of the truck Xavier and an ER nurse are rolling the woman through swinging doors and inside.

Abe sits on the loading dock, quivering a bit. A couple more ER nurses come out and he gets up, helps them get the dead driver onto a gurney. Inside. Back onto the rubber edge of the loading dock.

Xavier comes back out, sits heavily beside him. "They're working on it." All those years of medic work, the two tours in Indonesia and all, and still Xavier gets into it, every run. He lights a cigarette, hands trembling, takes a deep drag. Abe watches, feeling that he is just as bad as Xavier, though he tries not to care at all. Don't get into a savior complex! as the unit counselor would say. He looks at his watch: 7:30. Two hours since they got the call. Hard to believe; it feels longer, shorter—like six hours have banged by in fifteen minutes. That's rescue work for you. "Hey, we were off half an hour ago," he remembers. "Our shift is over."

"Good."

Time passes.

A doctor bumps out the swinging doors. "Bad luck this time, boys," he says cheerily. "Both dead on arrival, I'm afraid." Briefly he puts his hands on their shoulders, goes back inside.

For a while they just sit there.

"Shit," says Xavier, flicking his cigarette into the darkness. In the dim light Abe can just see the look on his face.

"Hey, X, we did what we could."

"The woman was *not* DOA! They let her go inside!"

"Next time, X. Next time."

Xavier shakes his head, stands up. "We're off, hey?"

"Yeah."

"Let's get out of here then."

Silently they roll. Abe puts them back on track, enters the program that will take the truck to MacArthur and the Del Mar Freeway, then up the Newport to Dyer. Everything seems empty, quiet. They track into the Fire and Rescue station, park the truck among a few dozen others, go inside, file reports, clock out, walk to their own cars in the employee lot. Abe approaches his car feeling the familiar drained emptiness. Every time he reaches for his own keys in this lot it's the same. "Catch you later, X," he calls at the dark figure across the lot.

"Doubtless. When we on again?"

"Saturday."

"See you then."

Xavier backs out, off to the depths of lower Santa Ana, and some life Abe can barely imagine: X has a wife, four kids, ten thousand in-laws and dependents . . . a life out of his grandfather's generation, as full of melodrama as any video soap. And X, supporting the whole show, is right on the edge. He's going to crack soon, Abe thinks. After all these years.

He gets back onto the Newport Freeway, great aorta of all the OC lives. River of red fireflies, bearing him on. He punches the program for South Coast Plaza south, sits back. Clicks in a CD, need something loud, fast, aggressive . . . Three Spoons and a Stupid Fork, yeah, powering out their classic album *Get the Fuck Off My Beach.*

What would your carbrain say if it could talk?
Would it say Jump In? Would it say Get Out and Walk?
(You are a carbrain
You're firmly on track
You're given your directions
And you don't talk back)
You are a carbrain
And your car is going to crash!
On the cellular level
Everything'll go smash!
(And you'll be inside
You'll be taken for a ride)

Abe sings along at the top of his lungs, tracks into SCP, finds parking almost directly below Sandy's place, takes the elevator up, pops on in. Blast of light, loud music, it's the Tustin Tragedy on the CD here, singing "Happy Days" in Indonesian gamelan style, punctuated by machine-gun fire. The rhythms perk Abe up immediately, and Erica gives him a peck on the cheek. "Tashi was looking for you." Good. Sandy barges around a corner, "Abra*ham*, you look wilted, you just got off work, right?" The Sandy grin, an eyedropper appears in his fingers and it's head back, lids pulled open, drip drip drip. Abe offers it back to Sandy; "Polish it, there's more." Drip, drip, drip, his spinal cord is suddenly snapping off big bursts of excess electricity and he wanders into the next room, they're dancing there and he feels great shocks of energy coursing up his spine and out his fingertips, he dances hard, leaping for the ceiling, shaking it all out, now that feels good. He tilts his head back, "Yow! Yow! Yoweeee!" Coyote time at Sandy's place, traditional high point of the parties, everyone just hauls back and lets loose, they must be audible all the way to Huntington Beach. Great.

Feeling much better, he goes out onto the balcony. Still no sight of Tash, though the balcony's his spot; Tash never goes indoors when he can help it. Even lives on a roof, in a tent. Abe loves it; Tash, his closest friend, is like a cold salt splash of the Pacific.

Instead he encounters Jim. Jim's a good friend too, no doubt about it. But sometimes . . . Jim's so earnest, so unworldly; Abe has to be in the right mood to really enjoy Jim's intense meaningfulness. Or whatever it is. Not now. "Hey there, bro," Abe says, "Howzit." Pretty lidded, he is.

"Good. Hey, you worked today, huh? How'd it go?"

Ah, Jimbo. Just what he doesn't want to talk about. "Fine." Jim cares, and that's nice, but Abe wants some distraction, here, preferably Tash, or one of his young women friends . . . a little chat and he's off.

Still no Tash on the balcony. To his surprise, he runs into Lillian Keilbacher instead. "Hello, Lillian! I didn't know you knew Sandy!"

"I didn't, till tonight." She looks thrilled to have been introduced, which is funny since Sandy knows everyone.

Lillian is maybe eighteen, a fresh-faced cute kid, blond and suntanned, a lively innocent interest in things. . . . Her mother and Jim's mother and Abe's mother are stalwarts of the tiny church they all attended as kids; the mothers are still into it, Abe and Jim have fallen away like the rest of civilization, Lillian . . . perhaps in that transition zone, who knows. Shit, Abe thinks guiltily, she shouldn't be at a party like this! But that almost makes him laugh. Who is he, anyway? He realizes he's holding the eyedropper sort of hidden, and thinks he's probably insulting her by being condescending to her youth. Besides, they lid out in second grade these days. He offers it to her. "No thanks," she says, "it just makes me dizzy."

He laughs. "Good for you." He lids a drip, laughs again. "Shit, what are you doing here? Last I saw you you were about thirteen, weren't you?"

"Probably. But, you know, it doesn't last."

He cracks up. "No, I guess not."

"I probably know more than you think I do."

Utterly transparent come-on in her eyes as she sidles up to him, so girlish that he wonders if it's actually a sophisticated come-on in clever disguise. He laughs and sees she's hurt, instant contraction back into herself as when you touch a sea anemone, ah, clearly she knows just as little as he suspected she did, maybe less. A girl, really. "You shouldn't be here," he says.

"Don't you worry about me." She sniffs disdainfully. "We're leaving soon to go to my friend Marsha's to spend the night anyway."

Jesus. "Good, good. How are your folks?"

"Fine, really."

"Say hello to them for me." Lillian agrees and with a last winsome over-the-shoulder smile she's off with her buddies. Abe remembers the girlish come-on and cracks up. Maybe she had in mind a first kiss from this handsome dashing old acquaintance, an older man no lie. A nice kid, truly; Sandy's seems definitely the wrong place for her, and he's glad to see her and her young friends giggling together out the door, the brave exploration into the den of sin completed.

He's even gladder half an hour later when Tash is pulled dripping from the Jacuzzi, naked and totally lidded. Giggling young women, friends of Angela's that Sandy calls the Tustin Trollops, maneuver Tashi onto the surfboard surrogate and urge him to ride some video waves for them, which he does with a perfect stoned grace, unaware of anything but the video wave, a Pipeline beauty twenty feet tall and stretching off into eternity. "Whoah," says Tash from deep in his own tube. Erica, Tash's ally, watches him with a look of sharp disapproval; Abe laughs at her.

Jim says "Hey, with his arms out like that he looks just like the statue of Poseidon in the Athens museum, here wait a second."

He goes to the video console and starts typing at the computer, and suddenly the wave is replaced by the motionless image of a statue: tall darkened-bronze bearded man, arms up to throw a javelin, eyes empty holes in the metal. Tash looks up, takes the pose instantly, and it brings down the house. "He does look just like him!" everyone exclaims. Jim, laughing, says, "Even the eyes are the same!" Tash growls in mock anger, without breaking the pose.

Abe laughs loud enough to draw the attention of a couple of the Tustin Trollops. Mary and Inez come over and join him on the couch; they're part of Abe's little fan club, and their lithe bodies press against his warmly, their fingers tangle in his black curls. Ah, yes, the blisses of unallied freedom. . . .

He's putting his arm around Inez when something—the give of soft flesh?—causes the image of the injured woman to strike him. Pulled from the wreck, bent, patched, braced, bloody—Fuck. Tension twists his stomach and he hugs Inez to him violently, clamping his eyes shut; his face contorts back to a mask of normality. "Where's that eyedropper I had with me?"

10

Dennis McPherson walks into his office one morning, just a mail visit before he runs over to White Sands, New Mexico, to oversee a test of the RPV system, now called Stormbee. He finds a note commanding him to go up and see Lemon.

His pulse goes up as the elevator rises. It's only been a week since Lemon flared into one of his tantrums, pounding his desk and going scarlet in the face and shouting right at McPherson. "You're too slow to do your job! You're a goddamned nitpicking perfectionist, and I won't abide it! I don't allow dawdlers on my team! This is a war like any other! You seize the offensive when the chance comes, and go all the way with it! I want to see that proposal for Stormbee *yesterday!''* And so on. Lemon likes to burst all constraints occasionally, everyone working for him agrees about that. This doesn't make McPherson like it any better. Lemon's been out of engineering so long that little matters like *weight* or *voltage* or *performance reliability* don't mean anything to him anymore. Those are things for others to worry about. For him it's *cost-effectiveness, schedules,* the team's *momentum,* its *look.* He's the team's fearless leader, the little führer of his little tin reich. If the project were perpetual motion he'd still be screaming about schedules, costs, PR . . .

This morning he's Mr. Charm again, ushering McPherson in, calling him "Mac," sitting casually on the edge of his desk. Doesn't he realize that the charmer routine means nothing when combined with the tantrums? Worse than that—the two-facedness turns him into a slimy hypocrite, a manic-depressive, an actor. It would be easier to take if he just did the screaming tyrant thing all the time, really it would.

"So, how's Stormbee coming along, Mac?''

"We've manufactured a prototype pod that is within the specs set by Feldkirk. The lab tests went okay and we're scheduled to test it on one of Northrop's RPVs out at White Sands this afternoon. If those go well we can either run it through some envelope testing or give to the Air Force and let them go at it.''

"We'll give it to the Air Force. The sooner the better.'' Of course. "They'll be testing it anyway.''

That's true, but it would be a lot safer for LSR if they found out about any performance problems before they let the Air Force see it. McPherson doesn't say this, although he should. This abrogation of his responsibility to the program irritates him, but he's sick of the tantrums.

Lemon is going on as if the matter is settled. That's the trouble with superblack programs; the contractor tends to do less testing than any competition for a white program could possibly get away with. And yet there's no good reason for it; they don't have a deadline. Feldkirk just said they should get back to him as soon as they could. So the haste is just Lemon's obsession; he's weakening the strength of their proposal by a completely irrational sense that they have to hurry. . . .

"We're going as fast as we can," McPherson allows himself to say. It's risking another outburst, but to hell with it.

"Oh I know you are, I know." A dangerous gleam appears in Lemon's eye, he's about to press home the point of how he knows—because he's the boss here, he's in charge, he knows all. But McPherson deadpans his way through the moment, passes through unscathed. Lemon trots out some more of his führer encouragements, then says, "Okay, get yourself out to White Sands," with a very good imitation of a smile. McPherson doesn't attempt to reciprocate.

He tracks to San Clemente and takes the superconductor to El Paso. Fired like a bullet in an electromagnetic gun.

It's been a tough couple of months, getting this test prepared. Every weekday he's gone into the office at six A.M., made a list of the day's activities that is sometimes forty items long, and gone at it until early evening, or even later than that. At first he had to deal with all of the tasks concerned with designing the Stormbee system: talking with the engineers and programmers, making suggestions, giving commands, coordinating their efforts, making decisions . . . It's good work at that point, responding to the technical challenge and dealing with the problems presented by them. And his design crew is a good group, resourceful, hardworking, quirky; he has to ride herd on the efforts of this disparate bunch, and it's interesting.

Then they got into the production and components testing phase, and the debugging of the programming. That was frustrating as always; it's beyond his technical competence to contribute much in the way of specifics at that point, and all he could do was orchestrate the tests and keep everyone working at them. It's a bit too much like Lemon's role at that point, not that he'd ever go about it in the same style.

Then it was time for the big components' tests. And now, time for the first test of the entire system.

The train arrives inside the hour, and from the tube station at El Paso the LSR helicopter lofts him over to White Sands Missile Range, the testing grounds that a consortium of defense companies leases from the government.

As he gets out of the helicopter McPherson reaches in his coat pocket for the sunglasses he brought with him. It really is uncanny how white the sand in this area is: a strange geological feature, for sure. Not that anyone actually visits the little national park on the edge of the testing grounds.

McPherson is carted to the LSR building on the range, and several of the engineers there greet him. "It's ready to go," says Will Hamilton, LSR's on-site testing chief. "We've got Runway Able for noon and one, and the RPV is fueled and prepped."

"Great," says McPherson, checking his watch. "That's half an hour?"

"Right."

They have coffee and some croissants in the cafe, then take the elevator up six floors to the observation deck on the roof. Cameras and computers will be monitoring all aspects of the test, but everyone still wants to see the thing actually happen. Now they stand on a broad concrete deck, looking out over the waves of pure white dunes, extending to the horizons like an ocean that has been frozen and then had everything but pure salt bleached away. Such a weird landscape! McPherson enjoys the sight of it immensely.

Over to the north are the runways that the companies all share, crossing each other like an X over an H, their smudged concrete looking messy in the surrounding pureness. Compounds for Aerodyne, Hughes, SDR, Lockheed, Williams, Ford Aerospace, Raytheon, Parnell, and RWD lie scattered around in the dunes, like blocks dropped by a giant child. There's a great plume of smoke out to the east, lofting some thirty thousand feet into the sky; someone's test has succeeded, or failed, it's hard to tell, although there's an oiliness to the plume that suggests failure. "RWD was trying out the new treetop stealth bomber's guidance system," Hamilton informs McPherson. "They say it didn't see a little hill over that way."

"Too bad."

"The pilot was automatically ejected no more than a second before impact, and he survived. Only broken legs and ribs."

"That's good."

"RPVs are the coming thing, there's no doubt about it. Everything moves too fast for pilots to be useful! They're just up there at risk, and it costs ten times as much to make a plane that will accommodate them, even though they can't do anything anymore."

McPherson squints. "As long as all the automatic systems work."

Hamilton laughs. "Like ours, you mean. Well, we'll find out real soon now." He gestures to the west. "The target tanks are out there on the horizon. We've followed your instructions, so they're equipped with the Soviets' Badger antiaircraft systems, and surrounded by Armadillo SAM installations. Those should give the plane a run for its money."

McPherson nods. The six tanks on the western horizon, also under remote control, are little black frogs trundling south in a diagonal pattern, churning up sugary clouds of sand. "It's a fair test."

They wait, and to pass the time they talk some more about the test, saying things they both already know. But that's all right. Everyone gets a little nervous when the time comes to see if all their efforts will actually amount to anything. Will the numbers translate into reality successfully? The talk is reassuring.

The deck intercom crackles as they're patched into air control for the runways. A hangar north of the runway has opened, and out of it rolls a long black jet with a narrow fuselage.

Below the fuselage are two pods.
They're as big as the fuselage itself: one black, one white.
Sensors. You can close your eyes, it won't matter.
Under each delta wing, flanking the turbines: arrays of
   little fletched missiles.
The front of the fuselage comes to a long point, like a
   narwhale's.
The rear flares out into stabilizers almost as big as the
   wings.
Under the fuselage, a small cylindrical rocket booster.
Understand: it doesn't look like a plane anymore.
And those brake lights, winking in the axons . . .

Altogether it's a weird contraption, appearing mole blind and not at all aerodynamic. There's something eerie about the way it rolls to the end of the runway, turns, fires up the jets and shoots down the runway and up into the dark blue sky. Who's minding the store? Hamilton is grinning at the sight, and McPherson can feel that he is too. There's something awfully . . . ingenious about the thing. It really is quite a machine.

The intercom has been giving takeoff specs and such; now, as the RPV's rocket booster cuts in and it recedes to nothing but a flame dot in the sky, they listen. "Test vehicle three three five now approaching seventy thousand feet. Test program three three five beginning T minus ten seconds. Test program beginning now."

Ten of the dozen men on the deck start the stopwatch functions of their wristwatches. Some of them have binoculars around their necks, but there won't be a chance to use them until after the test strike is made; there's nothing to be seen in the sky, it's a clean, dark blue, darker than any sky ever seen in OC. Nothing in it. McPherson finds that he's not breathing regularly, and he concentrates on hitting a steady rhythm. Scanning the sky, in the area where the RPV was last seen, probably not where it will reappear, look around more . . . his eyesight is remarkably sharp, and unfocusing his attention so that he sees all the expanse of blue above him, he notices a tiny flaw, there far to the north.

"Up there," he says quickly, and points. The chip of light moves overhead and then quicker than any of them can really follow it the black thing darts down zips over the *boom* white dunes and the tanks become orange blooms of fire as the thing turns up and fires back into the stratosphere like a rocket. Mach 7, really too fast for the eye to see: the whole pass has taken less than three seconds. The tanks are black clouds of smoke, *BoomBoom B-B-B-B-BOOOOM!* The sound finally reaches them. Empty blue sky, white dunes marred by six pillars of oily flame, off there on the horizon. Every tank gone.

They were shouting when the booms hit. Now they're shaking hands and laughing, all talking at once. No matter how many tests they've witnessed, the extreme speed of this craft, and the tremendous volume and power of the explosions, inevitably impresses them. It's a physical, sensory shock, for one thing, and then conceptually it's exhilarating to think that their calculations, their work, can result in such an awesome display. Hamilton is grinning broadly. "Those Badgers and Armadillos didn't even have time to register incoming, I'll bet! The data will show how far they got."

"And the pods all worked, " McPherson says. That was the crucial test, the one of the target designation and tracking. With all those things functioning, they've fulfilled the specs. The fact that the Soviets' best field SAM system isn't fast enough to stop the Stormbee is just gravy, confirmation that the Air Force has asked for the right things. The main fact is, they have a system that works.

They spend the next few hours going over the data that the test generated. It all looks very good indeed. They pop the cork on a bottle of champagne and click plastic cups together before McPherson gets on the helicopter with the data, to return to El Paso and OC.

Flying over the magnets in the soundless, vibrationless calm of the tube train, McPherson can't help but feel a little glow of accomplishment. He ignores the printouts in his lap and looks around the plush car of the train. Businessmen in the big seats are hidden behind opened copies of *The Wall Street Journal*. With no windows and no vibration and no noise, it's difficult to believe that they are moving at Mach 2. The world has become an incredible place. . . .

When he returns it'll be time for the painful task of writing up the description of the system, in proposal form. Several hundred pages it will run to, not as much as a bid proposal, it's true, but still, it will be his job to oversee and edit the ungodly number of descriptions, charts, diagrams and such. Not fun.

Still. Being at that stage means a lot; it means they have a working system, within the size and power specs given. It's more than a lot of LSR's programs can say, at the moment. McPherson thinks of Ball Lightning briefly, shoves the thought away. This is one of the rare times that a program director can say, The work is done, and it's a success. He hasn't been given all that many commands like this one, and it means a lot.

The image of the test comes back to him. That inhumanly swift stoop, attack, disappearance; the quick, precise, and total destruction of the six lumbering tanks; it really was quite extraordinary, both physically and intellectually.

And remembering it, McPherson suddenly sees the larger picture, the meaning of the event. It's as if he just stood back from a video screen, after months of examining each dot. Now the image is revealed. This system, this RPV with its Stormbee eyes, its armament of smart missiles, its speed, its radar invisibility, its cheapness and lack of a human pilot put at risk—this system is the kind of pinpoint weapon that can really and truly change the nature of warfare. If the Soviets roll out of Eastern Europe with their giant Warsaw Pact army—for that matter, if any army starts an invasion anywhere—then these pilotless drones can drop out of space and fire their missiles before any defensive system can find them or respond, and for each run a half dozen tanks or vehicles are gone. And quick as you can say wow the invading force is gone with it.

The net result of that, given that this technology is pretty much out there for anyone to develop—LSR is not a superinventor after all, nobody is—the net result is that when every country has systems like this one, then *no one will be able to invade another country*. It just won't be possible.

Oh, of course there will still be wars—he is not so idealistic as to think that pinpoint weapons systems will end war as an institution—but any major invasion force is doomed to a swift surgical destruction. So really, large-scale invasions become out of the question, which severely curtails how big a war can get.

And all this without having to use the threat of nuclear weapons. For a hundred years now, almost, NATO has used nuclear weapons as the ultimate stopper to any Warsaw Pact invasion. Battlefield nukes in artillery shells, nuclear submarines in the Baltic and Med, the illegal intermediate-range "messenger missiles" hidden in West Germany, ready to make a demonstration pop if the tanks roll . . . .It's one of the most dangerous situations in the world, because if one nuke goes off, there's no telling where it will stop. Most likely it won't stop until everyone's dead. And even if it does stop, Europe's cities will be wiped out. And all to resist tanks!

But now, now, with Stormbee . . . They can take the nuclear weapons out of there, and still have a completely secure defense against a conventional invasion. The cities and their populations won't have to go up with the invaders; nothing will be needed but a precise, limited, one could even say humane, response. If you invade us, your invading force will be picked off, by unstoppable robot snipers. Swift, surgical destruction for any invading force;

and the war wiped out with it. War—major wars of invasion, anyway—made impossible! My God! It's quite a thought! A weapon that will *make antagonists talk*—without the horrific threat of mutual assured destruction. In fact, with weapons like these, it really makes perfect sense to dismantle all the megatonnage, to get rid of the nuclear horror. . . . Can it really be true? Have we reached that point in history where technology finally will make war obsolete, and nuclear weapons unnecessary?

Yes, it seems it can be true: he has seen the leading edge of that truth, just barely seen it as it swooped down over the white sands of the desert like a Mach 7 mirage, a peripheral vision, that very day. It actually looks as if his work, the sweat of his brow, might help to lift from the world the hundred-year-long nightmare threat of nuclear annihilation. Might even help to lift the thousand-year-long threat of major, catastrophic war. It's . . . well, it's work you can take pride in.

And hurtling back over the surface of the desert, McPherson suddenly feels that pride more strongly than he ever has in his entire life, something like a radiant glow, a sun in his chest. It really is something.

11

In his dream Jim walks over a hillside covered with ruins. Below the hill spreads a black lake. The ruins are nothing but low stone walls, and the land is empty. Jim wanders among the walls searching for something, but as always he can't quite remember what it is he seeks. He comes across a piece of violet glass from a stained-glass window, but he knows that isn't what he is after. Something like a ghost bulges out of the top of the hill to tell him everything—

He wakes in his little apartment in Foothill, the sun beaming through the window. He groans, rolls onto the floor. Hangover here. What were they lidding last night? Groggily he looks around. His room is a mess, bedding and clothing scattered everywhere, as if a rainbow collapsed and landed in his bedroom.

Three walls of the room are covered with big Thomas Brothers maps of Orange County: one from the 1930s (faint tracing of roads), one from 1990 (north half of county gridded with interlocking towns, southern half, the hills and the Irvine and O'Neill ranches, still almost empty), one the very latest edition (the whole county gridded and overgridded). Kind of like keeping X-rays of a cancer on your walls, Jim has thought more than once. Surrealty tumor.

Stagger to the bathroom. Standing at the toilet he stares at a badly framed print of an old orange crate label. The bathroom walls are covered by these:

Three friars, taste-testing oranges by the white mission.
    Behind them green groves, and blue snow-topped
    mountains in the distance.
Portola, standing with Spanish flag unfurled, silent, on a
    peak in Placentia.
Two peacocks in front of a Disneyland castle: ''California
    Dream.''
Little bungalow in the neat green rows of a grove in
    bloom.
Beautiful Mexican woman, holding a basket of oranges.
    Behind her green groves, and blue mountains in the
    distance.
You have never lived here.

The labels, from the first half of the twentieth century, are the work of printer Max Schmidt and artists Archie Vazques and Othello Michetti, among others. The intensely rich, exotic colors are the result of a process called zincography. Taken together, Jim believes, these labels make up Orange County's first and only utopia, a collective vision of Mediterranean warmth and ease astonishing in its art deco vividness. Ah, what a life! Jim tries to imagine the effect on the poor farmers of the Midwest, coming in to the general store from the isolated wheat farm, the Depression, the subzero temperatures, the dustbowls—and there among the necessary goods in their drab boxes and tins, these fantasies in stunning orange, cobalt, green, white! No wonder OC is so crowded. These labels must have given those farmers a powerful urge to Go West. And in those days they really could move to the land pictured on the boxes (sort of). For Jim it's out of reach. He lives here, but is infinitely further away.

The utopias of the past are always a little sad. Jim steps into pants, pulls on a shirt, pads through his ap and looks out the front door.

Sunny day. Overhead looms the freeway, with its supporting pylons coming down in backyards or on streetcorners. Kind of a big concrete *thing*, squatting up there in the sky, crossing it side to side. The Foothill Freeway, in fact, extended into southern OC around the turn of the century. The land it needed to cross was by then completely covered by suburbia, and homeowners objected strenuously to having their houses bought up and torn down. The solution? Make the new freeway a viaduct, part of the elevated autopian network being built over the most congested parts of the Newport and Santa Ana freeways. Values for the homes below the flying concrete would plummet, of course, but they would still be there, right?

Now it's a perfect place for white-collar poor folk like Jim to live, in apartmentalized old suburban homes. The cars above aren't even that loud anymore. And the shade of the freeway can be pretty welcome on those hot summer days, as the real estate agents are quick to remind you.

Jim goes back inside, feeling blah. Hung over, confused. While he eats his cereal and milk he thinks about Arthur Bastanchury. Good old Basque name, from shepherds who came to OC when James Irvine used his land to raise sheep. Arthur still looks a little Basque: dark complexion, light eyes, square jaw. And they have a good long tradition of active resistance back home in Spain. Not to mention terrorism. Jim doesn't want to have anything to do with terrorism. But if there's something else that can be done —some other way . . . He sighs, eats his cereal, stares at his living room. His living room stares back at him.

Books everywhere. The OC historians, Friis, Meadows, Starr et al.

Volumes of poetry. Novels. Stacks and stacks, anything
anywhere.
In the corner under the window, the Zen center: mat,
incense, candle.
CD disks all over an old console, on a bookcase of bricks
and boards.
The desk is buried in paper. The couch is tattered, bamboo
and vinyl.
Paper everywhere. Newspapers, mail, scraps.
A poem is a grocery list.
We eat our culture every day.
How does it taste to you?
Oops! Someone's forgotten to do the dishes.
No one minds a little dust, either.

"We believe that the truly staggering amounts of money and
human effort (which is what money stands for, remember) that are
being invested in armaments represent the greatest danger of our
time," Arthur said to Jim later on the night of their poster blitz.
"Nothing that we've tried in the legal channels of American politics has ever slowed the military-industrial complex down. They're
the biggest power in the country, and nothing can stop them. We
wanted to stay nonviolent, but it was clear we had to act, to go
outside politics. The technology was available to attack the products without attacking the producers, and we decided to use it."

"How can you be sure you won't hurt anybody?" Jim asked
uneasily. "I mean, it always starts this way, right? You don't want
to be violent, but then you get frustrated, maybe careless, and
pretty soon you fall over the line into terrorism. I don't want to
have anything to do with that."

"There's a big difference between terrorism and sabotage,"
Arthur said sharply. "We use methods that harm plastics, programs, and various composite construction materials, without endangering people. Then we select what we think are the most
destabilizing weapons programs, and by God we take it to them.
Maybe later I can go into more detail. But we're patient, you see.
We aren't going to start escalating just because we don't get results
right away. It might take twenty years, forty years, and we know
that. And we are absolutely committed to making sure people aren't
physically hurt. It's vital to us, you see. If we don't hold to that

we become just another part of the war machine, a stimulus to the security police industry or whatever."

Jim nodded, interested. It made sense.

Now, eating his breakfast, he is less certain about it all. On the poster-blitz night he told Arthur he was interested in helping, and Arthur said he would get back to him. That was what, a week ago? Two weeks? Hard to say. Would Arthur bring the matter up again? Jim doesn't know, but he isn't easy about it.

Upset, he decides to meditate. He sits in his Zen corner and lights a stick of incense. Preparation for *zazen*; empty the mind. No thoughts, just openness. Watch sunlight pierce the sweet rising smoke.

The no-thoughts part is hard, damned hard. Concentrate on breathing. In, out, in, out, in, out, yeah there he was doing it! Oops. Spoiled it. Start over. Must have gotten off five or ten seconds, though. Pretty good. Shh! Try again. In, out, in, out, in, out, wonder who the Dodgers are playing today *oops*, in, out, in, out, pretty smoke curl *shh!*, in, what's that out there? Ah, hell. Don't think, don't think, okay I'm not thinking, I'm not thinking, I'm not thinking, hey look at that I'm not thinking! . . . Oh. Well. In? Out?

It's useless. Jim McPherson must be the most wired Zen Buddhist in history. How can he actually stop thinking? Impossible. It doesn't even happen in his sleep!

Well, he did it for about fifteen seconds there. Better than some mornings. He gets up, feeling depressed. Mornings are typically low for him, must be low blood sugar or the lack of the various drugs that are usually in him. But this one's a special bummer. He's pretty confused, pretty depressed.

Might as well go with the flow of it. Jim puts on his "Super-tragic Symphony," a concoction of his own made up of the four saddest movements of symphonic music that he knows of. He's recorded them in the sequence he thinks most effective. First comes the funeral march from Beethoven's Third Symphony, grand and stirring in its resistance to fate, full of active grief as an opening movement should be. Second movement is the second movement of Beethoven's Seventh Symphony, the stately solemn tune that Bruno Walter discovered could be made into a dirge, if you ignored

Beethoven's instruction to play it allegretto and went to adagio. Heavy, solemn, moody, rhythmic.

The third movement is the third movement from Brahms's Third Symphony, sweet and melancholy, the essence of October, all the sadness of all the autumns of all time wrapped up in a tuneful *tristesse* that owes its melodic structure to the previous movement from Beethoven's Seventh. Jim likes this fact, which he discovered on his own; it makes it look like the "Supertragic Symphony" was meant to be.

Then the finale is the last movement of Tchaikovsky's *Pathetique*, no fooling around here, all the stops pulled, time to just bawl your guts out! Despair, sorrow, grief, all of czarist Russia's racking misery, Tchaikovsky's personal troubles, all condensed into one final awful *moan*. The ultimate bummer.

What a symphony! Of course there's a problem with the shifting key signatures, but Jim doesn't give a damn about key signatures. Ignore them and he can gather up all of his downer feelings and sing them out, conduct them too, wandering around the ap trying feebly to clean up a bit, collapsing in chairs, crawling blackly over the floors as he waves an imaginary baton, getting lower and lower. Man, he's *low*. He's so low he's getting high off it! And when it's all over he feels drained. Catharsis has taken place. Everything's a lot better.

He even feels in the mood to write a poem. Jim is a poet, he *is* a poet, he is he is he is.

He finds it hard going, however, because the piles of poetry collections on his bookcases and around his junk-jammed desk contain so many masterpieces that he can't stand it. Every tap at the old computer keyboard is mocked by the volumes behind and around him, Shakespeare, Shelley, Stevens, Snyder, shit! It's impossible to write any more poetry in this day and age. The best poets of his time make Jim laugh with scorn, though he imitates them slavishly in his own attempts. Postmodernism, moldering in its second half century—what does it amount to but squirming? You have to do something new, but there's nothing new left to do. Serious trouble, that. Jim solves the problem by writing postmodern poems that he hopes to make post-postmodern by scrambling with some random program. The problem with this solution is that postmodern poetry already reads as if the lines have been scrambled by a random program, so the effects of Jim's ultraradical experimentation are difficult to notice.

But it's time to try again. A half hour's staring at the blank screen, a half hour's typing. He reads the result.

> Rent an apartment.
> There are orange trees growing under the floor.
> Two rooms and a bath, windows, a door.
> The freeway is your roof. What shade.
> The motorized landscape: autopia, the best ride.
> Magnetism is invisible, but we believe in it anyway.
> Step up the pylon ladder in the evening sun.
> Lie on the tracks to catch a tan.
> They truck the sand in for all our beaches.
> Do you know how to swim? No. Just rest.
> Eat an orange, up there. Read a book.
> Commuters running over you take a brief look.

Okay, now run this through a randomizer, the lucky one that seems to have such a good eye for rhythm. Result?

> The freeway is your roof. What shade.
> Eat an orange, up there. Read a book.
> The motorized landscape: autopia, the best ride.
> Rent an apartment.
> Lie on the tracks to catch a tan.
> Two rooms and a bath, windows, a door.
> Magnetism is invisible, but we believe in it anyway.
> They truck the sand in for all our beaches.
> Commuters running over you take a brief look.
> Do you know how to swim? No. Just rest.
> There are orange trees growing under the floor.
> Step up the pylon ladder in the evening sun.

There, pretty neat, eh? Jim reads the new version aloud. Well . . . He tries another variation and suddenly all three versions look stupid. He just can't get past the notion that if you can let your computer scramble the lines of a poem, and in doing so come up with a poem that's better, or at least just as good, then there must be a certain deficiency in the poem. In, for instance, its sequentiality. He thinks of Shakespeare's sonnets, Shelley's "Julian and Maddalo." Is he really performing the same activity they did? "Rent an apartment"?

Ach. It's a ridiculous effort. The truth is, Arthur was right. He doesn't have any work that means anything to him. And in fact he's almost late for this meaningless work, the one that brings in the money. That isn't good. He throws on shoes, brushes his teeth and hair, runs out to his car and hits the program for the First American Title Insurance and Real Estate Company, on East Fifth Street in Santa Ana. Oldest title company in Orange County, still going strong, and when Jim arrives at his desk there and boots up he finds that there's the usual immense amount of work waiting to be typed in and processed. Transfers, notices, assessments, the barrage of legal screenwork needed to make sales, move land in and out of escrow. Jim is the lowliest sort of clerk, a part-time typist, really. The three-hour shift is exhausting, even though he does the work on automatic pilot, and spends his time thinking about the recent conversation with Arthur. Everyone's typing away at their screens, absorbed in the worlds of their tasks, oblivious to the office and the people working around them. Jim doesn't even recognize anyone; there are so many people on the short shifts, and Jim has so few hours, that few of his colleagues ever become familiar. And none of them are here today.

It gets so depressing that he goes in to visit Humphrey, who is sort of his boss, in that Humphrey makes use of the services of Jim's pool. Humphrey is the rising young star of the real estate division, which Jim finds disgusting. But they're friends, so what can he say?

"Hi, Hump. How's it going."

"Real good, Jim! How about you?"

"Okay. What's got you so happy?"

"Well, you know how I managed to grab one of the last pieces of Cleveland when the government sold it."

"Yeah, I know." This, to Jim, is one of the great disasters of the last twenty years: the federal government's decision, under immense pressure from the southern California real estate lobby and the OC Board of Supervisors, to break up the Cleveland National Forest, on the border of Orange and Riverside counties, and sell it for private development. A good way to help pay the interest on the gargantuan national debt, and there wasn't really any forest out there anyway, just dirt hills surrounded by a bunch of communities that desperately needed the land, right? Right. And so, with the encouragement of a real estate developer become Secretary of the Interior, Congress passed a law, unnoticed in a larger package, and the last empty land in OC was divided into five hundred lots and sold at public auction. For a whole lot of money. A good move, politically. Popular all over the state.

"Well," Humphrey says, "it looks like the financing package is coming together for the office tower we want to build there. Ambank is showing serious interest, and that will seal things if they go for it."

"But Humphrey!" Jim protests. "The occupancy rate out in Santiago office buildings is only about thirty percent! You tried to get people to commit to this complex and you couldn't find anybody!"

"True, but I got a lot of written assurances that people would consider moving in if the building were there, especially when we promised them free rent for five years. The notes have convinced most of the finance packagers that it's viable."

"But it isn't! You know that it isn't! You'll build another forty-story tower out there, and it'll stand there empty!"

"Nah." Humphrey shakes his head. "Once it's there it'll fill up. It'll just take a while. The thing is, Jim, if you get the land and the money together at the same time, it's time to build! Occupancy will take care of itself. The thing is, we need the final go-ahead from Ambank, and they're so damn slow that we might lose the commitment of the other financiers before they get around to approving it."

"If you build and no one occupies the space then Ambank is going to end up holding the bills! I can see why they might hesitate!"

But Humphrey doesn't want to think about that, and he's got a meeting with the company president in a half hour, so he shoos Jim out of his office.

Jim goes back to his console, picks up the phone, and calls Arthur. "Listen, I'm really interested in what we talked about the other night. I want—"

"Let's not talk about it now," Arthur says quickly. "Next

time I see you. Best to talk in person, you know. But that's good. That's real good.''

Back to work, fuming at Humphrey, at his job, at the greedy and stupid government, from the local board of supervisors up to Congress and this foul administration. Shift over, three more hours sacrificed to the great money god. He's on the wheel of economic birth and death, and running like a rat in it. He shuts down and prepares to leave. Scheduled for dinner at the folks' tonight—

Oh shit! He's forgotten to visit Uncle Tom! That won't go over at all with Mom. God. What a day this is turning out to be. What time is it, four? And they have afternoon visiting hours. Mom's sure to ask. There's no good way out of it. The best course is to track down there real quick and drop in on Tom real briefly before going up for dinner. Oh, man.

12

On the track down 405 to Seizure World he clicks on the radio, they're playing The Pudknockers' latest and he blasts himself with a full hundred and twenty decibels of volume, singing along as loud as he can:

I'm swimming in the amniotic fluid of love
Swimming like a finger to the end of the glove
When I reach the top I'm going to dive right in
I'm the sperm in the egg—did I lose? did I win?

Seizure World spreads over the Laguna Hills, from El Toro to Mission Viejo: "Rossmoor Leisure World," a condomundo for the elderly that used to be only for the richest of the old. Now it's got its ritzy sections and its slums and its mental hospitals just like any other "town" in OC, and overpopulation sure, there's more old folks now than ever before, an immense percentage of the population is over seventy, and two or three percent are over a hundred, and they have to go somewhere, right? So there are half a million of them densepacked here.

Jim parks, gets out. Now this place: this is depression. He hates Seizure World with a passion. Uncle Tom does too, he's pretty sure. But with emphysema, and relying completely on Social Security, the old guy doesn't have much choice. These subsidized aps are as cheap as you can get, and only the old can get them. So here Tom is, in a condomundo that looks like all the rest, except everything is smaller and dingier, closer to dissolution. No pretending here, no Mediterranean fake front on the tenement reality. This is an old folks' home.

And Tom lives in the mental ward of it—though usually he is lucid enough. Most days he lies fairly calmly, working to breathe. Then every once in a while he loses it, and has to be watched or he'll attack people—nurses, anyone. This has been the pattern for the last decade or so, anyway. He's over a hundred.

Jim can't really bear to think about it for too long, so he doesn't. When he's out in OC it never occurs to him to think of Uncle Tom and how he lives. But during these infrequent visits it's shoved in his face.

Up the wheelchair ramp to the check-in desk. The nurse has a permanent sour expression, a bitchy voice. "Visiting hours end in forty-five minutes."

Don't worry.

Down the dark hallway, which smells of antiseptic. Wheelchair cases bang into the walls like bumper cars, the old wrecks in them drooling, staring at nothing, drugged out. A young nurse pushes one chair case down the hall, blinking rapidly, just about to cry. Yes, we're in the nursing home again. ("Did I lose? did I win?")

Tom's got a room just bigger than his bed, with a south-facing window that he treasures. Jim knocks, enters. Tom's lying there staring out at the sky, in a trance.

Wrinkled plaid flannel pajamas.
Three-day stubble of white beard.

Do you live here?
Clear plastic tube, from nostrils to tank under bed.
   Oxygen.
Bald, freckled pate. Ten thousand wrinkles. A turtle's
   head.

Slowly it turns, and the dull brown eyes regard him, focus, blink rapidly, as the mind behind them pulls back into the room from wherever it was voyaging. Jim swallows, uncomfortable as always. "Hi, Uncle Tom."

Tom's laugh is a sound like plastic crackling. "Don't call me that. Makes me feel like Simon Legree is about to come in. And whip me." Again the laugh; he's waking up. The bitter, sardonic gleam returns to his glance, and he shifts up in the bed. "Maybe that's appropriate. You call me Uncle Tom, I call you Nigger Jim. Two slaves talking."

Jim smiles effortfully. "I guess that's right."

"Is it? So what brings you here? Lucy not coming this week?"

"Well, ah . . ."

"That's all right. I wouldn't come here myself if I could help it." The plastic cracks. "Tell me what you've been up to. How are your classes?"

"Fine. Well—teaching people to write is hard. They don't read much, so of course they don't have much idea how to write."

"It's always been like that."

"I bet it's worse now."

"No takers there."

Tom watches him. Suddenly Jim remembers his archaeological expedition. "Hey! I went and dug up a piece of El Modena Elementary School. Shoot, I forgot to bring it." He tells Tom the story, and Tom chuckles with his alarming laugh.

"You probably got some construction material from the donut place. But it was a nice idea. El Modena Elementary School. What a thought. It was old when I went there. They closed it as soon as La Veta was finished. Two long wooden buildings, two stories high with a cellar under each. Big bell in one. The high school got the bell later and the principal, who had been principal of the elementary school years before. Went crazy at the dedication. Had a nervous breakdown right in front of us. Big dirt lot between the two buildings. They were firetraps, we had fire drills almost every day. I played a lot of ball on that lot. Once I singled and stretched it to two, they overthrew and I took third, overthrew again and I went home. They made a play on me there, and I was safe but Mr. Beauchamp called me out. Because he didn't like me hot-dogging like that. He was a bastard. We used to bail out of swings at the top of the swing. Go flying. I can't believe we didn't break limbs regularly, but we didn't.''

Tom sighs, looking out the window as if it gives a prospect onto the previous century. He recounts his past with a wandering, feverish bitterness, as if angry that it's all so far gone. Jim finds it both interesting and depressing at once.

"There were a couple of girls that hung together, everyone hounded them without mercy. Called them Popeye and Mabusa, meaning Medusa I suppose. Although it amazes me that any kid there knew that much. They were retarded, see, and looked bad. Popeye all shriveled, Mabusa big and ugly, Mongoloid. Boys used to hunt for them at recess, to make fun of them.'' Tom shakes his head, staring out the window again. "I had a game of my own that I played on the teacher who was recess monitor, a kind of hide-and-seek. Psychological warfare, really. I used the cellars to get from one side of the yard to the other to pop out and surprise her. The monitor would see me here, then there—it drove her nuts. One time I was doing that, and I found Popeye and Mabusa down there in the cellar hiding, huddled together. . . .'' He blinks.

"Kids are cruel,'' Jim says.

"And they stay that way! They stay that way.'' Coppery bitterness burrs Tom's voice. "The nurses here call us O's and Q's. O's have their mouths hanging open. Q's have their mouths hanging open with their tongues stuck out. Funny, eh?'' He shakes his head. "People are cruel.''

Jim grits his teeth. "Maybe that's why you became a public defender, eh?'' Seeing two retarded kids, huddled together in a cellar: can that shape a life?

"Maybe it was.'' The little room is taking on a coppery light, the air has a coppery taste. "Maybe it was.''

"So what was it like, being a public defender?"
"What do you mean? It was the kind of work that tears your
heart out. Poor people get arrested for crimes. Most crimes are
committed by really poor people, they're desperate. It's just like
you'd expect. And they're entitled to representation even though
they can't afford it. So a judge would appoint one of us. Endless
case loads, every kind of thing you can imagine, but a lot of
repetition. Good training, right. But . . . I don't know. Someone's
got to do that work. This isn't a just society and that was one way
to resist it, do you understand me boy?"

Jim nods, startled by this intersection with his own recent
thoughts. So the old man had tried to resist!

"But in the end it doesn't matter. Most of your clients hate
you because you're just part of the system that's snared them. And
a good percentage are guilty as charged. And the case loads . . ."
The plastic cracking, it really seems like something in him must
be breaking. "In the end it doesn't make any difference. Someone
else would have done it, yes they would! Just as well. I should
have been a tax lawyer, investment counselor. Then I'd have enough
money now to be in some villa somewhere. Private nurse and
secretary. . . ."

Jim shivers. Tom knows just exactly what he's living in, he's
perfectly aware of it. Who better? It's despair making all those
Q's and O's, in this old folks' mental ward. . . .

"But you did some good! I'm sure you did." Doubtfully:
"You saved some people from jail who were grateful for it. . . ."

"Maybe." *Crack crack crack.* "I remember . . . I got this
one Russian immigrant who could barely speak English. He'd only
been in the country a month or two. He was lonely and went into
one of the porno theaters in Santa Ana. The police were trying to
close those places down at the time. They made a sweep and
arrested everyone they could catch. So they got this Russian and
he was charged with public indecency. Because they said he was
masturbating in there. If you can believe that. When I first saw
him he was really scared. I mean he was used to the Soviet system
where if you're arrested then you're a goner. Guilty as charged.
And he didn't understand the charges and I mean he was *scared*.
So I took it to trial and just massacred the assistant D.A.'s case,

which was bullshit to begin with. I mean how can you prove something like that? So the judge dismissed it. And the look on that Russian's face when they let him out . . ." *Crack! Crack!* "Oh, that might have been worth a few days in this hole, I guess. A few days."

"So . . ." Jim is thinking of his own problems, his own choices. "So what would you do today, Tom? I mean, if you wanted to resist the injustices, the people who run it all . . . what would you do?"

"I don't know. Nothing seems to work. I guess I would teach. Except that's useless too. Write, maybe. Or practice law at a higher level. Affect the laws themselves somehow. That's where it all rests, boy. This whole edifice of privilege and exploitation. It's all firmly grounded in the law of the land. That's what's got to change."

"But how? Would you resist actively? Like . . . go out at night and sabotage a space weapons factory, or something like that?"

Tom stares out the window bright-eyed. As often happens, his bitterness has galvanized him, made him seem younger. "Sure. If I could do it without hurting anybody. Or getting hurt myself." *Crack!* "A liberal to the end. I guess that's always been my problem. But yeah, why not? It would take a lot of that kind of thing. But they should be stopped somehow. They're sucking the world dry to fuel their games."

Jim nods, thinking it over.

They talk about Jim's parents, a natural enough association, although neither of them mentions Dennis's occupation. Jim talks a bit about his work and friends, until Tom's eyes begin to blur. He's getting tired: slumping down, speech coming with an ugly hiss of breath. Jim sees again that the mind, that sharp-edged bitter quick mind, is trapped in an old wreck of a body that is just barely kept going by constant infusion of oxygen, of drugs. A body that poisons its mind occasionally, blunts all its edges . . . One gnarled hand creeps over the bedsheet after the other, like a pair of crabs; spotted, fleshless, the joints so swollen that the fingers will never straighten again. . . . That has to hurt! It all does. He must live with pain every day, just as a part of living.

Jim can't really imagine that, and the thought doesn't stay with him long. Too hard. It's getting time to go, it really is.

"Tell me one last Orange County story, Tom. Then I've got to go."

Tom stares through him, without recognition: Jim shivers.

The focus returns, Tom stares out the window at the sky. "Before they built Dana Point harbor, there was a beautiful beach down there under the bluff. Not many people went there. The only way down was a rickety old wood staircase built against the bluff. Every year steps came out and it got chancier to go down it. But we did. The thing was to go after a big storm had hit the coast. The beach was all fresh, sand torn out and flushed and thrown back in. And in the sand were tiny bits of colored stones. Gem sand, we called it. It was really an extraordinary thing. I don't know if they really were tiny bits of sapphires, rubies, emeralds —but they looked like it, and that's what we called them. Not driftglass, no, real stones. Walking along the beach real slow, you'd see a blink of colored light, green, red, blue—perfectly intense and clear against the wet sand. You could collect a little handful in a day, and if you kept them in a jar of water . . . I had one at home. Wonder what happened to that. What happens to all the things you own? The people you know? I'm sure I never would have thrown that out. . . ."

And Tom falls off into reverie, then into an uneasy sleep, tossing so that the oxygen tube presses against his neck. Jim, who has heard about the gem sand before, arranges the tube and the sheets as best he can, and leaves. He feels sad. There was a place here, once. And a person, with a whole life. Now hanging on past all sense. This awful condomundo—a jail for the old, a kind of concentration camp! It really is depressing. He's got to come by more often. Tom needs the company. And he's a historical resource, he really is.

But tracking up 5, Jim begins to forget about this. The truth is, the overall experience is just too unpleasant for him. He can't stand it. And so he forgets his visits there, and avoids the place.

On to dinner at the folks'. Then his class! It really is turning out to be a hell of a long day.

13

After Jim leaves, Old Tom continues the conversation in his head.

I played in the orange groves as a child, he tells Jim. When you lived on a street plunging into a grove that extended away in every direction, then you could go out any time you liked. Mid-afternoon when everything was hot and lazy was a good time. It was always sunny.

They cleared the ground around the trees, nothing but dirt. Around each tree was a circular irrigation moat maybe thirty feet across, which made the groves look strange. As did the symmetrical planting. Every tree was in a perfect rank, a perfect file, and two perfect diagonals, for as far as you could see. The trees were symmetrical too, something like the shape of an olive, made of small green leaves on small twisted branches.

There were almost always oranges on the trees, they blossomed and grew twice a year and the growing took up most of the time. Oranges first green and small, then through an odd transition of mixed green and yellow, to orange, darkening always as they ripened—until if not picked they would darken to a browny orange and then go brown and dry and small and hard, and then whitish brown and then earth again. But most of them were picked.

We used to throw them at each other. Like snowballs already formed and ready to go. Old ones were squishy and smelled bad, whole new ones were hard and hurt a little. We fought wars, boys throwing oranges back and forth and it was kind of like German dodgeball at school. Getting hit was no big deal, except perhaps when you had to explain it to your mother. During the fights itself it was kind of funny. I wonder if any of those young friends ended up in Vietnam? If so, they were poorly trained for it.

We took bows and arrows out into the groves to shoot the jackrabbits we often saw bounding away from us. They could really run. We never even came close to them, happily, so we shot at oranges on trees instead. Perfect targets, quite difficult to hit and a wonderful triumph if you did, the oranges burst open and flew off or hung there punctured, it was great.

We ate the oranges too, choosing only the very best. The green and slightly acrid sweat that comes out of their skin as you peel them, the white pulpy inside of the peels, the sharp and fragrant smell, the wedges of inner fruit, perfectly rounded crescent wedges . . . odd things. Their taste never seemed quite real.

I spent a lot of time out there in the groves, wandering in the hot dusty silence with my bow and arrow in hand, talking to myself. It was a very private world.

But when they started to tear the groves down I don't remember we ever cared all that much. No one could imagine that *all* the groves would be torn down. We played in the craters, and the piles of wood left when the trees were chopped up, and it was different, interesting. And the construction sites—new foundations, framing thrown up in hours—made great playgrounds. We swung from rafters and tested if newly poured concrete would melt if you held a candle under it, and jumped from new roofs down into piles of sand, and once Robert Keller stepped on a nail sticking up through a board. Fun.

And then when the houses were built, fences put up, roads all in—well—it was a different place. Then it wasn't so much fun. But by then we weren't kids anymore either, and we didn't care.

14

When Stewart Lemon hears the bad news—direct from LSR president Donald Hereford in New York—he can scarcely believe it. All of his premonitions have come true in the worst way. While on the phone with Hereford he has to keep cool, take it calmly, make assurances that it's all still under control, the contract virtually in the bag. In fact, Hereford's brusque, icy questioning frightens him considerably. So that when the call is done and Lemon is alone, he gets so angry, so frightened, that he locks his office, shuts down all the systems, and runs amok—kicks the desk and chairs, throws the paperweights against the wall, punches the soft backing of his swivel chair until he's thoroughly killed it.

Breathing heavily, he surveys the room, then very carefully puts everything back in order. He's still angry, but physically he feels less like he's going to explode. His health really can't take the pressures of this job, he thinks; it's a race between ulcers and heart attack, and both contestants are picking up the pace as they near the finish line. . . . He swallows a Tagamet and a Minipress, hits the intercom button, says to Ramona in his calmest voice, "Is McPherson back from White Sands yet?"

"Let me check. . . ." Ramona knows perfectly well that this dead-calm voice means he is furious. All the better, he likes people to know when he's mad. She gets back to him quickly: "Yes, he's just in."

"Get him up here now."

Actually it takes more like fifteen minutes for McPherson to show up. He looks annoyed in his usual minimalist way, mouth drawn tight, eyes staring an accusation. *He's* angry? Lemon stands up the moment he walks in, feels the pressure in him rising again.

Nearly shouting, he says, "I asked you to hurry on the Stormbee program, didn't I! And you gave me that what's-the-big-hurry look, there's no deadline, and now I'll *tell* you what the big hurry was, goddamn it!"

McPherson flinches under this immediate onslaught, then clams up completely. No expression on his face at all. Lemon hates this robot response, and he sets about cracking it open: "They've made your superblack program white, do you understand? If we'd gotten the proposal to the Pentagon when I wanted to they wouldn't have been able to do this, but *you* had to hold on to it! And now it's a white program and the RFP is out there for everyone to go after!"

That got him all right. McPherson has visibly paled, his mouth is nothing but a tight white line across his face. "When did you hear?" he manages to say, jaw bunching and unbunching.

"Just now! I'm not as slow as you are, I just got the call from New York. From Hereford himself."

"But—" The man is really in shock, or else he wouldn't deign to ask Lemon questions like this: "What happened? Why?"

"Why? I'll tell you why! You were too fucking slow, that's why!" Lemon pounds his desk hard. "Let me try to explain the Air Force to you again, McPherson. They like results! They don't have the patience of a hummingbird, and when they ask for something they want it now! If they don't get it they go somewhere else. So you didn't produce as fast as they wanted! It's been four months, for Christ's sake! Four months! And so now the RFP for the Stormbee contract is coming out this Friday in *Commercial Business Daily*, and after that we're just one of any number of bidders. If the Pentagon had already gotten our proposal and accepted it this couldn't have happened, but as it is now, we're fucked! We're back to square one!"

Lemon has worked himself into a therapeutic frenzy with this outburst, and he can see McPherson is infuriated too, the man's lips are going to fuse if he doesn't watch out. If he were a normal kind of guy they'd shout it out, get it all off their chests and be able to go out afterward and drink it off and plan some strategy, the hard words forgotten as things spoken in the heat of anger. But McPherson? No, no, he just holds it all in with an almost frightening compression, till it metamorphoses into a hate for Lemon that Lemon can see just as sure as he can see the man's face. And it makes Lemon mad. He hates that close-mouthed supercilious style, it angers him personally and it *loses them business*. Disgusted, he waves the man away. He can't stand to look at him. "Get out of here, McPherson. Get out of my sight."

"I take it we'll be making a bid?"

"*Yes!* For Christ's sake, do you think I'm going to let all that work go to waste? You get this thing whipped into proper proposal shape and do it *fast*. Was the test at White Sands successful?"

"Yes."

"Good! You get this proposal into the selection board first. With the head start we've had we should be able to make the strongest bid by a good margin."

"Yeah."

"You bet, *yeah*. I'll tell you this, McPherson—your ass is on the line, this time. After all the stunts you've pulled—you'd better win this one. You'd better."

Stiffly the man nods, stomps out. Goddamned robot. Lemon can't believe he's got such a tight-ass robot working for him still. It just isn't his style, he can't work with a man like that. Well— this is McPherson's last chance, he has tinkered around in per-fectionist dilettante style one time too many. Vengefully Lemon hits the intercom and tells Ramona to send a memo: "To Dennis McPherson. Tell him that along with program management for the Stormbee *proposal*, I want him co-directing the Ball Lightning program with Dan Houston. Tell him Houston remains head, but he is to render all assistance asked of him."

That'll give the bastard something to think about.

15

So Jim tracks up to his parents' home that evening, to join them for dinner. Up the knob of Red Hill, the first rise off the big flat plain of the OC basin, a sort of lookout point sticking out from the hills behind it. Jim's books say there was a mine there in the 1920s, the Red Hill mercury mine, with tailings that could be found decades later. And the soil of the hill had a reddish cast, because of the high amount of cinnabar in it.

Home is the same. Dennis is back from work, out in the garage working on his car's motor, which is already in perfect factory condition. He doesn't reply to Jim's hello, and Jim goes on into their section of the house. Lucy is making dinner; happily she greets him, and he sits down comfortably at the kitchen table. Quickly enough he's up on the latest developments at the little church: the minister still has some problem related to the death of his wife, the new vicar continues to vex the veteran membership, Lillian Keilbacher has started work as Lucy's assistant in the minister's office.

Then he hears about Lucy's friends, and then Dennis's work. This is the only way that Jim ever hears about his father's work, perhaps because Dennis assumes, correctly, that Jim is a pacifist bleeding-heart pseudoradical who wouldn't approve of any of it. So Dennis never speaks of it to Jim. Apparently he's almost as bad with Lucy; her account is fragmented and incomplete, consisting mostly of her own judgments and opinions, generated by the minute bits of evidence Dennis mutters when he arrives home, disgruntled and closemouthed. "He hates this Lemon he's working for," Lucy opines, shaking her head in disapproval. It's

83

not Christian, it's not good for his health, it's not good for his career. "He should try to like him more. It's not as if the man is the devil or something like that. He probably has troubles of his own."

"I don't know," Jim says. "Some people can be pretty awful to work for."

"It's what you make of it that counts." Sigh. "Dennis should have a hobby, something to take his mind off work."

"He's got the car, right? That's a hobby."

"Well, yes but it's just more of the same, isn't it. Trying to get some machine to work."

Jim has begun a radically censored account of his week, when Dennis comes in and washes up for dinner. Lucy sets out the salad and casserole and they sit down; she says grace and they eat. Dennis eats in silence, gets up and goes back out to continue his work.

Lucy gets up and goes to the sink. "So how is Sheila?" she asks.

"Well, um . . . ." Jim fumbles, feeling sudden guilt. He hasn't even thought of Sheila for a long time. "Actually, we aren't seeing each other as much these days."

A quick *tkh* of disapproval. Lucy doesn't like it. Jim gets up to help clean the table. Of course she's ambivalent about it; Sheila wasn't a Christian, and she'd really like Jim to settle down with a Christian girl, even get married—in fact she knows some candidates down at the church. On the other hand, she met Sheila many times and liked her, and the real and actual always count more for Lucy than the theoretical. "What's wrong?" she complains.

"Well . . . we're just not on the same track." It's a phrase of Lucy's.

She shakes her head. "She's nice. I like her. You should call her and talk to her. You've got to communicate." This is a sacred tenet with Lucy: talking will cure everything. Jim supposes she believes it because Dennis doesn't talk much. If he did, she'd know better that the tenet wasn't true.

"Yeah, I'll call her." And really he should. Have to tell her that he's, um, seeing other people. A difficult call at best. And so a part of him is already busy forgetting the resolution. Sheila will get the idea. "I will."

"Did you go see Tom?"

"Yeah."

"How was he?"

"Same as always."

She sighs. "He should be living here."

Jim shakes his head. "I don't know where you'd put him. Or how you'd take care of him, either."

"I know." There's a slight quiver at Lucy's jaw, and suddenly Jim perceives that she's upset. He doesn't have the faintest idea why. "But it isn't right."

Maybe that's it. "I'll go down there more often." This too he instantly begins to forget.

"Dennis has got to go to Washington again this week."

"He's been going a lot this year."

"Yes." She's still upset, throwing dishes into the dishwasher almost blindly. Jim doesn't want to ask her why, she'll start crying and he doesn't want to deal with it. He ignores the signs and tells her cheerily of his week, his classes and what he's been reading, while she pulls it together. Is she angry at Dennis about something? he wonders. He can't tell; there's lots he doesn't know or understand about his parents' relationship. He's more comfortable with it that way.

Dishes finished, the talk continues desultorily. Jim's mind wanders to his various problems and he doesn't catch one of his mom's questions. "What's that?"

"Jim. You don't *listen*." A cardinal sin, in this household where it happens so often. . . .

"Sorry." But at the same time he's glancing at a newsheet headline that's grabbed his eye. "I can't believe this famine in India."

"Why, what's it say?"

"Same old thing. Third major famine of the year in Asia, kills another million. And look at this! Fight in Mozambique killed a hundred!" From their kitchen window they can see the two giant hangars down at El Toro Marine Base, the helicopters rising and dropping like bees around a hive.

"They should learn to talk."

Jim nods, absorbed in the details of the second article. When he's done he says, "I'm off. Gotta go teach my class."

"Good. Don't forget about visiting Tom more often, now." She is serious, scolding, insistent: still upset about something.

"I won't, but remember I just saw him today. I'll go again next Thursday."

"Tuesday would be better."

Jim goes out to the garage. He doesn't notice the intensity of Dennis's silence, hasn't noticed the tension in him all evening long. Dennis is quiet a lot; and Jim hasn't really been paying attention.

He clears his throat; Dennis looks up from a bundle of colored wires running over the motor block of his car. "Um, Dad, my car's having some power troubles going uptrack."

Dennis pokes his glasses up his nose, glares at Jim. "How does it start?" he asks after a long pause.

"Not so well."

"Have you cleaned the track contacts lately?"

"Um . . ."

Angrily Dennis grabs up some tools, rags, leads Jim out to his car. It looks shabby and unkempt under the streetlight. Dennis pulls up the hood wordlessly, reaches down to shift the contact rod up into maintenance position. His back says he's sick of doing work on Jim's car.

"Look at these brushes, they're caked!" A black paste of oily scum adheres to the contacts where they come closest to the road and the track. "Here, you clean them."

Jim starts on it, fumbles with a screwdriver, gouges the side of one brush, propels a gob of the pasty black goo right past Dennis's eye.

Dennis elbows him aside. "Watch out, you're wrecking them. Watch how I do it."

Jim watches, bored. Dennis's hands move surely, economically. He gets every brush coppery clean, factory perfect. "I suppose you'll just let all this go to hell again," Dennis says bitterly as he finishes, gesturing at the car's motor.

"No," Jim protests. But he knows that after years of negligence and ineptitude with his car, there's nothing he can do now to convince Dennis that he is really interested. It is interesting, of course, in a theoretical way; forces of entropy, resistance to it, a great metaphor for society, etc. But ten seconds after the hood is down the actual physical details fade for Jim, the words turn back into jargon and he's as ignorant as he was when the lesson started. His memory is retentive, so maybe he truly isn't interested.

"Have you done anything about getting another job?" Dennis demands.

"Yeah, I've been looking."

Disgust twists Dennis's features. "You know I'm still making the insurance payments on this car?" he says as he gathers his tools. "Do you remember that?"

"Yeah, I remember!" Jim squirms at this accusation, feeling the shame of it. Still supported by his parents: he can't even make his own way in the world. He can see Dennis's contempt and it makes him defensive, then angry. "I appreciate it, but I'll take them over starting with the next one." As if Dennis has been keeping him from paying on his own.

The pretense makes Dennis angry too. "You will not," he snaps. "It's illegal to be without that insurance, and you can't afford it. If I gave it to you and you let it lapse and then got in an accident, then I'd be the one ended up paying the bills, wouldn't I?"

Stung that his father would imagine him capable of that, Jim scowls at the ground. "I wouldn't let it lapse!"

"I'm not so sure about that."

Jim turns and walks off across the lawn, circling. He's ashamed, hurt, furiously angry. There's nothing he can say. If he starts to cry in front of his father he'll . . . "I don't do things like that! I keep my commitments!" he shouts.

"The hell you do," Dennis says. "You don't even support yourself! Isn't that a commitment? Why don't you get a job where you can afford all your own expenses? Or why don't you budget what you make to pay for them? Are you going to tell me you don't spend any of what you make on entertaining yourself?"

"No!"

"So here you are twenty-seven years old and I'm still paying your bills!"

"I don't want you paying for them! I'm sick of that!"

"*You're* sick of it! Fine, I won't. That's it for that. But you'd better find yourself a decent job."

"I'm *looking*! At least the jobs I have are decent work!"

For a second it almost looks like Dennis is going to hit him; he even shifts all the tools to his left hand, instantly, without thinking. . . . Then he freezes, snarls, turns away and walks into the house. Jim runs to his car, jumps in, tracks off cursing wildly, blindly.

16

Inside the house Dennis hears Jim's old car click over the street track and hum away. It almost makes him laugh. When he was a kid, sons angry at their fathers could rev a car up to seven thousand RPM and burn rubber in a roaring, screeching departure; now all they can do is go hum, hum.

"Is that Jim?" says Lucy. "He didn't come in to say good-bye."

Damn. Dennis goes to sit before the video wall without a word.

"I wish you two wouldn't argue," Lucy says in a small, determined voice. "There aren't that many jobs to be had, you know. Half the kids Jim's age are unemployed."

"The hell they are." Dennis is angrier than ever. Now the kid's gotten Lucy upset too, and *he* doesn't like arguing with his son and having him tear off with that look of hurt resentment on his face: who would? But what can you do? And after a day like he's had . . . Remembering it just makes him feel worse. After a successful test like the one at White Sands, having the program jerked back out to the uncertainties of open competition . . . Lemon's fierce tongue-lashing . . . hell. An awful day. "I don't want to talk about it."

After a while he gets up from his chair, turns off the video; he's been blind to it, hasn't seen a thing. He goes to the sliding glass door, stares through his reflection at the lights of the condos of Citrus Heights, the pulsing head- and taillights of the Foothill Freeway viaduct, standing above the flats of Tustin. People everywhere. He'd like to go outside, into the house's little backyard, but it belongs to the Aurelianos who own the other side of the house. They wouldn't mind, but Dennis does.

He thinks of their land, up on the northern California coast near Eureka. Beautiful windswept pines, on a rocky hillside falling down into a wild sea. Ten years ago they bought five acres as an investment, and Dennis had even thought to retire up there, and build a home on the land. "Sometimes I'd like to just throw it in, move up to our land and get to work up there," he says aloud. To build something with your own hands, something physical that you could see taking shape, day by day . . . it's work he could love, work in stark contrast to the abstract, piecemeal, and endlessly delayed tasks he performs for LSR.

"Uh-huh," Lucy says carefully.

It's the tone of voice she uses when she wants to humor him, but doesn't agree with whatever point he's making. As Dennis well knows, Lucy hates the idea of moving north; it would mean leaving all her friends, the church, her job . . . Dennis frowns. He knows it's just a dream, anyway.

"Do you think the trees have grown back yet?" Lucy asks.

Just a year after they bought their land a forest fire burned over several hundred acres in the Eureka area, including everything they bought. They tracked up on vacation to have a look; the ground was black. It looked awful. But the locals told them it would all recover in just a few years. . . .

"I don't know," Dennis says, irritated. He suspects the fire did not bother Lucy all that much, as it made it impossible for them to move up there for a good long while. "I'll bet it has, though. The new trees will be small, but they'll be there. The land recovers fast from something like that—it's part of the natural cycle."

"Except they found out some kids set the fire, didn't they?"

Dennis doesn't reply to that. After a minute or two he sighs, answers what he takes to be Lucy's real point: "Well, we can't go up there anyway."

His black mood condenses to a big lump in his stomach. That bastard Lemon. He feels bad; certainly he transferred some of his anger at Lemon onto his idiot son, who surely deserved it, but still . . . that look on his face . . .

What a day.

"Did Jim say he was looking for a job?"
"I don't want to talk about it."

17

Tashi Nakamura gets to Jim's writing class just before starting
time. Tashi's interest in writing is minimal, but Jim's classes de-
pend on enrollment for survival, and this semester it looked like
there might not be enough students to keep the class going. So
Tashi decided to sign up. It was a typical Tashi act; he has a streak
of generosity that few know about, because of his shyness and
poverty.

Jim arrives ten minutes late, just as his students are packing
up to leave. Instantly Tashi can see that Jim is upset about something; he's flushed, his mouth is a tight line, he slams his daypack
down on his desktop and glares at it. Stands there pulling himself
together.

After a while he takes a deep breath, begins the night's lecture
in a monotone. His explanations of comma use, shaky at the best
of times, are now almost incoherent. In the middle of them he
stops, veers off into one of his historical jags. "So the Irvine
Ranch, which began as the county's only force for conservation,
ended up by selling out to a corporation that leased all its land to
developers, who made it into a replica of the northern half of the
county, ignoring all the lessons they should have learned and grad-
ing the hills with a complete disregard for the land. In fact our
fine college is part of that heritage. And this development came
at the time when the ballistic defense was being put into orbit, so
the arms industry expanded into this new land and increased a hold
on the county that was already completely dominant!"

Jim's other students blink at him, completely unimpressed.
In fact they're looking rather mutinous. Most have taken the class

to get by the minimal writing test necessary to graduate Trabuco, and they are impatient with Jim's digressions. Learning to write is hard enough as it is. One of the more aggressive men breaks into Jim's monologue to complain. "Listen here, Mr. McPherson, I still don't have the slightest idea when to use 'that' or 'which,' or which one goes with commas or how to use the commas." Really disgusted about it, too.

Jim, flustered and still really upset about something, Tash can't guess what, tries to return to the dropped explanation. He makes a hash of it. The students are looking openly rebellious. Rules of punctuation are not Jim's forté anyway; he's more an inspirational teacher than a technical one. But it's a student body looking for rules and regulations, and they are getting angry at him as he flounders.

"The example you used with me," Tash says in an ominously silent pause, "is definition versus added information. You use 'that' to help define, like in, 'On the day that it rained.' And there's never a comma there. 'Which' is for additional information—'Last Friday, which was rainy, turned out well.' And there you use commas to bracket the interjected phrase." Several students are nodding, and a relieved Jim is quickly writing examples on the blackboard, *screech!* Wow, got to watch that chalk, Jimbo. He's definitely not all there tonight. What's the problem? "That's how you put it when I asked you last week," Tash adds, and begins scribbling the examples in his own notebook.

Then when class is over, Jim packs up swiftly and is out the door and gone before Tash even has time to stand. Too upset to talk about it? Now that *is* unusual.

Tash shakes his head as he leaves the concrete bunkers above the Arroyo Trabuco condos. Too bad. Well, maybe he'll find out about it later, after Jim's had a chance to calm down. Meanwhile he can't worry about it; he's got to get ready to go surfing.

Yes, it is just after ten P.M., and Tashi Nakamura is going to go home and eat and do a little carbrain repair, and then drive down to Newport Beach and go surfing. This is his latest innovation; after all, the waves are jammed with hordes of surfers by day, and so—think about it—if you want to avoid them, there's no choice but to surf at night.

All his friends laughed themselves silly at this idea. It had the trademark Tashi characteristics, following a solution out to a logical but crazy end; Tashi, Jim said, just didn't believe in *reductio ad absurdum*. And they laughed themselves sick. *Ahhh, hahahaha*.

But did they ever try it? No, people tend to judge new ideas without actually testing them, and so they remain on track all their lives, a part of the great machine. That's fine with Tash, because among other things, it means he can have the nighttime waves all to himself.

The trick is to do it when there is a full moon, like tonight. So at 3:30 A.M. Tash parks in Newport Beach, walks down the dark, quiet street, surfboard under his arm. Curious how unanimously diurnal people are. Between the fashionable beachfront condos, with their walls of dark glass facing the sea. Onto the broad expanse of sand, milky in the moonlight, lifeguard stands looming on the bright surface like ritual statuary.

Stone groins extend into the water every four blocks; they're there to help keep the trucked-in sand on the beach. Just off their sea ends waves break, faint white in the darkness. That's another trick to night surfing: find a regular point break with a clear orienting marker. Each groin starts a left break when there's a south swell, as there is tonight; and they're easy to see. Perfect.

Tashi waxes his board, steps down to the water. He arrived in his wetsuit, so sweat reduces by a fraction the room for seawater. Still, wading in and strapping the board's leash onto his ankle, the soup surges up his legs and gives him the familiar shock. Cold! Lovely salt stimulation. He shoves the board into a broken wave, jumps chest first onto it and paddles out, puffing walruslike at the rush of chill water down the wetsuit's neck. Pull of the backwash, the rise into a wave almost breaking, slap of water into his face, the clean cold salt taste of it; he takes in a big mouthful of ocean, sloshes it around in his mouth till the taste fills him. Swallows some to get it down his throat. He's back in Mother Ocean, the original medium, the evolutionary home of the ancient ancestor species that he now feels cheering wildly, down there in his brainstem. Yeah!

Outside the break, paddling with smooth lazy strokes. Pretty

much directly out from the 44th Street groin, his favorite. Newport Beach now seems a long strip of white sand backed by hundreds of toy blocks. As usual there's no wind, and the water is
perfectly glassy, like dawn glass only better. A liquid heavier
than water.

Seeing the waves. It is a bit of a problem, naturally. But the
moon's millions of squiggled reflections rise and fall on the swells
outside, making a pattern. And close up the black wall of a wave
is hard to miss. It's a good sharp left tonight, lips pitching out and
dropping over with clean reports as they hit.

Tashi digs the board in, paddles to match the speed of a point
about to break, pushes up and stands in one fluid thoughtless
motion. Now he's propelled along without further effort, it's merely
a matter of balancing his weight in a way that will keep him moving
ahead of the break. There's a kind of religious rapture in feeling
this movement: as the universe is an interlocking network of wave
motions, hitting the stride of this particular wave seems to click
him into the universal rhythm. Nothing but gravitational effects,
slinging him along. Tuning fork buzzing, after a tap of God's
fingernail.

A wall in the wave that Tash doesn't see knocks him over,
however, and it's underwater night soup time, an eerie experience
of cold wet zero-gee tumbling, up to the roiling moonwhite surface,
where a million bubbles are hissing out their lives and popping a
fine salt rain into the air just above the water. Tug on leash, grab
board, get on, paddle hard to get over the next wave before it
breaks. Success, barely. Back over to the point off the groin. Try
another one.

It's a pas de deux with Mother Ocean at her most girlish and
playful. Quickly Tashi gets into a rhythm, the interval between
crests is known to his body more than his eyes, and sometimes he
takes off on a wave without even looking at it. He wonders if the
blind could surf, concludes it would be possible.

Well. Of course waves are variable; like snowflakes, there
are no two the same. And in the dark they bring a lot of surprises,
sudden wall-offs, unexpected bowls, backwash ripples and so forth,
which catch Tash off guard and knock him down. No big deal,
it's interesting, a challenge. But the neat thing is that about the
time he is getting tired of the unexpected variable dumping him,

the stars in the east dim, and the sky grows blue. The water is quick to soak up the sky's color, as always. Tash finds himself skimming over a velvet blue like the sky in Jim's orange crate posters, a pure, intense, glossy, rich, *blue* blue. Wow. And he can see a lot more of the wave's surface. It's so glassy that he looks at one smooth wall about to crunch him and decides he must need a haircut: wild-haired guy grinning back at him like an Oriental Neptune, surfing inside the wave like the dolphins do. Who knows, maybe it was Neptune.

The best part of the day. A renewable miracle: always so astonishing, this power of the ocean to resist humans. Here he lives in one of the most densely populated places in the world, and all he has to do is swim a hundred yards offshore and he's in a pure wilderness, the city nothing but a peculiar backdrop. Wildlife refuge, and him the wildlife.

Not only that, but the tide is going out and the waves are getting hollower and hollower, little four-foot tubes tossed into existence for the five seconds necessary to stall back into them, so that he can clip along in a spinning blue cylinder that provides swirling floor walls and roof, with a waterfall fringe at the open end, leading back out into the world. Might as well be in a different dimension when you're in the tube, it is such a wonderful feeling. Tubed, man! How tubular!

Ah, but good times are like tubes, here briefly and then gone forever. There's enough light now for anyone to surf; and within half an hour or so, just about anyone is surfing.

Little clumps of bright wetsuits up and down off each
    groin.
Scattered surfers between the clumps, hoping for
    anomalous waves.
Spectrum bands, magenta, green, orange, yellow, violet,
    pink:
Solids and stripes: wetsuits and boards.
Rising and falling.
The concept of play is either bourgeois or primitive, but
    does that matter?
Looks like a child's plastic bead necklace, thrown on the
    water.
The glassy blue water, the waves.

The real problem is that most of the occupants of these colorful wetsuits are assholes. They average about thirteen years old, and ruder little tykes couldn't be imagined. Densepacking at the takeoff point is intense, and the young surfnazis have dealt with the problem by forming gangs and taking off in groups. If two gangs take off on one wave, it's war. People are pushed off, fights are started. They think this is funny, surfing at its finest.

Tash just continues to do his thing, ignoring the crowd. Aside from a lot of violent threats he is rarely bothered. The truth is, the surfnazis think he is a kind of killer kung-fu character, Bruce Lee crossed with Jerry Lopez, and they leave him alone. But this time one of the more hostile kids deliberately drops in ahead of Tash, shouting "Get the fuck off, Grandpa!" and trying to drive him back into the break. Tash makes his normal bottom turn, comes up and is surprised when he knocks the kid off the wave.

As Tash paddles back out his harasser steams over toward him shrieking abuse and calling on his buddies to help beat up this intruder. Tash just sits up on his board and stares the kid down. Calling him names won't do any good; these poor masochistic sleepwalkers like to be called nazis, in fact it's a compliment among them: "Hey, fucker," one will say to another after a good ride. "That's real nazi."

So Tash just looks at the kid. The rest of the gang hangs back. Tash allows himself a little theatrics, says to the enraged surfer in a tiny horror-video whisper, "Don't cut me off again, my child. . . ."

That not only infuriates the young nazi, it gives him the creeps. Tash paddles back out to the point, chuckling.

But here he is chuckling over terror tactics, when just an hour ago he was involuntarily grinning at the sweet dark face of nature itself, as it rushed up to embrace him. Now it's mallsprawl on the water, surfing another video game. Tash rides a few more waves, and no one actively bothers him, but the mood is gone.

So he paddles out of the new machine, walks up the beach. Sits down to dry off, warm up.

Watches sand grains roll down the side of a hole his toe is making.

The sun gets higher, people begin to populate the beach. By

the time he picks his way across the expanse of sand it is dotted
with hundreds of figures on towels.

Let's spend a day at the beach!
Talk. Smell of oil, try this coconut!
Here I'll put it on you. Coconut is popular this month.
Thirty tunes clash in the baked shimmery air.
Lifeguard stands are open. Green flags on top.
Lifeguards in red trunks, burnt noses, aren't they cute?
Pastel colors of the old beachfront condos. Neon rainbow
   overlay.
You don't know how to make a book.
A seabreeze flutters the flags.
White sand, colored towels. See it!
Girls with lustrous dark skin, lying on their backs.
Bright patches of the *cache-sexe*:
Colors repeat the wetsuit array.
Your head aches when you think about it!
Oiled legs, arms, breasts,
Backbone lifting to a round bottom.
Skin poked out by shoulderblades.
Silky blond hairs, swirled in oil on inner thigh.
The erotic beach. Beautiful
animals.

Tash observes the sunbathers with the sort of godlike detach-
ment that a morning of surfing can bring. What is the cosmos for,
after all? If the highest response to the universe is an ecstatic
melding with it, then surfing is the best way to spend your time.
Nothing else puts you in such a vibrant contact with the rhythm
and balance of the cosmic pulse. No wonder the godlike detach-
ment afterward. And seen from that vantage, lying flaked on the
beach looks lame indeed. Minds turned off, or tuned to trivia (their
selves). Surfing calls for so much more grace, commitment, attention.

Or it can, anyway. Tash recalls the surfnazis. It depends on
what you make of it. Maybe there are people out there in the prone
zone turning the activity into a deep sunworshiping contemplation?
. . . No. They lie there chattering. Divorced from it all. No land,
seasons, fellow animals, work, religion, art, community, home,

world. . . . Hmm, quite a list. No wonder the erotic beach, the alliance merry-go-round. All they have left.

Oh well. Nothing to be done. Time to go home.

Tashi's home is a tent, set on the roof of one of the big condotowers in the Newport Town Center. The roof used to be a patio, but was closed when a resident fell over the too low railing to her death. Soon afterward Tashi saved the building manager from a bad mugging in Westminster Mall, and over drinks the manager told Tash about the roof, and later allowed him to move up there, with the understanding that Tash would never allow anyone to fall over the side. Tashi sewed a big tent, with three large rooms in it, and that has been his home ever since. In the concrete block that holds the elevator there is a small bathroom that still functions, and all in all it couldn't be nicer.

Tashi's friends tend to giggle about the arrangement, but Tash doesn't mind. His home is part of his larger theory, which goes like so: The less you are plugged into the machine, the less it controls you. Money is the great plug, of course; need money, need job. Since most jobs are part of the machine, it follows that you should lead a life with no need for money. No easy task, of course, but one can approximate, do what is possible. The roof is a fine solution to the major money problem, and it even helps with the other major need: he has vegetables growing in long boxes, most of them set in rows next to the railing, to provide a margin of safety. Neat. And he's out in the weather; has a view of the ocean, a great blue plain to the southwest; and above him, the ever-changing skyscapes. Yes, it's a fine home.

He washes down his wetsuit, showers. As he's finishing up in the bathroom the elevator door opens. Sandy and Tash's ally Erica Palme emerge. "In here!" he calls as they pass the bathroom headed for the tent. They look in. "We've brought some lunch along," Erica says.

"Good."

Sandy starts laughing, "*Ah*, hahahaha— Tashi! What are you *doing?*"

"Well—" He's about to brush his teeth, actually. It's obvious. "I'm brushing my teeth."

"But why are you tearing up the toothpaste tube?"

"Well, it's about out. I was just getting the last of it."

"You're tearing open a toothpaste tube to get out the last of the toothpaste?"

"Sure. Look how much was left in there."

Sandy looks. "Uh-huh. Yeah, that's right. You should be able to brush several teeth with that."

"Hmph! Oll sh' oo!" Tashi brushes triumphantly. Sandy cracks up while Erica drags him off to the tent.

Once inside they go to work on the bags from Jack-in-the-Box. Tashi finishes well ahead of the others, starts to work on a broken carbrain. He buys the little computers from car yards, fixes them and sells them to underground repair shops. Another part of OC's black economy. Income from this alone is almost enough to pay the bills, although it's only one of many activities that Tashi pursues, in a deliberately diffuse way.

Erica watches this work with a sour expression that makes Tash a little uncomfortable. A vice-president in the administration of Hewes Mall, she never seemed to mind Tashi's semi-indigence before; but lately that appears to be changing. Tashi doesn't know why.

Sandy notices Erica's stare and Tashi's discomfort under it, and says, "Last week I made a connection with my supplier at Monsanto San Gabriel, and I was tracking back home with about three gallons of MDMA on the passenger seat, when I ran into a Highway Patrol spot-check point—"

"Jesus, Sandy!" Erica purses her mouth.

"I know. It was one of those mechanical checks, to make sure all my track points were functional, which they were. But meanwhile one of the Chippies walks over to me and looks in, right at the container. He says, 'What's that?' "

"Sandy!" Erica cries, scolding him for getting into such a situation.

"Well, what could I do? I told him it was olive oil."

"You're kidding!"

"No, I said I worked for a Greek restaurant in Laguna and that this was a whole lot of olive oil. And there was so much of it there, he couldn't imagine that it would be anything illegal! So he just nodded and let me go."

"Sandy, sometimes I can't believe you."

Tash agrees. "You should be more careful. What if he had asked to taste it?"

After Sandy and Erica have left to get back to work, Tash operates on a circuit board and shakes his head, recalling Sandy's tale. Sandy's dealing is getting a little crazier all the time. For a while there he was talking about making a bundle, investing it, and retiring. He might have, too; but then his father's liver failed after a lifetime of abuse, and since then Sandy has been paying for regeneration treatments in Dallas, Mexico City, Toronto, Miami Beach. . . . Radically expensive stuff, and Sandy's been pushing hard for almost a year now, about to untrack under the stresses of his schedule. Only his closest friends know why; everyone else assumes it's just Sandy's manic personality, magnified by the effects of his products. Well, that might be part of it, actually. A tough situation.

Tash sighs. Sandy, Jim. Abe too. Everyone in the machine. Even if you aren't you are.

18

After a morning's work at the church, Lucy McPherson tracks under the Newport Freeway and into the depths of Santa Ana. Poor city. More than half of it is under the upper level of the freeway triangle, and the ground level, under a sky of concrete, has inevitably gone to slums. Lucy looks nervously through the windshield at the shadowy, paper-filled streets; she doesn't much trust the people who live down here.

She certainly doesn't approve of the woman she's been called to help. Her name is Anastasia, she's about twenty years old, Mexican-American, and she has two small children, although she's never been married. She lives in a run-down old applex under the upper mall at Tustin and 4th.

There's a sidewalk that crosses a dirty astroturf lawn to the front door of the beige stucco building; some fierce and unkempt young men are sitting on the lawn on both sides of the sidewalk. Lucy grits her teeth, lea res her car and walks past them, enters the smelly, olive-green hallway of the complex. Walking down it she can barely see a thing. Knock on the battered door.

"Hello, Anastasia!" Lucy's social mask is solid, and she projects all the sympathetic friendliness she can muster, which is a very considerable amount indeed. Although she can't help but note the dirty dishes stacked in the sink, the heaps of soiled laundry on the bed filling the bedroom nook. Anastasia's hair is oily and uncombed, and apparently the babe has scratched her cheek.

"Lucy, thank God you're here. I gotta go out and get some groceries or we'll starve! Baby's asleep and Ralph's watching TV. I'll just be a few minutes."

"Okay," Lucy says, but adds firmly, "I absolutely have to leave before eleven, I've got business I can't miss."

"Okay, sure. That won't be a problem." Out the door flies Anastasia, without brushing her hair.

Lucy hopes she'll come back on time; once she was stuck here for an entire day, and it's made her distrustful. In fact she didn't mention that her crucial business was a meeting with Reverend Strong, for fear that Anastasia wouldn't consider it important enough to return. She heaves a deep sigh. Some of these good works are really a pain.

Dishes washed, some of the laundry washed in the sink and hung up over the shower curtain rod to dry—not a laundromat within two miles, Anastasia has said—and Lucy sits down with Ralph, a passive six-year-old. She tries to teach him to read, using the only book in the house, a *Reader's Digest Condensed Books for Children*. Ralph stumbles over the first sentence and turns the page to the scratch-'n'-sniff pads that illustrate, or enscentify, the story. As usual, she ends up reading to him. How do you teach someone to read? She points to each word as she reads it. They go through the alphabet letter by letter. Ralph gets bored and cries to have the video wall put back on. Lucy, irritated, resists. Ralph screams.

Lucy thinks, I'm too old for this. Is this really the Lord's work? Baby-sitting? Does Anastasia regard it as such? Quite a few of Lucy's friends feel that they're being taken advantage of in this program of theirs, aiding young women who appear to be joining the church only to get free help. Well, if it's true, Lucy thinks, it still represents a chance to change people's minds, over time, perhaps. And if not . . . well . . .

> God does not expect us
> To cause the seed to sprout—
> He just said to plant it,
> And plant it all about.

She can talk to Anastasia about coming to Bible class when she returns. Speaking of which—it's 11:30. Lucy begins to get annoyed. By noon she's really angry.

Anastasia returns at 12:20, just as Lucy has settled down for an all-day rip-off. Stiffly Lucy reminds Anastasia that she had an appointment at eleven. Anastasia, already upset at something else, begins to cry. They put the meager supply of groceries into the filthy refrigerator: tortillas, soy hamburger, beans, Coke. Pampers into the bathroom. Anastasia has no money left, the utilities bill is overdue, Ralph has outgrown his shoes . . . Lucy gives her fifty dollars, they end up both in tears as she leaves.

Tracking away she can barely see. She just isn't a social worker, she hasn't got the mentality, the ability to distance herself. The people she helps become like family, and it's painful and frightening to see what sordid lives some people lead in this day and age. And so few of them Christian. No help for them from anywhere, not even faith in God. Reverend Strong has clipped a newspaper article that says that only 2 percent of Orange County residents are churchgoing Christians anymore, and he's stuck it to the office bulletin board as a sort of challenge; but Lucy has to sit at her desk and look at it all day as she works, and given everything else she has to face, she finds it depressing indeed.

Reverend Strong is finishing lunch at the vicarage when she

arrives, and he understands about her missing the meeting. "I figured it was Anastasia," he says with a cynical laugh. Lucy isn't yet to the point where she finds it funny. They go into the office and discuss the various works at hand.

Reverend Strong is a nice enough man, but sadly—tragically—his wife was killed in a bomb explosion while they were on a mission to Panama, and Lucy feels that the experience gave him a secret dislike for the poor. He tries to control it, but he can't, not really. And so he is surprisingly, almost shockingly, cynical about most of their good works programs, and he is prone to oblique and confused outbursts in his sermons, against sloth, ambition, political struggle. It leaves most of the congregation confused, but Lucy is sure she understands what is going on. It's the explanation for his frequent return to the parable of the talents. Some people are given only one talent, and instead of working with it they try to steal from the man given the ten talents. . . . Really, the more he harps on it, the more Lucy begins to wonder if the parable of the talents wasn't a bit of a mistake on God's part. In any case, she has the constant problem of getting the reverend's approval for the works that the church obviously has to undertake, in the poorer parts of the community. . . .

These days Reverend Strong says he is worrying intensely about the theological issues raised in the doctrinal negotiations with the Roman Catholics that have been going on for a year at the Vatican. He doesn't want to be bothered with practical problems concerning community work; he has to think about abstract theology, it takes up all his mental energy. This is what he tells Lucy over their late lunch.

Lucy ends up suggesting solutions to their most pressing problem—fund-raising—and absentmindedly he agrees to them. So, she thinks angrily: time for another futile, pathetic garage sale . . . because who cares if we don't have enough money to help out our poor neighbors? They don't deserve it anyway! They were only given their one talent. . . .

The afternoon goes to helping Helena, and to calling all the local newsheets to announce the garage sale, and to visiting four families in El Modena with care packages, and to teaching Lillian Keilbacher how to assist in the office, keeping the records. That last part is actually fun. Lillian, her friend Emma's daughter, is now being paid as a part-time assistant, which means she goes at it harder than most of the young people. Lucy really enjoys her company, especially after Anastasia, who must be just a year or two older.

"Lucy, I just hit the command key to get the mailing list and everything disappeared!"

"Uh-oh." They sit down looking at the computer screen, which stays stubbornly blank no matter what they try. "You sure you only hit the command key?"

"Well that's what I thought, but I must be wrong." Lillian is cross-eyed with consternation. Then the screen beeps for their attention and starts displaying a brightly colored sequence of graphs and figures.

"Wow!" They laugh at the extravagance of it. "Do you think this disk is damaged?" Lillian asks.

"I hope so. It's either that or the computer is haunted."

Lillian laughs. "Maybe we can get the reverend to, you know, cure it."

"Exorcise it, sure."

It's fun. A nice girl, Lucy says to herself after Lillian leaves; and that's her highest praise.

Office in order and closed, home to start dinner. Lucy chats on the phone with her friend Valerie while she chops up potatoes for a new casserole she's trying. Into the microwave.

Then Jim comes by. He looks messy, tired.

"You aren't going to teach looking like that, are you?"

He looks affronted. "Looking like what?"

"Those clothes, Jim. You look like you came out of lower Santa Ana."

"Now, Mom, don't be prejudiced."

"I am *not* being prejudiced." As if she were some bigoted recluse! When was the last time he was in lower Santa Ana? It's too much. But he doesn't understand, he's giving her the what-did-I-say-now look that she also gets from Dennis. They look surprisingly alike sometimes. Usually the wrong times. Lucy sniffs hard and collects herself while tending the microwave. "Anyway, you should try to look better. It would make you a better teacher."

"I look like what I look like, Mom."

"Nonsense. It's all under your control. And it sends out

signals about what you think of the people you're with. And of yourself, of course."

"Semiotics of clothing, eh Mom?"

"I don't know. Semiotics?"

"What you were saying about signals."

"Well, yes then. Go look in the mirror."

"In a bit."

"Are you staying for dinner?"

"No. Just dropped by to see if any mail's come for me."

Great. "No, nothing's here." And off he goes, hurrying a bit to make sure he's gone by the time Dennis gets home.

This worries Lucy greatly, this growing rift between Dennis and Jim. She knows very well that it's bad for both of them. Both of them need to have each other's respect to be fully happy, that's only natural. And when there are so many other forces in action to make them unhappy, it becomes more important than ever. It's support, mutual support, in a crucial area . . . Thinking these thoughts Lucy picks up the phone and calls Jim as he tracks east on the Garden Grove Freeway. "Listen, Jim, can you come to dinner tomorrow night? We haven't been seeing you often enough recently." Not at all, in fact, since he and Dennis had that fight out in the driveway. They haven't seen each other even once since then, and it's been over a week, and Lucy can feel the resentment and anger growing on both sides.

Jim says, "I don't know, Mom."

Annoyance and concern clash in her. "You don't just come by here and check for mail," she snaps. "We're more than a post office box. You come by and eat a meal with your father soon, do you understand me?"

"All right," he says, voice sharp. "But not tomorrow. Besides, I don't see what good it'll do—he'll just think it's another way that he's supporting me." And he hangs up.

Only minutes later Dennis stalks in, in a foul mood indeed. Lucy decides that he needs distraction from work thoughts, and she risks rebuff to tell him about Anastasia and Lillian. Dennis grunts his way through dinner. She tries another tack. Get him to talk it out, not bottle things up. "What did you do today?"

"Talked with Lemon."

Ah. That explains it. Really, this Lemon must be quite unpleasant, though Lucy has a hard time imagining it, given the charming man she has met at LSR parties. "What about?"

But Dennis doesn't want to go into it, and he retires to the video room table to get out the briefcase and pore over papers. Lucy cleans up, sits down to rest her feet. She's teaching the Bible class tomorrow morning and they're doing a chapter of Galatians that is problematic indeed. Paul is an ambiguous writer, when you read him closely; conflicting desires in him, some self-less and some not, make for a somewhat incoherent output. She reads over the teacher's manual again and worries about the class. She finds herself nodding off. Time for bed already; the evenings always disappear. Dennis is out there staring at nothing, head tilted at an angle. Probably thinking of their plot of land up near Eureka, dreaming of an escape. Lucy shudders at the thought; she didn't like that desolate coastline, its immense distance from her friends, family, work, the world. In fact she has wondered guiltily if the fire that burned the land was somehow an unwanted response to prayer, God granting her least worthy desire as a peculiar kind of lesson or warning to her. . . .

They retire. Another day done. Sleepy prayers. She's got to get Jim back up here. Work on that some more tomorrow. Important. After class. Or the session with Lillian. Or . . .

19

That Saturday morning the same old party is beginning at the spa when Sandy gets sick of it. It's sunny outside and the spa with its plants, mirrors, spectrum slide walls, clanking Nautilus machinery, gym shorts, leotards, and the sweet smell of clean sweat, just isn't big enough to do the day justice. *"Ahhhhhhh! Boring!!!!"* He lets the lat pull go and its weights crash down, then he fires off into the mall and comes back with softballs, bats, and a dozen gloves.

"Let's *go*! Play *ball*!" He dragoons the whole crowd and they're off.

It takes them a while to think of a park big enough to play softball in, but Abe does and they track south and east to Ortega, where a large grass park surrounded by eucalyptus trees lies empty. Perfect. There's even a backstop. They split into teams, lid some eyedroppers, and start up a game.

None of them have played since junior high school at best, and the first innings are chaotic. Sandy plays shortstop and does pretty well with the grounders, until one bad hop jumps up and smacks him right on the forehead. He grabs the ball in midair and throws out the speedy Abe by a step. His forehead has a red bruise that shows the ball's stitching perfectly; it looks like some of the surgical work on Frankenstein's monster. When Sandy's told this he starts acting the part, which makes for somewhat stiff short-stopping.

Tashi has apparently lidded some Apprehension of Beauty; he watches everything with the dazed wonder of a four-year-old, including, when he comes to bat, the first two pitches from Arthur. Openmouthed awe, bat forgotten—what an arc! Sandy runs up and reminds him of his purpose there, mimes a hit. Tashi nods. "I know—I was just getting the trajectory down." Next pitch he hits one so far over Humphrey's head in left field that by the time Humphrey even touches the ball Tashi has crossed the plate and sat down, looking more dazed than before. "Home run, huh? Beautiful."

Third out and Jim takes left field in a state of rapture. "I love softball!" "Jim, you never play." "I know, but I love it." Trotting out onto that pure green diamond time disappears, all the adult concerns of life disappear, and Jim feels like an eight-year-old.

Unfortunately for his team he also plays like an eight-year-old. Arthur is up, and he hits a fly ball toward Jim. The moment it's hit Jim begins to run forward, because after all the ball is in front of him, right? But while running in a little basic trajectory analysis shows him that in fact the ball is destined to fly far over his head. He tries reversing direction instantaneously and falls on his ass. Scrambles up, oh shoot there goes the ball, running desperately backwards trying to look over his shoulder for the ball, left shoulder, right shoulder, how do you decide? Now the ball's falling, awful acceleration as it does, Jim running full tilt makes a great leap, the ball hits his outstretched glove then bounces off and out, *no*, an inch more of leather and it would have been an unbelievable catch! He falls, runs to the ball, throws it wildly past Sandy as cut-off man, watches Angela recover it and fire it in sidearm as Arthur cruises across the plate. Damn! Virginia, on deck, is laughing hard. Jim throws his glove down, shrugs ruefully at his grinning teammates. "Hit another one out here!"

"I'll be trying," Virginia calls back.

More hits, more alarming misjudgments, awkward scrambles after the ball, wild throws back in. It's fun.

Next time at bat Tashi hits one even farther than the first time. Home run again. For his subsequent at-bat the outfielders have dropped back until they're standing in the eucalyptus trees, and Tash laughs so hard he can barely stand. "I couldn't hit it that far no matter what!" "Sure, sure. Go ahead and swing."

Moving the outfielders so far back does create some monster gaps up the alleys, and Tash proceeds to hit a screaming line drive that stays eight feet off the ground for about two hundred feet, then skips off the grass and rolls forever. Another homer. And the time after that he does it again. Four for four, all homers. Tash just stands there, mouth hanging open. "Four homers, right? Three? Four? Beautiful."

It's a different story in the field. Playing center, Tash catches a medium-deep fly and sees Debbie tag from third for home. Really a good chance to nail her at the plate, so Tash rears back and puts everything he's got into the throw. Unfortunately his release is a little premature. The ball is still rising as it rockets forty feet over the backstop and into the trees. Who knows where it'll land. Tash stands in center inspecting his right hand. Everyone sits down they're laughing so hard. Then they can't find the ball. Sandy declares the game over and they sit down in the hazy sun to eat Whoppers and fries and drink Coke and Buds. "Do you think it achieved orbit?" "Great game."

Great day. Jim sits on the grass and flirts with Rose and Gabriela, who have singled him out for the afternoon. They only pick on guys they can trust not to take them seriously, it's a sign they feel comfortable and friendly with you, and so of course Jim enjoys that part of it; also he can't help fantasizing that they really are serious this time. That would be a night to remember: what the screens would show!

Jim doesn't really notice Virginia, sitting on the other side of him. And unfortunately she appears to be peeved about something; she knocks his hands away from her when he does turn to her, snaps at him. "What's the problem?" he says, irritated.

She just snarls. And she won't confess to any reason for being disgruntled, which annoys Jim no end. He can't figure it out. He has to suffer the *sotto voce* lash of her sharp tongue, even while they're both being very hearty and friendly with everyone else. Great. Jim hates this kind of thing, but Virginia knows that and so she pours it on.

Finally Jim asks her to come along with him for a short walk, and they go off into the eucalyptus trees.

"Listen, what the hell are you so upset about?"

"Who's upset?"

"Oh come on, don't give me that. Why don't you tell me? It's stupid to be bitching at me when I don't even know what for."

"You don't, do you."

"*No!*"

"That's just like you, Jim. Off in your own little dreamworld, completely unaware of what's going on around you. People don't mean a damn thing to you. I could be dying and you wouldn't even notice."

"Dying! What do you mean, dying?"

Virginia just grimaces with disgust, turns to walk away. Jim grabs her by the wrist to pull her back around, and furiously she swings her arm free. "Leave me alone! You don't have the slightest idea what's going on!"

"You're right I don't! But I do know that I hang out with you by choice—I don't have to. If it's going to be like this—"

"Leave me alone! Just leave me alone!" And she storms off, back to the others out in the sun.

Well. So much for that alliance. Jim doesn't understand why it's ended, or why it began, but . . . Oh well. Confused, frustrated, angry, he walks back out onto the playing field. Beyond the seated group of friends, Virginia is conferring with Arthur; then, to Jim's relief, she walks off with Inez and they track away.

But the feelings generated by the fight don't go away; the real world has intruded back into Jim's afternoon, and anger makes the Whopper lie heavy on his stomach. Virginia's bad mood adds to the other more serious bummers of the last couple of days, forms a fierce brew, a desire to strike back somehow. . . .

When Arthur stands to leave Jim approaches him. "Arthur. You talked about real resistance work. Something more serious than the postering."

Arthur stops and stares at him. "That's right. And you called the other day. I was wondering if you'd ever do anything more."

Jim nods. "I had to think about it. But I want to do something. I want to help."

"There's something coming up," Arthur acknowledges. "It's a lot more serious, this time."

"What you mentioned before. Sabotaging weapons plants?"

Arthur looks at him even longer. "That's right."

"Which one?"

"I'd rather not say, till the time comes." And Arthur's look becomes sharp indeed. They both know what this means: Jim has to commit himself to sabotaging any of the defense corporations in OC, including, presumably, Laguna Space Research. His father's company.

"All right," Jim says. "No one will get hurt?"

"No one in the plants. *We* could get hurt—they've got some tough security on those places. It's dangerous, I want you to know that."

"Okay, but no one inside."

"No. That's the ethic. If you do it any other way, you just become another part of the war."

Jim nods. "When?"

Arthur looks around to make sure they are still quite alone. "Tonight."

The Whopper does a little backstroke in Jim's stomach.

But this is his chance. His chance to make some meaning out of his life, to strike back against . . . everything. Against individuals, of course—his father, Virginia, Humphrey, his students

—but he doesn't think of them, not consciously. He's thinking of the evil direction his country has taken for so long, in spite of all his protests, all his votes, all his deepest beliefs. Ignoring the world's need, profiting from its misery, fomenting fear in order to sell more arms, to take over more accounts, to own more, to make more money . . . it really is the American way. And so there's no choice but action, now, some real and tangible form of *resistance*.

"Okay," Jim says.

20

So that very night Jim finds himself tracking with Arthur through the network of little streets on the east side of the City Mall, in Garden Grove. They turn down Lewis Street, which is a tunnel-like alley through the underlevel, walled on both sides by warehouse loading docks, all of them closed in the late evening. Arthur turns his headlights off and on three times as they turn into a ten-car parking lot between two warehouses. Parked in this cubbyhole is a station wagon. Four men standing by it, a black a white and two Latinos, jump to the back of the station wagon as Arthur and Jim slide into the lot. They lift out some small but apparently heavy plastic boxes, put them in the backseat of Arthur's car. With a few muttered words and a quick wave he's out into the alley again, tracking toward the freeway.

"That's the usual method," he says matter-of-factly. "The idea is to keep hold of this stuff for as short a time as possible. No one has it for more than a couple of hours, and it's constantly on the move."

And no more than an hour after that, Jim finds himself crawling on his belly up the dry bed of the Santa Ana River, scraping over sand, gravel, rocks, plastic shards, styrofoam frag ments, bits of metal, and pools of mud. He's dressed in a head-to-foot commando suit Arthur has provided out of one of the four boxes. This suit, as Arthur explained, is completely covert. It holds Jim's body heat in, so that he gives out no IR signal; one layer is made of filaboy-37, Dow Chemical and Plessey's latest stealth material, a honeycomb-structured synthetic resin whose irregular molecules not only distort but "eat" radar waves; and it's a flat bland color called chameleon, very difficult to see.

Jim peers out through eyepieces that have some kind of head's-up display, green and violet visuals from covert low-frequency sensors giving him a fairly good view of the night world, though the colors are out of a bad drug hallucination. And he can't see Arthur at all. The suit's sauna effect is intense, he's soaked with sweat.

They get up to climb the east side of the riverbed. Jim is cooking. The world looks as if it's under very turbid green and violet water. "Thus they crossed the Lake of Fire . . ." Oh, it is weird, weird.

Here on the Newport Beach side, occupying the site of an old oil field now gone dry, is the physical plant of Parnell Airspace Corporation: fully lit (each light a white-green magnesium flare in Jim's bizarre field of vision), surrounded by a high fence that is electrically defended so conspicuously that the barbed wire on top can only be for decoration, or nostalgia—a symbol, like the mark of a brand over a modern cattle factory.

Jim bumps into Arthur, crouches beside him, puts down the box that he's been carrying or pushing along with him. It's heavy. The buildings of the Parnell complex are still some three or four hundred yards away, dark masses on a green plain of concrete, which is dotted here and there by lavender cars.

Arthur crawls up to the fence and gently hangs on it what looks like a tennis racket without a handle. The frame adheres to the fence, and the wire mesh of the fence caught inside the frame falls away. The frame is now giving out the proper response to the fence's sensors, convincing them that no hole exists—so Arthur has explained to Jim as they prepared for their raid.

"Where do you get all this stuff?" Jim asked at the time.
"We have our suppliers," Arthur said. "This is the crucial item here, the solvent missile. . . ."

Now he shuffles back to Jim and they quickly set up a missile launcher, with the missile already in it. They nail the base of it into the ground. It's got a covert laser targeter, and all in all it's the latest in microarmament: it looks like a Fourth of July skyrocket, or a kid's toy. When they fire it, it will shoot through the new hole in the fence and behave like a little cruise missile, following its laser clothesline into the door of Parnell's physical plant; impact will penetrate the door and release a gas containing degrading enzymes and chemical solvents, mostly a potent mix called Styx-90, another Dow product; and all the plastic, filaboy, reinforced carbon, graphite, epoxy resin, and kevlar reached by the gas will be reduced to dust, or screwed up in some less dramatic way. And Parnell, primary contractor for the third layer of the ballistic missile defense architecture, currently trying to make satellite mirror stations covert or semicovert, will have the bulk of its ground stock handed to it on a plate. Turned into dust and odd lumps on the floor.

Aiming the device is simple though a bit risky, as it makes them semicovert for that instant that the laser targeting is happening. Arthur does it, and they crawl down the fence fifty yards and repeat the whole operation, aiming at another building's door.

Now comes the hard part. The missiles have secondary manual starters, in case radio signals happen to be jammed or responded to with some kind of return fire. Arthur has judged either possibility to be all too likely, so they are using the manual starters, which are buttons at the end of cords connected to the minimissiles. The cords are about a hundred yards long. So Jim crawls backwards through the sage and the trash as far away as the cord lets him, and Arthur does the same from the first missile. They angle toward each other, but Jim can't see Arthur when he comes to the end of his cord. In the suits they're completely invisible to each other.

Arthur has anticipated this difficulty, however. He's given Jim one end of an ordinary length of string, and now Jim feels three tugs on it. They're ready to go. When he gets three more hard tugs he pushes the button on the firing cord, drops both cord and string, and starts running.

It really is a very simple business.

Hitting the button is like turning on all the alarm systems in the world at once; there's a wail of sirens and glare of supplementary floodlights back on the Parnell lot. There's no way of knowing exactly what the missiles did—not a chance of hearing any small crunches that they might have made on impact—but judging by the response, *something* sure happened.

Jim finds himself flying down the riverbed, crouched over so far that he's in danger of smacking his nose with his knees, and leading Arthur by a good distance. They reach Arthur's car, which he parked in the rivermouth beach parking lot; they jump in and track out of there, toward Newport Beach. The commando suits are stripped off in a panic hurry. They track into traffic, Arthur gets in the slow lane and tosses the suits out the window when they pass over Balboa Marina. Off the bridge and into the water. At that point they become two citizens out on the road, nothing to connect them to the buildings full of weapons-become-slag back on the old oil field.

They both smell strongly of sweat, it's like the spa's weight room in Arthur's car. The towels Arthur brought along are damp before they're through drying off, and they struggle back into street clothes still sticky and hot. Jim's hands shake, he can hardly button the buttons on his shirt. He feels a little sick.

Arthur laughs. "Well, that's that. Intelligence estimates we got about ninety million dollars of space weaponry. They'll find the missile stands, but that won't tell them anything." Suffused with energy that is still welling up in him, he sticks his head out the window, shouts "Keep—the sky—*clean!*"

Jim laughs wildly, and the fight-or-flight adrenaline of their run downriver courses through him—one of the most powerful drugs he's ever felt. The best stimulant in the world. "That was great. *Great.* I actually—did something."

He stops, thinks about that. "I've actually done something. You know"—he hesitates, it sounds silly—"I feel like this is the first time in my life that I've actually *done* something."

Arthur nods, stares at him with raptor intensity. "I know just what you mean when you say that. And that's what resistance can do for you. You feel you're in a system so big and so well entrenched that nothing at all could bring it down. Certainly nothing you can do individually will make the slightest bit of difference. But if you hold to that conviction and do nothing, then it's self-fulfilling—you create the very condition you perceive.

"But take that very first step!" He laughs wildly. "Take that first step, perform an act of resistance of even the smallest kind, and suddenly your perception changes. Reality changes. You see it can be done. It might take time, but—" He laughs again. "Yeah! You bet it can be done! Let's go celebrate your first act." He hits the dashboard, hard. "Here's to resistance!"

"To resistance."

21

They lived here for over seven thousand years, and the only sign they left behind were some piles of shells around the shores of Newport Bay.

This is all we know of them, or think we know:

They came down from the plains east of the Sierra Nevada, wandering members of the Shoshonean tribes, setting up camps and then wandering farther to trade and gather food. When they reached the sea, they stopped and set up camp for good.

They had many languages.

They were what we call hunter-gatherers, and did no cultivating, kept no animals. The men made weapons and hunted with bows and arrows. The women gathered berries and edible roots, and made thistle sage into a porridge; but acorns and pine nuts were their staples. They had to leech the tannin out of their acorn flour, and used a fairly complex set of drains and pits to do it. I wonder who invented the method, and what exactly they thought they were doing, changing this white powder from inedible poison to the daily bread. No doubt it was a sacred act. Everything they did was a sacred act.

They lived in small villages, their dwellings set in circles. In the gentle climate they had little need for protection from the weather, and they slept out except when it rained. Then they slept in simple homes made of willow frames and cattail thatch. The women wore rabbit-pelt skirts, the men animal pelts thrown over the shoulder, the children nothing. Fur cloaks were worn in the winter for warmth.

They traded with tribes from every direction. Obsidian and salt were obtained from the people in the desert. Branch coral came up from Baja. The pelts of sea mammals came from the Channel Island people, who paddled over from the islands ten to a canoe.

They smoked tobacco, and carved stone figures of birds and whales and fish.

The political system was like this: most of the people in a village were family. A headman guided the village with the permission of everyone in it. They changed the headman occasionally.

Sometimes they fought wars, but mostly they were at peace.

They made some of the finest baskets in America, weaving intricate symbolic patterns into them.

They spent part of every day in a sweathouse, pouring water over hot coals and talking in the steam.

In the centers of the villages, they built circular chambers of willow and cattail and brush. The tribes to the north called this sacred sweathouse a *yoba*, the southern tribes called it a *wankech*. Here they held their major religious ceremony, the *toloache* ritual, where the young men drank a jimsonweed liquid, and saw visions, and were initiated as adults. Each sacred chamber held an image of their most important god, *Chinigchinich*, the one who had named things. The complete skin of a coyote or wildcat was removed from a body, then filled with arrows, feathers, deer horns, lions' claws, beaks and talons of hawks, and sewn back up, so that it resembled the live animal, except that arrows came out of its mouth, and it wore a feather skirt. During the *toloache* ritual *Chinigchinich* spoke to the participants through this image, telling them the secret names of all things, which revealed their innermost identities, and gave humans power over them. And so the young became adults.

This is what we know of them; and we know that their village life went on, year after year, generation after generation, existing in an unobtrusive balance with the land, using all of its many resources, considering every rock and tree and animal a sacred being—for seven thousand years. For seven thousand years!

See them, in your mind's eye, if you can, living out their lives on that basin crowded with life. Doing the day's work in the steady sun. Visiting the neighboring village. Courting. Sitting around a fire at dusk. See it.

And then a band of men came by, looking kind of like crabs, wearing shells that they could take off. They could kill from a distance with a noise. They didn't know any of the languages, but had one of their own. History began.

When these soldiers left, the Franciscans stayed. After Junipero Serra founded San Juan Capistrano, in 1776, and went on up "El Camino Real" to found the rest of the missions, a Fray Gerónimo Boscana stayed behind to help run the mission, and convert the locals to Christianity. Those around the mission were called Juaneños, after the mission; those farther north were called Gabrielinos, after the mission at San Gabriel. Fray Boscana wrote, "I consider these Indians in their endowments like the soul of an infant."

And so he put them to good Christian work, cultivating the land and building the mission. Within fifty years all of them were dead. And all that went away.

22

For Abe as for most people, the weeks fly by in a haze of undifferentiated activity. He can never believe it as he tears the month past off the calendar: whatever happened to that one? His shifts on the job all blur together, especially since he deliberately tries to forget most of them. He couldn't tell you a thing about his mad drive from Laguna Canyon Road up to UCI hospital: did they lose the victim that time? Was he working with Xavier? He has no idea, and what was it, one, two months ago? No one can tell; no one is operating on that kind of long-term time scale anymore. Lucky if you can remember what happened day before yesterday.

Somewhere inside him, of course, it is all remembered: every crash, every drive, every expression flitting over X's face as he sweats it out with the victims in the gutbucket. But the recollection mechanism is firmly turned off. As far as Abe knows in his waking hours, it's completely gone. Two months ago?· Gone! It's present tense for Abe, the here and now his only reality, the moment and the only moment. This may account for the fact that he very seldom has an ally. He doesn't think about it. Alliance? With Inez, right? Or was it Debbie. He'll find out tonight at Sandy's party.

Tonight he's working with Xavier again, as usual. As long as one of them doesn't trade around off days to extend a vacation (which happens fairly frequently) they're a team. They like that. It gives the job some continuity, makes it a little more like ordinary jobs.

The radio crackles, X picks it up. "We hear you, All-Seeing One."

They're tapped out. Code nine, pile-up, five to eight cars,

118

Foothill Freeway just west of the Eastern Freeway, still up on the viaduct. They're on the Santa Ana Freeway in Tustin, they gun up the Eastern and then up onto the Foothill. The tracks are stacked, Abe drives them on the really narrow viaduct shoulder toward a seemingly airborne forest of flashing reds and blues, three CHPs and another rescue truck already on the scene. Abe and Xavier jump out. The other rescue pair is engaged at the front of the pile-up, so they go to work on the rear end. "X, see if you can get another truck or two here fast."

Third car in has been accordioned to a pancake of metal and glass no more than ten feet thick, and driver and passenger are still in it, both unconscious. Viciously Abe pulls over his primary cutter from the truck, goes to work on the passenger side. The passenger, an older woman, is dots. "A definitive case of the dots," as X mutters while crawling over her toward the driver. "Real chicken pox." Driver, an older man, is thrashing around suddenly. Abe leaps over to his side of the car, X is slapping on the drug patches and trying to assess the damage. "Here, Abe, chop a hole for me to get in th'other side." Screech of metal cut like paper, waldo Superman yanks the roof up and X slithers in, cursing at a sharp edge that catches at his crotch. He flops over the front seat and goes at the driver, Abe continues to widen the door, snip snip snip, Chippie puts a halogen floodlight on them and it's all overexposed, howl of approaching sirens, it's loud out here on the freeway but Abe doesn't hear a thing, it's only stubborn metal here. He chops away the whole side of the car, looks up to see the hundred cars passing slowly, vampire eyes feasting on the sight.

"Abe! *Abe!*" X is hanging down underneath the steering wheel. Abe leans in. "Look man, he's caught here, the driveshaft wall has snapped over and crushed the right ankle."

Abe can see that.

"Cut that loose, will you?"

Abe goes to work on it.

"Not so close!"

"Well shit, how else can I get that sheet turned back?"

"Work higher around it, man this guy's gonna bleed to death from his fucking foot! Can't get the patch all the way around—"

Snip. Crrk. Crrk. Crrk. Snip.

"The driveshaft and the motor are pressing down on that wall, I'll have to get the crane on it and yank it up—"

"No time for that! Okay—I got a tourniquet on the calf. That foot is almost torn off anyway, and he gonna die if we don't get him out of here right fast, so listen here Abe, take those snips and cut his foot clear—"

"What?"

"You heard me, amputate right here. I'll get him to the car. Do what I say, man, I'm the medic here!"

Abe set the edges of the cutter blades against a bloodied black sock, resists an urge to look away. Just like scissors. "That's it, right there." He squeezes the master handles together gently. "Quick now." There's no resistance at all to the flesh. Only a little resistance, a slight crunch, as the blades cut through the bone. The footless driver sighs. X slaps a fix on the stump, hands flying, breath *whoosh*ing in and out of him as he wiggles around, lifts the driver out, they pull him free of the dash and get him on a street gurney. "Cut that foot free and bring it along," X says as he runs the gurney to the truck.

"Fuck." Abe attacks the motor from the front, puts the snips to it and presses together hard as he can; it takes all of his and the teleoperator's strength to cut the driveshaft in half, but that done he can sink the cutter into the motor and pull it forward by main strength. Then he can get a grip on the driveshaft wall, a tricky maneuver, but he does it and bends the wall back, runs around to the driver's door, reaches in, yep, there, he can reach in and grab the thing, shoe all full of blood, and here he is running back to the truck with a foot and ankle in his hand. Part of him can't believe it's happening. He throws it in back on the bed with its owner, X looks up from his man, "Let's get this guy to an ER fast." Abe is in the driver's seat, seat belt on, off he goes, Mission Viejo's got a little hospital with a good ER to handle all their swimming casualties, no track now, it's full speed ahead and X's sweaty face in the window. "I got him stabilized, I think. He's looking good."

"Will they be able to graft that foot back on?"

"Yeah, sure. It's a clean cut. They could graft your head back on these days." He laughs. "You shoulda seen the look on your face when you tossed it in to me."

"Shit."

"Ha, ha! That's nothing. On Java once I was carrying a whole *leg* out, hip down, and damned if it didn't keep *kicking* me."

"Shit."

"You didn't feel anything twitching or anything? Ha, ha. . . ."

"Please, X."

Abe flies down La Paz and up the tortured curving streets that are supposed to make old Mission Viejo somehow different. To the hospital, onto the ER dock, wheel the guy and his foot inside. Whew. They sit on the dock.

X gets up and gets towels and water bottle from the ambulance compartment. They towel off their faces, drink deeply. Abe feels the shakes begin to hit. The kinetic memory of the amputation returns, that crunch when the waldo suddenly overcame the bone's resistance. "Man," he says. X laughs softly.

Brrk! Crrk! "Truck five twenty-two, code six, a two car head-on where the Coast Highway meets Five in Capistrano Beach—"

Tapped out again. Reflexively they're up. Xavier yells in to the ER nurses, Abe gets the truck started. X jumps in. Seat belts on. "Man they're densepacked tonight."

"Drive, road pilot, drive this baby."

23

Dennis McPherson reads of the sabotage at Parnell on the morning wall news, shoots air between his teeth. A bad business. There have been several attacks by saboteurs on defense contractors recently, and it's hard to tell who's behind them. It's beginning to look like more than intercompany rivalries. Every company's security division, including LSR's, is involved in some questionable activities, usually concerned with getting their hands on classified military documents or the plans of other companies; this Mc-

Pherson is aware of, as is everybody. And in isolated cases a zealous or desperate security team may have gotten out of hand and done some mischief to a rival. It's happened, sure, and in recent years, with the Pentagon's budget leveling off a little, the competition has become more and more unscrupulous. But mostly it's been confined to intelligence and minor-league tampering. This widespread sabotage appears to be something new. The work of the Soviets, perhaps, or of some Third World power; or of home-grown refusniks.

Dennis laughs without humor to read that the composite-compound solvents used in the attack were mostly Styx-90, made by Dow. Parnell is owned by Dow. And he laughs again when it occurs to him that these companies, whose main business it is to defend America from ICBM attack, cannot even effectively protect themselves from little field cruisers. Who anymore can possibly believe in Fortress America?

Certainly not the security men at the gate of the LSR complex. They look distinctly unhappy as they check to see if McPherson is the correct occupant of his car. They're there to defend against industrial espionage, not guerrilla attack. They've got an impossible job.

And the people inside?

For the last several weeks McPherson has been whipping the informal Stormbee proposal into formal shape. Going from su-perblack to white. There are advantages to a white program that McPherson appreciates. Everything's on the table, the specs are there in the RFP and can't be changed by some clown in the Air Force who happens to come up with a new idea. And they're forced by the intense competition to do a thorough job, including tests that are run until every part of the system has been proved to work, under all kinds of circumstances. And that's good in the long run, as far as McPherson is concerned. He's been out to White Sands seven times in the last month, working on further tests of the system, and in the tests they discovered, for instance, that if the target tanks were grouped in a mass the laser target designator tended to fix only on the tanks on the perimeter, leaving those in the middle alone. Some work by the programmers and the problem was solved, but if they hadn't even known about it? Yes, this is the way McPherson likes to work. "Let's get it right," he tells his crew almost every day. In fact his programmers call him LGIR behind his back, pronounced "Elgir," which has led certain music-minded programmers to speak of cello concertos, or to whistle "Pomp and Circumstance" to indicate the boss's arrival on the scene. . . .

So, McPherson sits down at his desk and looks at the list of Things To Do that he left the night before. He adds several items that have occurred to him over the night, and on the drive in.

> 9:00 meet Don F. re Strmbee prop printing
> see Lonnie on CO_2 laser problems
> work Strmb prop introduction
> 1:30 meeting software group re guidance
> call Dahlvin on Strmb power
> work Strmb prop
> 4:00 meet Dan Houston on Ball Lightning

He lifts the phone, punches the button for Don Freiburg. The day begins.

Becoming a white program means that the Stormbee proposal is now part of the mainstream of public military procurement in America. This is a vastly complicated process that contains hundreds of variables, and very few people, if any, understand all the facets of it. Certainly McPherson does not; he concentrates on the part of the process that is important to his work, just as everyone else does. Thus he is an expert in the Air Force's aerospace technology procurement, and knows little or nothing about other areas. Just learning his own little area is difficult enough.

It begins within the Air Force itself, like so: One of the operating commands, say the Strategic Defense Phase One Group (SDPOG), makes a Statement of Operational Need (SON) with a Mission Element Need Analysis (MENA) to the United States Air Force Headquarters (HQ USAF). If HQ USAF decides that the SON represents a major program, they make a Justification for Major Systems New Start (JMSNS), which is reviewed by the Requirements Assessment Group (RAG), and this review is then submitted to the Secretary of the Air Force (SAF). If SAF decides that the JMSNS represents an Air Force Designated Acquisition Program (AFDAP), he approves the JMSNS, and it becomes an AFJMSNS. The SAF then submits the AFJMSNS as part of the next Air Force Program Objectives Memorandum (POM) to the Secretary of Defense (SECDEF). If the SECDEF approves the POM, and thus the AFJMSNS, the HQ USAF prepares and issues a Program Management Directive (PMD), and Planning, Programming and Budgeting System (PPBS) action is taken. The Concept Exploration Phase (CEP) has begun. In this phase the various Preliminary System Operational Concepts (PSOCs) are explored, and altogether they constitute the Phase Review Package (PRP). From the PRP a System Concept Paper (SCP) is prepared by HQ USAF, and it is again reviewed by the RAG, and by the Air Force Systems Acquisition Review Council (AFSARC), after which it is submitted to the SAF. If the SAF approves the SCP, it is reviewed by the Defense Systems Acquisition Review Council (DSARC), which recommends it to the SECDEF. If the SECDEF approves the SCP—a Milestone I decision—then HQ USAF issues another PMD and the program enters the Validation and Demonstration Phase (VDP).

All clear? Well, it's at that point that the program first connects with private industry. If the SAF and the SECDEF have agreed that the program must remain top secret, then the program becomes a superblack program and a single contractor or two is contacted by Air Force personnel directly in the Pentagon. At least usually. There are also the ordinary black programs, which are given directly to contractors like the superblacks; a few people in Congress are told about these as well, so they can think that they are in on all the Pentagon's secrets.

But by far the majority of the programs are so-called white programs, and these require more complicated procedures. During the VDP, HQ USAF begins floating draft Requests For Proposals (RFPs) and Requests For Information (RFIs) to relevant defense contractors, asking for comments. The interested companies respond with technical suggestions based on their evaluations of the RFP, and these become part of the Decision Coordination Process (DCP). Eventually HQ USAF issues a final RFP, which is usually published in *Commerce Business Daily*. At this point there has already been an important tactical struggle between the interested contractors, as each attempted to get things written into the RFP that only they were competent to do. But now the RFP is out there for anyone to respond to, and the race is on.

Typically companies have ninety days to submit proposals to the Program Manager (PM), who is an Air Force colonel or brigadier general. After submission, the proposal evaluation process begins. Part of it is conducted by the Air Force Test and Evaluation Center (AFTEC), which is part of the Air Force Systems Command (AFSC) based at Andrews AFB; part of it is conducted out of HQ USAF in the Pentagon, or under the PM. From these units and others a Source Selection Evaluation Board (SSEB) is convened, under the command of a Source Selection Authority (SSA), who is usually but not always the PM. The various proposers are brought in and grilled over every detail of their proposals, and when that six-week process is over, the SSEB makes its evaluation, which is then summarized by the SSA, who uses his summary to justify his decision to the people above him. The decision to award the program to a bidder (or to award it to two bidders in a competitive development, or in a so-called leader-follower arrangement) is thus ultimately the SSA's decision, but he usually follows the recommendations of the SSEB, and he also has to secure the approval of his superiors, up to the SAF or even the SECDEF.

All clear?

But meanwhile, at this point, all Dennis McPherson has to worry about is putting together a proposal that will stand up under the technical testing and budgetary demands that the SSEB will soon be making. Not too many days left; and so it is nearer five-thirty than four when he finally gets free for the first conference with Dan Houston about the Ball Lightning program, which Lemon has vengefully commanded him to work on, in his ''spare time'' from the Stormbee proposal.

McPherson can still remember perfectly the mistake that got him stuck with this. He was down in LSR's executive restaurant, walking in with Art Wong, and in response to something Art said, without pausing to think (or look around), he said, ''I'm damned glad I don't have the job you guys do. The whole ballistic defense program is nothing but a black hole for money and effort if you ask me.'' And then he turned around and there was Stewart Lemon, standing right there and glaring at him.

And so now he's assigned to Ball Lightning. Lemon never forgets.

Dan is ready to quit for the day, and he's about to go with some of his crew to the El Torito just down the road. He wants McPherson to come along and join them for margaritas, and McPherson hides his irritation and agrees to it. On the short drive over he calls Lucy to let her know he'll be home late, and then ascends the office complex's maze of exterior staircases to the restaurant on the top floor. Fine view of the Muddy Canyon condos, and in the other direction, the sea.

Dan and Art Wong and Jerry Heimat are already there at a window table, and the pitcher of margaritas is on its way. Mc-Pherson sits and starts in on the chips and salsa with them. They're talking shop. Executives at Grumman and Teledyne have been indicted for taking kickbacks from subcontractors. ''That's why they call the Grumman SAM the 'Kicker,' I guess,'' says Dan. This gets them on the topic of missiles, and as the pitcher of margaritas arrives and is quickly disposed of, they discuss the latest performances in the war in Indonesia. It seems a General Dynamic antitank missile has gotten nicknamed ''the Boomerang'' for persistent problems with guidance software or vane hinges, no one is quite sure yet. But they just keep on flying in curved trajectories, a weird problem indeed. No one wants to use these devices, but they're ordered to anyway because the Marines have huge quantities of them and won't acknowledge that the problems have gotten above an acceptable percentage. So soldiers in the field have taken to firing their GDs ninety degrees off to the side of the target tanks . . . or so the gossip mill says. No doubt it's a pack of lies, but no one likes GD so it makes for a good story.

''Did you hear about Johnson at Loral?'' asks Art. ''He's in charge of the fourth-tier ICBM program, shooting down leakers. So, one day he gets a directive from SDC, and it says, Please assume that you will have to deal with twenty percent *more than* the total amount estimated to be launched in a full-scale attack!'' They all laugh. ''He almost has a heart attack, this is a couple of orders of magnitude more incoming than he thought the system was going to have to deal with, and all his software is shit out of luck. The whole system is overwhelmed. So he calls the Pentagon just before his ticker says good-bye, and finds out that whoever wrote 'twenty percent *more than*' should have written 'twenty percent *of*.' . . .''

"He's still got trouble," Dan says when they stop laughing. "They can't even knock down one incoming with more than fifty percent reliability, so they're going to have to at least double the number of smart rocks, and the Pentagon is already threatening to dump him." This reminds Dan of his own troubles, and with a grim smile he downs the rest of his margarita.

Art and Jerry, aware of their boss's moods, sense this change of humor. And this is supposed to be a conference between the two managers. So they chat for a while longer, and finish their drinks, and then they're up and off. Dan and Dennis are left there to talk things over.

"So," Dan says, smiling the same unhumorous smile. "Lemon has stuck you into the Ball Lightning program, eh?"

"That's right."

"Worse luck for you." Dan signals to a passing waitress for another pitcher. "He's running scared, I'll tell you that. Hereford is calling from New York and putting the pressure on, and right now he's feeling it but good, because we are stuck." He shakes his head miserably. "Stuck."

"Tell me about it."

Dan gets out a pen, draws a circle on the yellow paper tablecloth. "The real problem," he complains, "is that the first tier has been given an impossible job. Strategic Defense Command has said that seventy percent of all Soviet ICBMs sent up in a full attack are to be destroyed in the boost phase. We won a development contract using that figure as the baseline goal. But it can't be done."

"You think not?" McPherson suspects that Dan may just be making excuses for his program's problems. He sips his drink. "Why?"

Houston grimaces. "The necessary dwell time is just too long, Mac. Too long." He sighs. "It's always been the toughest requirement in the whole system's architecture, if you ask me. The Soviets have got their fast-burn boosters down to sixty seconds, so most of their ICBMs will only be in boost phase for that minute, and half that time they'll be in the atmosphere where the lasers won't do much. So for our purposes we're talking about a window of thirty seconds.''

He scribbles down the figures on the tablecloth as he talks, nervously, without looking at them, as if they are his signature or some other deeply, even obsessively memorized sign. $t_B = 30$.

''Now, during that time we've got to locate the ICBMs, track them, and get the mirrors into the correct alignment to bounce the lasers. Art's team has got that down to around ten seconds, which is an incredible technical feat, by the way.'' He nods mulishly, writes $t_T = 10$. ''And then there's the dwell time, the time the beam has to be fixed on the missile to destroy it.'' He writes $t_D = $, hesitates, leaves the other side of the equation blank.

''You told the Air Force we could pulse a large burst of energy, right?'' McPherson asks. ''So the damage is done by a shock wave breaking the skin of the missile?''

Dan nods. ''That's right.''

''So dwell time should be short.''

''That's right! That's right. Dwell time should be on the order of two seconds. That means that each laser station can destroy N missiles, where,'' and he writes:

$$N = \frac{t_B}{t_D + t_T}$$

''However,'' Dan continues carefully, looking down on the simple equation, one of the basic Field-Spergels that he has to juggle every day, ''dwell time in fact depends on the hardness of the missile, the distance to the target, the brightness of the laser beam, and the angle of the incidence between the beam and the surface of the missile.'' He writes down H, B, R, and 0, and then, obsessively, writes down this equation too, another Field-Spergel:

$$t_D = \frac{4\partial^2 HR^2}{\pi PD^2 \cos 0}$$

''And we've been getting figures for hardness of about forty kilojoules per square centimeter.'' He writes H = 40 KJcm^2. ''Our lasers have twenty-five megawatts of power hitting ten-meter-diameter mirrors at wavelength two point seven nanometers, so even with the best angle of incidence possible, dwell time is,'' and he writes, very carefully:

$$t_D = 53\ seconds.$$

"What?'' says McPherson. "What happened to this pulse shock wave?''

Dan shakes his head. "Won't work. The missiles are too hard. We've got to burn them out, just like I used to say we'd have to, back before we got this development contract. The mirrors are up there and they won't be getting any bigger, the power pulse is already incredible when you think that over a hundred and fifty laser stations will have to be supplied all at once, and we can't change the wavelength of the lasers without replacing the entire systems. And that's the whole ball game.''

"But that means that dwell time is longer than boost time!''

"That's right. Each laser can bring down about eight-tenths of a missile. And there's a hundred and fifty laser stations, and about ten thousand missiles.''

McPherson feels himself gaping. He takes the pen from Houston, starts writing on the tablecloth himself. He surveys the figures. Takes another drink.

"So,'' he says, "how did we get this development contract, then?''

Dan shakes his head. Now he's looking out the window at the sea.

Slowly he says, "We got the contract for Ball Lightning by proving we could destroy a stationary hardened target in ground tests, with the sudden pulse shock wave. They gave us the contract on that basis, and we were put in competition with Boeing who got the same contract, and after three years we have to show we can do it in boost phase, in real-time tests. It's getting close to time for the head-to-head tests. The winner gets a twenty-billion-dollar project, just for starters, and the loser is out a few hundred million in proposal and development costs. Maybe it'll get a follower's subcontract with the winner, but that won't amount to much.''

McPherson nods impatiently. "But if we could do it on the ground?"

Dan polishes off another glass in one swallow. "You want another pitcher?"

"No."

He pours foam and ice into his glass. "The problem," he says carefully, "is that the test wasn't real. It was a strapped chicken."

"*What?*" McPherson sits up so fast his knee knocks the table and almost tips his glass over. "What's this?"

But it's clear what Dan means. The test results didn't mean what LSR said they did.

"Why?"

Dan shrugs. "We were out of time. And we thought we had the problem licked. We thought we could send a beam so bright that it would create a shock wave in even the hardened skins, the calculations made it look like all we needed was a little more power and the brightness would be there. So we simulated what would happen when we did solve the problems, and figured we could validate the tests retroactively, after we had the contract. But we've never been able to." He stares at the table, unable to meet McPherson's gaze.

"For God's sake," Dennis says. He can't get over it.

"It's not like no one has ever done it before," Dan says defensively.

"Uhn."

In fact, as they both know, the strategic defense program has a long history of such meaningless tests, beginning under its first R&D PM. They blew up Sidewinder missiles with lasers, when Sidewinders were designed to seek out energy sources and therefore were targets that would latch on to the beams destroying them. They sent electron beams through rarefied gases, and claimed that the beams would work in the very different environments of vacuum or atmosphere. They bounced lasers off space targets and claimed progress, when astronomy rangers had done the same for decades. And they set target missiles on the ground, and strained them with guy wires so that they would burst apart when heated by lasers, in the famous "strapped chicken" tests. Yes, there's a history of PR tests that goes right back to the beginning of the whole concept. You could say the ballistic missile defense system was founded on them.

But now—now the system is being produced and deployed. It's the real thing now, sold to the nation and in the sky, and with a strapped chicken in their part of the system, they're in serious trouble. The Pentagon is not as lenient with private contractors as they were with their own research program, needless to say. The company could even be liable to prosecution, though it seldom comes to that. It doesn't have to to ruin the company, though.

And here Lemon has put him into this program! McPherson already knew that Lemon gave him the task out of malice; it complicated his primary work quite a bit; but this! This! It goes beyond malice.

"Does Lemon know?"

". . . No."

But McPherson can see in Dan's face that he's lying, trying to cover for his boss, his friend. Amazing. And there's no way Dennis can call Dan on it, not now. "My God." He stops a waitress and orders another pitcher of margaritas.

They sit in silence until the new pitcher arrives. They fill up. "So what do you think we should do?" Dan says hesitantly. There's a certain desperation in his voice; and he's drinking the margaritas as fast as he can.

"How the hell should I know?" Dennis snaps. The question makes him suddenly furious. "You've got Art and Jerry's people working on the pulse problem?"

"Yeah. No go so far, though."

McPherson takes a deep breath. "Would more power help?"

"Sure, but where will we get it?"

"I don't know. I suppose . . ." He is thinking to himself now. "I suppose the best thing to do is try jamming all the power we do have into as short a burst as we can manage. And focus it to as small a space." He sighs, picks up the pen and starts scribbling formulas. The two of them bend their heads over the table.

24

—*RRKK!*—"Slightly radioactive still. On the foreign front the score is still in our favor in Burma—as for Belgium, I don't want to talk about it, all right? Now let's put an ear to the new hit by our favorite group The Pudknockers, 'Why My Java Is Red White and Green'—"

Sandy Chapman turns off the radio. Groan, moan. Stiffness in the joints, he feels like an old man. Sunlight streams into the plant-filled, glass-walled bedroom; it's warm, humid, smells like a greenhouse. Sandy manages to lever himself into a seated position. Angela is long gone, off to work in the physical therapy rooms at St. Joseph's Hospital.

All the glossy green leaves blur. Bit of fuzz vision, too much eyedropping yesterday as usual, leads to a sort of eyeball hangover, as if he'd been teargassed or had his corneas sandblasted or something. He's used to it. He gets up, pads off to the bathroom. The face in the mirror looks wasted. Dark circles under bright red eyes, stubble, mouth caked white, long red hair broken out of ponytail, looking electrocuted. Yes, it's morning time. Ick.

In the kitchen he starts the coffee machine, sits staring out at the San Diego Freeway until it's ready. Back to the bedroom, where he sits on the floor among the plants. Eyedrop a little Apprehension of Beauty . . . ah. That's better. Just the lubrication feels good. He sips coffee, relaxes, thinking nothing: no worries, no plans. Odors of coffee, hot plants, wet soil. "Hey this is why my Java is red white and green," he sings, "the blood in the jungle, the smoke white machine. . . ." This is the sole moment of peace in his day, waxy leaves around him glowing translucent

132

green in the mote-filled sunny air, everything visible, a world of light and color. . . .

Need another cup of coffee. Fifteen minutes later the thought occurs to him again, and he stands. Oops got up too fast. Through warm patches to the kitchen. Ah, feeling much better now. Sensuousness of feet on warm tile, taste of coffee cutting through fuzz in mouth, video of Angela getting undressed last night, running on the kitchen screens. Ready to get a start on the day's business. A day in the life, sure enough.

But first he stops to call his father, down at the experimental clinic in Miami Beach. They talk on the video link for twenty minutes or so: George seems good today, hearty and cheerful despite the pallor and the IV lines. Sandy finds it reassuring, sort of.

Then he's dressed, alert, out the door to work like any other businessman.

Sandy begins his day on time. And while he's only depending on himself, he stays on schedule. He tracks to a rundown area of the underlevel of Santa Ana, a mile or so north of South Coast Plaza, and unlocks the door to the warehouse he rents, after turning off all the alarms. Inside is his laboratory.

Today he starts with cytotoxicity assays, one of the most crucial parts of his work. Anyone can make drugs, after all; the trick is finding out if they'll kill you or not without testing them personally. Or giving them to rats. Sandy doesn't like killing rats. So he likes these assays.

Since the cornea's epithelium will be the first place the drugs hit, epithelial cells get the first tests. A couple of days ago Sandy joined the crowd of biochem techs at the slaughterhouse and bought a package of cow eyeballs; now he takes them from the fridge and uses a device called a rubber policeman to scrape the epithelial cells off the basement membrane. Tapped into a petri dish with some growth medium, and a carefully measured dose of the drug in question—a new one, a variant of 3,4,5 trimethoxyamphetamine that he's calling the Visionary—these cells will either proliferate or die or struggle somewhere in between, and staining them at the end of a week will tell the tale.

That assay set up, Sandy moves on to trickier stuff. The new drug's effect on lymphocytes has to be checked as well, because blood will be carrying it a lot of the time. So Sandy begins a chromium release assay, injecting chromium 51 into lymphocytes, then centrifuging them so only the cells remain. At that point all the chromium in the mix is within the cells. Then the Visionary is added—in doses ranging from femtomolars up through picomolars, nanomolars, micromolars—and it all goes into a growth medium that should keep lymphocytes happy. But with the drug in there who knows. In any case dying or dead cells will release the chromium, and after another centrifuging, the free chromium found will be a good measure of the drug's toxicity.

Later more tests of stationary cells and organ cells, particularly bone marrow cells, will be necessary. And eventually, after a lot of hours in the lab, Sandy will have a good idea of the Visionary's toxicity. Neat. As for long-term negative effects of the new drug, well, that's not so clear. That's not in the guarantee. That's not something he likes to think about, and neither does anybody else. None of these new drugs are well understood on the long-term level. But if there are problems down the road, they will no doubt come up with something, like they did for the various viral killers. Make the body into a micro-battlefield and win it all: the brain can finally prove it is smarter than viruses. Who knows what demon will fall next?

So, not to worry about long-term physical effects. As for the new drugs' effects on the mind, well, it isn't so cut and dried, but he does have a collection of cross spiders, building their webs under the influence of the new products. The particular nature of the altered state induced by the drug can be partially predicted by the computer's Witt analysis of the webs. Amazing but true. More precise knowledge in this area will come after some extensive field testing; he has a lot of volunteers.

The fact is, he buys his drugs in an advanced state, so the molecular engineering he does to make his new products is nothing really supercomplex, though he has a reputation for genius that he does nothing to try to dispel. Actually, he has got a talent for pharmacometrics—taking the basic drugs from the companies and then guessing, with the aid of a structure/activity relationships program pirated from Upjohn, which alterations in chemical structure will shift the psychoactive properties of the drugs in an interesting way. Pharmacometrics is really quite an art, still, even with the program's indispensable aid: structure/activity relationships is a big and complex field, and no one knows it all. So to that extent he is a kind of artist.

Into the second hour of work. Sandy moves among the various endomorphins and alkaloids and solutions on the shelves in their bottles and flasks, and the reference texts and papers that spill over one big bookcase, and the bulks of the secondhand centrifuges, refrigerators, the g.c./mass spec . . . It would be easy to impress any visitors allowed to drop by. For a few minutes he attacks again the problem of the synergistic self-assembly effects of La Morpholide 15 and an enkephalin introduced into the brain at the same time—a sophisticated problem in pharmacokinetics, sure, and interesting as hell, but a little bit much for this morning. Easier to return to the final plans for fitting 5-HIAA to the serotoninergic neurons, which he's already almost mastered. Should be a nice hallucinogen, that.

So it's a fascinating couple of hours in the lab, as always. But he's supposed to meet one of his suppliers, Charles, at noon, and looking up at the clock he finds he'd better hurry. Sure enough, he shows up at Charles's place in Santa Ana at 12:05. Nothing to complain about, right?

However, the inevitable process of getting behind schedule begins immediately, with Charles inviting him in to share an eyedropper, followed by a close discussion of Charles's difficulties in life. So the simple pickup of a liter of Sandoz DMT takes him until 1:30.

He then heads to the first of his distributors, in Garden Grove, and discovers no one home. Twenty minutes of waiting and they show up, and it's the same program there; only really need to lay twenty eyedroppers on them and collect the money for them, could take five minutes, right? But no. Got to blink another eyedropper of Social Affability, light up a Sandy spliff, and socialize for a bit. That's sales for you, it's a social job and you can't escape that. Not many people realize how full Sandy's schedule of deliveries actually is, and of course he doesn't want to make too big a point of saying so. It's a test of his diplomacy to get out in under an hour; so now it's almost three. He hurries up to Stanton to make a drop at June's, then tracks at street level to La Palma to meet Sidney, hits the freeway to get back to Tustin and the Tunaville drug retailers' weekly meeting, down to Costa Mesa to see Arnie Kalish, on to Garden Grove to see those Vietnamese guys in Little Saigon . . . until he's over three hours behind schedule and losing ground fast, with a dozen more people who want to see him before dinner. Whew.

Luckily this happens every day, and so everyone expects Sandy to be late. It's an OC legend; stories abound of Sandy showing up for lunches at dinner, for dinners at midnight, for parties the next day . . . By this time it would no doubt actually shock people if he showed up on time. But, he thinks, it's never my fault!

So he works his way along, tracking like a maniac to sit through one glacial transaction after another. It's a bit of an effort, when he's tired or depressed, living up to the task of being Sandy Chapman; he's expected to show up at a friend/client's house and galvanize the day, burst in with manic energy and his crazy man's grin, discuss all the latest developments in music, movies, sports, whatever, shifting registers from full-blown culturevulturehood to astonishing mallworld ignorance . . . pull out yet another eye-dropper, of Affability or Funny Bone or California Mello or the Buzz, whatever seems to be called for at the moment, eyes bugging out with manic glee as he holds up the dropper and pulls his face under it. . . . He's used to operating rationally under the weight of monumental highs; in fact it's just everyday reality for him, stonedness, it's a handicap he barely notices anymore. His tolerance level is so high that he only really notices the effect of that first drip of Apprehension of Beauty at the beginning of each day. So he lids with whatever household he has reoriented to party mode, smokes dope with them, inhales capsules of snapper, giggles at them as they exhibit the first signs of brain damage, fills them full of that comic spirit that is surely the main thing he is selling. It's quite a performance, though he seldom feels it as such. Method acting.

Long after sundown he finishes making his last delivery, some five hours late. On the way home he stops and buys the ten-trillionth Big Mac fries and a Coke, eats while tracking home. Reaches home, but it's no rest for the weary; the party there is in dormant mode and reflexively he sparkplugs it, gets it ontrack and rolling. Then into his bedroom, to check on phone messages.

The answering machine can barely hold all the messages that have been left, and Sandy sits on the bed buzzing like a vibrator, watching the surfing on the wall screens and listening to them. One catches his wandering attention and he repeats it from the start:

"Hey, Sandy. Tompkins here. We're having a small party tonight at my place and we'd like to see you, if you can make it. We want to introduce you to a friend from Hawaii who has a proposal, too. It'll go late so don't worry about when you arrive. Hope this reaches you in time—later—"

Sandy goes out to the game room. Jim is absorbed in the hanging video screens, and Sandy checks them out. Collage city. "What's on, Jim Dandy?"

Jim gestures at one flickering black-and-white square. "Best *Hamlet* ever filmed. Christopher Plummer as the Dane, shot by the BBC at Elsinore years ago."

"I like the old Russian one, myself. His father's ghost, ten stories tall—how could you beat it?"

"That's a nice touch, all right." Jim seems a bit down. He and Virginia looked to be in a heated discussion when Sandy walked in, and Sandy guesses they have been arguing again. Those two are not exactly the greatest alliance ever made; in fact they both keep saying it's over, although it seems to be having a long ending. "Do you think you can drag yourself away from the Bard for a jaunt to La Jolla? My big-time friends have invited us to a party at their place."

"Sure, I've got this at home."

Sandy collects Arthur, Abe, Tashi. "Let's see if we can get Humphrey to drive," he says with his wicked grin.

They laugh; Humphrey keeps his electric bill down by driving as little as possible. He's an almanac of all the shortest distances, he can give you the least expensive route between any two points in OC faster than the carbrains can. They approach him in a gang,

Sandy says, "Humphrey, you've got a nice big car, give us a ride down to La Jolla and I'll get you into a party there you won't forget."

"Ah, gee, what's wrong with this one? Can't ask for more, can you?"

"Of course you can! Come on, Humphrey. . . ." Sandy waves a fresh eyedropper of the Buzz, Humphrey's favorite, in front of his eyes.

"Can't leave your own party," Humphrey starts to say, but founders in the face of the statement's absurdity. Sandy steers him to the door, stopping for a quick kiss and an explanation for Angela. Remembering Jim and Virginia, he runs back in and kisses her again. "I love you." Then they're out, followed by Arthur, Abe, Tashi and Jim, who elbow each other and snicker as they all clump down the rarely used stairwell. "Think Humph's got the coin slots installed on his car doors yet?" Abe asks under his breath, and they giggle. "Taxi meter," Tashi suggests. "Better profit potential."

"Subtler," Arthur adds.

Humphrey, next flight down, says to Sandy, "Maybe we can all go shares on the mileage, huh?" The four above them nearly explode holding the laughs in, and when Sandy says, "Sure thing, Humphrey, and maybe we should figure out the wear on the tires, too," they experience catastrophic failure and burst like balloons. The stairwell echoes with howls. Tashi collapses on the banister, Abe and Arthur and Jim crumple to the landing and take the next flight down on hands and knees. Humphrey and Sandy observe this descent, Humphrey perplexed, Sandy grinning the maniac's grin. "You men are stoned." Which lays them out flat. Maybe they are.

They scrape themselves off the floor in the parking lot and get in Humphrey's car, carefully inspecting the door handles and the car's interior. "What are you guys looking for?" Humphrey asks.

"Nothing, nothing. Can we go now? Are we gone yet?"

They're gone. Off to San Diego.

25

On the track down 405 they sit in the three rows of seats in Humphrey's car and talk. Sandy, slumped in the front passenger seat, just smiles; he looks zoned, as if he's catching some rest before he dives back into it in La Jolla.

Humphrey tells them about a trip he and Sandy and some others took to Disneyland. "We had been in the line for Mr. Toad's Wild Ride for about forty-five minutes when Chapman went nuts. You could see it happen—we were all standing there just waiting, you know, hanging out and moving with the line, and suddenly his eyes bug out past his nose and he gets that happy look he gets when he's got an idea." The others laugh, "Yeah, yeah, show us the look, Sandy," and half-asleep Sandy shows them a perfect simulacrum of it. "So he says real slow, 'You know, guys, this ride only lasts about two minutes. Two minutes at the most. And we'll have been in line for it an hour. That's a thirty-to-one ratio of wait to ride. And the ride is just a fast trackcar going through holograms in the dark. I wonder . . . do you think . . . could it be . . . that this is the *worst* ratio in Disneyland?' And he gets the insanity look again and says, 'I wonder, I just wonder . . . which one of us can rack up the *worst* ratio for the whole day?' And we all see instantly we've got a new game, a contest, you know, and the whole day is transformed, because it's a miserable day at Disneyland, totally densepacked, and there's some real potential here for racking up some fantastic scores! So we call it Negative Disneyland and agree to add points for stupidest rides combined with the worst ratios."

The four in back can't believe it. "You've got to be kidding."

"No, no! It's the only way to go there! Because with Sandy's idea we weren't fighting the situation anymore, you know? We were running around finding the longest lines we could, stepping through our paces like we were on the ride itself, and timing everything on our watches, and every time we turned another corner in the line we'd see Sandy standing there up ahead of us towering over the kids, eyes bugged out and grinning his grin, just digging these monster delays to get on Dumbo the Elephant, Storybook Canal, Casey Junior, the Submarine . . ."

Sandy's smile turns blissful. "It was a stroke of genius," he mutters. "I'll never do it any other way, ever again."

"So who won?" Jim asks.

"Oh Sandy, of course. He totaled five and a half hours of waiting for eighteen minutes of ride!"

"I can beat that," Tashi says promptly. "Hell, I've beaten that trying *positive* Disneyland!" Sandy denies it and they make a bet for next time.

They leave OC and track through the immense nuclear facility at San Onofre, eighteen concrete spheres crowding the narrow valley like buboes bumping out of an armpit, powerlines extending off on ranked towers to every point of the compass, glary halogen and xenon and mercury vapor lamps peppering spheres, towers, support buildings. "Camp Pendleton," Jim announces, and they all pitch in together: "Protecting California's Precious Resources!" Or so the neon sign says. The motto is a joke; aside from the nuclear plant, the Marines have contracted with the towns of south OC to take all their sewage into a gigantic treatment facility, which covers the hills south of San Onofre. Concrete tanks and bunkers resemble an oil refinery, and altogether it's as extensive as the power plant north of it. Then comes the land they've leased for the desalination plant that provides OC with much of its water; that means another immense complex of bunkers and tubes, nearly indistinguishable from the nuclear facility, and a whole stretch of the coast blasted by salt mounds and various processing tanks.

After that they're into the supercamp for Marine recruits, then into Oceanside, and the precious resource is passed. Past Oceanside it's like OC on a rollercoaster, same condomundo and mallsprawl and autopia, broken up only by some small dead marshes in the low parts of the rollercoaster ride. Yes, San Diego, along with Riverside and Los Angeles and Ventura and Santa Barbara, is nothing more than an extension of OC. . . .

They get off on La Jolla Village Drive and track west, around the megaversity to La Jolla Farms Road. Here they are stopped at the security gate, Sandy calls his friends, and they're in. La Jolla Mansion Road, it should be called; they track slowly by a long series of multimillion-dollar homes, all single-family dwellings. Abe, who lives in an annex of his parents' house on Saddleback Mountain, isn't impressed, but the rest of them stare. Humphrey goes into his real estate mode and estimates values and mortgage payments and the like in religious tones.

Sandy's friends' house is near the end of the road, on the ocean side, therefore on the crumbling edge of Torrey Pines Cliff. They find parking with difficulty, go to the door and are only let in after Sandy's friend Bob Tompkins comes and okays them. Bob is fortyish, tanned, golden-haired, perfectly featured, expensively dressed. He shakes all their hands, ushers them in, introduces them to his partner Raymond. Raymond is if anything even more perfect than Bob; his jawline could open letters. Perhaps they got their start in modeling.

But now the two are partners in major minor drug dealing, and this is sort of a party for field reps. Sandy recognizes quite a few people he knows. He starts pingponging among them, and rather than follow him his OC friends grab drinks and go out onto the cliff-edge lawn, which is on three terraced levels some three or four hundred feet over the black sea. They've got a perfect view of the hilly curve of La Jolla jutting into the dark water, its sparkling skyscraper hotels reflecting like fire off the bay in between; and to the north stretches the whole curve of the southern California coast, a white pulsing mass of light. *Major* light show, here.

It's a class-A party. Among the guests on the lawn are some Lagunatics they know, and happily they fall to drinking and talking and dancing.

Jim notices Arthur disappearing down the wooden staircase that leads down to the beach below, following—was that Raymond? Arthur was caustic indeed about the mansions on this road, so seeing him with Raymond is a bit of a surprise to Jim.

This turns some key in Jim's sense of curiosity. Ever since

their raid on Parnell Jim has been asking Arthur questions, and Arthur has been putting him off. It's better if Jim doesn't know too much, he says. Jim is up on the theory of revolutionary cells, sure, but it seems to him to be going too far not even to know the name of the group he's part of. Sure the cause is just, but still . . . And Arthur—well, who knows exactly why he came along tonight? It isn't something he'd ordinarily do. And once he said he got his equipment from "the south" . . . could be that Raymond used drug smuggling as a cover . . . well, that would be crazy, but . . .

Jim's curiosity is aroused. He wanders down the wooden steps of the staircase, into the dark.

The stairs switch back from platform to platform down the steep sandstone cliff: thick planks are nailed into parallel four-by-fours that are bolted to telephone poles driven into the cliff face, and the whole structure is painted some bright color, yellow or pink or orange, hard to tell in the dark. Spectrum band, no doubt. Iceplant and some bushy trees have been planted all around the staircase in semisuccessful efforts to stop the erosion of the cliff. Through one thick clump of trees the stairway proceeds in a groomed tunnel of foliage, and beyond that, on the next platform, Jim sees two dark figures standing. Above them stereo speakers facing westward challenge the even roar of the surf with the majestic end of *The Firebird Suite*, cranked to high volume.

Curious, and pitched to a bolder level by the music, Jim slips off the staircase into the iceplant. Ho, it's steeper than it looks! But he can hold his footing, and very slowly he descends through the bushy trees. Any noise he is making is overwhelmed by waves below and music above, which has segued from the Firebird to "Siberian Khantru," brilliant lead guitar piercing the night and leading the supple bass on a madcap ramble. Fantastic. The last knot of trees overhanging the stairway is just above the platform, fine, Jim wiggles his way down through the low branches, slips on iceplant and jerks to a halt jammed down into the fork of two thick branches. Ribs a little compressed. Hmmm. Seems he might be a little stuck, here. On the other hand, he's just above the platform, and the two figures, seated on the rail looking down at the faint white-on-black tapestry of breaking waves, are just within earshot. Wouldn't want to be much closer, in fact. Jim gives up struggling to escape, accepts the salt wetness of his perch, concentrates on listening.

Arthur seems to be making a report, although the booming of the surf makes it difficult to hear everything. "What it comes . . . the campaign has got its own momentum . . . supply material and give . . . do a one-night . . . bigger operation than there really is."

"Do any of your" *krkrkrkrkrkrkrr* asks Raymond.

" . . . assume, well, whatever. They don't *know* anything."

"So you guess."

"I'm pretty sure."

"And you think a concerted action could bring in the people we're trying to find?"

"Makes sense, doesn't it? They" *krkrkrkrkrkrkrrrr*

"Possibly. Possibly." Raymond jumps down and stalks the deck of the platform nervously, looking right up at the clump of trees that holds Jim. "If that happens, we might have a hard time finding out about it. Being sure."

Arthur's back is now to Jim, and Jim can't hear his voice at all. But he can hear Raymond's reply:

"That'd be one way to find out, sure. But it would be dangerous, I mean some of you might just disappear."

Jim feels his throat and stomach take a big swallow. Disappear?

His paranoia quotient soars into the megapynchons, his understanding of his sabotage adventure with Arthur trapdoors out from under him, leaving him hanging like, well, yes, like a man stuck in a tree on the side of a cliff. His ribs begin to complain vociferously. But he definitely doesn't want to move until Arthur and Raymond leave.

Relief for his ribs, and frustration for his mounting curiosity, arrive in the form of night beach partyers climbing back up the stairs. Raymond greets them cheerily, and he and Arthur ascend with them. Soon Jim is alone with Torrey Pines Cliff, in his tree. He'd love to take time and think over what he's just heard, sort it out some, but his ribs protest at the idea and he tries to extricate himself. Arms up, hands on branches to each side, push out. This frees him to fall down the iceplant slope, he lets the branches go when his arms begin to snap out of their sockets, and one branch clips him in the ear as he slides by, heading down here uh-oh, turn into the iceplant and clutch, feet digging, thump, thump, thump! Stopped, thank God. Below him it gets markedly steeper, in fact kind of vertical. All alarms go off in the McPherson body, he convinces one hand to declutch with great difficulty, resets it a foot over toward the stairway. Footwork is trickier, need knobs or clumps of iceplant, the usual spread of the stuff is damned slippery, not that he's complaining; without it he would be one with the sandstone blocks on the beach, still a couple hundred feet below. Carefully he makes ten or twelve heartstopping handhold transfers, and traverses to the stairway. Leeches onto it, heaves up and over the banister. A group descending the stairs catches him in the final act of rolling over the banister to safety, and they laugh at his evident inebriation. "Fell off, hey? Come on down with us and swim it off."

"Is he sober enough to swim?"

"Sure, a blast of ocean water will do him good."

Jim agrees in as calm a voice as he can muster. It'll be a good way to wash some of the dirt and crushed iceplant off of his hands and face. They descend to the beach, strip, walk to the water. The white, almost phosphorescent rush of broken waves over Jim's ankles feels good. It's cold but not anywhere near as bad as he expected. He runs into the water, dives into the chill salt waves. A great rush, cleansing and refreshing. Broken waves tumble him about and he lets them. Maybe Tashi has something in this night surfing idea. Jim does a little desultory bodysurfing in the shore break.

While he's at it he tumbles into a young lady from the group; she squeaks, clings to him, her body incredibly warm in the ocean chill. Legs wrapped around his middle, arms around his neck, a quick kiss, whoah! Then a wave knocks them apart and she's off, he can't find her.

He swims around in an unsuccessful search, chills down, walks out of the water and up the beach. Major refreshment. Remarkably warm out. Beautiful naked women emerge from the surf and walk up to him, give him one of their towels, towel-dry before him. Dryads would they be, or Nereids?

Some quality of the encounter in the dark sea has quickened something in him; it's not the same as his usual lust, not at all. The others dress, he dresses. Up the stairway, back to the party. No time to sort it out; but some part of him remembers. . . .

Up top people are dancing in three rooms. Tashi and Abe are in one, doing the beach boy bounce, dance considered as a helix of pogo hops. "Been swimming?" Abe asks, panting. "Yeah. Plus a small mystical experience." And a big mysterious conversation. Jim joins in the dance. It's The Wind'n'Sea Surf Killers, singing their latest hit "Dance Till Your Feet Are Bloody Stumps." Perfect.

And so the party progresses as parties do. Jim never manages to identify his oceanic love. Along about three he finds himself very tired, and unenthusiastic at the prospect of any chemical reascendance. No. He sits in a fine leather chair in the front room, where he can see the entryway. Lot of people in and out. Humphrey and Tash come sit with him and they talk about San Diego. Humphrey enjoys it because of all the deals down in Tijuana. "Of course," Abe cries as he joins them and sits on the floor. "You should see Humphrey in Tijuana! He grinds those shopkeepers like you can't believe! 'Two hundred pesos, shit, you must be joking! I'll give you ten!' " The others laugh as Abe catches Humphrey's tone of indignation and pleasure exactly. Humphrey nods, grinning. "Sure."

"Man, those poor people open up on a Saturday morning and see Humphrey coming in first thing in the day, and it's like *disaster* for them, they know they're going to end up selling half their stock for a couple handfuls of pesos."

"Rather see an armed robber come in the door," Tash adds.

"Better deal—"

"Less pain—"

"*Safer*—"

Arthur shows up. They sit and wait for Sandy. Quietly Jim watches Arthur, who seems the same as always. No clues there.

26

Sandy, however, has only just now been able to get off with Bob Tompkins for a little conference. They retire to Bob's bedroom with a friend of Bob's that Sandy hasn't met yet, and sit on a gigantic circular bed.

Eight video cameras:
Two walls of screens show them sitting cross-legged, from
    eight angles.
Life in the kaleidoscope: which image is you?
Bedspread of green silks. Wallpaper bronze flake. Carpet
    silver gray.
Oak dressers, topped by a collection of ornate hookahs:
Ceramic jars, copper bowls, woven tubes,
Six speakers play soft zither music.
A poem is a list of Things To Do.
Have you done them yet?

"This is Manfred," Bob says to Sandy. "Manfred, Sandy."

Manfred nods, his eyes bright and very dilated. "Good to meet you." They shake hands across the green silk.

"Well, let's try out some of my latest while we talk about Manfred's proposition." Bob puts a big round wooden platter on the middle of the bed, between the three of them. He gets a smallish hookah from the collection, puts it on the platter, sits down, fills one part of the multichambered bowl with a black tarry substance. There are three tubes coming out of the bulbous ceramic base of the pipe, and they each take one and breathe in as Bob waves the flame of a lighter over the bowl. The moment the smoke hits his throat Sandy begins coughing his lungs out. The other two are coughing too, more moderately but only just. On the wall screens it looks like a whole gang of men have just been teargassed in a bordello.

"Gee," Sandy chokes out. "Great."

The other two wheeze their laughter. "Just wait a couple of minutes," Bob advises. He and Manfred take another hit, and Sandy tries, but only starts coughing again. Still, the pattern of the bedspread has lifted off the bed and begun to rotate clockwise as it becomes ever more elaborate; and the bronze flake wallpaper is glittering darkly, breaking up the subdued lamplight from the dresser into a trillion meaningful fragments. Strangely beautiful, this chamber. "A great reckoning in a little room," Sandy mutters. He puts his thumb over the soapstone mouthpiece of his tube while the other two smoke on. Advanced-lane opium smokers, here. Pretty primitive stuff, opium—noisy as hell, kind of a sledgehammer effect to the body. Sandy finds himself thinking he can do better than this in his lab. Still, as a sort of archaeological experiment . . . Jim should be in on this, didn't the Chinese who built the California railroads use this stuff? No wonder there are no more railroads.

When Manfred and Bob are done smoking, they sit back and talk. The talk flows in unexpected channels, they laugh a lot.

Finally Manfred tells Sandy their proposition. "We've got a very illegal drug from Hong Kong, by way of Guam and Hawaii. The amounts are fairly large, and the DEA has got a spike into the source, so it all added up to trying a different channel for getting it in."

"What is it?" Sandy asks bluntly.

"It's called the Rhinoceros. The tricky thing about sexual arousal is that you have to be stimulated and relaxed in the right degrees of both, and in the right synergy. Two systems are involved and both have to be squeezed just right. So we've got a couple of compounds, one called Eyebeep and the other a modified endomorphin imitant. They self-assemble in the limbic region."

"An aphrodisiac?" Sandy says stupidly.

"That's right. A real aphrodisiac. I've tried it, and, well . . .''
Manfred giggles. "I don't want to talk about it. But it works."
"Wow."

"We're sailing it over from Hawaii, that's our new route. Our idea is to make a brief rendezvous with a small boat that will come out from Newport and meet us behind San Clemente Island. Then the small boat will bring it on in. I realize it's a risk for the last carrier, but if you were willing to do it, I'd be willing to pay you for that risk, in cash and in a part of the cargo."

Sandy nods noncommittally. "How much?"

"Say, twenty thousand dollars and six liters of Rhino."

Sandy frowns. Is there really going to be a demand for six liters of some strange new aphrodisiac? Well . . . sure. Especially if it works. OC's new favorite, no doubt.

Still, the plan goes against Sandy's working principle, which demands a constant low profile and labor-intensive work in small quantities. "And what percentage of the total does that represent?"

They begin to dicker over amounts. It goes on slowly, genially, as a kind of theoretical discussion of how much such a service *would* be worth if one were to contemplate it. A lot of joking from Bob, which the other two appreciate. This is the strange heart of drug dealing; Sandy has not only to come to a financial agreement with Manfred, but also to reach a certain very high level of trust with him. They both have to feel this trust. No contract will be signed at the end of their dealing, and no enforcement agency will come to one's aid if the other breaks their verbal agreement. In this sense drug dealers must be much more honest than businessmen or lawyers, for instance, who have contracts and the law to fall back on. Dealers have only each other, and so it's crucial to establish that they're dealing with someone they can trust to stick to their word. This, in a subculture of people that includes a small but significant number of con artists whose very art consists in appearing trustworthy when they are not. One has to learn how to distinguish between the false and the real, by an intuitive judgment of character, by probing at the other in the midst of the joking around: asking a sudden sharp question, making a quick gesture of friendliness, making an outright, even rude, challenge, and so on; then watching the responses to these various maneuvers, looking for any minute signs of bad faith. Judging behavior for what it reveals of the deeper nature inside.

All this subtle business taking place, of course, under a staggering opium high; but they're all used to that kind of handicap, it can be factored in easily. Eventually Sandy gets a secure feeling that he is talking to a good guy, who is acting in good faith. Manfred, he can tell, is coming to a similar conclusion, and as they are both pleased the meeting becomes even friendlier—a real friendliness, as opposed to the automatic social imitation of it that they began the meeting with.

Still, the basic nature of the deal is not something Sandy likes, and he stops short of agreeing to do it. "I don't know, Manfred," he says eventually. "I don't usually go in for this kind of thing, as Bob probably told you. For me, in my situation you know, the risks are too high to justify it."

Manfred just grins. "It's always the high-risk projects that bring in the highest profits, man. Think about it."

Then Manfred gets up to go to the bathroom.

"So what does Raymond think of this?" Sandy asks Bob. "How come he isn't doing the pickup himself?" For Raymond has done a whole lot of major drug smuggling from offshore in his time, and claims to enjoy it.

Bob makes a face. "Raymond is really involved in some other things right now. You know, he's an idealist. He's always been an idealist. Not that it keeps him from going after the bucks, of course, but still it's there. I don't know if you ever heard about this, but a year or so ago some of Ray's friends in Venezuela were killed by some remotely piloted vehicles that the Venezuelan drug police had bought from our Army. They were good friends, and it really made Ray mad. He couldn't really declare war on the U.S. Army, but he's done the next best thing, and declared war on the people who made the robot planes." He laughs. "At the same time keeping an eye out for profits!" He laughs harder, then looks at Sandy closely. "Don't tell anyone else about this, okay?" Sandy nods; he and Bob have done a lot of business together over the years, and it's gone on as long as it has because they both know they form a closed circuit, as far as information goes, including gossip. And Bob appreciates it, because he does love to gossip, even—or especially—about his ally Raymond. "He's been importing these little missile systems that can be used perfectly for sabotaging military production plants."

"Ah, yes," Sandy says carefully. "I believe I've read about the results of all that."

"Sure. But Raymond doesn't just do it for the idea. He's also finding people who want these things done more than he does!"

Sandy opens his eyes wide to show how dubious he is about this.

"I know!" Bob replies. "It's a tricky area. But so far it's been working really well. There are customers out there, if you can find them. But it's murky water, I'll tell you. Almost as bad as the drug scene. And now he thinks he's been noticed by another group who are into the same thing."

"Uh-oh."

"I know. So he's all wrapped up in that now, trying to find out who exactly is out there, and whether he can come to terms with them."

"Sounds dangerous," Sandy says.

Bob shrugs. "Everything's dangerous. But anyway, you can see why Ray isn't interested in this smuggling deal. His mind is occupied with other things these days."

"You bet."

Manfred comes back from the bathroom. They try a few more puffs of the harsh black smoke, talk some more. Manfred presses Sandy to commit himself to the aphrodisiac smuggling enterprise, and carefully, ever so diplomatically, Sandy refuses to make the commitment. What he has just heard from Bob isn't any encouragement. "I'm going to have to think about it, Manfred. It's really far out of my usual line."

Manfred accepts this with grace: "I still hope you'll go for it, man. Think about it some more and then let me know—we've still got a week or so."

Sandy looks at his watch, rises. "I've got a working day tomorrow, starts in about four hours actually. I should get back home." Farewells all around and he's off, into the living room where Tashi, Jim, Humphrey, Abe and Arthur are sitting around talking to people. "Let's go home."

27

Tracking back north Jim dozes. He's sitting in the middle seat, leaning against the right window. Arthur is beside him, Abe and Tash behind him in the backseat. Jim finds it difficult to joke around with Arthur; easier to doze. The act of falling asleep often brings hypnagogic visions to him, and the sensation of falling down a black cliff jerks him awake. "Whoah!" Arthur and Raymond, on the cliffside platform. Snatches of a conversation. Warm body in the ocean's chill. It's been a strange night.

Out the window is the single stretch of southern California's coast left undeveloped: the center of U.S. Marine Camp Joseph H. Pendleton. Dark hills, a narrow coastal plain cut by dry ravines, covered with dark brush. Grass gray in the moonlight. Something about it is so quiet, so empty, so pure. . . . My God, he thinks. The land. A pang of loss pierces him: this land that they live on, under its caking of concrete and steel and light—it was a beautiful place, once. And now there's no way back.

For a moment, as they track up the coast and out of the untouched hills, into the weird cancerous megastructures of the desalination plant and the sewage plant and the nuclear facility, Jim dreams of a cataclysm that could bring this overlit America to ruin, and leave behind only the land, the land, the land . . . and perhaps—perhaps—a few survivors, left to settle the hard new forests of a cold wet new world, in tiny Hannibal Missouris that they would inhabit like foxes, like deer, like real human beings. . . .

They track on into the condomundo hills of San Clemente, and the absurdity of his vision, combined with its impossibility, and its cruelty, and its poignant appeal, drive Jim ever deeper into depression. There is no way back; because there is no way back. History is a one-way street. It's only forward, into catastrophe, or the track-and-mall inferno, or . . . or nothing. Nothing Jim can imagine, anyway. But no matter what, there is no going back.

Humphrey gets them up the empty freeway to Sandy's place, and they all get out to go to their own cars. Humphrey says, "Listen, the odometer shows about a hundred and forty miles, divide it among the six of us and it'll be really cheap—"

"*Really* cheap," say Tashi and Abe together.

"Yeah, so let me just figure it out here and we can even up before you guys forget."

"Figure it out and bill me," Sandy says, walking off toward the elevator. Even Sandy seems a little weary. "We will recompense you *fully*." Arthur's off without a word. Tashi and Abe are emptying their pockets and giving Humphrey their change, "Sure that covers wear on the brake pads, Humph?" "Don't forget oil, Bogie, that big hog of yours just *sucks* the oil." "No lie."

"Yeah, yeah," Humphrey says seriously, collecting their coins. "I took all that into my calculations." He drives off without a blink at Tash and Abe's gibing, perfectly unaware of it. Jim laughs to see it. The guy is so perfectly unselfconscious! And of his chief characteristic!

As he walks to his car Jim marvels over it. And tracking home he wonders if everyone is, perhaps, unaware of the principle aspect of their personality, which looms too large for them to see. Yeah, it's probably true. And if so, then what part of his own character doesn't he see? What aspect of him do Tash and Abe giggle over, behind his back or even right in front of him, because he doesn't even realize it's there to be made fun of?

It comes to him in a flash: he's got no sense of humor at all!

Hmm. Is that right? Well, it certainly is true that he has about the same amount of wit as a refrigerator. His carbrain would be quicker with repartee, if it only had a speaker. Yes, it's true. Jim has never really thought of it this way before, but many's the time when he's recalled a funny conversation, Abe and Sandy and Tash jamming on one comic riff or another, and a great line to throw into the hilarious sequence will come to him!—only a week or so too late. A bit slow in that department, you could say.

Of course his friends are perfectly aware of this; now Jim

sees it clearly. They'll get on a jag and everyone'll be laughing hard and Sandy will get that gleam in his eye and demand swiftly of Jim, "What do *you* say about that, Jimbo?" and Jim will conquer his giggling and puff and wheeze and blow out all his mental circuits trying to think of just one of the kind of witticisms that are flying out of his friends as natural as thoughts, and finally he'll say something like, "Well . . . *yeah!*" and his three friends will collapse, howling like banshees. Leaving Jim grinning foolishly, only dimly aware that in a gang of wits a dorker can be more valuable than another quick tongue.

What joy it would be to convulse the crowd with an ad-libbed one-liner, tossed into a long sequence of them! But it's not something Jim, Mr. Slow, has ever managed. He's just a convulsee, a one-man audience, the great laugher; when they get Jim going they can drive him right to the floor with laughing, he gasps and chuckles and screams and beats the floor, stomach muscles cramping, Sandy and Tash and Abe standing over him giggling, extemporizing one comic theme or another, Sandy saying "Should we kill him right now? Should we asphyxiate him right here on the spot?"

Sigh. It's been a long night. Partying can be damned hard work. And rather disturbing as well.

Mr. Dull walks in the door of his little ap just before dawn. In the gray light it looks messy, stupid. Books in the city built tomorrow. Sigh. Go to sleep.

28

But he hasn't been sleeping for long when he wakes to the sound of Virginia Novello coming in the door.

"What are you doing, still sleeping?"

"Yeah." Didn't she give her key to his place back to him last week? Throw it at him, in fact?

"Christ, this place is a mess. You are so lazy." She sits on the bed hard, rolls him over.

"Hi," he says fuzzily.

Kiss on the forehead. "Hello, lover."

And suddenly he is in the world of sex. Virginia gets up, turns on his bedroom video, undresses, climbs into the rumpled bed with him. He watches the screens goggle-eyed.

"Want me to cook you some breakfast?" she says when they're done.

"Sure."

Jim rolls over and begins to wonder what Virginia is doing there. Officially they broke up their alliance at the famous softball game, but since then they have gotten together pretty frequently, for no real reason that Jim can see. Except for some easy sex, and perhaps a stimulating fight or two. . . . He gets up, feeling uneasy, and goes to the bathroom.

From the shower he can just hear her voice, raised to carry over the sound of the freeway. "You really should try to keep your kitchen cleaner. What a mess!" After a bit: "So where were you last night?"

"San Diego."

"I know. But I don't know why you didn't ask me along."

"Um," Jim says, drying off. "Couldn't find you at Sandy's, you know—"

"Bullshit, I was there the whole time!" She appears in the bathroom doorway, potholder on one hand clenched like a boxing glove. Jim pulls up his shorts more quickly than usual.

"The truth is," she says sadly, "you'd rather be away from me than with me."

Sigh. "Come on, Virginia, don't be ridiculous please? I just woke up."

"Lazy bastard."

Sigh. From endearment, to complaint, to recrimination: it's a familiar pattern with Virginia. "Give me a break?"

"Why should I, after you skipped off my track last night?"

"I just went with the guys to another party. You and I didn't have anything on last night."

"Well whose fault was that?"

"Not mine."

"Oh yeah? You *wanted* to go off with your friends that you're so queer for. Sandy, Tashi, Abe, you'd rather do *anything* with them than *something* with me."

"Ah come on."

"Come on where? Admit it, you and those guys—"

"We're friends, Virginia. Can you understand that? Friendship?"

"*Friends*. Your friends are all heroes to you."

"Don't be silly." Actually that may be true, sure; Jim's best friends are heroes to him, each in his different way. "Besides, what's wrong with liking your friends?"

"It's more than that with you, Jim, you're weird about it. You idolize them and try to model your life on theirs, and you aren't up to it. I mean none of you even have jobs."

Jim has gotten used to Virginia's logic, and now he just follows wherever it leads. "Abe has a job. We all have jobs."

"Oh, *grow up*! Will you grow up? Ever?"

"I don't know—"

"You don't know!"

"I don't know what you mean, I was going to say. Let me finish what I'm saying, all right?"

"Are you finished?"

"Yeah, I'm finished."

Jim stalks past her to the kitchen, disgusted by the stupidity of their debate. Scrambled eggs have gone black in the pan. "Shit."

"Now look what you made me do," Virginia cries, rushing past him and putting the pan under the faucet.

"Me? Get serious!"

"I am serious, Jim McPherson. You don't have a real job and you don't have a real future. Your little jobs are just part-time excuses for work. You laze around all day writing stupid poems, while I work and make the money we use to go out, when you can be dragged away from your friends to go!"

Part of Jim is thinking, Fine, if that's what you think then leave, quit bothering me. This alliance is over anyway! Another part is remembering the good times they've had, with their friends, out together, talking, in bed. And that part hurts.

Jim shakes his head. "Let me make some breakfast," he says. Why does she even bother, he thinks, if she feels this way about him? Why did she come by? Why doesn't she make it easy for him and leave for good? He doesn't have the courage to tell her to leave him alone; she would crucify him with how cruel he was being to her. Besides, is he sure that's what he wants? She's smart, beautiful, rich—everything he desires in an ally, in theory. When she sloshes across the jacuzzi with everyone watching her, to sit on his lap with that perfect rounded bottom, he thinks that it's worth all the fights, right? That's right. Jim likes that. He wants that.

Ach. Just another tricky day with Virginia Novello. How long have they been doing this? One month, two? Three? And it's been like this from the start. It's gotten so he can cook and eat and carry on a fight and at the same time be considering what else he should read before tackling his next poem. Sure, why not? Everyone can run parallel programs these days.

But this time he really loses his temper. They aren't allies anymore, they're ex-allies, there's no reason he has to stand for this kind of thing! He tells her that in a near shout and then storms out the front door.

Oops. He's on his street; he's just stormed out of his own ap. Bit of a mistake. He had thought, momentarily, that he was at Virginia's. Now he's in kind of an embarrassing position, isn't he. What to do?

He drives around the block, returns, looks in his window surreptitiously. Yes, she's gone. Whew. Got to remember where he is a little more securely.

Well, enough of that. The day can begin.

But when he sits down to write, a knot in his stomach forms that won't go away: he keeps reimagining the argument in versions that leave Virginia repentant, then naked in bed; or else crushed by his bitter dismissal, and gone for good. And yet those and all the other self-justifying scenarios leave him feeling as sick as the reality has. He doesn't write a single word, all day; and everything he tries to read is dreadfully boring.

He turns on the video and replays the tape of this morning's session in bed. Watches it morosely, getting aroused and disgusted in equal measure.

He's twenty-seven years old. He hasn't learned anything yet.

29

Stewart Lemon wakes early and pads out to his sunlit kitchen. His house is on Chillon Way in the Top of the World complex in Laguna Beach, and from the kitchen windows there's a fine view out to sea. Lemon goes to the breadbox on top of the orange ceramic countertop, and judges that the sourdough bread there is stale enough to make good French toast. He puts a pan on the stove and whips up the egg and milk. A little more cinnamon than usual, today. Slice the bread, soak it, throw it in the pan. Sweet cinnamon smell as it sizzles away. Shafts of sunlight cutting in the windows, one of them lighting the Kandinsky in the hall. Lemon likes the Kandinsky better than their little Picasso, and has hung it where he can see it often. It soothes the spirit. A beautiful morning.

Still, Stewart Lemon is not at peace. Things are not going well at LSR these days, and Donald Hereford, the company's president and an ever-growing power at Argo/Blessman, is really putting the heat on. Ball Lightning is in trouble and about to go into a showdown with Boeing, one of the giants. That's enough cause for worry right there, but in addition to that Hereford is demanding a yearly growth rate of several percent, and the only chance that that will happen this year lies with the Stormbee proposal, another project in trouble. If both of these were to go down, LSR would not only not show any growth, it would without a doubt be a loss for Argo/Blessman for the year. And probably longer. And Hereford, and the people above him, aren't the kind that will stand for that very long. They might sell LSR, they might send in a new team to take it over and turn it around; either way, Lemon would be in big trouble. A whole career . . . and at a time when it seems everyone else in the defense industry is prospering! It's maddening.

And worrying, to the point that Lemon barely tastes his French toast. He leaves the dishes for Elsa—give her at least that to do —goes in and dresses. "I'm off," he says brusquely to the sleeping form, still in her bed. Elsa just mutters something from a dream, rolls over. She hasn't spoken to him for . . . Lemon's mouth tightens. He leaves the house and tries to forget about it.

Into the Mercedes. A Vivaldi oboe concerto for the ride along the coast to work. In his mind are mixed images of Elsa in bed, the Ball Lightning proposal, Hereford watching him over the video from his desk in the World Trade Center. Dan Houston's hangdog look, the Ball Lightning figures. Ach—the pressures on the executives are always the most extreme; but it's what he's trained for, what he's always wanted. . . .

First meeting of the day is with Dennis McPherson, to go over the numbers for the Stormbee proposal. The proposals are due in just over a week, and McPherson is still dawdling; it's time to get serious. Time to decide the amount for the bid, the money total, the number of dollars. This is probably the crux of the whole process, the moment when they will either win or lose.

"All right, Mac," Lemon begins impatiently. Might as well settle immediately into their usual dialectic, Lemon sarcastic and oppressive, McPherson stiff and steaming. "I've looked over the numbers you've sent up, and my judgment is that the final total is considerably too high. The Air Force just doesn't want to pay this much for unmanned systems, they still have a strong prejudice against planes without pilots and they're only going for this stuff because the technology makes it inevitable. But we've got to play to that, or we're going to be left out."

McPherson shrugs. "We've kept everything down as much as we could."

Lemon stares at him. "All right. Pull your chair over to the desk here, and let's go into it line by line."

Micromanagement. Lemon grits his teeth.

McPherson's people have got all the figures printed out in a sheaf of graph-filled sheets. First comes the full-scale engineering development costs. Prime mission equipment, $189 million. Training, less than a million, as always. Flight test support equipment,

$10 million. System test and evaluation, $25 million. System project management, $63 million. Data, $18 million. Total, $305 million.

Lemon presses McPherson on the prime mission equipment figures, running through the subtotals and pointing items out. "Why should it take that much? I've done a rough estimate using prices of the components we're buying from other companies, and it shouldn't be more than one thirty."

McPherson points to the breakdown sheet, which has all the components priced exactly. "The CO-two laser is being modified to match the specs in the RFP. We can't buy that off the shelf. Then the pods have to be assembled, which is accounted for in this category. The robotics for that are going to be expensive."

"I know, I know. But do we have to use Zenith chips, for example? Texas Instruments are a quarter the cost, and there's nine million right there."

"We need Zenith chips because there's a complete reliance on them for the whole system to work. As a criticality they get top priority."

Lemon shakes his head. Texas Instruments chips are just as good, in his estimation, but there's no denying the industry thinks otherwise. "Let's go on and come back to this."

They go on to production readiness. Here the figures are less firm, as it is a step beyond the FSED. Still, McPherson's team has worked up the totals. Each category—the same group of them as for the FSED—has a few pages of explanations. Total, $154 million. They go over it line by line, Lemon objecting to equipment decisions, estimates of LSR's labor costs, everything he can think of. McPherson stubbornly defends every single estimate, and Lemon gets irritated. The figures can't possibly be that firm. McPherson just doesn't think about money; it isn't a factor for him.

An hour later they move on to the estimate sheet for production lot one, which would consist of eighty-eight units. Prime mission equipment, $251 million, system test and evaluation $2 million (it had better be working by then!), system project management, $30 million, data, $30 million. Total, $313 million. Lemon is fierce in his denunciation of the management and data costs. Here he knows more than McPherson, he's got the authority to bend these figures down. McPherson shrugs.

So, the complete bid comes to $772 million dollars. "You've got to get that down!" Lemon orders. "I don't have exact figures on the bids of McDonnell/Douglas or Parnell, but the feelers are out and it's looking like the low seven hundreds will be common."

McPherson just shakes his head. "We've cut it to the bone. You've just seen that." He looks tired; it's been a long onslaught. "If we try to slash numbers, the Air Force will just go over the proposal and bump them back up in their MPCs." Members of the SSEB will do Most Probable Cost estimates on all the bids, and depending on whether they're feeling friendly or not, the results can be devastating. "If they bump them up far enough we'll look like monkeys."

Lemon stands, irritated anew. "You don't have to teach me my job, Mac."

"I'm not." He must be tired, to speak out like this! "You asked me how much the system will cost. I've told you. I'm not telling you how much our bid should be. That's your decision. You can order us to make the system cheaper by downgrading the product, or you can keep the system the same and adjust the bid anyway. That's your decision. But you can't get me to tell you this system as designed will cost less than it does, because I won't do it. My job is to tell you how much this system costs. I've done that. You can take it from there."

So he has finally gotten McPherson to speak up! But it doesn't make him any less angry, as he always imagined it would. In fact, he's stung to the point that he forgets his persona. "Take that stuff and leave," he says violently, and abruptly he goes to the window so that McPherson won't see his face. Something—something in what McPherson has just said, perhaps—has given Lemon a fright, somehow, and it's made him unaccountably furious. "Get out of here!"

McPherson leaves. Lemon heaves a sigh of relief, sits down and regains control of himself. That arrogant son of a bitch has put him on the spot again. The bid is too high, the system over-designed. But he can't change that without endangering the bid from the technical point of view. You've got to balance quality and cost, but how to do that with a man like McPherson designing the thing? The man is crazy!

When he's completely calm again he calls Hereford on the video link.

Hereford comes onscreen; he's at his desk, before the window. Behind him is a fine view of New York harbor. They express pleasure at each other's views, the usual opening between them.

Lemon hesitates, clears his throat nervously. He's more than a little in awe of Donald Hereford, and he can't help it. Lemon has driven himself all his life, and he's risen at LSR very quickly indeed—about as fast as one can, he thinks. And yet Hereford is about his age, perhaps even a year or two younger, and there he is high in the complex power structure of Argo/Blessman, one of the biggest corporations in the world, sixtieth in the Fortune 500 the year before. . . . Lemon can't really imagine how the man did it. Especially since he is by no means a monomaniac; on the contrary, he is very urbane, very cultured; he has Manhattan's cultural world, perhaps the richest anywhere, at his fingertips, as he proves every time Lemon comes for a visit. Small galleries, the Met, theater on Broadway and off, the Philharmonic, dance . . . it's admirable. In fact, Lemon finds it incredibly impressive.

So he gives the facts to Hereford in as casual and efficient a tone as he can muster. Hereford pulls at his lean jaw, scratches his silver hair, straightens a five-hundred-dollar tie. His face remains impassive. "This man McPherson is good, you say?"

"Yes. But he's a bit of a perfectionist, and in the art of presenting a proposal, balancing all the factors involved . . . well, he's still an engineer at heart."

Hereford nods briefly, his aquiline nose wrinkling. "I understand. In fact, I was wondering why you described him as good, when his previous two proposals lost."

Yes, yes; Lemon is perfectly aware of Hereford's powerfully retentive memory, thanks. He shrugs, scrambling mentally, says, "I meant from the engineering standpoint, of course."

Hereford looks down at Manhattan. Finally he speaks. "Cut everything by five percent, and the management and data costs by ten. Any more than that and the MPCs are likely to be embarrassing. But that'll bring it down into the range of the other bids, right?"

"I think so, yes."

"Good. When's the proposal due?"

"A week from today."

"Talk to me then. I've got to go now." And the video screen goes blank.

30

Abe and Xavier are driving back from Buena Park Hospital after working a nasty head-on in Brea, and Abe can feel that Xavier has about gone over the redline. The torque has been too heavy for too long, all the parts are fatigued to shear points, Abe can hear the gears grinding within and it sounds like all the teeth are about to strip out and fly away. . . . The truth is that they're both stressed, to the burnout point and beyond. Making up for clumps of vacation time in the past, setting up clumps of vacation time in the future, filling in for other friends on the squad: one way or another they have arranged for too many hours on in the last month, and the effects are showing.

So they get a call from the radio dispatcher and they both groan and then just stare at the thing. Tapped out again. Slowly, very slowly, Xavier presses the transmit button. "What do you want."

They're directed to a side street near Brookhurst and Garden Grove avenues, in Garden Grove. "How could anybody get up enough speed in that neighborhood to make more than a fender-bender?" Xavier wonders.

"The call was not too coherent, I'm told," says the voice of the dispatcher. "No idea of the code or anything. There might even have been a relevant address—1246 Emerson."

"Sure this one isn't a police matter?"

"Said rescue squad."

Xavier clicks off. "Don't kill us getting there. This one has got to be bullshit somehow."

So Abe drives then to Brookhurst and Garden Grove, and
they find no sign of a wreck. They see only:

A Jeans Down discount clothing store.
A Seedy audio outlet, a See-All Video Rental.
The Gay/Lesbian Adult Video Theater, A Kentucky
    Colonel's.
Your dingy apartment complex. You live there.
A retail furniture warehouse outlet.
A robotics and camera discount repair shop.
Two used-car lots. A Pizza Hut.
Yes, despite theory, the monad still exists.
Here you are, right?
A coin and map store. A dance hall.
The parking lot fronting all these establishments. The cars.
Billboards, traffic signals, street lights, street signs,
Telephone wires scoring the sour milk sky,

and so on, out to where parallax brings the tracks and the two
sides of the long straight boulevard together. In short, the OC
commercial street, which one can see repeated a hundred times
anywhere in the county. But no sign of an accident.

"Well?" says Abe.

"Let's try the address they gave us."

"But,"—they track around to Emerson Street backing Garden Grove Avenue—"it's just the back lot for the furniture outlet,
isn't it?"

"Yeah, but observe, there's maybe some aps tucked on top
of it there. A look is in order."

Abe shakes his head. "Looks suspiciously like police work
to me."

They get out of the truck and walk up the outside of the
building on concrete stairs that rise above an alley between buildings. The alley is filled with gray metal trash dumpsters and flat-
tened cardboard boxes of immense size. At the top of the stairs is
a wooden door that's been kicked open a lot, once painted an
orange that's faded to dusty yellow. Xavier raises a fist to knock
and there's a sudden yelping, like a dog in pain. They look at each
other. Xavier knocks.

"Keep out! Ah, God—get the fuck out of here!" It's a woman's voice, hoarse and wild.

"Hmm," says Xavier. Then he calls out: "Rescue squad, ma'am!"

"Oh! Oh, you! Help! Help!"

Xavier shrugs, tries to open the door. It's locked. "Your door is locked!"

"Don't bust it! He'll evict me—ahh! Ahh! *Help!*"

"Well, come open up, then!"

"Can't!"

"Well." Xavier looks at the door, jiggles the knob. Nothing doing.

"Help, damn you!"

"We're trying, lady! It'd be easier if you hadn't locked your door!" X looks around. "Here, Abe, the kitchen window is just over the rail, and it's open. It looks like you'd just about fit in."

Abe looks at the little window dubiously. "It's too small. Besides, it's hanging out over the alley!"

"No it's not. Give it a try, I'll hold on to you."

So Abe climbs over the flimsy black-iron railing, reaches inside and finds nothing to hold on to except the sink faucet. The window really is too small. But . . . he steps onto the railing and squirms inside. Powerful stench of garbage left under the sink too long. His shoulders just make it through, then it's a matter of twisting over the sink and pulling his legs in. X gives him a final shove that catapults him onto a dirty kitchen floor. "Hey!"

"Help! Oh—oh—help!"

Abe gets to his feet and rushes into the little living room/bedroom of the ap. A black-haired woman in a sweat-soaked long T-shirt is on her back on the floor. And unless she's unfashionably fat—nope—pregnant woman here, gone into labor. Abe rushes to the door. "Hey!" the woman shouts. "Over here!"

"I know!"

He unlocks the door and Xavier hurries in. The woman jerks back awkwardly against an old green vinyl couch. "Hey! Who are you!"

"Rescue squad." Xavier kneels beside her, holds her wrist and moves her hand off her belly. "Relax, lady—"

"Relax! Are you kidding? What took you so long? Ahh!

ahh!'' Her face is dripping with sweat, she rolls her head from side to side. "I wanted an ambulance!"

"We are the ambulance, lady. Try to relax." Xavier checks her out. "Hey, how long have you been in labor?"

"Couple hours. I guess."

"Say, you're making awfully fast progress."

"You're telling me! Listen who the fuck are you?"

"Rescue squad."

"I don't want some spade playing around down there while I'm trying to—ahh!—have a baby!"

Xavier frowns at her. "I'll try to refrain from molesting you till you're done, all right? It's a little too crowded in there to rape you just now."

The woman takes a weak swing at him. "Get away from me! Leave me alone! Ah, God!"

"We're the rescue squad, ma'am," Abe tries to explain.

"Will you cut that *ma'am* shit! All I need is the ambulance!"

"We can do that too," Xavier says. "Abe, run down quick and get the stretcher. I think we've got time to get her over to St. Joe's."

Abe runs down and grabs the furled stretcher, carries it back upstairs. Back in the ap Xavier and the woman are arguing loudly. "They can't hold your kid hostage, woman! If you can't pay, you can't pay! You're going too fast here, and it's pretty sure to rip you up some. You'd best be in the hospital!"

The woman is hit by a severe contraction and can't reply. Abe can see she wants to reply, her eyes are fixed on Xavier's and she's glaring fiercely, shaking her head. "Don't—want—to go!"

"That's tough. We're not allowed to just let you bleed to death, are we."

Abe finishes getting the stretcher unfurled and set up. As they lift the woman onto it she arches, sobbing with pain. "Try to push in a rhythm, will you?" Xavier says. "Don't you know anything about how to do this?"

"Fuck you!" the woman cries, trying again to hit him. "God-damned molesters! I didn't even know—ahh!—didn't know I was pregnant until two months ago."

"Great. Here, Abe, hold her shoulders up for her. Push, woman, push!"

"No!" But push she does, an awful straining effort, the veins and tendons in her neck standing out like pencils under the skin. Abe finds that he's a little freaked, here; paramedics are supposed to run into this situation all the time, but it's a first for him, and the way that she's writhing under his hands is disconcerting indeed. He isn't so sure he doesn't prefer them a little more comatose.

They're about to pick up the stretcher when the contractions begin again, and Xavier stops to check her out once more. "Oops, top of its head is showing here, I don't think we've got time anymore. Push, woman."

"Can't—"

"Yes, you can, here when I press on your belly. Legs up, hands down here. A big push, hold it, let off. Rest for a bit. Now again."

"X, have you done this before?" Abe asks.

"Sure."

"Are you going to do an, an episiotomy?"

"Are you kidding? This kid's doing it himself."

"Great!" the woman cries in a break between pushes. "Just what I want to hear! What kind of medic are you?"

"Army. Here, pay attention to what you're doing."

"As if I've—got any choice!"

The woman gasps, bears down again. She's gasping for more air. Abe had no idea they had to work so hard at it. He jumps up and gets a grayed towel from the bathroom, wipes off her face. Her belly heaves again, she squeaks, teeth clamped, eyes squeezed shut so hard the lids are white in a bright red face. "Breathe in, push on the exhale," Xavier says softly. "Okay, push. Push."

"Fuck off."

Suddenly Abe notices that the light has dimmed; there's a big crowd of neighbors in the doorway! The woman notices them and curses between gasps. "Hey, get out of here!" Abe says. "Unless you're a doctor or a midwife, go wait outside! And close the door!" He gets up and chases them off, having trouble with the smallest kids, who are fast. Mostly kids and teenagers, looking in round-eyed with curiosity.

"Push! Push, yeah! Here we go, head's out. Now push those shoulders out right quick." Xavier's hands are busy at the woman's crotch, Abe glances and sees a wet blood-and-mucus-streaked baby, rubbery-looking red in X's black hands, just about clear of her, sliding out the last part of the way. Amazing. Xavier starts working on the umbilical cord and the placenta. He flicks the infant on the side and it wails. "Here, Abe, take it." Abe crouches and is handed a baby. Wet, warm, sticky. It hardly weighs a thing, and its whole head fits in one hand easily.

"A little hemorrhaging," Xavier remarks, frowning.

"Hey—when do I push!"

"You're done, lady. The kid is born."

"What? Why didn't you tell me!" The woman takes a weak swing at the air. "What kind of doctor are you, anyway? Hey! Boy or girl?"

"Umm . . ." Abe checks. "Boy, I think."

"You *think*?" the woman demands. She and Xavier laugh. "What you got here, spade, some kind of medical student or something?"

"Come on," Xavier says. "We've still got to get to the hospital. Lady, can you hold the kid on top of you while we carry you downstairs?"

She nods, and they arrange the little creature on the wet T-shirt, in her arms. It makes quite a picture—messy, but . . . good.

As they maneuver her down the stairs, however, shooing the neighborhood kids ahead of them, the woman fades a little. She lets the kid slip off to the side; they have to drop the stretcher and grab the baby fast before it goes over the railing and into the dumpsters. Thump, thump, the stretcher and the woman land half on Xavier, who almost falls down the stairs; he has to sit fast to avoid it. "Lady, what are you *doing*?"

"Who are you guys anyway! Trying to kill me! Give me my kid back!"

"Try holding on to it this time, okay?" X is disgusted. "Little tip for mothers, I give to you free—don't drop your kid into trashbins when you can help it."

They make it down the stairs and to the truck. Xavier jumps in back with her, Abe drives them off toward St. Joe's.

Xavier calls out from the ambulance chamber. "Make it snappy, Abe, I can't really get the compresses up where the bleeding is."

"You damn well better not try!" Abe hears the woman say sharply. "It was one of your spade brothers knocked me up in the first place."

"Uh-huh. You just relax, lady, and shut up if you can. I'll keep a hold on myself."

X sticks his head through the window, into the cab beside Abe. "Ungrateful bitch."

"So you've done deliveries before?" Abe asks.

"Yeah, couldn't you tell? That was the real midwife touch, there."

"I see. Was this one unusual?"

"Awful fast."

"That's what you think!" the woman cries from the back.

"Quiet, lady. Save your strength."

Abe says, "I didn't know it was such hard work. I mean I'd heard, but I'd never seen it."

"No? Man, you are a rookie. Yeah, it wipes them out. Brains have gotten bigger a lot faster than cunts, and that makes it dangerous. You got two healthy people there and they can still both die on you. In fact, step on it, will you?"

When they get to St. Joe's, and get the woman and her child onto a gurney at the ER entrance, she gets sentimental and starts to cry. "I really appreciate it—I was really scared. I'm sorry I said all those things about you. You aren't really a spade."

"Well," X says, compressing his lips to keep a straight face.

"What's your names? Abe? Okay. Xavier? Xavier? How do you spell that? Okay. I'm gonna name him William Xavier Abraham Jeffers, I really am. I really am. . . ."

She's wheeled away. They wash up in the ER men's room, then go back to the waiting room.

A doctor comes out in a few minutes and tells them that the woman is fine, the baby is fine, there are no problems. No problems at all.

Back out in the truck. Abe has kind of an unreal feeling. They're both grinning like fools. "So," Abe says. "William Xavier Abraham Jeffers, eh?"

"Got any cigars?" X asks.

And they both start to laugh. They laugh, they shake hands, they pound each other on the arm, they laugh. "Could you believe it when the whole neighborhood came in to watch?'' ''Or when the kid fell off into the trashbins!'' ''Hey, aren't we about done for the night? Let's go get a drink.''

So they go to celebrate at the Boathouse in lower Santa Ana, on Fourth Street. One of X's regular hangouts. They drink a lot of beer. Abe relaxes, feeling good to be a part of X's off-work life, to be accepted in this black bar, if only for a little bit, as a friend of X's. Xavier tells their story to the guys and the whole place howls, immediately sets to retelling the story with a million elaborations. ''Why you ain't no spade after all! *Heeee*, heee heeee *heeeee* . . .''

Abe and Xavier get drunk. Abe watches X's laughing face, and feels his own grin. He hasn't seen X this relaxed in . . . well, whenever. Abe squeezes his eyes shut, trying to hold on to the moment, the smell of smoke and sweat, the rowdy voices of X's friends, the look on X's face. Hold, time. Stop.

31

But time, of course, does not stop. And eventually they take the truck back to headquarters, and Xavier goes home.

Abe tracks to Sandy's place, still feeling high. Into the endless party, and for once he's in sync with the prevailing mood. There's been a headline in the *Los Angeles Times* that morning:

DEA DECLARES ORANGE COUNTY
''DRUG CAPITAL OF THE WORLD''

and Sandy has therefore declared the day a local holiday. He and Angela have gone all out to decorate the ap, with balloons, ribbons, confetti, streamers, noisemakers, and big strips of paper that have the headline reproduced on them in various spectrum bends. Samples of every recreational drug known to science are on hand and in action, Sandy is in the kitchen singing along with the blender as it grinds up quantities of ice cream, chocolate sauce, milk, and, well, Abe isn't too sure what else, but he has his suspicions. "Rnn rnn rnn, rnn rnn rnn!" Sandy sings, and grabs the blender from its base. He pours the frothy milkshakes into tall plastic glasses, handing them to whoever gets a hand out first, "Hey, drink this! Try this!" His pupils are flinching just inside the blue rims of the irises as he sees Abe and hands him a glass. Cold in the hand. Sandy uses the blender itself to clink a toast. "To the day's work!" with that Sandy grin blazing at San Onofre–level megawatts. Now how did he know that his toast would be appropriate on this night of all nights? Another drug mystery. Abe drinks deep. No taste but chocolate, though it's maybe a bit chunky. What might it be? He'll soon find out. Best to establish a transitional period by lidding as much as possible.

A lot of people are already pretty stoned, they've got eyes like black holes and their mouths are stretched wide like they're trying to do imitations of Sandy's ordinary smile, they're grinding their teeth and giggling a little and staring around like the walls have sprouted fantastic morphological formulations out of the usual condo cottage cheese ceilings, say, is that, could that be a, a stalactite there? Abe can only laugh. But Sandy splutters with dismay. "No zoning out here, this is a celebration, get on your feet!" People stare at him like he's maybe part of the ceiling's deformations. "Uh-oh. Jim! Jim! Jim—put something inspiring on the CD."

Happily Jim hurries to the collection of tattered old CDs, bought in boxfuls by Sandy and Angela at swap meets, no idea what's in the boxes, a perfect situation for Jim, who is in heaven bopping from box to box and rooting around. Abe laughs again, lidding from an eyedropper of the Buzz and feeling his spine begin to radiate energy. Jim, King of the Culturevultures. Hopping bird-like box to box, talking as fast as he can to people who clearly aren't understanding a word he says. Head still as a bird's, snapping instantaneously from position to position just like a finch's, except that now Abe sees a kind of after-image of Jim, trailing behind him. A hallucinogen, eh? Fine by Abe. He can't help laughing at his good friend Jim, who would no doubt look for the perfect music till dawn; but Sandy returns and grabs him by the elbow. "Now, huh? Desperate need for music *now*!"

Jim nods, his face suddenly twisted with nervousness. They're really going to play his choice? What if he has gone off on some spiral of reasoning that has led him to a completely stupid choice, he can't be at all sure that he hasn't! Abe can read all this perfectly in Jim's comically exaggerated expression of alarm, and he starts laughing hysterically. Jim trails Sandy to the CD player changing his mind, trying to get more time to think it over, but Sandy beats him away with one arm while inserting the CD with the other, and suddenly the speakers are roaring out some big symphonic fanfare. What's this?

" 'Pomp and Circumstance'! " Jim shouts at Sandy and Abe, scowling with desperate uncertainty. Sandy grins, nods, turns the volume up so that the people on Catalina can enjoy it too. Then the march begins and Sandy high-steps around the rooms of the ap, leaning over to scream in the face of anyone who has remained sitting. Soon everyone's up and marching like toy soldiers with scrambled circuits, banging into walls and knocking over plants and each other. Abe marches behind Jim and feels the dust in the blood begin to fly in him, the dumb old march has somehow acquired this immense *majesty*, now everyone's out on the balcony, marching: twenty drum majors, a can-can line over by the railing, goose-steppers trying some kick-boxing. . . . Abe jumps up and down in place, feeling the glory of pure Being surge all through him. Incredible rush of exhilaration, face to the stars, it's clear tonight and up there on the fuzzy black vault of the night are the big fast satellites, the solar panels in their polar orbits, the microwave transmitters, the ballistic missile mirrors to the north—all the new artificial constellations, swimming around up there and nearly blocking out the little old twinkly stars. And planes falling onto John Wayne Airport like space stations landing, like fireflies in formation: what an amazing sky! Abe leans all the way back and howls. Coyote's entrance, here, the others take it up, and they howl and yip at the blinking night sky.

Angela, always first in these things, pulls off her blouse and throws it on the floor of the balcony, in the middle of the marchers. Bra next. Can she get her jeans off while doing the can-can? In a manner of speaking. Howls scale the sky. Clothes begin to fly onto the pile, a flurry of shirts, pants, blouses, silk underwear, boxer shorts. Quickly they're a ring of naked dancers, as in some pagan rite of spring, they can all feel it and for once it has that quality of primitive sensuousness, no all-American tits-n-ass consciousness in Abe tonight, it's just the clean joy of having a body, of being able to dance, of Being and Becoming. The way the pink of skin jumps out of the night's smeary darkness is just part of the joy of it. Freckled Sandy tosses all the couch cushions in the ap onto the big pile of clothing, and then he dives on, swims into the pile, ah-ha, a pile-on here. Naked Humphrey is dancing wallet in hand, can't just throw *that* in a pile of other people's clothes, right? Abe starts howling again, laughing and howling, he can't get over how good everything feels, how happy every face looks to him, there's Jim happy, Sandy happy, Angela happy, Tashi and Erica happy, Humphrey happy, all of them dancing in a circle and howling at the sky, Abe dives into the great mass of clothes and people and cushions, clean laundry smell, he's buried, he's coming up for air, coming up to be born, like the baby he helped bring into the world just hours before—born out of their clothes, naked, shocked at the pure glossy presence of things, their sensuous reality, their there-ness. For the second time that night Abe Bernard squeezes shut his eyes and wills the moment to stop, to stop while he and all his friends are happy, to stop, stop, stop, stop, stop.

32

... In the 1790s the area still belonged mostly to the Indians, now called Gabrielinos. The Spanish rarely ventured away from San Juan Capistrano and the El Camino Real, and they avoided the swamps and marshes above Newport Bay, because these were difficult to traverse on foot or horseback.

But during those years the bay had some visitors. A party

of French-American colonists, en route to Oregon by way of the long trip around Cape Horn, sailed into the bay and wintered there. The next year a small group returned from Oregon, and they lived on the mesa above Newport Bay for nearly twenty years. These were the first non-Indian residents of the area.

History doesn't tell us much more about these French-Americans than that. But we can deduce a fair amount about the lives they must have led. They were from Quebec, they were used to the wilderness, and they knew the crafts necessary for survival in it. They must have been fishermen, and perhaps they did some farming as well. We don't know if they were literate, but they easily could have been; they may have had some books along with them, a Bible perhaps.

They must have had contact with the Indians who lived on the bay; perhaps they learned where to dig for clams, where to set snares, from Indian friends. There was an Indian village on Newport Mesa, called Genga; they must have spent some time there, learned a bit of the Gabrielino language. The Spanish called the bay Bolsa de Gengara, after this village; what did these French call it? If we knew what the Indians called it, perhaps we could guess.

At that time, in the same years that the French Revolution and Napoleon were causing such upheavals in Europe, Newport Bay did not look like it does now. The Santa Ana River, which ran all year around, drained into the vast marshes at the upper end of the bay; these marshes extended all the way in to Santa Ana and Tustin. And the upper section of Newport Bay was open to the sea. Balboa Peninsula did not then exist; it was created by flooding of the Santa Ana River in 1861. The river itself did not swing into its new delta at 56th Street until the 1920s, in another great flood.

Ocean, estuary, marsh, grasslands, hillsides; it was a land of great variety, teeming with life. And this little group of French-Americans—how many were there?—lived in the midst of this wilderness, with their Indian neighbors, in peace, for over twenty years.

What must their lives have been like? They must have made their own clothes, shoes, boats, homes. Children must have been born to them, raised until they were perhaps twenty years old.

Perhaps some of them died there. Their days must have been spent hunting, farming, fishing, exploring, making, talking—speaking French, and Gabrielino.

Why did they leave? Where did they go, when they left? Did they return to Oregon, to Quebec, to France? Were they in Paris when the Napoleonic wars ended, when the train tracks were laid? Did they ever think back to the twenty years they had spent on the California coast, isolated from all the world?

Perhaps they never left. Perhaps they stayed on the shores of the primeval bay, in a little bubble of history between the dream time of the Indians and the modern world, until they were exterminated with the rest of the Gabrielinos when the Europeans came up from Mexico—killed by people who couldn't tell them from Indians anymore.

33

Next time Arthur comes by, Jim decides to take the direct approach.

"We have another strike planned," says Arthur.

And Jim replies, "Listen, Arthur, I want to know more about who you are, who we are. Who exactly we're working for and what the long-range goals are! I mean, the way it is now, I don't really know."

Arthur stares at him, and Jim swallows nervously, thinking that he may have gone too far somehow. But then Arthur laughs. "Does it really matter? I mean, do you want a name? An organization to pledge allegiance to?"

Jim shrugs, and Arthur laughs again. "Kind of old-fashioned, right? The truth is that it's more complicated than you probably think, in that there is more than one so-called group doing all this. In fact, we're stimulating a lot of the action indirectly. It's getting so that half of the attacks you hear about are not actually our doing. And it seems to be snowballing.''

"But what about us, Arthur. *You*. Who supplies you, who are you working for?''

Arthur regards him seriously. "I don't want to give you anybody's name, Jim. If you can't work with me on that basis, you can't. I'm a socialist and a pacifist. Admittedly my pacificism has changed in nature since I've decided to join the resistance against the weapons industry. But like I told you, the methods I tried before—talking to people, writing, lobbying, joining protests and sit-ins—none of them had any tangible impact. So, while I was doing that I met all sorts of socialists. You wouldn't think any existed anymore in America.''

"I would,'' Jim says.

Arthur shrugs. "Maybe. It's almost a lost concept, that individuals shouldn't be able to profit from common property such as land or water. But some of us still believe in it and work for it. There could be a combination of the best of both systems—a democratic socialism, that gave individuals the necessary freedoms and only prohibited the grossest sorts of profiteering. Everyone has a right to adequate food, water, shelter and clothing!'' Frustration twists Arthur's face into the intense mask Jim remembers from their poster raid on SCP. "It's not that radical a vision—it could be achieved by votes, by an evolutionary shift in the law of the land. It doesn't have to be accomplished by violent revolution! But . . .''

"But it doesn't happen,'' Jim prompts him.

"That's right. It doesn't happen. But do you know what to do about it? No. None of us do. But now, after everything else, I'm convinced that unless the plan includes active, physical resistance, it isn't going to work. It's like the defense industry is the British before the revolution—they control us in the same way— and we're the small landowners in Virginia and Massachusetts, determined to take our lives into our own hands again. *We* being a group of Americans who are determined to fight the military-industrial complex on every front. There are lobbying groups in Washington, there are newsheets and videos and posters, and now there's an active arm, dedicated to physical resistance that hurts nothing but weaponry. Since there's so much public about this group, it's absolutely necessary to keep the active arm of it secret. So. I know a couple of people—just a couple—who supply me with the equipment, and the intelligence necessary to carry out the operations. That's all I really know. We don't have a name. But you can tell by the public statements, really, who we're a part of.''

Jim nods.

Arthur watches him closely. "So. Is it okay?"

"Yeah," Jim says, convinced. "Yeah, it is. I was worried by how little I really knew. But I understand, now."

"Just think of it as you and me," Arthur suggests. "A personal campaign. That's what it all comes down to in the end, anyway. Not the name of the organization that you belong to. Just people doing what they believe in."

"True."

And so that night they track into the warren of streets behind the City Mall, to the little parking lot between the warehouses at Lewis and Greentree. There they flash their headlights three times and meet the same four men and their station wagon full of boxes, and the four men help them load the boxes into Arthur's car. Their leader pulls Arthur aside for a brief muttered conversation.

And then they track into the Anaheim Hills, putting on another pair of stealth suits as they take the Newport and Riverside freeways north. Once off the freeway they track up to the edge of a tiny park in an applex, one dotted with long-neglected slides and swings and benches. They crawl to the edge of the park, where a small slope of grass overlooks the Santa Ana Canyon. Below them and across the freeway-filled gorge, on a knoll, sprawls the big manufacturing plant of Northrop. And in the northeast corner of the expanse of buildings, all lit by blazing xenon lights, with a perimeter fence that is swept by roving searchlights, are the three long warehouselike buildings that hold the production facilities for the third tier, midcourse layer of the ballistic missile defense—that is to say, space-based chemical lasers, which will be transported to Vandenberg and hauled up into orbit. The "High Fire" system.

Quickly they hammer four little missile stands into the grass, and Arthur aims them at four doors in these buildings. This is the dangerous moment, the semicovert moment, and if the defenses are sensitive enough . . .

Arthur, Jim has time to think, is connected up with some excellent intelligence sources: he knows the right buildings, the correct doors, he knows the buildings will be empty, the night security forces elsewhere in the complex . . . Such information must be top secret in the companies involved, so that the espionage involved in getting hold of it must be sophisticated indeed.

Missiles set and targeted, they trail the ignition cords across the tiny park, back toward Arthur's car. Buttons pushed, run to the car, track away, tear the suits off, dump them down a storm drain. No sign at all of pursuit; in fact, they can't even tell what the missiles might have done, because they're on the other side of the hill now, getting onto the Riverside Freeway with all the rest of the cars. They never even heard a siren this time, because the little condo park was over a mile from the Northrop complex. It really is *very simple*. But one can assume that the little missiles have followed the laser light directly to their targets, and have dissolved the materials in the plant susceptible to the solvents in the payloads. . . .

Despite the ease of the attack, Jim's heart is racing, and he and Arthur shake hands and pound the dash with the same sharp exhilaration that they felt in the first raid against Parnell. Jim becomes more certain than ever that he is only really alive, really living a meaningful life, when he is doing this work. "Here's to resistance!" he cries again. He has a slogan now.

34

In the month after LSR submits its bid for the Stormbee program, Dennis McPherson flies to Dayton four times to meet various members or subcommittees of the Source Selection Evaluation Board. The questions are tough and exacting, and each session drains McPherson completely. But so far as he can tell, they are faring well. Except for a whole day's worth of questions concerning the laser system's abilities in bad weather, the so-called blind let-down issue, he has satisfactory answers for all of their technical questions, and these in turn justify the estimated costs of the system. As for blind let-down, well, there's nothing much they can do about that. The RFP asked for a covert system, so they're stuck with the CO_2 laser's inability to see well through clouds. McPherson tries not to worry about it; he figures that the SSEB is merely trying to find out which of the bidders' proposed systems will deal with this handicap the best.

So. Four intense grillings, each with its ritual humiliations, the various reminders that the Air Force is in control here, it's the biggest buyer's market of all history and so everyone gathering around to sell has to do a little submission routine, rolling on their backs and exposing throat and belly like dogs . . . at least in certain ritual moments, as when beginning or ending presentations, or answering irrelevant, insolent questions, or greeting members of the board at the occasional lunch or cocktail party on the base. McPherson goes through all that grimly and concentrates on the actual sessions, on clear concise answers to the questions asked. It really is wearing.

But eventually the time runs out, and the SSEB has to stop and make its report, and the Source Selection Authority—General Jack James, a serious aloof man—has to stop and make his decision, and this decision has to be reviewed by HQ USAF, and then it finally comes time for the Air Force to award the contract for Stormbee. Somewhere in there the decision has been made. One company will have its bid chosen and will be in charge of a $750 million system, the other four competitors will be sent home to try again, each some several million dollars out of pocket as a result of their attempt.

Because of McPherson's reports on the grillings, and the original choice of LSR by the Air Force back when the program was superblack, Lemon is confident that their bid is going to be the one chosen. All the Dayton questions indicate a strong interest in the problems of development and deployment, and Lemon thinks the proposal is so strong that no weaknesses have been found. Donald Hereford, in New York, appears convinced by Lemon, and on his orders a big contingent of LSR people travel to Crystal City for the Air Force's announcement of the award. Hereford himself comes down, with a small crew of underlings. The night before the announcement they have a party in the restaurant above the LSR offices in the Aerojet Tower, and the mood is celebratory. The rumor, spreading industrywide, is that LSR has indeed nailed the contract.

McPherson is politely cheerful at the party, but as for the rumor, he's trying to wait and see. He's too nervous to make any assumptions. This is his program, after all. And rumors are worthless. Still, it's impossible not to be infected by the mood a little bit, to allow hope to break out of its hard tight bud. . . .

The next day, in one of the Pentagon's giant white meeting rooms, McPherson feels talons of nervousness digging into him. A whole lot of people fill the room, including big groups from all five bidders: Aeritalia, Fairchild, McDonnell/Douglas, Parnell, and LSR, each team gathered in knots around the room. McPherson eyes the other companies' teams curiously. Jocularity with the rest of his own group is a tough bit of acting, and it's doubtful that he really pulls it off. Really all he wants is to sit.

It's actually a relief to see the Air Force colonel come into the room and stride to the flag-bedecked podium at the front. Video lights snap on and a microphone in the cluster of them at the podium begins to hum. It's another big media conference, the Pentagon's idea of high entertainment. And everyone else seems to agree. Several cameras are trained on the speaker, and McPherson recognizes many of the trade reporters, from *Aviation Week and Space Technology, National Defense, SDI Today, Military Space, L-5 Newsletter, The Highest Frontier, Electronic Defense*, and so on; ID badges also announce reporters from *The Wall Street Journal*, AP, UPI, *Science News, Science, Time*, and many newspapers. This is big news, and the Pentagon has been canny about turning the award ceremonies into PR events for itself. The colonel who will be their master of ceremonies is obviously an experienced PR man: a handsome flyboy, McPherson thinks sourly, about to award the contract that will make pilots obsolete.

For the sake of the reporters and cameras, they first have to endure a glowing description of the Stormbee system and its tremendous importance for American security. Also its great size and monetary worth, of course. Tension among the competitors present reduces them all to a state of sullen, tight attentiveness. Nearly seventy minds are thinking, Get to it, you bastard, get to it. But it's part of the ritual, one of the reminders of who is boss in this game. . . .

For a moment McPherson is distracted by these thoughts, and then he hears: "We're pleased to announce that the contract for the Stormbee system has been awarded to Parnell Aviation Incorporated. Their winning bid totaled six hundred ninety-nine million dollars. Details of the decision process are available in the document that will now be distributed."

McPherson's stomach has closed down to a singularity. Lemon is red-faced with anger, and something in his expression ignites fury in McPherson more than the announcement itself did. He snatches one of the booklets being passed around, reads the basic information page feverishly. When he finishes he is so surprised that he stops and goes back to read it more slowly, blinking in disbelief.

Apparently they're using a YAG laser system, in a two-pod configuration. And $669 million! It's impossible! It's instantly clear that Parnell has made a lower bid than they can possibly stick to. And the Air Force has let the fraud pass. Has, in fact, colluded in it. The room is filling with incredulous or angry voices, enough to overwhelm the happy chatter of the Parnell team, as more and more people get the gist of the booklet. Reporters are scurrying around, surrounding the Parnell group, faces bright under the video lights—disembodied pink faces, smiles, eyes—

Something snaps in McPherson. He stands, speech spills out of him. "By God, they've rigged it! We've got the best proposal in there, and they've given it to one that's an obvious lie!"

Lemon and the rest of the Laguna Hills folks are staring at him in amazement. They've never in their lives heard such an outburst from Dennis McPherson, and they're really taken aback. Art Wong's mouth hangs open.

Donald Hereford, silver-haired and calm, just looks at McPherson impassively. "You think their bid is unrealistically low?"

"It's impossibly low! I can't imagine the MPC evaluations letting this crap pass! And the proposal itself—look how they've ignored the specs in the RFP—two pods, YAG laser, eleven point eight KVA, why the planes won't have the power to run these rigs!'' Heart racing, face flushed hot, McPherson slams the booklet down on the back of a chair. ''We've been screwed!''

Hereford nods once, no expression on his face at all. ''You're certain our proposal is superior to this?''

''Yes,'' McPherson grates out. *''We had a better proposal.''*

Hereford's mouth tightens. After a moment he says, ''If we let them do it this time, they'll feel free to do it again. The whole bid process will unhinge.''

He looks at Lemon. ''We'll file a protest.''

The possibility hadn't even occurred to McPherson. His eyes fix on Hereford. A protest! . . .

Lemon starts to say something: ''But—''

Hereford cuts him off with a hand motion, a quick chop. Perhaps he's angry too? Impossible to tell. ''Contact our law firm here in Washington, and start giving them all the particulars. We need to hurry. If there are irregularities in their compliance with the RFP, then we may be able to get a court injunction to halt the award immediately.''

Court injunction.

McPherson's stomach begins to return to him, a little at a time. They have recourse to some legal action, apparently. It's a new area for him, he doesn't know much about it.

Lemon is swallowing, nodding. ''Okay. We'll do it.'' He looks confused.

McPherson forces down a few deep breaths, thinking *court injunction, court injunction.* Meanwhile, across the room, the Parnell people are still in paroxysms of joy, the dishonest bastards. They know better than anyone else that they can't possibly build the Stormbee system for only $699 million. It's just a ploy to get the bid; later they can get into the matter of some unfortunate ''cost overruns.'' It can only be a deliberate plan on their part, a deliberate lie. That's the competition, the people he has to put his own work up against: cheaters and liars. With the Air Force going along with them all the way, completely a part of it, of the cheating and lying. In control of it, in fact. Feeling physically ill, McPherson sits down heavily and stares through the booklet, seeing nothing at all.

35

Sandy Chapman is in the middle of an ordinary business day, snorting Polymorpheus and listening to The Underachievers with his friend and client John Sturmond, watching the hang-gliding championships at Victoria Falls on John's wall video and talking about the commercial possibilities of a small-scale aural hallucinogen. Suddenly John's ally Vikki Gale bursts in, all upset. "We've been ripped off!"

Turns out that she and John fronted nearly a liter of the Buzz to a retailer of theirs named Adam, who has now disappeared from the face of OC. No chance of finding him, or collecting the bill, which means they are out some ten thousand dollars. Gone like a dollar bill dropped in the street, and with no lost and found. And no police to call. It's gone. The price you pay for bad character judgment.

Vikki is collapsed on the couch crying, John is up striding around, shouting, "Fuck! Fuck! Fuck! I knew I shouldn't have trusted that guy!"

Heavy gloom ensues. Sandy sighs, roots around in his Adidas bag and pulls out a large eyedropper of California Mello. "Here," he says. "There's only one solution to a situation like this, and that's to get as stoned as you can."

So they start lidding. "Think of it as an event," Sandy drones. "An experience. I mean, how often does it happen? It's great, in a way. Teaches you some about the realms of experience and emotion."

"For sure," Vikki says.

"I'm with you there," says John.

182

"Besides, I fronted you, and okayed the front to this thief Adam, so I'll halve the loss with you. We'll just have to sell more and make it back."

"For sure."

"That's really tubular of you, man. Absolutely *untold*."

They lid some Funny Bone. Now the whole thing strikes them funny, but they're too mellow to laugh.

"It's a high-risk industry." Giggles.

"Investment portfolio just walked off on us." Chuckles.

"We've been completely fucked."

But beneath all that, under the attempt to take the bummer in style, Sandy is thinking furiously. He had expected to be paid several thousand by John and Vikki, which apparently they thought they were going to get from the absent Adam. So much for that.

But he needs that several thousand to buy the supplies for the next shipment from Charles, who works C.O.D. only. Without the several thousand, he is into a serious cash-flow problem, especially given the giant bills from the medical center in Miami. He starts doing some serious accounting in his head, where all the books are anyway, at the same time holding down his part of the conversation with John and Vikki.

Somewhere in that conversation John says something that Sandy finds particularly interesting, and after he's done with his calculations—which remain disheartening—he tries to track back to it.

"What did you say a second ago?"

"Huh?" John says. "What?"

"I say, say what? What did you say? Say it again?"

"Oh man, you're asking a lot! What were we talking about?"

"Um, dangerous work, something about chancy occupations like ours, and you said something about aerospace plants?"

"Oh yeah! That's right. This guy I know, Larry, he's working for a friend in San Diego who does industrial espionage. He slips into offices as a repairman or janitor and rips off paperwork and disks. Now that's already chancy enough, but he tells me that it's escalated into sabotage recently."

"Yeah, yeah, I've read about some of that I guess," Sandy says. This is connecting up with something he heard . . . when was that? "Do you know the friend?"

"Larry didn't mention the name. But they're hiring out to people that want the work done, apparently, and Larry is freaked. Even though the pay is good he's not too comfortable with the way things are trending."

"He's doing the actual sabotage himself?"

"Some of it. And then he's got people working for him too. Like your friend Bastanchury."

"Arthur's one?"

Dispassionately Sandy considers it. Up until this point he hadn't placed the earlier conversation he remembers having on this topic, but now with the mention of Arthur the party on Torrey Pines Cliffs comes back to him, the opium conference with Bob Tompkins. What was it Bob had been saying? Whew. There is this problem with drug taking at Sandy's level: functioning in the present is possible, just barely, with the most intense concentration; but the past . . . the past tends to disappear. A lot of tracks branch back up into the hippocampus there, and he doesn't seem to have much of a program for navigating them.

Well, he couldn't give a word-for-word transcript, but finally he does recall the gist of it. Something about Raymond taking revenge against the military, which is a funny idea on the face of it, although it's developing disturbing aspects. Instinctively he is curious. He wants to know what is going on. Partly this is because it is going on in his territory, the black economy of OC, and it's important for him to know as much as he can about the territory. Then partly it's because he has the feeling that the whole affair might have something to do with his friends, through Arthur. Jim hangs out with Arthur a lot these days, and probably he doesn't know what Arthur's gotten himself into. . . .

For the moment, however, he's distracted by the memory of Raymond and Bob Tompkins. That was the night that Bob's friend Manfred made the proposal concerning the aphrodisiac coming in from Hawaii, that's right. A little smuggling for twenty thousand and a lot of aphrodisiac, which no doubt there would be a good demand for. Of course it goes against Sandy's usual operating principle, but in a situation like this one . . . necessity makes its own principles. Now when was that conference? Just a week or so ago, wasn't it? So there might still be time. . . .

Vikki starts crying again. She was the one who first met this disappearing Adam, and introduced him to John and Sandy, and so she feels responsible. "Let's lid some more," John suggests morosely.

Without a word, Sandy shifts back into support mode, pulls another eyedropper from his bag. Impassively he watches his friends blink Mello into their tears. We use drugs as a weapon, he thinks suddenly; a weapon to kill pain, to kill boredom. The thought shocks him a little, and he forgets it.

After cheering them up again he makes his way out. He types in the program for his next appointment, and sits in the driver's seat watching the cars tracking around him. Ten thousand dollars. John and Vikki won't be able to repay him for months and months, if ever, so essentially the loss is entirely his. Ach. Thieves, frauds, con men, do they ever think how their victims feel? He redoes the accounting, confirms the results; he is in a bad cash crunch.

Bleakly he picks up the car's phone, calls Bob Tompkins. "Bob? Sandy here . . . I'm calling about your friend Manfred . . ."

So he agrees to do it. Bob says he has a few days before the transfer is to take place. The boat is all ready, in a slip in Newport harbor. Fine.

Once or twice during the next couple days Sandy remembers to ask casually about the industrial sabotage thing. It turns out that there are a whole lot of rumors about sabotage attacks on defense contractors—that they're being made by members of the black economy's extended family. But the rumors tend to contradict each other. No one but John Sturmond has heard Arthur's name connected with it. Eveline Evans believes that the security chief at Parnell is behind it all, and that it's all a manifestation of an intercorporations war. But Eveline is a big fan of intercorporate espionage videos, so Sandy is suspicious. This is a problem; filtering through rumors to real information is not an easy task. But Sandy keeps at it, when he remembers.

One night around 2:00 A.M. he's talking with Oscar Baldarramma, a friend and a big distributor of the lab equipment and tissue cultures Sandy needs for his work. They're out on Sandy's balcony, near the end of the nightly party. And Oscar says, "I hear that Aerojet is going to get hit tonight by those saboteurs."

"Is that right? How do you know?"

"Ah, Raymond himself was up here last night, and he let it slip."

"Not very good security."

"No, but Raymond likes to show off."

"Yeah, that's what Bob says. Is that all Raymond's doing this stuff for, though?"

" 'Course not. He's doing it for money, just like he does everything. There's lots of people happy to pay to see some of these companies suffer a setback or two."

"Yeah." And Sandy is thinking of Arthur, who left the party a couple hours before, after turning down an eyedropper of the Buzz, which surprised Sandy. And, for that matter, what happened to Jim?

36

Hurrying to his night class Jim stops at Burger King for a quick hamburgerfriesandcoke. He picks up the little free paper, the *Register*, and scans it briefly. Among the personals and real estate ads that constitute the bulk of the paper is a small OC news section; the headline reads, AEROJET NORTH LATEST VICTIM OF SABOTAGE. Yes, that's Jim and Arthur's work again. Jim reads the details with interest, because just as at Northrop and Parnell, they never got to see the effects of their action. Appears the ballistic missile defense software program has taken a serious blow, according to the Aerojet PR people. Fantastic, Jim thinks. He throws the paper in the trash on the way out, feeling that he is becoming a part of history. He is now an actor on the stage of the world.

Thus it's difficult to concentrate on the grammatical problems of his little class. Tonight one of his students hands in a gem: "We can take it for granite that the red gorillas will destroy Western civilization if they can." Jim shudders to think of the student's conception of the wars in Indonesia and Burma: Marines being hunted down by giant crimson apes . . . And take it for granite! It's perfect, really; the way the student has heard the phrase even makes sense, as metaphor. Solid as granite. Jim likes it. But it's one more sign among many others that his students don't read. Thus writing is completely foreign to them, a different language. And it's impossible to teach a language in one short semester. They've all got an impossible task. Why even try?

Class over, Jim collects the papers on the table. Turns off the room's light, walks into the hall. The door to the room across from his is open, which is unusual. Inside it a black-haired woman is lecturing vigorously.

Wild black frizzed-out mane, flying behind her.
She's big: tall, bulky, big-boned.
Army fatigue pants, frumpy wool sweater rucked up over
    the arms.
Boots.
Working at an easel: ah. An artist. That explains it, right?
Wrong. Brake light. A poem is a list of
Things To Do.

Jim moves to one side of the doorway, to try and see what's on the easel. Black lines. She sketches with careless boldness, sometimes looking at the class while she does it. "Try that," she commands. Try drawing while looking the other way?

While they try she comes to the door. "You lost?"

"No! No, I just finished teaching across the hall here." Though, still, I may be lost. . . . "I was just watching."

"Come in if you're going to watch."

Jim hesitates, but she's back at the easel, and just to disappear seems impolite. So he slips in and sits at a desk by the door. Why not?

The students are at tables, desks, easels, drawing away. The teacher's sketch is a landscape, in an Oriental style: mountain peaks piled on each other, disappearing in cloudbanks and reappearing. At the bottom, tiny pine trees, a stream, a teahouse, a group of fat monks laughing at a bird. It's like the illustrations in one of his books on Zen. He's given up on Zen as hopelessly apolitical, but still, the art has something. . . . The teacher looks at the clock, says, "We're going overtime. Time to stop." While the students pack up, she says, "You practice the strokes until you can do them without thinking, so that it's your head painting. That takes a long time. And all that time you've got to practice seeing too. It's a matter of vision as much as technique. Using the white spaces, for instance. Once you've learned washes, it's entirely a matter of vision." She walks among them. "We sleepwalk our way through most of this life, and it won't do. It won't do. You've got to throw your mind into your eyes and see. Always be watching." She takes her paintbox to a sink in the corner, where some others are washing brushes. "When it becomes a habit you begin to see the world as a great sequence of paintings, and the technique you know will help get some of them onto a surface. Tonight when you walk out the door, remember what I've said, and wake up! Okay, see you Thursday."

The students leave, talking in small groups. Jim sits and watches her. She tosses her equipment into a large briefcase, almost a suitcase. Snaps it shut. "Well?" she says to Jim.

"I'm learning how to see."

She wrinkles her nose. "Watch out you don't break something."

Jim hesitates. "Want to get something at the Coffee Hut?"

She looks away from him uncomfortably. He thinks she's shy, and almost smiles; would her students believe it possible? "All right." She pulls the suitcase off the table and barges out the door.

Jim follows. They exchange names. Hers is Hana Steentoft. She lives up in Mojeska Canyon, not all that far from the college. "And you're an artist?" Jim asks.

"Yes." She's amused for some reason.

They enter Trabuco J.C.'s pathetic attempt at a coffee house in the Bohemian style: plastic wood ceiling beams, dimmed lighting, old posters of European castles, a wall of automatic food and drink dispensers. Nothing can hide the fact that Trabuco is a commuter's junior college. The place is empty. They sit in the corner opposite the janitor washing the imitation wood floor.

"Do you paint in the style you were teaching tonight?"

"No. I mean it's a tool, a stylistic resource. I love the look of some dynasties, and Ming Dynasty painting is perfect for some of what I do, but . . . you teach writing? It's like if you taught a class in sonnet writing, and I asked you if you wrote sonnets. You probably don't, but you might use what you learned from sonnets in other poems."

Jim nods. "So you sell your paintings?"

"Sure. Can't live on what they pay us here, can you." She laughs.

Jim doesn't reply to that one. "So who are your customers?"

"Individuals, mostly. A group in the canyons, and in Laguna. And then some banks. Murals for their offices." She changes the subject. "And what do you write?"

"Ah—poetry, mostly. But I'm teaching bonehead English."

"You don't like it?"

"Oh, it's all right, it's all right." He regrets calling it that.

She chugs down most of her beer. They talk about teaching. Then about painting. Jim knows the Impressionists, and the usual culturevulture selection of others. They share an enthusiasm for Pisarro. Hana talks about Cassatt, then about Bonnard, her special hero. "Even now we haven't fully understood aspects of his work. That coloration that at first looks so bizarre, and then when you look closer at the real world you see it there, kind of underneath the surface of things."

"Even those white shadows in that one painting?"

She laughs. "*Cabinet de Toilette*? Well—I don't know. That was for the composition, I guess. Haven't seen any white shadows, myself. But maybe Bonnard did, I wouldn't doubt it. He was a genius."

They talk about genius in art, what it consists of and how those without it can best learn from it. Jim, who will concede in an instant that he is no artistic genius, and only hope that he is not pressed further to concede that he is in fact no artist at all, notices that Hana never makes any of these concessions. She makes no claims, either. This is intriguing. They continue to share enthusiasms, they find themselves interrupting each other to elaborate on the other's remarks. Jim is intrigued, attracted.

"But you can't just mean that paying closer attention to what you see is all of it, can you?" Jim asks, referring to her lecture to her class. "I mean, that's just like getting a good focus on a camera, or a telescope—"

"No no," she says. "We don't see like cameras at all. That's part of what makes photographs so interesting. But focusing your eyesight and your vision aren't the same thing, you see. Focusing your vision means a change in the way you pay attention to things. A clarification of your aesthetic sense, and of your moral sense as well."

"Vision as moral act?"

She nods vigorously.

"Now *that's* not postmodernism."

"No, it isn't. But now we're leaving postmodernism, right? Changing it. It's a good time for artists. You can take advantage of the open space left by the death of postmodernism, and the absence of any replacement. Help to shape what comes next, maybe. I like being a part of that."

Jim laughs. "You're ambitious!"

"Sure." She looks at him briefly; mostly she watches the table when she talks. "Everyone's ambitious, don't you think?"

"No."

"But you—aren't you?"

"Ah." Jim laughs again, uncomfortable. "Yeah, I guess so." Of course he is! But if he says so, doesn't it underline his lack of accomplishment, his lack of effort? It isn't something that he likes to talk about.

She nods, watching the table again. "Everyone is, I think. If they can't admit it, they're scared somehow."

A bit of mind-reading, there! And Jim hears himself say, "Yeah, it scares me, actually."

"Sure. But you admitted it anyway, didn't you."

"I guess so." Jim grins. "I'd like to see some of your work."

"Sure. And maybe I can read some of yours."

Stab of fear. "It's terrible."

She smiles at the table. "That's what they all say. Uh-oh, look. They're closing the place."

"Of course, it's eleven!" They laugh.

They gather their things and leave. As they walk under the light in the entryway Jim notices how wild looking she is. Hair unbrushed, sweater poorly knitted, she really is strange looking. Couldn't be more out of fashion if she tried. Jim supposes that's the point, but still . . .

"We should do this again," he says. She's looking off at the ground, maybe checking out the way ground bulbs underlight the shrubbery edging the quad. It is a weird effect. Ha—here's Jim seeing things, all of a sudden.

"Sure," she says indifferently. "Our classes end the same time."

He walks her to her car. "Thursday, then?"

"Sure. Or whenever."

"Okay. See you." Jim gets in his car and drives off, thinking of things they have talked about. Is he really ambitious? And if so, for what? You want to make a difference, he thinks. You want to change America! In the writing, in the resistance work, in the teaching, in everything you do! To change America, whoah—you can't get much more grandiose than that. Remarkable, then, how lazy he is, and what a huge gap there is between his desires and his achievements! Big sigh. But there, look at that string of headlights snaking along the shore of Rattlesnake Reservoir, reflected in the black water as a whole curved sequence of squiggly S-blurs . . .

It's a question of vision.

37

Dennis McPherson is not surprised to find that Lemon is furious about all aspects of the Stormbee decision, including the protest. Since the protest was Hereford's idea, stimulated by McPherson's outburst and made before the whole traveling crew of the company, it makes Lemon look like he is not crucial to the policy-making process of LSR, and he can't stand it. So with his most malicious smile he gives McPherson the job of representing LSR in the long and involved matter of the appeal. He guesses that McPherson will hate it, and he is right. Now McPherson has two main tasks: flying to Washington and talking to their law firm, appearing before committees and making depositions and the like; and helping Dan Houston, back in Laguna, with the disaster that Ball Lightning is about to become. Great. McPherson can feel his stomach shrinking, a little more every day.

So he's off to Crystal City again. In for consultation with LSR's law firm, Hunt Stanford and Goldman Incorporated. One of the most prosperous firms in the city, which is saying a lot.

It's Goldman who has been put in charge of their case; Louis Goldman, who is fortyish, balding, handsome, and a very snappy dresser. McPherson, who for years has believed lawyers to be one of the principal groups of parasites in the country, along with advertisers and stockbrokers, was at first quite stiff with the East Coast smoothie. But it turns out that Goldman is a nice guy, very sharp, and someone who takes his job seriously, and McPherson has grown to respect and then like him. For a lawyer he isn't bad.

Tonight they're having dinner up in Crystal City's finest restaurant, a rotating thing on the roof of the forty-story Hilton. Planes landing at National Airport cruise down the Potomac River basin, already below them: a strange sight.

McPherson asks about the appeal and Goldman makes a little flow chart on a napkin. "The whole history of the project prior to the Air Force's RFP is out, of course," he says. "No one wants these superblack programs acknowledged in public, and there's nothing written down concerning it anyway, so for our purposes it's irrelevant."

McPherson nods. "I understand that. But the RFP as published matched the specs they gave us for the superblack program, so any deviation from that—"

"Sure. That could be grounds for a successful challenge. Let's see if I've got the main points as you see them. Air Force asked you for a covert guidance system for a remotely piloted aircraft that could be dropped from low orbit, to underweather but without blind let-down, where it would be navigated at treetop level. Then it was to locate enemy military vehicles and lock on air-to-surface missiles it would be carrying."

"That's what they wanted."

"And they wanted it in one pod, preferably, and it was to use less than eleven KVA."

"Right. And yet they chose a system that uses two pods, and although Parnell claims they only need eleven point five KVA, they appear to be lying, according to our calculations of the needs of their system. The Air Force should have been able to see that too."

Goldman jots down these points on a pad he's put by his dessert plate. No napkin for this stuff. "And they've got a radar system, you say?"

"Right. See, the RFP repeats the original request that the system be covert, that it doesn't give itself away by its outgoing signals. Parnell has ignored that feature of the RFP and put in a radar system. So they won't be covert, but it does mean that they'll be able to do a blind let-down. And now the Air Force is listing that capability as a plus for Parnell, even though it's not asked for in the RFP." McPherson shakes his head, disgusted.

"It's a good point. And there are other discrepancies?"

"That's the main one, but there's others." They go over them, and Goldman fills out his list. The Air Force has listed Parnell's accelerated schedule as an advantage, then given them a contract with a relaxed schedule. And the Air Force's most probable cost estimates of the LSR and Parnell proposals consistently upped LSR's figures, while leaving Parnell's alone, or even lowering them. Then the lower cost of the Parnell system, as determined by the Air Force, was listed as a plus for them.

"It's pretty clear from all this that the Air Force wanted Parnell, no matter what the proposals were like," Goldman remarks. "Do you have any idea why that might be?"

"None." McPherson's anger over the matter is getting its edge back. "None whatsoever."

"Hmm." Goldman taps his pen against a tooth. "I've got some of my moles looking into the matter, actually. Don't tell anyone that. But if we can figure out their motive for doing this, and find any way of proving it, that would be a big help to the appeal."

"I believe it." They order brandies and sit back as the table is cleared. "So where do we go from here?" McPherson asks.

Back to the flow chart on the napkin. "Two approaches initially, see? First, we've petitioned the courts in the District to make an injunction halting the award of the contract until an investigation by the General Accounting Office is made. At the same time we've asked the GAO to make the investigation. Results so far have been fifty-fifty. The GAO has agreed to investigate, and that's very good. They're an arm of Congress, you know, and one of the most impartial bodies in Washington. One of the only real watchdogs left. They'll go after it full force, and I think we can count on a good effort from them.''

Goldman swirls his brandy, takes a sip. "The other front has brought some bad news, I'm afraid. In the long run it could be pretty serious."

"How so?" McPherson feels the familiar tightening in the stomach.

"Well, you make a request for an injunction to the judiciary system, and in the District of Columbia it goes to the federal court system and is given to one of four appellate courts, each with a different presiding judge. It's not a regional thing, so someone in the system makes a decision and sends your request to one court or another. Mostly it's a random process, as far as we can tell, but it doesn't have to be. And in this case, our request for an injunction has been given to court four, Judge Andrew H. Tobiason presiding."

Another sip of brandy. Goldman seems to have the habit of courtroom timing: a little dramatic pause, here. "So?" McPherson says.

"Well, you see," says Goldman, "Judge Andrew H. Tobiason is also Air Force Colonel Andy Tobiason, retired."

Stomach implosion. A peculiar sensation. "Hell," says McPherson weakly, "how could that be?"

"The Air Force has its own lawyers, and many of them work in the District of Columbia. When they retire, some are made judges here. Tobiason is one. Giving him this particular case is probably a bit of mischief worked by the Air Force. A few phone calls, you know. Anyway, Tobiason has refused to make the injunction; he's decided the contract is to be carried out as awarded, until the GAO finishes its investigation and its report is conveyed to him." Goldman smiles a wry smile. "So, we've got a bit of an uphill battle. But we've also got a lot of ammunition, so . . . well, we'll see how it goes."

Still, he can't deny it's bad news. McPherson sits back, drains the brandy snifter. A terrible singer is moaning ballads over bad piano work, in the center of the revolving restaurant. Their table's window is now facing out over the lit sprawl of Washington, D.C. The dark Mall is a strip across the lights, the Washington Monument white with its blinking red light on top, the Capitol like an architect's model, same for the Lincoln Monument there in the trees . . . all far, far below them. Washington has kept its maximum height law for buildings, and everything over there is under ten stories, and far below them. And of course height means the same thing it always has; the isobars for altitude and prosperity, that is to say altitude and power, are an almost perfect match in every city on earth. Height = power. So that here in Crystal City they look down on the capital of the nation like gods looking down on the mortals. And it isn't just a coincidence, McPherson thinks; it's a symbol, it says something very real about the power relationship of the two areas, the massive Pentagon and its lofty crowd of luxury-hotel sycophants densepacked around it—looking across the river and down, on the lowly government of the people. . . .

"The Air Force has a lot of power in this town," Goldman says, as if reading his mind. "But there's a lot of power in other places as well. So much power here! And it's scattered pretty well. Could be better, but there are some checks and balances still. All kinds of checks and balances. We'll get our chance to manipulate them."

To be sociable McPherson agrees. And they talk in an amiable way for another hour. He enjoys it, really. Still, on his way back to his hotel room, his mood is black. A retired Air Force colonel for a judge! For Christ's sake!

A well-dressed woman gets into the elevator with him. Perfume, bright lipstick, glossy hair, backless yellow dress. And alone, at this hour. McPherson's eyes widen as it occurs to him that she is probably one of the Crystal City prostitutes, off to fulfill a contract of her own. Stiffly McPherson returns her smile as she gets off. Just another military town.

38

Now Jim looks forward to seeing Hana Steentoft, but he certainly can't count on it happening; she doesn't seem quite as interested in getting together. Some nights she's gone before Jim dismisses his class. Other nights she has work to do; "Sorry," she says diffidently, looking at the ground. "Got to be done." Then again there are the nights when she nods and looks up briefly to smile, and they're off to the pathetic Coffee Hut, to talk and talk and talk.

One night she says, "They've given me a studio on campus. I've got to work in a while, but do you want to come see it first?"

"Sure do."

They walk over dark paths, between concrete buildings lit from below. Sometimes they get wedge views of the great lightshow of southern OC. Nobody else is on campus; it's like a big video set, the filming completed. One of the concrete blocks holds Hana's studio, and she lets them in. Lights on, powerful glare, xenon/neon mix.

Piled against the walls are rows of canvases. Jim looks through one stack while Hana goes to work mixing some paints, in a harsh glare of light. The canvases are landscapes, faintly Chinese in style, but done in glossy blues and greens, with an overlay of dull gold for pagoda roofs, streams, pinecones, snowy mountaintops in the distance.

The results are . . . odd. No, Jim is not immediately bowled over, he does not suffer a mystical experience looking at them. That isn't the way it works. First he has to get used to their strangeness, try to understand what's going on in them. . . . One looks totally abstract, great stuff, then Jim realizes he's got it upside down. Oops. Real art lover here. Reversed, it's still interesting, and now he understands to look at them as abstract patterns as well as mountains, forests, streams, fields. "Whoah. They're wonderful, Hana. But what about—well, what about Orange County?" She laughs. "I knew you'd ask that. Try the stack in the corner. The short one." Laughter. "It's harder, of course."

Well. Jim finds it extremely interesting. Because she's used the same technique, but reversed the ratios of the colors. Here the paintings are mostly gold: gold darkened, whitened, bronzed, left itself, but all arranged in overlapping blocks, squares tumbled one on the next in true condomundo style. And then here and there are moldlike blotches of blue or green or blue-green, trees, empty hillside (with gold construction machinery), parks, the dry streambeds, a strip of sea in the distance, holding the gold bar of Catalina. "Whoah." One has an elevated freeway, a fat gold band across a green sky, bronzed mallsprawl off to the side. Like his place, under the freeway! "Wow, Hana." Another abstract pattern, Newport harbor, with the complex bay blue-green, boats and peninsula gold blocks. "So how much do you charge for these?"

"More than you can afford, Mr. Teacher."

"Sandy could afford it. Bet he'd like one of these in his bedroom."

"Uh-huh."

Jim watches her mixing a couple of gold paints together in blue bowls, the paint sloshing bright and metallic in the light, Hana's tangled black hair falling down over her face and almost into the bowl. It's a picture in itself. Some unidentifiable feeling, stirring in him. . . .

As she mixes paints he talks about his friends. Here's Tashi writing tales of his surfing with a clarity and vividness that put Jim's work to shame. "Because he isn't trying for art," Hana says, and smiles at a bowl. "It's a valuable state of mind."

Jim nods. And he goes on to talk about Tashi's great refusal, his secret generosity; about Sandy's galvanic, enormous energy, his complex dealing exploits, his legendary lateness. And about Abe. Jim describes Abe's haggard face as he comes into the party after a night's work, transformed by an act of will into the funtime mask, full of harsh laughter. And the way he holds himself at a distance from Jim now, mocking Jim's lack of any useful skills, teaming with Tash or Sandy in a sort of exclusion of Jim; this combined with flashes of the old sympathy and closeness that existed between them. "Sometimes I'll be talking and Abe will give me a look like an arrow and throw back his head and laugh, and all of a sudden I realize how little any of us know what our friends are, what they're thinking of us."

Hana nods, looking straight at him for once. She smiles. "You love your friends."

"Yeah? Well, sure." Jim laughs.

"Here, I'm ready to work. Get out of that light, okay? Sit down, or feel free to track or whatever."

"I'll look at the other ones here." He studies painting after painting, watching her as well. She has the canvas flat on a low table, and is seated next to it, bent over and dabbing at it with a tiny brush. Face lost in black hair. Still bulky body, hand moving deftly, tiny motions . . . it must take her hours to do one painting, and here there are, what, sixty of them? "Whoah."

After a while he just sits by one stack and watches her. She doesn't notice. Every once in a while she heaves a big breath, like a sigh. Then she's almost holding it. Cheynes-Stokes breathing, Jim thinks. She's at altitude. Once he comes to and realizes he's been watching her still form without thought, for—he doesn't know how long. Like the meditation he can never do! Except he's about to fall asleep. "Hey, I'm going to track." "All right. See you later?" "You bet."

On the drive home he can hear a poem rolling around in his mind, a great long thing filled with gold freeways and green skies, a bulky figure perched over a low table. But at home, staring at the computer screen, he only hears fragments, jumbled together; the images won't be fixed by words, and he only stares until finally he goes to bed and falls into an uneasy insomniac's slumber. He dreams again that he is walking around a hilltop in ruins, the low walls broken and tumbled down, the land empty out to the horizon . . . and the thing rises up out of the hill to tell him whatever it is it has to say, he can't understand it. And he looks up and sees a gold freeway in a green sky.

39

Sandy manages to talk Tash into accompanying him on his sailing trip to rendezvous with the incoming shipment of Rhinoceros. As always it's the personal plea rather than financial arguments that convince Tash.

Soon after that Sandy is visited by Bob Tompkins, who gives him the latest information on the smugglers, and the keys to the boat moored in Newport harbor. When that business is done they retire to Sandy and Angela's balcony for a drink. Angela comes out and joins them.

"So how's Raymond doing?" Sandy asks casually when they are suitably relaxed.

"Oh, okay."

"Is he still involved with this thing in OC, the defense industry vendetta?"

"Yeah, yeah. More than ever."

"So he has people up here that he's recruited, then?"

"Hired, to be exact. Sure. You don't think Raymond would do all this by himself?"

Sandy hesitates, trying to figure out an unobtrusive opening; Angela takes the direct approach. "We think some of our friends might be working for him, and we're worried that they'll get in trouble."

Bob frowns. "Well . . . I don't know what to say, Angela. Raymond's going about it with his usual security measures, though. He swears it's all going very quietly."

"Rumors are flying up here," Sandy says.

"Yeah?" Bob frowns again. "Well, I'll tell Raymond about that. I think it'd be nice if he stopped, myself, but I don't know if he will."

Sandy looks at Angela, and they let the conversation drift to other topics. Afterward, thinking about it, Sandy decides he didn't really find out much. But he might have sent some useful news up the line to Raymond.

The next afternoon Sandy goes down with Tash to the upper bay. They've got all the keys they need: one for the marina parking lot, one for the marina, one for the cage around the boat's slip, one to turn off the boat's alarm system, three to get into the boat, and one to unlock the beam and the rigging.

It's a thirty-three-foot catamaran, big-hulled and slow as cats go, named *Pride of Topeka*. Solid teak paneling, dark blue hull and decking, rainbow sails, little auxiliary engines in each hull. They get it out of the slip and putter down the waterways of Newport harbor.

> Past five thousand small boats.
> Past Balboa Pavilion, and the ferry kept running for
>   tourists.
> Past the house split in two by feuding brothers. That's
>   History.
> Past the buoy marking where John Wayne moored his
>   yacht.
> Past the Coast Guard station (look innocent).
> Past the palm trees arched over Pirate's Cove. That's your
>   childhood.

And out between the jetties. They're caught in the five-mile-per-hour traffic jam of the busiest harbor on earth. Might as well be on the freeway. To their left over the jetty is Corona del Mar, where Duke Kahanamoko introduced surfing to California. To their right over the longer jetty is the Wedge, famous bodysurfing break. "I wonder where they got the boulders for the jetties," Sandy says. "They sure aren't local."

"Ask Jim."

"Remember when we were kids and we used to run out to the end?"

"Yeah." They look at the metal tower at the end of the Corona del Mar jetty, the green light blinking on its top. Once it was one of their magic destinations. "We were crazy to run over those boulders."

"I know!" Sandy laughs. "Just one slip and it's all over! I wouldn't do it now."

"No. We're a lot more sensible now."

"*Ahhh*, hahaha. Speaking of which, it's time for an eye-dropper, eh?"

"Let's get the sails up first so we don't forget how."

They put up the mainsail, the boat heels over, they sail south.

Engines off. White wake spreading behind.
Sun on water. Wind pushing onshore.
The sail bellies
Full.

Sandy takes a big breath, lets it out. "Yes, yes, yes. Free at last. Let's celebrate with that eyedropper."

"Really change the routine."

After a few blinks Sandy sighs. "This is the only way to travel. They should flood the streets, give everyone a little Hobie cat."

"Good idea."

They're headed for the backside of San Clemente Island, some sixty miles off the north San Diego coast. It's owned by the government, inhabited only by goats, and used by the Navy and the Marines to practice amphibious landings, helicopter attacks, parachuting, precision bombing, that sort of thing. Sandy and Tash are scheduled to rendezvous sometime the next day or night with the boat from Hawaii, off the west side of the island.

They sail in a comfortable silence, broken only occasionally by stretches of talk. It's an old friendship, there's no pressure to make conversation.

That's the sort of companionship that brings people out; even the quiet ones talk, given this kind of silence. And suddenly Tash is talking about Erica. He's worried. As Erica rises ever higher in the management of Hewes Mall, her complaints about her layabout ally and his eccentric life-style become sharper. And no one can get sharper than Erica Palme when she wants to be.

Sandy questions Tash about it. What does she want? A businessman partner, kids, a respectable alliance in the condomundos of south OC?

Tash can only blink into an eyedropper and declare "I don't know."

Sandy doubts this; he suspects Tash knows but doesn't want to know. If Sandy's guesses are correct, then Tash'll have to make changes he doesn't want to make, to keep the ally he wants to keep. Classic problem.

Sandy has the solidest of allies in Angela; she's biochemically optimistic, as he's joked more than once, she appears to have equal amounts of Funny Bone, Apprehension of Beauty, the Buzz, and California Mello running in her veins. If he could get his clients to Angela's ordinary everyday mental state, he'd be rich. Sandy treasuresher, in fact they're really old-fashioned that way; they're in love, they've been allies for almost ten years. Some kind of miracle, for sure. And the more Sandy hears from all his friends, the more he sees of their shaky, patched-up, provisional alliances, the luckier he feels.

So he can only sympathize with Tash concerning his problem; he can't really claim to offer any help out of his own experience. It's a difficult situation, no doubt about it; it is, in fact, a dilemma. Choosing either course of action means painful consequences. Change to suit Erica, remain the same and lose her; what will Tash do?

As night falls they talk less and less. Events from their childhood, events from the world news. Among the blurry stars overhead the swift satellites and the big mirrors slowly move, north, south, east, west, like stars cast loose and spinning off on crazy courses of their own. "Death From the Stars." "No lie." Sandy shivers in the wind, watching them. He pulls out soggy Togo's sandwiches and they eat. Afterward Sandy feels a bit queasy. "Marijuana reduces nausea, right?"

"So they say."

"Time to test it out."
It works only indifferently.

To their left OC bounces up and down.
The coast an unbroken bar of light.
The hills behind bumpy loafs of light.
Lights stationary, lights crawling about.
A flat hive of light, squashed between black sea and black
    sky.
The living body of light.
A galaxy seen edge-on.

Sandy retires to the cabin in the left hull, leaving the first watch to Tashi. He wakes to find Tashi drowsing over the tiller in gray predawn.
"Why didn't you wake me?"
"Fell asleep."
"I take it they didn't show."
"That's right."
"Tonight, then. Hopefully."
Tashi retires to his cabin in the right hull. Sandy has the dawn to himself. Gentle offshore breeze blowing. Tash had the tiller and sail set perfectly, even in his sleep. Sandy can see Catalina to the north behind him, and San Clemente Island poking up over the horizon to the south, perhaps another ten or fifteen miles ahead.
The stars and satellites wink out. Color comes to sea and sky. The sun rises over the mountains behind San Diego. Morning at sea. Sandy thinks about his usual schedule and feels blessed. Hiss and slap of water under the hulls. So peaceful. Maybe it's true, what Jim always says; there was a better way of life, once, a calmer way. Not in OC, of course. OC sprang Athena-like, full blown from the forehead of Zeus Los Angeles. But somewhere, somewhere.
Midmorning Tash comes up, they eat oranges and make cheese sandwiches. They sail around San Clemente Island just to pass the day. It's strange: scrub-covered, except where erosion has ripped out raw dirt watersheds, the hills are everywhere littered with wrecked amphibious landers, tanks, helicopters, troop carriers.

And the west side, the side away from the mainland, is heavily pocked with bomb craters. Top of one hill gone. Another is covered by a mass of concrete, from which springs scores of radar masts and other protuberances.

"Is it really a good idea to pick up sixty liters of illegal aphrodisiac right under the Navy's nose?" Tash inquires.

"Purloined letter principle. They'll never expect it."

"They won't have to! Those surveillance arrays up there will probably analyze the goods by molecular weight. And hear our conversations."

"So let's not talk about it."

Their instructions are to lay to, four miles directly west of the southernmost tip of the island. They do some compass work and establish triangulated landmarks that will keep them near the spot after dark.

The southwest end of the island is benched in a series of primordial beaches that terrace the hills a hundred feet high or more. They can see some goats on one terrace. "Those must be the most paranoid goats on earth," Tash remarks. "Can you imagine their lives? Just peacefully eating sage, when suddenly wham bang, they're being strafed and bombed again."

Sandy can't help but laugh. "Horrible! Can you imagine their world view? I mean, how do they explain it to each other?"

"With difficulty."

"Like flies to small boys are we to the gods, or something like that."

"I wonder if they have a civil defense program."

"Something about as good as ours, no doubt. 'Hey, here they come! Run like hell!' " They laugh. "Like flies to small boys . . . how does that go?"

"Need Jim here."

Sandy nods. "He'd enjoy this, those benches and all."

"Should have brought him instead of me."

"He's got class tonight."

"So do I!"

"Yeah, but you don't have to teach it."

"Not most nights, anyway." They laugh. "Hey, did you know he's seeing a woman who teaches across the hall from us?"

"Good for him. Beats suffering with Virginia."

"No lie. . . . I wonder what ever happened with Sheila. I liked her."

"Me too. But Jim is . . ."

"An idiot?"

"*Ah*, hahahahaha. No, no, you know what I mean. Anyway, maybe with this teacher."

"Yeah."

After dark the island gets more active. As they eat more sandwiches they hear roars, clanking, grinding, the soft feathery whirr of combat helicopters. All without a single light anywhere, except for one red on-and-off to mark the high point of the island. Once or twice Tash spots the bulk of a helicopter against the stars. Then *swu*BAM, BOOM, and the island is momentarily lit by a ball of orange fire blackened with the dirt it's thrown up. Both of them jump convulsively. "Damn!"

Tash laughs. "Let's hope none of those things' heat-seeking targeters lock on to us."

"Tash, don't say that!"

"They're like clotheslines, tied from firing platform down to the target, which is located by its heat. Infrared system. Then you clip a bomb on the clothesline, and down it slides."

The island elaborates: *whoosh*BOOM.

"Lucky we don't have any heat here."

"Just us."

"Well hey! Maybe we ought to go in the cabins?"

"Nah. These are the best fireworks we'll ever see, unless they draft us. Every burst probably costs a hundred thousand dollars."

"Man, that's a lot of money!"

"No lie."

The battle exercises go on for an hour, until their ears begin to hurt. When it ends Sandy retires again. "Wake me this time."

Tashi does, at 3:00 A.M. They appear to be at the same heading off the island. All is dark and calm, there's hardly a breeze. Up and down on a deep groundswell. Salt air fills Sandy to the brim; he's suddenly happy.

Tash is in no hurry to retire. "Do you ever think about leaving OC?" he asks.

"Ah, yes, I suppose so. Sometimes." Actually it has never

occurred to Sandy; he never has time to think about that kind of thing. "Santa Cruz, maybe."

"That's just OC north."

"What isn't?"

"I was thinking of Alaska."

"Wow. I don't know, man. Those winters. The people I've talked to from up there say it's a manic-depressive life, manic in the summer and depressed in the winters, with the winters twice as long. Doesn't sound like such a deal to me."

"Yeah, I know. But it'd be a challenge. And it'll always stay empty, because of those winters. And it means I could get out into the real world every day, you know?"

There's a strain in Tashi's voice, a kind of poignant longing that Sandy hasn't heard before. He thinks, When you're on the horns of a dilemma, you do your best to find a third way. But he doesn't say this. "That would be something, wouldn't it. Surfing might be a problem, though."

Tash laughs. "No more so than here. The crowd scene is too much."

"Even at night?"

"Nah, but look around—can you see the waves? It beats war with nazis, but still, it's not the same."

"Alaska, then. Hmm. Sounds like a possibility. Maybe you can grow pot for me."

"Maybe."

"Speaking of which . . ." They rock on the water. Tash falls asleep. Sandy keeps a hand on the tiller, worrying about his friend. Maybe he'll mention it to Jim. Maybe Jim will think of something to say to Tashi. So many troubles, these days . . . alliances going bad left and right . . . things falling apart. What to do, what to do?

In the predawn he starts awake, then falls into a doze. He's half-awake, now, watching gray swells surge up and down under his fingertips, up and down, up and down, up and down. There's a light mist smoking off the swell tops, liquid turning to gas. There is a lovely glassy sheen to the water's surface, it's so smooth, so smooth. Maybe he's dreaming. The terraced benches of the island are obscured by mist, the gray hills rise out of it as on the first day, an unreal solidity intruding into a liquid world. Everything seems surreal, dreamlike, mesmerizing.

Suddenly there's a creak, and a forty-foot yacht has hove to alongside them. Three men jump down onto the deck of the cat, frightening Sandy. The thumps and the sudden tilt of the deck wake Tash, and he appears out of his cabin to stand beside Sandy. Sandy still feels like he's in a dream, he's too groggy to move. The three strangers form a chain and small metal drums are hefted over the water onto the cat's middeck, behind the mast.

While they're at it, right in the middle of their operation, there's a deep *crump* from the island, followed by a huge sonic boom. BOOOOMM!!!! Whoah!

That'll wake you up. Tash stares out to sea. "Look there, quick," he says urgently, and points. Sandy looks. A black dot, just over the water out on the horizon, skimming in over the mist . . . it's moving fast and jinking from side to side as it approaches, *zoom* past the two boats faster than Sandy can turn his head, and *crump* into the island. BOOOM! a racking sonic boom, like the fabric of the world has been ripped. And another dot has appeared out there. . . .

Bizarrely, the strangers from the yacht have continued to sling the drums over onto their deck, not missing a stroke, completely ignoring the missiles screaming overhead. When there's twelve drums on board they stop. One man comes back to them. "Here." A card is put in his hand, the man hops up to the deck of the yacht. It pulls away, all its sails angel-wing white over the mist. Around the southern tip of the island, and gone.

Sandy and Tash are still staring at each other, wordless and bleary-eyed. Here comes another skittering black dot, another *crump*, another shattering roar. "What *are* they?" Sandy cries.

"Cruise missiles. Look how fast and low they fly! Here comes another one—"

Skimming black dot. One every couple minutes. Each sonic boom smacks their nerves, makes them jump. Finally Tash stops waiting for them to cease. He checks the drums on the middeck, returns. "I guess we're the proud owners of twelve drums of aphrodisiac," he says. BOOM! The mast is quivering in the blasts of air. "Let us get the fuck out of here."

40

Late that afternoon they are approaching Dana Point harbor, under the fine rugged bluff of Dana Point. This is where Bob Tompkins asked them to bring the boat. But then Tash spots two Coast Guard cutters, lying off the jetty. They appear, through binoculars, to be stopping boats and boarding them. "Sandy, I don't think we should try to go in past those two, not with this cargo."

"I agree. Let's change course now before it gets too obvious we're avoiding them."

They tack and begin a long northwesterly reach to Newport, using the auxiliary engines to gain speed. Sandy will just have to call Tompkins and tell him the goods are elsewhere. Tompkins won't be overjoyed, but that's life. No way they can risk a search by the Coast Guard, and it looks like that's what they're doing. Could they be searching for Sandy and Tash's cargo? Sandy doesn't like to think such obviously paranoid thoughts, but it's hard to avoid them with what they've got aboard.

An hour later Tashi climbs the minimal mast halyards, with some difficulty, for a look north using the binoculars. "Shit," he says. "Look here, Sandy, let's cut back toward Reef Point."

"Why?"

"There's Coast Guard off Newport too! And they're stopping boats."

"You're kidding."

"I wouldn't kid you about something like that. There's a lot of them, in fact, and I think—I think—yeah, a couple of them are coming this way. Making a sweep of the coast, maybe."

"So, you're thinking of dropping the stuff off?"

"Right. And we'd better be quick about it—it looks to me like they're only stopping cats of about our size."

"Damn! I wonder if they've been tipped off?"

"Maybe so. Let's get the drums back on deck."

Tashi descends and they quickly lift the metal drums out of the cabins. The cat is slower in the water with the drums aboard, but the effect is least when they're clumped right behind the mast, so that's where they put them.

Tashi takes the tiller and brings them in past the reefs of Reef Point, a beachless point on the continuous fifty-foot bluff that makes up the old "Irvine coast," from Corona del Mar to Laguna. The top of the bluff in this area is occupied by a big industrial complex; just to its right are the condos of Muddy Canyon.

Tash motors them further in, out of view of the buildings on the bluff above them. "That's where Jim's dad works," Tashi says as he luffs to a stop in waist-deep water, just outside the shorebreak. Happily it's a day without surf. "That's Laguna Space Research, right above us." He tosses the boat's little anchor over the side. "Hurry up, Sandy, those cutters were coming south pretty fast."

He jumps overboard and Sandy picks up the drums and hands them down to him. Both of them handle the drums as if they were empty; adrenaline is about to replace their blood entirely. Tash takes the drums onto one shoulder and runs them up the mussel-and-seaweed-crusted boulders at the base of the sandstone bluff. He puts them into gaps between boulders, roots around like a mad dog to find small loose boulders to place over them. Sandy jumps in and rushes from boat to shore with the drums, huffing and puffing, splashing in the small shorebreak, skidding around on the slick rock bottom in search for better footing. They both are panting in great gasps as the sprint exertions catch up with them.

Then all the drums are hidden and they're back on the boat and motoring offshore. No sight of other boats. Ten minutes, perhaps, for the whole operation, although it felt like an hour. Whew.

They motor west until they can circle around and approach Newport again, from out to sea. Sure enough, off Newport harbor they're stopped by a Coast Guard cutter, and searched very closely indeed. It's a first for both of them, although it resembles police searches of their cars on land. Sandy has thrown all the eyedroppers overboard, and he is polite and cooperative with the Guardsmen. Tash is grumpy and rude; they're doing good detainee/bad detainee, just out of habit.

Search done, the Guardsmen let them go impassively. They motor on into the harbor, subdued until they get into the slip and are off the boat, onto the strangely steady, solid decking. Back to the parking lot and Sandy's car, away from the scene of the crime, so to speak. Now, no matter what happens to the Rhinoceros, they are safe.

"Pretty nerve-racking," Tash says mildly.

"Yeah." Despite his relief, Sandy is still worried. "I don't know what Bob is going to say about this." Actually, he does know; Bob will be furious. For a while, anyway.

"Well hey, it looks to me like they had a pretty bad information leak."

"Maybe. Still, to put the stuff right under LSR. They're sure to have security of some kind. I suspect I am going to be status but not gratis with the San Diego boys."

"To hell with them."

"Easy for you to say."

And there won't be any payment without the goods delivered. Sigh. "Well. We'd better go get stoned and think it over."

"No lie."

41

Sandy decides that the best thing to do is return immediately to Reef Point and recover the drums, and he calls Bob Tompkins to explain about the delay, also to complain about the apparent information leak. But Tompkins is in Washington to do some lobbying, and that same afternoon Sandy is visited by a worried-looking Tashi. "Did you see the news?" Tashi asks.

"No, what's up? San Clemente Island blown to smithereens?"

Jim looks up from Sandy's computer. "Where'd that word come from?"

"Ignore him," says Sandy. "He's testing my new drug, Verbality."

"Verbosity, more like. Here, check out the news." Tash clicks on the main wall screen and taps in the command for the *Los Angeles Times*. When it appears he runs through it until he reaches the first page of the Orange County section. The screen fills with a picture of what appears to be a twentieth-century newspaper page, a formatting gimmick that has gotten the *Times* a lot of subscriptions down at Seizure World. "Top right."

Sandy reads aloud. "LSR Announces Increased Security For Laguna Hills Plant, oh man, because of recent spate of sabotage attacks, defense contractors in OC, perimeter now patrolled, blah blah blah so what," so Tashi cuts in and reads a sentence near the bottom of the article: "The new measures will include cliff patrols and boat patrols in the ocean directly off LSR's seacliff location. 'Any sea craft coming within a mile of us is going to be under intense surveillance,' says LSR's new security director Armando Perez."

"They must be joking," Sandy says weakly.

"I don't think so."

"It's illegal!" Panic seeping in everywhere. . . .

"I doubt it."

Jim looks up. "What could be the difficulty that is encumbering and freighting your voices with the sounds of *sturm und drang*, my brethren?"

"Scrap that new drug," Tashi suggests.

"I will. The difficulty," Sandy explains to Jim, "is that we have stashed twelve big drums of an illegal new aphrodisiac at the bottom of a bluff now under the intense scrutiny of a trigger-happy private security army!"

"Zounds! Jeepers!"

"Shut up." Sandy rereads the article, turns it off. The initial shock over, he is again thinking furiously. "I've got an idea."

"What's that?"

"Let's go to Europe."

"Taking the constructive approach, I see."

"No, let's go!" Jim says. "Semester break frees me after Wednesday's class! On the other hand"—crestfallen—"I am a trifle short of funds."

"I'll loan it to you," Sandy says darkly. "High interest." Actually, he's short of funds himself. But there's always Angela's emergency account. And this is an emergency; he needs to be out of town when Bob gets this news, to give him time to adjust to it. Bob's like that; he has two- or three-day fits of anger, then collects himself and returns to cool rationality. The important thing is to be out of reach during those first two or three days, so that nothing irrevocable can happen. "Bob's in Washington for a couple days, so I'll leave a message on his answering machine outlining the situation. By the time we get back, he'll have had time to cool down."

"And you'll have time to think of something," Tash says.

"Right. You coming, Tash?"

"Don't know."

The news spreads quickly: they're going to Europe. Jim asks Humphrey for time off work, and Humphrey agrees to it, as long as he can come along. Angela agrees to the use of her emergency account, takes her vacation time, and is coming too. Abe can't get the time off. Tashi is thinking of splurging for it, but Erica's angry about it—"*I've* got to work, of course"—and he decides against going.

Humphrey takes over arrangements for the trip and finds them a low-budget red-eye no-frills popper that will put them in Stockholm two hours after departure. After they arrive they'll decide where to go; this is Sandy's decree.

Following his last class on Wednesday, Jim tells Hana that he's off to Europe with friends. "Sounds like fun," she remarks, and wishes him bon voyage. They make arrangements to meet again when the next semester begins, and happily Jim goes back home to pack.

"Off to the Old World!" he says to his ap. "I'll be walking waist deep in history wherever we go!" And as he packs he sings

along with Radio Caracas, playing the latest by the Pentagon
Mothers:

We only want to take you to the thick of the fray!
World War Three? It isn't just on its way!
You're in it, you're a part of it, you win every day!
So come on everybody, let's all stand up and say:
Mutual Assured Stupiditee-uh-*eeeeeeeee*!

42

On the next trip to Washington Dennis McPherson is taken by
Louis Goldman to a restaurant in the "old" section of Alexandria,
Virginia. Here prerevolutionary brick is shored up by hidden steel,
and the old dock warehouses are filled with boutiques, ice-cream
shops, souvenir stands, and restaurants. Business is great. The
seafood in the restaurant Goldman has chosen is superb, and they
eat scallops and lobster and enjoy a couple bottles of gewürz-
traminer before getting down to it.

Plates cleared, glasses refilled, Goldman sits back in his chair
and closes his eyes for a moment. McPherson, getting to know
his man, takes a deep breath and readies himself.

"We've found out some things about the decision-making
process in your case," Goldman says slowly. "It's a typical Pentagon procurement story, in that it has all the trappings of an
objective rational process, but is at the same time fairly easy to
manipulate to whatever ends are desired. In your case, it turns out
that the Source Selection Evaluation Board made its usual detailed
report on all the bids, and that report was characterized as thorough
and accurate by our information source. And it favored LSR."

"It favored us?"

"That's what our source told us. It favored LSR, and this report was sent up to the Source Selection Authority without any tampering. So far so good. But the SSA takes the report and summarizes it to use when he justifies his decision to the people above him. And here's where it got interesting. The SSA was a four-star general, General Jack James, from Air Force Systems Command at Andrews. Know him?"

"No. I mean I've met him, but I don't know him."

"Well, he's your man. When he summarized the SSEB's report, he skewed the results so sharply that they came out favoring Parnell where they had originally favored you. He's the one that introduced the concern for blind let-down that's not in the RFP, and he's the one who oversaw the most probable cost evaluations, to the extent of fixing some numbers himself. And then he made the decision, too."

Remarkable how this Goldman can spoil a good dinner. "Can we prove this?" McPherson asks.

"Oh no. All this was given to us by an insider who would never admit to talking with us. We're just seeking to understand what happened, to find an entry point, you know. And some of this information, conveyed privately to the investigators at the GAO, might help them aim their inquiries. So we've told them what we know. That's how these legal battles with the Pentagon go. A lot of it consists of subterranean skirmishes that are never revealed or acknowledged to be happening. You can bet the Air Force lawyers are doing the same kind of work."

This news sends a little chill through McPherson. "So," he says, "we've got a General James who didn't want us to get the contract. Why?"

"I don't know. I was hoping you could tell me. We're still trying to find out, but I doubt we will any time soon. Certainly not before the GAO releases their report. It's due out soon, and from what we hear it's going to be very favorable to us."

"Is that right?" After all he has heard so far, McPherson is surprised by this. But Goldman nods.

All of a sudden the possibility of getting these men—James, Feldkirk, the whole Air Force—Parnell—the possibility of taking their corrupt, fraudulent, cheating decision and stuffing it back down their throats and *choking* them on it—the possibility of forcing them to acknowledge that they have some accountability to the *rules*—oh it rises in McPherson like a great draft of clean fresh air; he almost laughs aloud. "And if it is favorable to us?"

"Well, if their report is stated in strong enough terms, Judge Tobiason won't be able to ignore it, no matter what his personal biases are. He'll be forced to declare the contract improperly awarded, and to call for a new process under the Defense Procurement statutes of 2019. They'd have to repeat the bidding process, this time adhering very closely to the RFP, because the courts would be overseeing it."

"Wow." McPherson sips his drink. "That might really happen?"

Goldman grins at his skepticism. "That's right." He raises his glass, and they toast the idea.

So McPherson returns to California feeling as optimistic about the whole matter as he has since the proposal went from superblack to white.

Back at the office, however, he has to turn immediately to the problem of Ball Lightning. Things are as bad as ever on that front. McPherson's role has been deliberately left vague by Lemon, as part of the punishment; he is to "assist" Dan Houston, whatever that means, Dan Houston who has had less time with the company and is clearly not competent to do the job. Galling. Exactly what Lemon had in mind.

But worse than that are the problems with the program itself. The Soviets' new countermeasure for their slow-burning boosters, introducing modest fluctuations in their propulsion—called "jinking"—has made LSR's trajectory analysis software obsolete, and so their easiest targets have become difficult. Really, offensive countermeasures to the boost-phase defenses are so easy and cheap that McPherson is close to convinced that their free-electron laser system is more or less useless. They'd have better luck throwing stones. (In fact there's a good rival program at TRW pursuing a form of this very idea.) But the Air Force is unlikely to be happy to discover this, some thirty billion dollars into the project, with test results in their files that show the thing is feasible. Strapped chicken results.

Dan Houston, bowed down by all these hard facts, has already given up. He still comes into the office, but he's not really thinking anymore. He's useless. One day McPherson can barely keep from shouting at the man.

That afternoon, after Dan has gone home early, his assistant Art Wong talks to McPherson about him. "You know," Art says, hesitant under McPherson's sharp gaze, "Dan's having quite a bit of trouble at home."

"What's this?"

"Well, he made some bad investments in real estate, and he's pretty far in debt. I guess he might lose the condo. And—well—his ally has left. She took the kids and moved up to L.A. I guess she said he was drinking too much. Which is probably true. And spending too much time at work—you know he never came home in the evenings when he first started on this program. He really put in the long hours trying to get it to work, after we won the bid."

"I'll bet." Considering the tests that won it. Ah, Dan . . .

"So . . . well, it's been pretty hard on him. I don't think . . ." Art Wong doesn't know what else to say.

"All right, Art," McPherson says wearily. "Thanks for telling me."

Poor Dan.

That night at the dinner table Dennis watches Lucy bustle around the kitchen telling him about the day's events at the church, which as usual he is tuning out entirely; and he thinks about Dan. McPherson has spent much of his life—too much of it—at work. On the weekends, in the evenings . . . But he can see, just by looking at her, that it has never even occurred to Lucy to leave him because of that, no matter how sick of it she may have gotten. It just isn't something she would do. He can rely on that, whether he deserves it or not. As she passes his chair he reaches out impulsively and gives her a rough hug. Surprised, she laughs. Who knows what this Dennis McPherson will do next, eh? No one. Not even him. He gives her a wry grin, shakes his head at her inquiries, eats his dinner.

And at work he tries to treat Dan with a little more sympathy, tries to lay the eye on him a little less often. Still, one day he can hardly contain himself. Dan is moaning again about the impossibility of their task, and says in a low voice, as if he has a good but slightly dangerous idea, "You know, Dennis, the system makes a perfectly fine weapon for fixed ground targets like missile silos. We've worked up its power so much for the rapidly moving targets that stationary ones wouldn't stand a chance. Missile silos hit before they launch, you know.''

"Not our job, Dan.'' Strategy. . . .

"Or even cities. You know, just the threat of a firestorm retaliation for any attack—who could ignore that?''

"That's just MAD all over again, Dan,'' McPherson snaps. He tries to control himself. "It wasn't what they bought this system for, so really, it's irrelevant. We just have to try to track and hold the boosters long enough to cook them, that's all there is to it. We've done everything possible to the power plant—let's work on tracking and on phased-array to increase the brightness of the beam, and just admit to the Air Force that the kill process will take longer than expected. Call it a boost phase/post–boost phase defense.''

Dan shrugs. "Okay. But the truth is that every defense system we've got works even better at suppressing defenses. Or at offense.''

"Just don't think about that,'' McPherson says. "Strategy isn't our area.''

And they get back to it. Software design, a swamp with no bottom or border. With the deadline closing in on them.

Dennis is in Laguna when he gets the next call from Louis Goldman. "The GAO report is out.''

"And?'' Heartbeat accelerating at an accelerating rate, not good for him. . . .

"Well, it concludes that there were irregularities, and recommends the contract be bid on again.''

"Great!''

"Well, true. But it's not really as gung-ho as I expected, frankly. The word is that the Air Force really put the arm on the GAO in the last couple of weeks, and they managed to flatten the tone of the report considerably.''

"Now how the hell can they do that?'' McPherson demands. "I mean, what sort of power could the Air Force have over the GAO? Isn't GAO part of Congress? They can't possibly threaten them, can they?''

"Well, it's not a matter of threatening physical violence, of course. But you know, these people have got to work with each other in case after case. So if the Air Force cares enough, they can say, Listen, you lay off us on this or we'll never cooperate with you again—we'll make sure any dealings you have with us are pure torture for you, and you won't be able to fully function in this realm anymore. So, the folks at GAO have to look beyond this particular case, and they're realists, they say, this one is top priority for them, but not for us. And so the report gets laundered a little. No lies, just deemphasizing.''

McPherson doesn't know what to say to this. Disgust makes him too bitter to think.

''But listen,'' Goldman goes on, ''it isn't as bad as I'm making it sound. In the main the GAO stuck to their guns, and after all they did recommend a new bidding process. Now we'll just have to wait and see what Judge Tobiason decides in the case.''

''When will that take place?''

''Looks like about three weeks, judging by his published schedule.''

''I'll come out for it.''

''Good, I'll see you then.''

Thus McPherson is in a foul mood, apprehensive and angry and hopeful all at once, when Dan Houston comes by at the end of the day and asks him to come along to El Torito for some drinks.

''Not tonight, Dan.''

But Dan is insistent. ''I've really got to talk to you, Mac.''

Sigh. The man's hurting, that's clear. ''All right. Just one pitcher, though.''

They track over and take their usual table, order the usual pitcher of margaritas, start drinking. Dan downs his first in two swallows, starts on a second. ''This whole BM defense,'' he complains. ''We can barely make these systems work, and when we do they work just as well against defensive systems, so in essence they're another offense. And meanwhile we aren't even paying attention to cruise missiles or sub attack, so as for a real umbrella, well that isn't even what we're trying for!''

McPherson nods, depressed. He's felt that way about strategic defense for years. In fact that was his big mistake, accidentally letting Lemon know how he felt. And his dislike for the concept springs from exactly the reasons Dan is speaking of; every aspect of it has spiraled off into absurdity. "You'd think the original system architects would have thought of these kinds of things," he says.

Dan nods vehemently and puts down his margarita to point, spilling some ice over the salt on the rim. "That's right! Those bastards . . ." He shakes his head, is already drunk enough to keep going: "They just saw their chance and took it. During their careers they could make it big designing these programs and selling them to the Air Force, making it all look easy! Because for them it meant bucks! It meant they had it made. And it's only after it was put in space and began to come on line that the next generation of engineers had to make the system work. And that's us! We're the ones paying for their fat careers."

"Well, whatever," McPherson says, uncomfortable with Dan's raw bitterness. There is a sort of team code in the defense industry, and really, you don't say things like this. "We're stuck with it, anyway, so we might as well make the best of it."

Here he is, sounding like Lucy. And Dan, drunk and miserable, far past the code, will have none of it: "Make the best of it! How can we make the best of it? Even if we could get it to work, all the Soviets have to do is put a bucket of nails in orbit and wham, ten of our mirrors are gone. Talk about cost-effective at the margin! A ten-penny nail will take out a billion-dollar mirror! Ha! ha! So we defend those mirrors by claiming that we will start a nuclear war with anyone who attacks them, so it comes right back to MAD to defend the very system that was supposed to get us away from all that."

"Yeah, yeah. I know." McPherson can feel the margaritas fuzzing his brain, and Dan has had about twice as many as he has. Dan's getting sloppy drunk here, McPherson can see it. So he tries to prevent Dan from ordering another pitcher, but Dan shoves his hand away angrily and orders another anyway. Nothing McPherson can do about it. He feels depression growing in him, settling into a knot around the tequila in his stomach. This is a waste of his time. And Dan, well, Dan . . .

Dan mutters on while waiting for the next drink to arrive. "Soviets get their own BMD and we don't like it, no no no, even though the whole strategy demands parity. All sorts of regional wars start so our hard guys can express their displeasure without setting off the big one. Boom, bam, hook to the jaw, jab in the eye, *Bulletin of Atomic Scientists* sets the war clock at one second to midnight— one second to midnight, man, set there for twenty years! And, and the Soviets' beam systems could be trained on American cities, burn us to toast in five minutes, and we could do the same to them like I was saying today but we all ignore that, that's not real no no no, we pretend they're defensive systems only and we work on knocking each other's stuff down before the other side does, so we can MIRV each other right into the ground—''

"All right, all right," McPherson says irritably. "It's complicated, sure. No one ever said it wasn't complicated."

A tortilla chip snaps in Dan's fingers. "I'm not saying it's just complicated, Mac! I'm saying it's crazy! And the people who designed this architecture, they knew it was crazy and they went ahead and did it anyway. They went along with it because it was good for them. The whole industry loved it because it was new business just when the nukes were topping out. And the physicists went along with it because it made them important again, like during the Manhattan Project. And the Air Force went along with it because it made them more important than ever. And the government went along with it because the economy was looking bad at the end of the century. Need a boost—military spending—it's been the method of choice ever since World War Two got them out of the Great Depression. Hard times? Start a war! Or pump money into weapons whether there's a war or not. It's like we use weapons as a drug, snort some up and stimulate the old economy. Best upper known to man."

"Okay, Dan, okay. But calm down, will you? Calm down, calm down. There's nothing we can do about that now."

Dan stares out the window. The next pitcher arrives and he fills his new glass, spilling over the edge so all the big grains of salt run in yellow-white streams down onto the paper tablecloth. He drinks, elbows on the table, leaning forward. He stares down into the empty glass. "It's a hell of a business."

McPherson sighs heavily; he hates a maudlin drunk, and he's about to physically stop Dan from refilling his glass yet again when Dan looks up at him; and those red-rimmed eyes, so full of pain, pierce McPherson and hold him in place.

"A hell of a business," Dan repeats soddenly. "You spend your whole life working on *proposals*. Bids, for Christ's sake. It isn't even work that is ever going to see the light. The Pentagon just sets companies at each other's throats. Group bids, one-on-one competitions, leader-follower bids. Kind of like cockfighting. I wonder if they bet on us.''

''Stimulates fast development,'' McPherson says shortly. There's no sense talking about this kind of thing. . . .

''Yeah, sure, but the waste! The waste, man, the waste. For each project five or six companies work up separate proposals. That's six times as much work as they would need to do if they were all working together in coordination, like parts of a team. And it's hard work, too! It eats people's lives.''

Now Dan gets an expression on his face that McPherson can't bear to watch; he's thinking of his ally Dawn now, sure. McPherson looks around for the waitress, signals for their check.

''All their lives used up in meeting deadlines for these proposals. And for five out of every six of them it's work wasted. Nothing gained out of that work, nothing made from it. Nothing *made* from it, Mac. Whole careers. Whole lives.''

''That's the way it is,'' McPherson says, signing the check.

Dan stares at him dully. ''It's the American way, eh Mac?''

''That's right. The American way. Come on, Dan, let's get you home.''

And then Dan slips in the attempt to stand, and knocks the pitcher off the table. McPherson has to hold him up by the arm, guide him between tables as he staggers. My God, a sloppy drunk; McPherson, red-faced with embarrassment, avoids the eyes of the other customers as they watch him help Dan out.

He gets Dan into his car, fastens his seat belt around him, reaches across his slumped body to punch the car's program for home. ''There you are, Dan,'' he says, irritation and pity mixing about equally in him. ''Get yourself home.''

''What home.''

43

...Under the Spanish and then the Mexicans, Orange County was a land of ranchos. To the north were Ranchos Los Coyotes, Los Alamitos, Los Bolsas, La Habra, Los Cerritos, Cañon de Santa Ana, and Santiago de Santa Ana. Midcounty were Ranchos Bolsa Chica, Trabuco, Cañada de Los Alisos, and San Joaquín. In the south were Ranchos Niguel, Misión Vieja, Boca de La Playa, and Lomas de Santiago.

To give an idea of their size: Rancho San Joaquín was made up of two parts; first Rancho Ciénega de las Ranas, "Swamp of the Frogs," which extended from Newport Bay to Red Hill—second Rancho Bolsa de San Joaquín, which contained much of the land that later became the Irvine Ranch. Say 140,000 acres.

These huge land grants were surveyed on horseback, with lengths of rope about a hundred yards long. They used landmarks like patches of cactus, or the skull of a steer. More precise than that they didn't need to be; the land remained open, and cattle roamed over it freely.

In the spring, after the calving, the roundups took place. Horsemen, reputed to be among the best who ever lived, and including among them a good number of the rapidly disappearing Indians, rounded up the cattle and led them to the branding stations, several for each rancho, as they were all so large. The stations became festival centers, with tables set out and decorated, and great feasts of meat, beans, tortillas, and spicy sauces spread out on them. After the new calves were branded, and strays sent back to their correct ranchos, the celebrating began. The most important events were the horse races; many took place over a nine-mile course.

Other games were more bloody: trying to grab the head from a rooster buried to the neck, while galloping by it at full speed, for instance. Or the various forms of bull-baiting.

Then in the evenings there were dances, using forms invented at San Juan Capistrano, which throughout this period remained the biggest settlement in the area.

Houses were one story, adobe, with simple furnishings made in the area. Clothing fashions were those of Europe some fifty to eighty years before, transformed by local manufacture and custom. There was no glass. They were rich only in cattle, and in open land.

It was a life lived so far away from the rest of the world that it might as well have been alone on the planet: backed by empty mountains and desert, facing an empty sea.

When Jedediah Smith traveled overland from Missouri in 1826, the Mexican governor of California tried to kick him out of the state. But ten years later, when other Americans arrived to trade, they were welcomed. They brought with them various goods of modern Europe, and took away tallow and hides.

Some of the Americans who came to trade liked the look of the land, and stayed. They were welcomed in this as well. Learn Spanish, become a Catholic, marry a local girl, buy some land: more than one American and Englishman did just that, and became respected members of the community. Don Abel Stearns and Don John Forster (known better as "San Juan Capistrano" for his obsession with the old mission, which he bought after its secularization) did even better than that, and became rich.

All the Americans who came in contact with the Californians, even the most anti-Papist among them, came away impressed by their honesty, dignity, generosity, hospitality. When Edward Vischer visited Don Tomás Yorba, head of the most distinguished family in the area, he complimented Don Tomás on a horse that the don rode while seeing Vischer off his rancho; and as Vischer boarded his ship in San Diego the horse was ridden up to the dock and given to him, along with a message from Don Tomás asking him "to accept his beautiful bay as a present and a remembrance of California."

Cut off from the world, existing in the slow rhythms of cattle raising, the ranchos of Orange County gave their people a slow, pastoral, feudal life, dreamlike in its disconnection from Europe, from history, from time. For four generations the cycle of ranch existence made its simple round, from branding to branding. Little changed, and the dominant realities were the adobe homes, the hot sun in the clear blue sky, the beautiful horses, the cattle out on the open hillsides, on the great broad coastal plain. The few foreigners who arrived to stay were welcomed, taken in; the traders brought glass. They didn't make any difference to the Californians.

But then the United States declared war on Mexico, and conquered California along with the rest of the great Southwest. And then gold was discovered in the Sierra Nevada, and Americans flocked to San Francisco, crazed by a gold rush that has never stopped. History returned.

The cattle of the south were driven north to feed these people, and Los Angeles grew on the business. As Americans poured into southern California, the immensity of the Spanish and Mexican land grants gained immediate attention; they were rich prizes to be captured. The Treaty of Guadalupe Hidalgo, which ended the Mexican War, guaranteed the property rights of Mexican citizens in California; but that was just a treaty. Like the treaties the United States made with the Indian tribes, it didn't mean a thing. Two years later Congress passed a law that forced the rancheros to prove their titles, and the hunt was on.

The old rancheros were asked to provide documentation that there had never been any need for, in earlier times, and court cases concerning the ownership of the land took up to twenty years to settle. The rancheros' only assets were their land and their cattle, and most of the cattle died in the great drought of 1863–64. To pay their lawyers and their debts, in the fight for their land, the rancheros had to sell parcels of it off. And so win or lose the court fights, they lost the land.

By the 1870s all the land was owned by Americans, and was being rapidly subdivided to sell to the waves of new settlers.

And so all that—the cattle roaming the open land, the horsemen rounding them up, the adobe homes, the huge ranchos, and the archaic, provincial dignity of the lives of the people on them—all that went away.

44

They land in Stockholm after a two-hour flight over the North Pole—just enough time to catch the in-flight movie *Star Virgin*. Once in the city they quickly decide that the Great Stagemaster in the Sky has shifted San Diego east and north to give them a surprise. Everyone speaks English, even. They eat at a McDonald's to confirm the impression and hold a conference in Sandy and Angela's hotel room to decide what to do next. Jim is for going north to the Arctic Circle and above, but no one else has much enthusiasm for the idea. "You can get reindeer steaks at Trader Joe's," Sandy tells him, "and snow on Mount Baldy. Midnight sun in the tanning parlor. No, I want to see someplace *different*."

"Well shoot," Humphrey says, "why don't we just go visit the Disneyland near Paris? That's bound to be different! We can walk around and note all the differences between it and the original Disneyland."

"The real Disneyland."

"The true Disneyland."

"The one and only and forevermore always the *best* Disneyland!"

Sandy nods. "Not a bad idea. But I've got a better one. We'll fly to Moscow."

"Moscow?"

"That's right. Get behind that Iron Curtain and see how the Russkies really live. It's bound to be different."

"It would be a challenge to the businessman," Humphrey says dreamily. "I'd have to do some shopping first."

Jim is in favor of the idea, he wants to see this Great Adversary that America has worked so hard to create and support. Angela is up for it.

So they go to Moscow. Well, sure. It reminds Humphrey of Toronto, his childhood home. Streets are clean. A lot of well-dressed people are out walking. Little untracked gas-engine cars roar about on the streets, which the travelers find delightfully quaint and noisy. At their hotel, recommended by the Intourist Bureau at the airport, they ask where they can rent a car and are told they cannot. "We'll see about that," Humphrey declares darkly. His eyes gleam crazily. "Time for some private sector enterprise." He has smuggled a number of videocassettes in, and as soon as they've unpacked in their rooms he stuffs several in his jacket and goes out to flag a taxi. Half an hour later he is back, pockets crammed with rubles. "No problem. Asked my driver if he knew anyone interested, and of course he was. The cab drivers are the big black market dealers here. The bellboy wants some too."

He looks affronted as Jim and Sandy and Angela laugh themselves silly. "Well, it's not so funny. We've got a serious problem here, in that they won't let you exchange rubles for real money. So this is like Monopoly money, you know?"

Sandy's eyes light up. "So while we're playing the game we might as well move to Boardwalk, is that it?"

"Well, yeah, I guess so." This is against Humphrey's grain entirely, but he can't figure out why he should object.

"What's the most expensive hotel in town?" Sandy asks.

They end up just behind Red Square in an immense old hotel called the Rijeka, and take up a suite on the top floor. Their window view of Red Square, filtered though it is, is impressive. "What a set, eh?" Sandy orders champagne and caviar from room service, and when it arrives Humphrey goes to work on the hotel employees, who speak excellent English. It's actually a disadvantage for the employees in this case, as it allows Humphrey to work them over more completely. When they leave the gang is many rubles richer, and Humphrey marches about the room ecstatically quoting long extempore passages from *Acres of Diamonds* in between attacks on the caviar, waving fistfuls of rubles in each hand.

They leave the hotel and go touristing, all ready to explore Red Square and say hello to Lenin and infiltrate the Kremlin and buy out GUM and do all the other great American-in-Moscow activities. In GUM they stand in a basement sale with hundreds of Russian women, and shout to each other across the crowds; they're a head and more taller than any of the locals there. Funny. The clothes on sale are remarkably gauche and Angela falls in love with several outfits. Back outside Humphrey flags a taxi and they sing "America the Beautiful" over Sandy's McCarthyite rap, "Better dead—than red, yeah better dead—than red."

They instruct their stoical driver to take them into the residential areas of the city, where great applexes are grouped around green parks. Up on a hill they figure they're in Party territory, everything's upscale as always in the hill districts of a city. And in fact they reach one cul-de-sac with a view over much of Moscow, and stare about them amazed. Sandy sputters: "Why it's—it's—it's *condomundo*! It's just like—*just like*—" and they all pitch in: *"Orange County!"*

Total collapse. They must return immediately to the hotel and order more champagne. OC has conquered the world. "James Utt would be proud," Jim says solemnly.

As soon as they can spend all Humphrey's rubles they're gone. "We still haven't seen anything *different*," Sandy complains.

"The Pyramids," Jim suggests. "See how it all began."

They fly to Cairo. The airport is in a desert of pure sand, even the Mojave can't compare to it. At the baggage collection they're met by an enterprising "agent of Egyptian tourist police" who is happy to offer them all of his private tourist firm's tours. He is smooth, but hasn't reckoned on Humphrey, who takes note of the many rival agencies in a long string of booths next to the agent's, and uses that fact to grind the man until he's sweating. Sandy, Angela and Jim just keep standing up and sitting back down on Humphrey's orders, depending on how the negotiations are going. In the end they have a free ride to a big hotel on the Nile offering half-price rooms, and transport to Giza for quarter-price tours and free tickets to the sound and light show here. The agent is punch-drunk by the time they leave, he looks like he's been mugged.

Cairo turns out to be the same color as the desert. The buildings, the trees, the billboards, even the sky, all are the same dust color. The Nile Hilton, across the river, has been painted turquoise to combat the monochrome, but the turquoise has turned sand-colored as well. Only the old snake river itself achieves a certain dusty dark blue.

When they leave the funky old freeway and hit the streets they see that the city is terrifically densepacked. Most of the buildings are tenements. Every street is stopped up by cars and pedestrians; they can't believe how many people are actually *walking*. Their hotel, old and dusty, is a welcome refuge. They chatter with excitement as they unpack and wait for the tour guide and driver to arrive and take them to Giza. Humphrey goes down to investigate currency exchange rates and comes back excited; there's an official rate, a tourist rate, various black market rates, and some theft rates, designed to tempt greedy people into exposing lots of cash. With some manipulation of this market Humphrey figures he can generate hundreds of Egyptian pounds, and he is about to start with the hotel staff when their guide arrives. Off they go to the Pyramids of Giza.

The Pyramids are to the west, in a morass of hotels and shops. When they get out of their car they are inundated by street merchants and the guide can't beat them away, especially with Humphrey asking about wholesale deals and the like. They dismiss their guide for saying "ThegreatandancientpyramidsofGiza" once too often, and walk up to the broad stone deck between pyramids one and two.

"Gee, they're not all that big, are they?" says Humphrey. "Our office building is bigger."

"You have to remember they were built by hand," Jim objects, resisting a certain disappointment that he too feels.

Sandy sees a chance to kid him a bit and chimes in with Humphrey. "Man they're nowhere near as big as South Coast Plaza. They're not even as big as Irvine City Hall."

"Kind of like the Matterhorn at Disneyland," Humphrey says. "Only not as pretty."

Jim is outraged. He gets even more distressed when he finds out no one is allowed to climb the Pyramids anymore. "I can't believe it!"

"Unacceptable," Sandy agrees. "Let's try the backside." They find guards on all sides of it, however. Jim is distraught. Their affronted guide retrieves them; it's time for the sound and light show, apparently a major spectacle. Sunset arrives, and with it busloads of tourists to see the show.

Tonight's show is in English, unfortunately. Between great sweeps of movie soundtrack romanticism a booming voice cracks out of twenty hidden speakers with a pomposity utterly unballasted by factual content. "THE PYRAMIDS . . . HAVE CONQUERED . . . TIME." The laser lights playing across the Pyramids and the Sphinx use the latest in pop concert technology and aesthetics, including a star cathedral effect, some satellite beaming down thick cylinders of light, yellow, green, blue, red, bathing the whole area in a lased glow. Amazing display. "Never let them tell you there haven't been useful spin-offs from the space defense technology," Sandy growls.

The booming voice carries on, more fatuous by the second. Angela leans over Sandy to whisper heavily to them all, "I am the Great and Powerful Wizard of Oz," and with the vocal style of the narrator pegged they can't restrain themselves, they get more hysterical at every sentence, and they're attracting a lot of irritated looks from the reverent tourists seated around them. Well, to be obnoxious is un-Californian, so they sit up rigidly and nod their heads in approval at each new absurdity, only giggling in little pressure breakthroughs. But on the drive back they simply roll on the seats and howl. Their guide is mystified.

But that night—that night, after the others have retired—that night, Jim McPherson wanders down to the hotel bar. He feels unsettled, dissatisfied. They aren't doing the Old World justice, he knows that. Going to see the Pyramids turned into bad pop video; that isn't the way to do it.

The hotel bar is closed. The clerk recommends McDonald's, then when she better understands Jim's desires, the Cairo Sheraton, just a few blocks away. It's simple to get there, she says, and Jim walks out into the dry, warm night air without a map.

There's a desert wind blowing. Smell of dust, static cling. Neon scrawls of Arabic script flicker over green pools of light that spill out into the dark streets. A few pedestrians, hardly any cars. From one shop comes the pungent smell of roasting spiced lamb, from another the quarter-tone ululations of a radio singer. Men in caftans are out doing the night business. Hardly anyone glances at Jim, he feels curiously accepted, part of the scene. It's peaceful in a way, the bustle is half-paced and relaxed. Men sit in open cafes over games that look a bit like dominos, smoking from giant hookahs whose bowls seem to contain chunks of glowing red charcoal. What are they smoking? Sandy would want to inquire, analyze a chunk for chemical clues; Humphrey would want to buy a bushel just in case. Jim just looks and passes on, feeling a ghost. The wailing music is eerie. Arab voices in the street are musical too, especially when relaxed like this. A cab driver plays the fanfare from "Finlandia" on his horn; all the cabbies here use that rhythm.

It occurs to Jim that he should have reached the Sheraton by now. It's on the Nile and shouldn't be that hard to find. But where, exactly, is the Nile? He turns toward it and walks on. Auto mechanics work on a car jacked up right in the street. Policemen stay in pairs, carry submachine guns. Jim seems to have gotten into a poorer neighborhood, somehow. Has he gotten his orientation off by ninety degrees, perhaps? He turns again.

The neighborhood gets poorer yet. Down one alley he can see the tower of the Sheraton, so he is no longer lost and all at once he pays real attention to what lies around him.

> The street is flanked by four-story concrete tenements.
> Doors are open to the night breeze.
> Inside, oil lamps flicker over mattresses on the floor.
> A stove.
> Each family or clan has one room.
> Ten faces in a doorway, eyes bright.
> Other families sleep on the sidewalks outside.
> Their clothing is sand-colored. A torn caftan hood.
> You live here, too.
> A man in a cardboard box lifts a little girl for Jim's
>   inspection.

Jim retreats. He thinks again, returns, hands the man a five-pound note. Five pounds. And he retreats. Off into the narrow alleys, he's lost sight of the Sheraton and can't recall where it was. Arms are extended out of piles of darkness, the cupped palms light in the gloom, the eyeballs part of the walls. It's all palpably real, and he is there, he is right there in it. He picks up the pace, hurries past with his head held up, past the hands, all the hands.

He makes it to the Sheraton. But past the guards, in the big lobby, which could be the lobby of any luxury hotel anywhere, he experiences a shiver of revulsion. The opulence is dropped on the neighborhood like a spaceship on an anthill. "There are people out there," he says to no one. With a shock he recalls the title of Fugard's play: *People Are Living Here*. So that's what he meant. . . .

He leaves, forces himself to return to the street of beggars. He forces himself to look at the people there. This, he thinks. This man, this woman, this infant. This is the world. This is the real world. He scuffs hard at the sidewalk, feels his breath go ragged. He doesn't know what he's feeling; he's never felt it before. He just watches.

Faces in the open doors, people sitting on the floor. Looking back at him.

This moment seems never to end—this moment does not end—but has its existence afterward inside Jim, in a little pattern of neurons, synapses, axons. Strange how that works.

Next morning he says, "Let's leave. I don't like it here."

45

So they fly to Crete, another of Jim's ideas. "We'll give you one more chance, Jimbo. . . ." They land at Heraklion, eat at Jack-in-the-Box, rent a Nissan at the Avis counter. Off to Knossos, a gaily painted reconstruction of a Minoan palace. It's quite crowded, and just the slightest bit reminiscent of the Pyramids.

Jim is disappointed, frustrated. "Damn it," he says, "give me that map."

Sandy hands him the Avis map of the island. Minoan ruins

are marked by a double axe, Greek ruins by a broken column. Jim looks for broken columns, understanding already that on this island Minoan ruins are first-class ruins, Greek ruins are second-class ruins. Find one away from towns, at the end of a secondary road, on the sea if possible. "Whoah." Several fit all the criteria. His mood lifts a bit. He picks one at random. "Humphrey, drive us to the very end of the island."

"Right ho. Gas is expensive here, remember."

"Drive!"

"Right ho. Where are we headed?"

"Itanos."

Sandy laughs. "World famous, eh Jim?"

"Exactly not. The Pyramids are world famous. Knossos is world famous. Red Square is world famous."

"Point taken. Itanos it is. What's there?"

"I don't have the slightest idea."

So they drive east, along the northern coast of Crete.

It strikes them all at the same time that the land looks just like southern California—to the extent that they know what southern California looks like, that is. Like the middle section of Camp Pendleton. Rocky dry scrubland, rising out of a fine blue sea. Dry riverbeds. Bare bouldery hilltops. Some tall mountains inland. "The first wave of American settlers always called southern California Mediterranean, when they tried to tell the people back east what it was like," Jim says slowly, staring out the window. "You can see why."

It's the same land, the same landscape; but look how the Greeks have used theirs.

Scrub hills.
Scattered villages. Concrete blocks, whitewashed. Flowers.
Untidy places, but not poor; Jim's ap is smaller than any
    home here.
Olive groves cover the gentler hills.
Gnarled old trees, crooked arms, silver-green fingers.
The road is spotted with black oily circles: crushed olives.
Do you live here?
Blue-domed, whitewashed church, there on the hilltop.
    Inconvenient!
An orange grove. . . .

"This is how it looked," Jim says quietly. And his friends listen to him, they stare out the windows.

They stop in at a village store and buy yogurt, feta cheese, bread, olives, oranges, a salami, retsina, and ouzo, from a very friendly woman who has not a single word of English. After Egypt's ceaseless venality her friendliness pleases them no end.

Late in the day they drive down one last blacktop ribbon of road, which follows a dry streambed to the sea.

Scrub hills flank them on both sides.
Hills breaking off in the dark blue sea.
A beach, divided into two by a knoll sitting in a small
    bay.
The knoll is covered with ruins.
The landscape is empty, abandoned. Nothing but the ruins,
    the scrub.

"My God!" Jim jumps out of the car. His recurrent dream, walking about in some great ruin of the past—ever since the effort to find El Modena Elementary School, it's been haunting him. On waking he always scoffed. No site exists without fences, ticket booths, information plaques, guides, visiting hours, lines, roped-off areas, snack bars, hordes of tourists milling around and wondering what the fuss was about; isn't that right?

But here they are. He pushes through shrubs, climbs a tumble of broken blocks, stands in the shattered entrance of an ancient church. Cruciform floor plan, altar against the back wall, which is dug into the knoll. Columns rolled against the walls.

The others appear. "Look," Jim says. "The church is probably Byzantine, but when they built it they used the materials at hand. The columns are probably Roman, maybe Greek. The big blocks in the walls that are all spongy, those are probably Minoan. Cut two thousand years before the church was built."

Sandy nods, grinning. "And look at the stone in the doorway. They had a locking post on the door, and as it swung open it scraped this curve here. Perfect semicircle." He laughs the Sandy laugh, a stutter of pure delight.

Humphrey and Angela walk to the north side of the knoll, investigating what looks like a small fortress, its walls intact.

"Well preserved," Sandy remarks. "It's probably Venetian," Jim says. "A thousand years newer than the church."

"Man, I can't really grasp these time scales, Jimbo."

"Neither can I."

On the beach below them are a pair of decrepit boats, pulled onto the sand. One appears to have an outboard motor under a tarp. From their vantage on the knoll they can see far out to sea, and back inland. Emptiness everywhere; the land deserted, the Aegean a blank plate.

"Let's camp here tonight," Jim suggests. "Two can sleep in the car, and two on our beach towels in the sand. We can eat the rest of the lunch food."

It's late and they've spent the day traveling; they all like the plan.

The sun nears the hills to the west as they bring the food up to the ruined church. The slightly hazy evening light brings out the orange in the rock, and the entire knoll turns deep apricot. Frilly pink herringbone clouds are pasted to the sky. The fallen blocks on the church entryway make perfect stools, tables, backrests.

They eat. The food and drink have vivid tastes. There's a group of goats on the hillside to the south of them. Sandy holds his hand up to the light, framing a pair of black rams. "Back in the Bronze Age."

After dinner they sit back and watch the florid twilight clouds as the light leaks away from the land. An abandoned, still, dusky landscape. "Tell us about this place, Jim," Angela says.

"Well, the back of the map has a few sentences about it, and that's all I know, really. It began as a Minoan town, around 2500 B.C. Then it was occupied by the Greeks, the Romans, and the Byzantines. Under the Greeks it was an independent city-state and coined its own money. It was abandoned around either 900 A.D. or 1500 A.D., because of earthquakes."

"Only six hundred years' difference," Sandy says. "My Lord, the time scales!"

"Immense," Jim says. "We can't imagine them. Especially not Californians."

Sandy takes this as a challenge. "Can too!"

"Cannot!"

"Can too!"

About five reps of that, and Sandy says, "Okay, try this. We'll go backwards from now, generation by generation. Thirty-three years per generation. You tell us what they were doing, I'll keep count."

"Okay, let's try it."

"Last generation?"

"Part of Greece."

Sandy makes a mark in the dirt between flagstones. "Before that?"

"Same."

Five generations go by like that. Jim has his eyes squeezed shut, he's concentrating, trying to recall Cretan history from the guidebooks, his history texts back home. "Okay, this guy saw Crete deeded over from Turkey to Greece. Before him, under the Turks."

"And his parents?"

"Under the Turks." They repeat these two sentences over and over, slowly, as if completing some ritual, so that Jim can keep track of the years. Sixteen times! "That's one big Thanksgiving," Humphrey mutters.

"What's that?"

"Lot of Turkey."

Then Jim says, "Okay. Now the Venetians."

So the response changes. "And their parents?" "Venetian." Ten times. At which point Jim adds, "We've just now reached the end of Itanos, by the way. The end of this city."

They laugh at that. And move to the Byzantines. Seven times Jim answers with that. Then: "The Arabs. Saracen Arabs, from Spain. Bloody times." Four generations under the Arabs. Then it's back to the Byzantines, to the times when the church before them was functioning, holding services, having its doorsill scraped by the door's locking post, again and again. Fifteen times Jim answers "Byzantine," eyes screwed shut.

"And their parents?"

"In Itanos. Independent city-state, Greek in nature."

"Call it Itanos. And their parents?"

"Itanos."

Twenty-six times they repeat the litany, Sandy keeping the

pace slow and measured. At this point none of them can really believe it.

"Dorian Greeks." After a few more: "Mycenaean Greeks. Time of the Trojan War."

"So this generation could have gone to Troy?"

"Yes." And on it goes, for eight generations. Sandy's shifting to get fresh dirt to scratch. Then: "Earthquakes brought down the Minoan palaces for the last time. This generation felt them."

"Minoan! And their parents?"

"Minoan." And here they fall into a slow singsong, they know they've caught the rhythm of something deep, something fundamental. Forty times Sandy asks "And their parents?", and Jim answers "Minoan," until their voices creak with the repetition.

And finally Jim opens his eyes, looks around as if seeing it all for the first time. "This generation, it was a group of friends, and they came here in boats. There was nothing here. They were fishermen, and stopped here on fishing trips. This hill was probably fifty feet inland, behind a wide beach. Their homes down near the palace at Zakros were getting crowded, they probably lived with their parents, and they were always up here fishing anyway, so they decided to take the wives and kids and move up here together. A group of friends, they all knew each other, they were having a good time all on their own, with their kids, and this whole valley for the taking. They built lean-tos at first, then started cutting the soft stone." Jim runs his hand over the porous Minoan block he is leaning against. Looks at Sandy curiously. "Well?"

Sandy nods, says softly, "So we can imagine it."

"I guess so."

Sandy counts his marks. "A hundred thirty-seven generations."

They sit. The moon rises. Low broken clouds scud in from the west, fly under the moon, dash its light here and there. Broken walls, tumbled blocks. A history as long as that; and now the land, empty again.

Except headlights appear on the road inland. Their beams lance far over the dark land, fan across it as they turn onto the side road to Itanos. The group falls silent. The headlights go right down to the beach below them. Car doors slam, cheery Greek voices chatter. A Coleman lantern is lit; its harsh glow washes the beach, and the Greeks go to work on the two old boats. "Fishermen!" Sandy whispers.

After leisurely preparations the boats are launched, their motors started. What a racket! They putter out of the bay and to sea, lanterns hung from their bows. After a time they're only stars on the water's flat surface, far out to sea. "Night fishing," Jim says. "Octopus and squid."

Sandy and Angela find a spot to lie down and sleep. Humphrey returns to the car. Jim climbs to the top of the knoll and watches the boats at sea, the moon and its flying clouds, the rough town map below him, defined by its tumbledown walls. Again he's filled with some feeling he can't name, some complex of feelings. "The land," he says, speaking to the Aegean. "It's not abandoned after all. Fishing, goat keeping, some kind of agriculture on the other side of the valley. Empty-looking, but used as much as scrubland can be. After all these many years." He tries to imagine the amount of human suffering contained in a hundred and thirty-seven generations, the disappointments, illnesses, deaths. Generation after generation into dust. Or the myriad joys: how many festivals, parties, weddings, love trysts, in this little city-state? How often had someone sat on this knoll through a moony night, watching clouds scud by and thinking about the world? Oh, it makes him shiver to think of it! It's a hilltop filled with spirits, and they're all inside him.

He tries to imagine someone sitting on top of Saddleback, to look across the empty plain of OC. Ah, impossible. Unimaginable.

How could history have coursed so differently for these two dry coasts? It's as if they're not part of the same history, they are separated by such a great chasm; how to make any mental juncture? Are they different planets, somehow? It is too strange, too strange. Something has gone wrong back home in his country.

He sits there through the night, dozing once, waking to the boats puttering back in, dozing again. He dreams of rams and fallen walls, of his father and licorice sticks, of a bright lantern under a cloudy moon.

He wakes to a dawn as pink as the sunset was orange, a woven texture of cloud over him. Pink on blue. In the bay below

Angela is swimming lazily. She stands on the smooth pebble bottom and walks out of the water, wet, sleek, supple. It's the dawn of the world.

A little later a pickup truck drives slowly down the road, honking its horn. A horde of sheep and goats come tumbling out of the hills at this signal, *baa*ing and clanging their bells. Feeding time! Far up the valley someone is burning trash.

Well, Angela has to be back to work in a couple of days, and so they have to start back home. Reluctantly they pack up. Jim takes a last walk over the site. He surveys the scene from his hilltop. Something about this place . . . "They're part of the land, it's not abandoned. The story's not over here. It'll go on as long as anything else." Humphrey honks. Time to go. "Ah, California. . . ."

46

. . . The first wave of American settlers trickled in by wagon from New Mexico, or came around the Horn in ships, or rode down from San Francisco after trying their luck in the gold rush. There weren't very many of them. The first new town, Anaheim, was begun by a small group of Germans determined to grow grapes for wine. They arrived from San Francisco in 1859, and there were only a hundred or two of them. The town was platted in the middle of open cattle range, and so they put up a willow pole fence that took root and became a living wall of trees, a rectangle with four gates in it, one on each side. They dug a ditch five miles long to obtain water from the Santa Ana River. And they grew grapes.

The other towns followed quickly after the partitioning of the great ranchos. When the ranchos were broken up and sold off, the new owners made advertisements to sell the land, and started towns from scratch.

Some of the landowners were interested in the new ideas of social organization circulating at the time, and several of the towns began as utopian efforts in communalism: the Germans in Anaheim were a cooperative, the Quakers helped to found El Modena on Society principles, Garden Grove began as a temperance community, and Westminster was a religious commune. Later the Polish group led by the Modjeskas settled in Anaheim and began a separate little utopia, although it fell apart almost at once. El Toro was founded by some English, who made it another outpost of the Empire, celebrating Queen Victoria's birthday and forming the first polo team in America: the British notion of utopia.

When the Southern Pacific Railroad extended from Los Angeles to Anaheim, a boom began that lasted through the 1870s. Santa Ana was founded, with lots sold at twenty to forty dollars apiece, when they weren't given away. Two years later there were fifty houses erected in the town. East of Santa Ana, Tustin was founded by Columbus Tustin, and the rivalry between the two new villages for the spur rail line from Anaheim was intense. When Santa Ana won the spur, Tustin was destined to remain a village for many years, while Santa Ana went on to become the county seat.

Orange was founded by Andrew Glassell and Alfred Chapman, two lawyers who were active in the rancho-partitioning lawsuits, thus becoming rich in both land and money. The town began with sixty ten-acre lots, surrounding a forty-acre townsite.

Southwest of these towns, on the coast, the lumbermen James and Robert McFadden built a landing that became an important point for shipping. The wharf was known as McFadden's Landing, and the town that grew around it was called Newport. The McFaddens had bought the land from the state for a dollar an acre.

Soon towns had sprung up everywhere across the county. In Laguna Beach because of the pretty bay. In El Modena because there was good land for vineyards, and the water from Santiago Creek. In Fullerton because the train line passed that way. And so on. Developers bought pieces of the ranchos, set out some streets, held a big party and brought out some of the crowds arriving in Los Angeles for a free lunch and a sales pitch. Sometimes it worked, sometimes it didn't. Towns like Yorba, Hewes Park, McPherson, Fairview, Olinda, Saint James, Atwood, Carlton, Catalina-on-the-Main, and Smeltzer, didn't last much longer then their opening days. Others, like Buena Park, Capistrano Beach, Villa Park, Placentia, Huntington Beach, Corona del Mar, and Costa Mesa, survived and grew.

In 1887 this growth was accelerated when the Santa Fe Railroad completed a line across the continent to Los Angeles and immediately began a rate war with the Southern Pacific, which had been the only line. Fares that had been $125 from Omaha plunged to a rate war special of $1 before leveling off at around $25 for a year or two. The trickle of settlers became a small flood, and sixty towns were founded in forty years.

The only area of Orange County that did not experience this blossoming of towns was the great landholding of James Irvine. Irvine came penniless from England to San Francisco during the gold rush, and engaged in land speculation in the city until he was rich. Then he and his partners moved to southern California, and they bought the entirety of the old Ranchos San Joaquín and Lomas de Santiago, which meant that, after Irvine bought out his partners, he owned one-fifth of all the land in Orange County, in a broad band that extended from the ocean far into the Santa Ana Mountains. His land crossed all the possible train routes from Los Angeles to San Diego, and he was powerful enough to hold off the Southern Pacific Railroad, which could be said of no one else in the state; his ranchers fought off forced efforts by the Southern Pacific construction crews to push a line through, and he granted permission of passage to the Santa Fe Railroad just so he could balk Southern Pacific for good.

The Irvine land itself was kept free of new towns, and after a decade or two of sheep ranching it was cultivated, in hay, wheat, oats, alfalfa, barley, and lima beans, and much later in orange groves. For a hundred years the marked distinction between the heavily developed northwestern half of Orange County, and the nearly empty southeastern half, was due to the 172 square miles of the Irvine Ranch, and Irvine and his heirs' policy of keeping the land free.

In 1889 the county of Orange was carved out of Los Angeles County. With the help of some money slipped to legislators in Sacramento, the border was set at Coyote Creek rather than the San Gabriel River, so that when it came time to choose the county seat, Santa Ana was more central and was chosen over Anaheim. Anaheim's citizens were very upset.

So the little towns grew, and the farms around them. Despite all the feverish land speculation and real estate development going on, the actual number of people involved was not great. The largest towns, Santa Ana and Anaheim, had populations of only a few thousand, and the newer towns were much smaller than that. Between each town were miles of open land, covered by farmland or the old range, head high in mustard. The roads were few, the little rail systems even fewer. Under the constant sun there was an ease to life that drew people from the east, but in small waves that grew very slowly in size. Publicists based in Los Angeles trumpeted the virtues of southern California; it was America's own Mediterranean, the golden land by the sea. The new orange groves contributed to that image, and orange growing was sold as a middle-class agriculture, more socially and aesthetically pleasing than the giant isolated wheat and corn farms of the Midwest. And perhaps it was so, at first; though many a man found himself working his grove and another job as well, to pay the grove off.

An American life of Mediterranean ease: perhaps. Perhaps. But there were disasters, too. There were floods; once it rained every day for a month, and the entire plain, from the mountains to the sea, was covered with water. All the new adobe buildings of Anaheim were melted back to mud. And once there was an outbreak of smallpox that finished off the last of the Indians at San Juan Capistrano, which remained as a silent remnant of the mission past. And the crops failed often; brought in from afar and usually planted in monocultural style, the grapes, the walnuts, and even the oranges suffered from blights that killed thousands and thousands of plants.

But by and large it was a peaceful life here, at the Victorian end of the frontier. Under the hot sun Americans from the East arrived and started up new lives, and most were happy with the results. The years passed and new settlers kept arriving and starting little towns; but it was a big land and they were accommodated without much change or sign of their arrival; they disappeared into the groves, and life went on.

The new century arrived, and the sun-drenched life by the sea fell into a pattern that it seemed would never end. In 1905 the young Walter Johnson, pitching for Fullerton High School, struck out all twenty-seven batters in a game with Santa Ana High. In 1911 Barney Oldfield raced his car with a plane, and won. In 1912 Glenn Martin flew a plane he had built himself from Newport to Catalina, the longest flight over water ever. In fact you could say that Martin began the aeronautics industry in Orange County, by building a plane in a barn. But no one could guess what would come of that kind of ingenuity, that pleasure taken in the possibilities of the mechanical. At that time it, like life itself, seemed a marvelous game, played in the midst of a prosperous, sunny peace.

And all that—and all that—and all of that—
All that went away.

47

Back in OC Jim can't shake a feeling of uneasiness. It's as if somewhere the program and the magnetic field keeping him on his particular track have been disarranged, fallen into some awful loop that keeps repeating over and over.

And in fact he falls into the habit of tracking about for several hours each day, all his free time spent in a big circle pattern on the freeways, Newport to Riverside to San Gabriel to San Diego to Santa Ana to Trabuco to Garden Grove to Newport, and so on.

While he stares out the window looking down at his hometown. Around and around the freeways he goes, stuck in a loop program that resembles a debugging search pattern caught by a bug itself. Software going bad.
Once he stops to cruise through South Coast Plaza.

Twelve department stores: Bullock's, Penney, Saks, Sears,
    KlothesAG, J. Magnin's, I. Magnin's, Ward's,
    Palazzo, Robinson's, Buffum's, Neiman-Marcus.
Three hundred smaller shops, restaurants, video theaters,
    game parlors, galleries . . .
A poem is a laundry list.
You wear your culture all over you.
Chrome, and thick pile carpets.
Mirrors everywhere, replicating the displays to infinity.
Is that an eye I see in there?
Escalators, elevators, half-floors of glass, fountains.
Lots of plants. Most are real, from the tropics. Hothouse
    blooms.
Spectrum bends, rack after rack after (mirrored) rack.
Entering Bullock's, Magnin's, Saks: thirteen counters of
    perfume each.
Perfume! Earrings, scarves, necklaces, nylons, stationery,
    chrome columns, blouse racks, sportswear, shoes—
You complete the list (every day).

Jim walks through this place untracked, his uneasiness bouncing back from every mirror, every glossy leaf and fabric. The memory of his night in Egypt is overlaid on his sight like the head's-up display of a fighter pilot's helmet. IR images in a faint green wash: of beggars in Cairo, too poor even to live in the jammed miserable tenements around them. How many people could live in a structure like SCP? The luxury surrounding him, he thinks, is a deliberate, bald-faced denial of the reality of the world. A group hallucination shared by everyone in America.
Jim wanders this maze, past the sleepwalkers and the security police, until he has to sit down. Disoriented, dizzy, he might even be sick. Some mall kids hanging out by the video rental window stare at him curiously, suspecting an OD. They're right about that, Jim thinks dully. I have ODed on South Coast Plaza. The kids

stand there hoping for some theatrics. Jim disappoints them by
getting up and walking out under his own power. His damaged
autopilot gets him through the maze of escalators and entry levels
to the parking lot, to his car.

He calls Arthur. "Please, Arthur, give me some work. Is
anything ready to go?"

"Yeah, as a matter of fact there is. Can you do it tonight?"

"Yes." And Jim feels immense relief that he can *act* on this
feeling of revulsion.

That night he joins Arthur enthusiastically as they stay up all
night to arrange a successful strike against Airspace Technology
Corporation, which makes parts for the orbiting nuclear reactors
that provide the old space-based chemical lasers with their power.
Off to the rendezvous at Lewis and Greentree, in the little warehouse parking lot; the same men load the boxes into Arthur's car;
and they're off to San Juan Hot Springs Industrial Park. Despite
security precautions that include fence-top heat-seeking missiles,
the strike succeeds; in Airspace Tech's main production plant, all
that was composite has fallen apart. . . .

But the next morning, back in his ap, exhausted to emptiness,
Jim has to admit that the operation hasn't changed all that much
for him. He's still sitting in his little ap under the freeway looking
around. Nothing in it soothes him. He's heard his music too often.
He's read all the books. The orange crate labels mock him. He's
looked at the maps till he knows them by heart, he's seen all the
videos, he's scanned every program in the history of the world.
His home is a trap, the complex and massively articulated trap of
his self. He has to escape; he looks around the dusty disorderly
room, with its treasured shaft of nine A.M. sunlight, and wonders
how he ever stood it.

The phone rings. It's Hana. "How are you?" she says.

"Okay! Hey, I'm glad you called! You want to come down
to my place for dinner tonight?"

"Sure."

And the flood of relief that fills him has other components in
it he can't tag so readily; it's the kind of pleasure he gets when
Tash or Abe give him a call to arrange something, the sense that
one of his good friends reciprocates his regard, and will actually

take the trouble to initiate a get-together, something that is usually left for Jim to do.

So he goes out and buys spaghetti and the materials for the sauce and a salad. A bottle of Chianti. Back home for some hapless, hopeless attempts to clean the place, or at least order it a little.

Hana shows up around seven.

"I'm really glad you called," Jim says, stirring the spaghetti sauce vigorously.

"Well, it's been a while." She's sitting at the kitchen table, staring past him at the floor, throwing her sentences out casually. Attack of shyness, it seems. Her black hair as tangled as ever.

"I—I think I'm losing it, somehow," Jim says, surprising them both. "This trip, it just reinforced everything I was feeling before!" And it all spills out of him in a rush, Hana glancing up now and then as he rattles on about Cairo and Crete and California. He mixes his account of them so that it must be impossible for her to figure out which place he's talking about, but she doesn't interrupt until a desperate edge tears his voice. Then she stands, briefly, puts a hand to his arm. This is so unlike her that Jim is struck dumb.

"I know what you mean," she says. "But look. Your dinner's almost ready, and you shouldn't eat when you're upset."

"I'd starve if I didn't."

But he pours the spaghetti into the colander with a wry grin, feeling a bit more relaxed already. There's something new floating in the steam between them, and he likes it. As they sit down to eat he goes and puts on one of his amalgamations of classical music, and they eat.

"What's the music?" Hana asks after a while.

"I've taken all the slow movements from Beethoven's five late string quartets, and also the slow movement from the *Hammerklavier* Sonata as the centerpiece. It has a very serene effect—"

"Wait a minute. You mean all these movements come from different quartets?"

"Yeah, but they're unified by a similar style and—"

She is laughing fit to burst. "What a terrible idea! Ha, ha, ha, ha! . . . Why did you do that?"

"Well." Jim thinks. "I found when I put on the late quartets I was usually doing it to hear the slow movements. It's for a mood I have that I like to, I don't know. Soundtrack, or reinforce, or transform into something higher."

"You've got to be kidding, Jim! You know perfectly well Beethoven would cringe at the very idea." She laughs at him. "Each quartet is a whole experience, right? You're cutting out all the other parts of them! Come on. Go put on one of them complete. Choose the one you like best."

"Well, that's not so easy," Jim says as he goes to the old CD console. "It's odd. Sullivan says in his book on Beethoven that opus 131 is by far the greatest of them, with its seven movements and the spacy opener and so on."

"Why should that matter to you?"

"What Sullivan says? Well, I don't know . . . I guess I get a lot of my ideas out of books. And Sullivan's is one of the best biographies in the world."

"And so you accepted his judgment."

"That's right. At first, anyway. But finally I admitted to myself that I prefer opus 132. Beethoven wrote it after recovering from a serious illness, and the slow movement is a thanksgiving."

"Okay, but let's hear the whole thing."

Jim sticks in the CD of the LaSalle Quartet performance, and they listen to it as they finish dinner. "How you could pass on this part?" Hana says during the final movement.

"I don't know."

After dinner she wanders his ap and looks at things. She inspects the framed orange crate labels with her nose about an inch from their surfaces. "These are really nice." In his bedroom she stops and laughs. "These maps! They're great! Where did you get them?"

Jim explains, happy to talk about them. Hana admires the Thomas Brothers' solution to the four-color map problem. Then she notices the video cameras in the corners where walls meet ceiling; she wrinkles her nose, shudders. Back into the living room, where she goes over the bookcase volume by volume, and they talk about the books, and all manner of things.

She notices the computer on Jim's battered old sixth-grade

desk, and the piles of printout beside it. "So is this the poetry, then? Do I get to read some?"

"Oh no, no," Jim says, rushing to the desk as if to hide the stuff. "I mean, not yet, anyway. I haven't got any of it in final form, and, well, you know. . . ."

Hana frowns, shrugs.

They sit on the bamboo-and-vinyl couch and talk about other matters. Then suddenly she's standing and looking at the floor. "Time to go, I have to work tomorrow." And she's off. Jim walks her to her car.

Back in his ap he looks around, sighs. There at the desk, all those feeble half-poems lying there, broken-backed and abandoned. . . . He compares his work habits to Hana's and he is ashamed of his laziness, his lack of discipline, his amateurishness. Waiting for inspiration—such nonsense. It really is stupid. He doesn't even like to think about his poetry anymore. He's an activist in the resistance, it's time for praxis now rather than words, and he only writes when he has the time, the inclination. It's different for him now.

But he doesn't really believe that. He knows it's laziness. And Hana—how is he ever going to show her any of his work? It just isn't good enough; he doesn't want her put off by his lack of talent. He's ashamed of it. He identifies the feeling and that makes him feel even worse. Isn't this his work, his real work?

48

The pace never slackens for Lucy McPherson; on the contrary, it seems there's a little more to do every day. One morning she wakes up alone. Dennis is off in Washington and Lucy's been up later than usual the night before watching the video, and now she's slept right through her alarm. Late from the word go. She hustles out without breakfast, down to the church, gets the office opened and starts the day's opening round of calls. The organizational routine ticks off fairly well. The fund-raising is more problematic. Then it's down to Leisure World for a too-brief visit with Tom. Tom looks worse than usual, complains of coming down with a cold. He listens to Lucy's associational rattle of news with his eyes, nodding occasionally.

"How's Jim?" he says.

"Okay, I guess. I haven't seen him much in the last month. He and Dennis . . ." She sighs. "Hasn't he been down to see you?"

"Not for a while."

"I'll tell him to come."

Tom smiles, eyes closed. He looks so old today, Lucy thinks. "Don't pester the boy, Lucy. I think he's having a hard time."

"Well, there's no reason for it. And no reason he can't come down here once in a while."

Tom shakes his head, smiles again. "I do enjoy it."

Then it's back on the freeway, to an early lunch with her study group. And back to the office, back to the fund-raising. Lillian comes in at two and they work together at it. Lucy was flagging, but now she picks up; it's more fun with Lillian there, someone to talk to.

"Well, he did it again," Lillian says after looking around conspiratorially.

"Reverend Strong?"

"Yep. Right at the end of class." Lillian is in the church's little confirmation class, which the reverend teaches on Thursday evenings.

"Better the end than the beginning."

Lillian laughs. "Less people listening, I know. But still, it isn't fair! It isn't the poor people's fault if they're poor, is it?"

"I don't think so," Lucy says slowly. She remembers Anastasia; got to visit her again next week. "Sometimes, though, you wonder. . . . Well, you can see where Reverend Strong gets his ideas."

Lillian nods. The lesson last week was based on the parable of the prodigal son. Why, the reverend demanded, should God value the prodigal son more than the one who had been faithful all along? This was clearly unfair, and the reverend spent over half an hour discussing the problems in the Greek text and the likelihood of a mistranslation from the original Armenian dialect. "So that by the end of it," Lillian says with a laugh, "he was basically saying that the Bible had got it backwards!"

"You're kidding."

"No. He said that it was the elder son who would always be God's favorite, for never having strayed away. The ones who stray can't be trusted, he said. You can forgive them but you can't trust them."

Lucy shakes her head. The parables—some of them are just too ambiguous. The prodigal son story never seemed quite fair to the elder son, it's true, and as for the parable of the talents . . . well, the way the reverend can *use* these stories! She finds it hard to think about them. And these are New Testament stories, too, the ones she has really committed herself to. The story of Job, and God and Satan betting over him—of Abraham and Isaac, and the faked sacrifice—she doesn't even try to understand those anymore. But Christ's parables . . . she's obliged to acknowledge the authority of them. Still, when the reverend can take the parable of the talents and use it to prove that the poor in OC are poor because it was meant to be . . . and imply that the church shouldn't waste its time trying to help them! Well, that was the reverend's fault, but the parable sure gave him room to run with it.

So Lucy and Lillian discuss strategies for getting around the reverend's biases. The programs that are already under way are the obvious channels to work through; keep the momentum going with those, and the fact that the reverend will never start another won't really matter. It's a question of fund-raising, of getting volunteer help, of going out there and working. Between them they should be able to do it.

There's only one problem; they need a new fund-raiser with all its funds tagged for the neighborhood poverty program, or it won't survive. It's the kind of thing Reverend Strong is sure to deny approval for. "I've got a plan," Lucy says. "See, it's me that the reverend is beginning to associate with these programs, and now it's getting so that every time I suggest something he turns it down. So what we should do, I think, is present the mail campaign idea as yours—something that you and the other people in the confirmation class thought up.''

''Sure!'' Lillian says, pleased at the subterfuge. ''In fact I can suggest it to the class, and then we can tell the reverend about it together!''

Lucy nods. ''That should work.''

They discuss the upcoming garage sale. ''I'll try again to get Jim to come and help,'' Lucy says, mostly to herself.

Lillian cocks her head curiously. ''Do Jim or Mr. McPherson ever come to church anymore?''

Lucy shakes her head, coloring a little. ''I tell them they should, but they don't listen to me. Dennis thinks he's too busy, I guess, and Jim has all sorts of reasons why it isn't a good idea. If he came and heard a sermon like the reverend's last one he'd go crazy. Even though he sounds like the reverend himself sometimes. But he just doesn't understand that the church isn't the individual people and their weaknesses. And it isn't the history, either. It's faith. And I guess he doesn't have that, at least right now.'' She sighs. ''I feel sorry for him. I suppose I'll talk to him again.''

''Maybe you can talk to them both together.''

''Just getting them together would be the problem.''

''Why's that?''

Lucy sighs. She doesn't like to talk about it, but . . . she's noticed already that what she says to Lillian stays with Lillian; even Emma doesn't hear it. And she needs to talk with *someone*. ''Well, they're not getting along. Dennis is tired of Jim not working in a better job, and Jim is mad at Dennis because of it. Or something like that. Anyway, they've had a couple of arguments, and now Jim isn't coming around anymore.''

''They need to talk to each other,'' Lillian says.

''Exactly! That's just what I say.''

A small smile from Lillian, but Lucy doesn't notice it. Lillian says, ''If I were you I'd try to get them together and talking again.''

''I have been, but it just isn't working.''

''You have to keep trying, Lucy.''

Lucy nods. ''You're right. I will.''

And that night she tries, to the extent she can with Dennis back in Washington. Well, it's simple enough; she needs to get

Jim up to dinner some time when Dennis is home. She gives Jim a call. "Hi, Jim? Mom here."

"Oh hi, Mom."

"How was the trip to Europe?"

"It was really interesting." He tells her briefly about it.

"It sounds like you had a good time. Listen, Jim, how about coming up for dinner next week? Dad will be back home then."

"Oh."

"Jim. Dad hasn't seen you for over two months, isn't that right? And it isn't right. He needs you just as much as you need him."

"Mom . . ."

"Don't Mom me. All these silly arguments, you should have more faith."

"What?"

"You'll come next week?"

"What?"

"I said, you'll come up next week for dinner?"

"I'll try, Mom. I'll think about it. But he's just going to think I'm leeching dinner from you guys again."

"Don't be ridiculous, Jim."

"I'm not!"

"You are. You're both too stubborn for your own good, and you're just hurting yourself by it. You come up here, you understand?"

"All right, Mom, don't get upset, okay? I'll . . . I'll try."

"Good."

They hang up. Lucy goes out to the video room, into the chair. The cat sits on her lap while she reads from next week's lesson. Paul's letter to the Ephesians, the verses swimming into double focus as she tries to stay awake and concentrate on them. On the screen a hot-air balloon is floating over a snowy peak, in a dark blue sky. The verses are floating about, big and black on the white page . . . She jerks to, finds it's after midnight. She's been sleeping in the chair, the Bible open on her lap. She lifts the cat off, gets up stiffly to go to bed.

49

Hana's too busy to see Jim for several nights running, and he goes down to Sandy's party depressed. She's working, he's not. What must she think of him?

At Sandy's he stands leaning against the balcony wall, watching cars flow through the great interchange pretzel of the five freeways. Something to stare at for hours.

Suddenly there's Humphrey's younger sister Debbie Riggs, standing beside him and elbowing his arm to get his attention. "Oh hi, Debbie! How are you?" He hasn't seen her in a while. They're good friends, they've known each other since junior high; in years past she's been sort of a sister to him, he thinks.

"I'm fine, Jimbo. You?"

"Okay, okay. Pretty good, really."

They chat for a bit about what they've been up to. Same things. But there's something bugging her. Debbie is one of the most straightforward people that Jim knows; if she's irritated with you she just comes right out with it.

And she's a good friend of Sheila Mayer's.

So without too much delay it bursts out of her. "Jim, just what did you think you were doing about Sheila? I mean, you guys were allies for over four months, and then one day, wham, not a visit not a call! What kind of behavior is that?"

"Well," Jim says uncomfortably. "I tried to call—"

"Bullshit! Bullshit! If you want to call someone you can get through to them, you know that. You can leave a message! There's no way you tried to call her." She points a finger at him accu-

satively and anger makes her voice harsh: "You screwed her, Jim!
You fucked her over!"

Jim hangs his head. "I know."

"You don't know! I visited her after you suddenly disappeared
out of her life, and I found her sitting in her living room, putting
together one of Humphrey's jigsaw puzzles, one of those ten-
thousand-piece ones. That's all she would do! And when she was
done with that one she went out and bought some more, and she
came back home and that's all she did was sit there in her living
room and put together those stupid fucking jigsaw puzzles, for a
whole month!"

Eyes flashing, face flushed, relentlessly she holds Jim's gaze:
"And you did that to her, Jim! You did that to her."

Long pause.

Jim's throat is constricted shut. He can't take his eyes from
Debbie. He nods jerkily. The corners of his mouth are tight. "I
know," he gets out.

She sees that he has gotten it, that he sees the image of Sheila
at that coffee table, understands what it means. Her expression
shifts, then; he can see that she's still his friend, even when she's
furious with him. Somehow that makes the anger more impossible
to deny. And even though he's gotten it, Debbie is so angry that
that isn't, at the moment, quite enough. Perhaps she has thought
it would mean more to her. Jim can see her remembering the sight
herself; her friend studiously sifting through the pieces, focusing
on them, not letting her attention stray anywhere else; suddenly
Debbie's blinking rapidly, and abruptly she turns and walks off.
And he sees the image better than ever; it's burned into him by
Debbie Riggs's distress.

"Oh, man," he says. He turns and leans on the balcony rail.
Headlights and taillights swim through the night. He feels like he's
swallowed one of the flower pots by his elbow: giant weight in
his stomach, tasting like dirt.

Jigsaw puzzles.

Why did he do it?

For Virginia Novello. But what about Sheila? Well, Jim didn't
think of her. He didn't really believe that he mattered enough that
anyone would care about him. Or he didn't really believe in the

reality of other people's feelings. Of Sheila Mayer's feelings. Because they got in the way of what he wanted to do.

He sees these reasons clearly for the first time, and disgust washes over him in a great wave.

Suddenly he sees himself from the outside, he escapes the viewpoint of consciousness and there's Jim McPherson, no longer the invisible center of the universe, but one of a group of friends and acquaintances. A physical person out there just like everyone else, to be interacted with, to be judged! It's a dizzying, almost nauseating experience, a physical shock. Out of body, look back, there's this skinny intense guy, a hollow man with nothing inside to define him by—defined by his fashionable ally and his fashionable beliefs and his fashionable clothes and his fashionable habits, so that the people who care about him—Sheila—

Empty staring at a jigsaw puzzle. Concentrate on it. The headlights all blur out.

50

Stewart Lemon's sitting at his desk, in a reverie. It's been another miserable morning, Elsa keeping up the silent treatment and walking around the house mute, like a naked zombie . . . how long has it been since she stopped speaking? Lemon sits and dreams of leaving her for his secretary, starting a new alliance, free of such a long history of pain. But if he leaves he'll lose the house. And doesn't Ramona have an ally? Ah, it's a fantasy; looked at realistically it falls apart. So that means he has to continue with Elsa. . . .

Ramona buzzes. Donald Hereford is in Los Angeles on Argo/Blessman business, and has decided to drop on down for a visit. He'll be here in half an hour.

Lemon groans. What a day! It's always tense for him when Hereford comes by, especially lately. Given the various troubles

LSR is having, the visits can only be in the nature of judgments
—check-ups to see whether Argo/Blessman's aerospace subsidiary
is worth keeping. . . . This is even more true when there is no
specific reason for the visit, as in this case.

So as much as he tries to compose himself, he is nervous as
Hereford arrives. He leads him into his office and they sit down.
Hereford looks at the ocean as he listens to Lemon go over the
latest on the various LSR projects of note.

"How's the appeal of the Stormbee decision coming?"

"The court rules on it end of this week or the beginning of
next. Did you see the GAO report?" Hereford shakes his head
briefly. Lemon describes the report. "It's pretty favorable," he
concludes, "but our lawyers can't tell if it will be enough to sway
Judge Tobiason. They think it should, but given Tobiason's back-
ground they aren't making any promises."

"No." Hereford sighs. "I wonder about that case."

"Whether it was . . ." Lemon was going to say, "a good
idea to protest the decision," when he recalls that it was Hereford's
idea.

Hereford looks up at him from under mildly raised eyebrows,
and laughs. "A good idea? I think so. We had to show the Air
Force that they can't just flaunt the rules and walk over us. But
we've done that, now, I think. They've had to kowtow to the GAO
pretty seriously. So that whatever Tobiason says, we may have
accomplished our goals in the matter."

"But—winning the contract?"

"Do you think the Air Force would ever allow that, now?"
Lemon considers it in silence.

Hereford says, "Tell me all the latest about the Ball Lightning
program."

Now it's Lemon's turn to sigh. In a matter-of-fact voice he
describes the latest round of troubles the program has been ex-
periencing. "McPherson has put them onto tracking the ICBMs
longer, in a phased array, so that their defenses can be overcome,
and it looks as promising as anything we've tried. But the Air
Force specs don't really allow for anything more than the first two
minutes after launch, so we don't know what they'll make of this."

"You have asked them?"

"Not yet."

Hereford frowns. "Now the Air Force already has test results that show we could do it in the two minutes, right?"

"Under certain special circumstances, yes."

"Which are?"

"Well, a stationary target, mainly. . . ."

Slowly and patiently Hereford drags the whole story out of Lemon. He gets Lemon to admit that the early test results reported by Dan Houston's team could be interpreted as fraudulent if the Air Force wanted to get hard about it. And since LSR has gotten hard in the Stormbee matter. . . .

Lemon, squirming in his seat, gets the strong impression that Hereford already knew all these details, that he has been making him go through them again just to bake him a little. Lemon tries to relax.

"McPherson's involved with this one too?"

"I assigned him to it to help Houston out. McPherson is a good troubleshooter." And troublemaker, he thinks. Don't the two always go together?

Hereford nods. "I want to see the on-site facilities for the Ball Lightning program." He stands. Lemon gets to his feet, surprised. They walk to the elevator, take it down to the ground floor and leave the executive building. Over to the engineer's offices, and the big building housing the labs and the assembly plant. It's your typical Irvine Triangle industrial architecture: two stories high and a couple hundred yards to a side, the walls made of immense squares of coppery mirrored glass, reflecting the obligatory lawns and cypress trees.

They enter and Lemon leads Hereford, by request, through all the labs and assembly rooms that have any part in the Ball Lightning program. Hereford doesn't really look at any single one very closely, but he seems interested in determining their locations in the building, strangely enough. When he's done doing that, he wants to survey the grounds outside the plant: the picnic benches in the small groves of cypress, the high security fence surrounding the property . . . it's strange. Lemon's beginning to get a headache thinking about it, out in the bright sun, coffee wearing off, stomach growling. . . . Finally Hereford nods. "Let's go have some lunch."

Orange County just can't provide the kind of culinary sophistication that Manhattan boasts, which is galling to Lemon when

he has to try to impress Hereford. He takes him down to Dana
Point, and they eat at the Charthouse over the harbor. Hereford
concentrates on the salad bar, eats with obvious relish. "They still
can't do this properly in New York, I'm not sure why." A couple
of young women in bathing suits sit at the next table, and Lemon
says, "Yes, there are certain advantages to living in California."
Hereford smiles briefly.

When they're done eating Hereford asks, "So what do you
make of this rash of sabotages against defense contractors in this
area?"

Ah ha. Here might be the explanation for the inspection of
the grounds. Lemon says, "Our security thinks it's a local group
of refusniks, and they're working with the police on it. Apparently
they won't attack any place where there are people working, because they don't want to kill or injure anyone. So we've taken the
precaution of having several night watchmen in the plant, as well
as people patrolling the perimeter of the grounds, and the beach
below us. And we announced the fact at a press conference—it
was pretty well reported."

Hereford is disturbed by this. "You mean you're assuming
these saboteurs won't make a mistake, or change their policy? If
it is indeed their policy?"

"Well . . ."

Hereford shakes his head. "Get all the night watchmen out
of the building."

"But—"

"You heard me. The risk is too great. I don't like the idea
of using people's lives as a shield, not when we're dealing with
an unknown enemy." He pauses, purses his lips. "The truth is,
we've got reason to believe that the sabotage out here is backed
by a very large, very professional group."

Lemon raises his eyebrows in unconscious imitation of Hereford. "Not the Soviets!"

"No no. Not directly, anyway. The truth is it may be one of
our competitors, providing the money, anyway."

Lemon's eyebrows shoot up for real. "Which one?"

"We're not sure. We've penetrated the organization on a
lower level, and naturally the links between levels are well concealed."

"I suppose it would have to be one of the companies that hasn't been hit."

"Not necessarily."

Now, this statement turns certain tumblers in Lemon's mind. He's silent for a time as he considers the implications of what Hereford has said. A company attacks others to harm their work and eventually damage their reputation for efficiency with the Air Force. Then it attacks itself to keep suspicion away from it. And, at the same time, it could use the attack on itself to get rid of something potentially damaging in and of itself. Sure, it makes sense.

But say another company learned it was going to be attacked; and say it had something, say it had a program that was in really serious trouble for one reason or another. . . .

"Should we increase our security on the perimeter?" Lemon asks, testing his hypothesis.

"No reason to." Around Hereford's eyes there is an amused crinkle; perhaps he thinks that Lemon is dense, perhaps he is amused that Lemon has finally gotten it; no way of telling. "We've done what we can, I think. Our insurance is in good shape, and all we can do is hope for the best."

"And . . . and get the night watchmen out of there."

"Exactly."

"Do you . . . do you have any information that indicates we might become . . ."

"A target?" Hereford shrugs. This goes too far, it shouldn't be talked about. "Nothing definite enough to go to the police with." But his eyes, Lemon thinks, his eyes; they look through the map of the Caribbean on their table, and they know. They know.

Lemon sits back in his seat, sips at his Pinot blanc. He's been let in on it, really. If he's smart enough to put it together, then he's in the know. Maybe he had to be. Still, it's a good sign.

And this means that maybe, just maybe, something will happen soon that will get him off the hook with the Ball Lightning program. Get LSR off the hook as well. And insurance . . . incredible. He swallows the wine.

51

Back at work in the First American Title Insurance and Real Estate Company, back at work in his night classes, Jim finds he cannot keep Sheila Mayer and her jigsaw puzzles from his mind. Now it's the principal element of the uneasiness that oppresses him. And he can't escape it.

Hana is still working hard, she has no time. Hana is working, he is not.

Finally, impelled to it, he sits at his computer and stares at the screen. He's got to work, to really work, he's *got to*. Tonight it's as much an escape from his life, from his uneasiness, as anything else. But any motive will do at this point.

He thinks about his poetry. He considers the poetry of his time. The thing is, he doesn't like the poetry of his time. Flashy, deliberately ignorant, concerned only with surfaces, with the look, the great California image, reflected in mirrors a million times. . . . It's postmodernism, the tired end of postmodernism, which makes utterly useless all his culturevulturing, because for postmodernism there is no past. Any mall zombie can write postmodern literature, and in fact as far as Jim can tell from the video interviews, that's who is writing it. No, no, no. He refuses. He can't do that anymore.

And yet this is his time, his moment; what else can he write about but now? He lives in a postmodern world, there is no way out of that.

Two of the writers most important to Jim wrote about this matter of one's subject. Albert Camus, and then Athol Fugard, echoing Camus—both said that it was one's job to be a *witness* to one's times. That was the writer's crucial, central function.

Camus and the Second World War, then the subjugation of Algeria—Fugard and apartheid in South Africa: they lived in miserable times, in some ways, but by God it gave them something to write about! They had something to witness!

While Jim—Jim lives in the richest country of all time, what's happening man, nothing's happening man. . . . Jack-in-the-Box is faster than McDonald's!

My Lord, what a place to have to be a witness to.

But how did it get this way?

Hmm. Jim mulls that over. It isn't really clear, yet; but something in that question seems to suggest a possible avenue of action for him. An approach.

But that brings up a second problem: it's all been done before.

It's like when his English teacher at Cal State Fullerton told the class to go out and write a poem about autumn. Great, Jim thought at the time. First of all, we live in Orange County—what is autumn to us? Football season. Wetsuits for surfing. Like that. He's read that Brahms's Third Symphony is autumnal, he's read that the rhythms of the Book of Psalms are autumnal—okay, so what's autumn? Brahms's Third Symphony! The Book of Psalms! That's the kind of circles you run in, when the natural world is gone. Okay, take those fragments and try to make something of it.

> I listen to Brahms
> And watch the Rams
> I read from Psalms
> We are only lambs
> Putting on our wetsuits
> To surf the autumn waves.

Hey, pretty good! But then the professor gets out "To Autumn" by John Keats, and reads it aloud. Oh. Well. Take your poem and eat it. In fact scratch that topic entirely, it's been done before to perfection. Well fine! Ain't no such topic in OC anyway!

The trouble is that if you start that process you quickly find that every topic in the world goes out the window the same way. It's either been covered to the max by the great writers of the past, or else it doesn't exist in OC. Usually both.

Be a witness to what you see. Be a witness to the life you live. To the lives we live.

And why, why, why? How did it get this way?

Back to that again. All right. Make that the orientation point, Jim thinks, the organizing principle, the Newport Freeway of your writing method. He thinks of *In the American Grain*, by William Carlos Williams. Williams's book is a collection of prose meditations on various figures of American history, explaining it all with that fine poet's eye and tongue. Of course Jim can't duplicate that book: he doesn't have any more writing ability than Williams had in his little fingernail. Every time WCW cut his fingernails, Jim thinks, he lopped off ten times more talent than I will ever have, and wrapped it in newspaper and tossed it in the wastebasket. He giggles at the thought. Somehow it makes him feel freer.

Duplication isn't the problem, anyway. It's OC Jim is concerned with, Orange County, the ultimate expression of the American Dream. And there aren't any great individuals in OC's history, that's part of what OC means, what it is. So he couldn't follow Williams's program even if he wanted to.

But it gives him a clue. Collectively they made this place. And so it has a history. And tracing this history might help to explain it, which is more important to Jim, now, than just witnessing. How it got to its present state: "The Sleepwalkers and How We Came to Be." He laughs again.

If he did something like that, if he made that his orienting point, then all his books, his culturevulturing, his obsession with the past—all that could be put to use. He recalls Walter Jackson Bate's beautiful biography of Samuel Johnson, the point in it where Bate speaks of Johnson's ultimate test for literature, the most important question: Can it be turned to use? When you read a book, and go back out into the world: *can it be turned to use?*

How did it get this way?

Well, it's a starting point. A Newport Freeway. You can get anywhere from the Newport Freeway. . . .

52

How did it happen?

It was World War Two that began the change, World War Two that set the pattern.

After Pearl Harbor the two thousand Orange County citizens of Japanese origin were gathered up and relocated in a shabby desert camp in Poston, Arizona. And people poured west to wage war. President Roosevelt called for the construction of fifty thousand planes a year, and the little airplane factories in Los Angeles and Orange had room to grow, they had empty farmland around them, every one. Thus the aeronautics industry in southern California had its start.

And the soldiers and sailors came west. They saw Orange County, and it looked just like the labels on the orange crates back home: the broad flat plain, covered with orange trees in their symmetrical rows; long lines of towering eucalyptus trees breaking the land into immense squares; the bare foothills behind, and the snowy mountains behind them; the wide, sandy, empty beaches down at Newport and Corona del Mar; the little bungalows tucked in their gardens, under the grapevine bowers, nestled each in an orange grove all its own.

There were only a hundred and thirty thousand people in all the county, lost in the millions of trees. City boys from the East, farmers from the cold Midwest and the poor South, all children of the Depression—they came out and saw the dream, the Mediterranean vision of a rich and easeful agricultural life, under an eternal sun. They went to the beach on Christmas day. They laughed punch-drunk in warm salt waves. They drove old

Fords down the country roads, flashing through the ranked shadows of the eucalyptus trees, drinking beer and laughing with local girls and breathing in the thick scent of the orange blossoms, in the bright sun of February. And they said: When this war is over, I'm coming back here to make my home.

There was land, empty farmland, that the military could use. And people were happy to see the military there, it meant good business. Patriotism, good business: the equation took root in Orange County, beginning with this war. The Santa Ana City Council, for instance, rented four hundred acres of the Berry ranch, for $6,386 a year, then turned around and rented the land to the War Department for a dollar a year, inviting the department to use the land for whatever they liked. It was patriotic, it was good business. The War Department made the ranch into the Santa Ana Army Air Base, and through the war 110,000 men trained there. They saw the land.

Next to the air base was established the Army Air Forces Flying Training Command, the "University of the Air." Sixty-six thousand pilots got their wings there. They all saw the land.

The Navy established one U.S. Naval Air Station at Los Alamitos, and another in Tustin, to house its blimps. It dredged the harbor at Seal Beach, and relocated two thousand residents, and established the U.S. Naval Ammunition and Net Depot, at a cost of $17 million—all of it paid to the local construction industry.

Groves in El Toro were torn out to make room for the U.S. Marine Corps Air Station, El Toro, one of the biggest in the country.

Orange County Airport became the Santa Ana Army Airdrome. Irvine Park became Camp George E. Rathke, infantry training center. And through all of these military bases poured the men, and the money.

So much of the population was directed to the war effort that not enough were left over to farm. Mexican braceros were brought in to pick the oranges. German POWs were brought in to pick the oranges. A group of Jamaicans were brought in to pick the oranges. ("These Negroes have Oxford accents!" a resident said.)

But the soldiers, the sailors, the fliers, the airplane factory workers, they all served the war. Orange County became part of a war machine; and this military-industrial infrastructure was built, and left in place, and it provided work for the thousands of men who returned after the war, with their new families; they came, and bought houses built by the construction industry that had been so well primed by military construction, and they went to work. In the 1950s the Santa Ana Freeway was extended down into Orange County from Los Angeles, and then you could work in L.A. but live in Orange County; like the coming of the railroad, like all the other improvements in the efficiency of transportation, it fueled the boom, and the military-industrial machine grew again. And so the machine served the Korean War, and the Cold War, and the Vietnam War, and the Cold War, and the Central American War, and the Cold War, and the African War, and the Cold War, and the Indonesian War, and the Cold War, and the Space War . . . a war machine, ever growing.

And none of that ever went away.

53

Sandy's return from Europe is a bit hectic. His answering machine goes on for two and a half hours, at a minute maximum per message. It seems that half the messages are from Bob Tompkins, too. So he calls Bob. "Hi, Bob, Sandy here."

"Ah, Sandy! You're back!"

"Yeah, I decided to, to—"

"To let things cool down a little, eh Sandy? Well, it worked."

Bob laughs, and Sandy nods to himself. It did indeed work. Talking to Bob on the day he got the news would have been blistering.

"You shouldn't worry so much about things, Sandy. I mean when I first got your message I was upset, sure, but it didn't take me a week to get over it, for Christ's sake! I mean when you've got the Coast Guard breathing down your neck, what else can you do? You could have dumped those barrels over the side, right? So just the fact that we might be able to recover them is a big plus. Listen, if you can liberate that stuff, there'll be a bonus in it for you, for duty above and beyond the call.''

"That's great, Bob, I'm glad you feel that way about it. But there's a certain problem with where we stashed the stuff. We just picked the nearest isolated spot on the coast, you know, and dumped them in a bunch of boulders. But then we noticed that the buildings for Laguna Space Research were on the top of the bluff above us. And they've just announced an increase in security around their facility, because of the recent sabotages. Including a watch against boats landing.''

"Ah ha. That is a problem. So . . . this company is a defense contractor, then?''

"Yeah.''

"I see.'' Long pause. "Okay, well listen Sandy, we'll have to figure something out to help you, then. I'll get back to you on this, okay? Meanwhile just let it ride.''

Fine with Sandy. He's free to concentrate on some heavy-duty dealing. He's got quite a bit of ground to make up, and so for the next few days he goes into overdrive, working sixteen, sometimes eighteen hours each day, to the point where he has to put some serious effort into supply as well as sales. Angela, who sees the need, is doing overtime herself taking care of him and the ap and their meals and the nightly party, which has regained its momentum in the days since their return. The constant running around in traffic, keeping track of handshake deals, doing the bookkeeping in the head, all over a ground base of massive drug intake, is exhausting in the extreme. In fact he's finding it hard to come home at night and really enjoy the party.

"Wow, burnout,'' he says to Angela.

"Why don't you take tomorrow night off. In the long run it'll help you keep this pace.''

"Good idea.''

So the next night he comes home early, around eleven, and corrals Abe, Tashi, and Jim. "Hey you guys, let's cruise.''

The others like the idea. They get in Sandy's big car and track onto Newport Freeway north. Sandy programs a loop into the car: Newport Freeway north, Riverside west, Orange south, Garden Grove east, and then north on the Newport again: it's upper level all the way in each of these directions, so that it's like going for a little plane ride on autopia, with the great lightshow and all the other cars and their passengers for entertainment.

They started doing this together on the wrestling team, when they first got driver's licenses. Starving and thirsty high school kids, trying to make weight, or celebrating the end of the weekly necessity to make weight by pigging out. . . . Tonight there's a strongly nostalgic feeling about it; they're cruising the freeways, a basic OC activity. How could they have lost the habit?

Sandy is driving, Abe's in the front passenger seat, Jim is behind Abe, Tash behind Sandy. The first order of business is to deploy a few eyedroppers, in fact there's a sort of synergistic capacity upgrade when these four get together like this, and they really drown their eyes, according to long-standing tradition.

"Nothing like coming down to the old club and settling in," Jim says blissfully. "The lightshow is good tonight, isn't it? Look there, you can see in the pattern of the streetlights, the original plattings for the first towns in the area. See the really tight squares of streetlights are the oldest towns, when the platting was into really small blocks. There's Fullerton . . . there's Anaheim, the oldest . . . pretty soon we'll see Orange . . . and in between the pattern stretches way out, see? Longer blocks and twisty housing tracts."

"Yeah, I see it!" Sandy says, surprised. "I never noticed that before, but it's there."

"Yep," Jim says, proudly. He goes rattling on about real estate history, which his employer First American Title Insurance and Real Estate has all the records for; then about First American and Humphrey's attempt to build his office building on the land of the dismembered Cleveland National Forest; then about a new computer system that the company has installed in the offices, very advanced, "I mean you really can talk to it, not just simple commands but really complicated stuff, it's like the real beginning of the man-computer interface, and it's really going to mean a lot for," and then suddenly all three of his friends have turned to stare Jim in the face.

He comes to a halt and Sandy giggles. Abe, shaking his head, says in a pitying, exasperated voice: "Jim, no one gives a fuck about computers."

"Ah. Yes. Well. You know." And Jim starts to giggle himself. Must have been an eyedropper of Funny Bone, that last unmarked one.

Abe is pointing down at the Orange Mall. "Sandy, did you ever tell these guys about the time we were in the parking garage there?"

"No, don't think I did," Sandy says, grinning.

Abe turns to the two in the backseat. "We were leaving the mall and driving out of the big parking garage they have, you know, the thirty-story one, and we're following the arrows down the ramps from floor to floor, and it's not a simple spiral staircase situation at all, they've got it screwed up and you have to go to successive corners of each floor to get down, or something like that. So here we are following the arrows down, and Sandy's eyes do their bug-out-of-his-head thing, you know?"

Tashi and Jim nod, imitating the look in tandem.

"Exactly." Abe laughs. "And he says, 'You know, Abraham, if it weren't for these arrows . . .' and I say uh-huh, yeah, what? And he says, 'Stop the car! Wait a minute! Stop the car, I forgot something!' So I sit there while he goes back in the mall, and then he comes running back out with two big cans of paint— one can white, one a gray the color of the garage floors. And two brushes. 'We'll start at the bottom,' he says, 'and no one will ever escape.' "

"*Ahhh*, hahaha."

"The labyrinth without the thread," Jim says.

"You aren't kidding! I mean, think about it! So we drive around and at every arrow Sandy jumps out and quick paints over the old one and puts a new one down, pointing in a new direction—not necessarily the opposite direction, just a new one. And finally we reach the top floor. Already we can hear the honking and the cursing and all from the floors below. And then Sandy turns to me with this puzzled expression, and says, 'Hey, Abe— how are we going to get out of here?' "

Sandy's manic laugh dominates the rest.

They're tracking south on the Orange Freeway, coming to the giant interchange with the Santa Ana and the Garden Grove freeways—another immense pretzel of concrete ribbons flying through the air, lightly buttressed on concrete pillars. Their change to the Garden Grove east will take them right through the middle of the knot. Great views over Santa Ana to the south, then Orange to the north; just names in the continuum of the lightshow, but given what Jim has said about the pattern of the streetlights, interesting to observe.

Tashi rises up like he's achieved enlightenment, and speaks the message from the cosmos: "There are only four streets in OC."

"What?" cries Abe. "Look around you, man!"

"Platonic forms," Jim says, understanding. "Ideal types."

"Only four." Tash nods. "First there's the freeways."

"Okay. I'll grant you that."

"Then there's the commercial streets, big ones with parking lots flanking them and all the businesses behind the parking lots, or on them. Like Tustin Avenue, right down there." He points north.

"Or Chapman." "Or Bristol." "Or Garbage Grove Boulevard." "Or Beach." "Or First." "Or MacArthur." "Or Westminster." "Or Katella." "Or Harbor." "Or Brookhurst."

"Yeah yeah yeah!" Tashi interrupts them. "Point proven! There are many commercial streets in OC. But they all are one."

"I wonder," Sandy says dreamily, "if you blindfolded someone and spun them around to disorient them, then took off the blindfold somewhere on one of the commercial streets, how long it would take them to identify it?"

"Forever," Tash opines. "They're indistinguishable. I think they made a one-mile unit and then just reproduced it five hundred times."

"It would be a challenge," Sandy muses. "A sort of game."

"Not tonight," Abe says.

"No?"

"No."

"The third kind of street," Tashi forges on, "is the residential street, class A. The suburban streets of the housing tracts. Please don't start naming examples, there are ten zillion."

"I like the cute curly ones in Mission Viejo," Sandy says.

"Or the old cul-de-sac exclusive models," Jim adds.

"And the fourth type?" says Abe.

"Residential street, class B. The urban ap streets, like down there in Santa Ana."

"A lot of that's original platting," Jim says. "Now it's as close to slums as we've got."

"As close to slums?" Abe repeats. "Man, they're there."

"I guess you're right."

"There's a fifth kind of street," Sandy announces.

"You think so?" Tash asks, interested.

"Yeah. I guess you could call it the street-freeway. It's a street, but there's nothing facing it at all—it's backed by housing-development walls, mostly, and there's no shops, no pedestrians—"

"Well, none of them have pedestrians."

"True, but I mean even less than usual. They're just avenues for tracking fast where there aren't freeways."

"Negative numbers of pedestrians?"

"Yeah, we use those a lot," Abe says. "Like Fairhaven, or Olive, or Edinger."

"Exactly," Sandy says.

"Okay," Tash agrees. "We'll make it five. There are five streets in OC."

"Do you think it's because of zoning laws?" Jim asks. "I mean, why is that?"

"More use habits than zoning, I'd bet," Tash says. "Stores like to be together, housing developments are built in group lots, that kind of thing."

"Each street has a history," Jim says, staring out the window with his mouth hanging open. "My God!"

"Better get writing, Jim. . . ."

"Speaking of streets and history," Sandy says, "I was driving east on the Garden Grove on a really clear morning a few weeks ago, first morning of a Santa Ana wind, you know? You could see Baldy and Arrowhead and everything. And the sun was just up, and I looked north to where the old Orange Plaza used to be —a little west of that, I'd guess. And I couldn't believe my eyes! I mean, down there I suddenly saw this street that I'd never seen before, and it had really tall skinny palm trees on one side of it, and the street surface was like white concrete, wider than usual, and the houses on each side were solo houses with yards, little bungalows with enclosed porches and grass lawns, and sidewalks and *everything*! I mean it was like one of those old photos from the 1930s or something!''

Jim is bouncing in his seat with excitement, leaning over into the front. ''Where, where, where, where!''

''Well, that's the thing—I don't know! I was so surprised that I got off at the next exit and tracked on over to take a look for it. I thought you'd be interested, and I even thought I might want to buy a house there if I could, it looked so . . . So I tracked around for about a half hour looking for it, and I couldn't find it! Couldn't even find the palm trees! Since then every time I drive that stretch I look for it, but it just *isn't there*.''

''Whoah.''

''Heavy.''

''I know. I figure it had something to do with the light or something. Or maybe a time warp. . . .''

''Oh, man.'' Jim hops up and down on his seat, thinking about it. ''I want to find that.''

They track some more. In the cars around them other people live their lives. Occasionally they track by freeway parties, several cars hooked together, people passing things between them, music all the same from every car.

''Let's fuel up,'' Tashi says. ''I'm hungry.''

''Let's swing into one of the drive-thrus,'' Sandy says, ''so we don't have to leave the loop. Which shall it be?''

''Jack-in-the-Box,'' says Abe.

''McDonald's,'' says Jim.

''Burger King,'' says Tashi.

''Which one?'' Sandy shouts as they pass one of the drive-thru complex offramps. The others all shout their choices and Tash reaches over Sandy's shoulder for the steering switch. Abe and Jim grab his arm and try to move it, and the struggle begins. Shouts, curses, wrestling holds, karate chops: finally Sandy cries, ''Taste test! Taste test!'' The others subside. ''We'll try all of them.''

And so he gets off at the Lincoln exit in Orange and they drive-thru the Burger King and the Jack's, stopping briefly to order pay and collect from the little windows on the upper level; then around the bend to the Kraemer exit in Placentia, for Jim's Big Macs.

"See, look. The Burger King Whopper has indisputably got the best meat. Check it out."

"Isn't that some kind of bug there, Tash?"

"No! Let's look at yours if you dare, you know they make those Big Macs out of petroleum byproducts."

"They do not! In fact they won the slander case in court on that!"

"Lawyers. Look at that meat, it's sludge!"

"Well, it's better than the double Jack Abe's got, anyway."

"Sure, but that's saying nothing."

"Hey," says Abe. "The Jack's are adequate, and look here at the malt and fries you get at Jack's. Both absolutely unmatchable. Burger King malts are made of air, and McDonald's malts are made of styrofoam. You only get a real ice-cream malt at Jack's."

"Malt? Malt? You don't even know what malt tastes like! There hasn't been malt in this country since before the millennium! Those are shakes, and the McShake is just fine. Orange-flavored, even."

"Come on, Jim, we're trying to eat here. Don't make me puke."

"And the McFries are also the best. Those Jackfries, you could inject drugs with those things."

"Ho, Mr. Get Tough! Your fries are actually shot puts in disguise! Get serious!"

"I am serious! Here, Sandy, you be judge. Eat this, here."

"No, Sandy, mine first! Eat this!"

"Mmff mmff mmff."

"See, he likes mine better!"

"No, he just said Burger Whop, didn't you hear him?"

Sandy swallows. "They taste the same."

"What kind of a judge are you?"

Abe says, "Best malt—"

"Shake! Shake! No such thing as malt! Mythical substance!"

"Best malt, best fries, perfectly standard burger."

"In other words the burger is disgusting," Tashi says. "There's no fighting it, the basis of the American body is the hamburger, the rest is just frills. And Burger King has the best burger by miles. And so there you have it.''

"All right," Sandy says. "Tashi, give me the patty out of yours."

"What? No way!"

"Yeah, come on. There's only half left anyway, right? Give it to me. Now Abe, give me the bun with the secret sauce. Not the other one, that's blank! *Ahhh*, hahahahahahaha, what a burger, Jesus, give me the secret sauce. Jim, hand over that smidgin of lettuce, right, okay, and the ketchup in its convenient poison-proofed pill-sized container. Fine, fine. Abe, hand over the malt. Yeah, you win! Hand it over. The fries, hmm, well, let's just mess them all together here, on the seat here, that's okay. Where'd that ketchup go? Slip down the straw, did it? Squirt it on there, Abe, and watch out you don't get it all on one fry. Right. There we have it, bros. Le Grand Compromis, the greatest American meal of all time! Fantastic! Dig in!''

"Whoah."

"Think I've lost my appetite, here. . . . ''

When they're done eating, Sandy takes over the controls and turns them back toward home. It's late, he's got another full day tomorrow.

They track down the Newport Freeway, on the underlevel, the adscreens hanging from the underside of the upper level, flashing over them is a colorful subliminal parade of words, images, images, words. BUY! NEW! LOOK! NOW! SPECTAC! They slump back in their seats, watch the lights streak in the car windows.

No one speaks. It's late, they're tired. There's a feeling in the car that is somehow . . . elegiac. They've just performed one of their rituals, an old, central ritual that seems to have been a part of their lives always. How many nights have they cruised autopia and talked, and eaten a meal, and looked at the world? A thousand? Two thousand? This is how they were friends together. And yet this night it feels, somehow, as if this may have been the last time they will perform this particular ritual. Nothing lasts forever. Centrifugal forces are tugging on all their lives, on their collective life; they feel it, they know that the time is coming when this long childhood of their life will have to end. Nothing lasts forever. And this feeling lies as heavy in the car as the smell of French fries. . . .

Sandy punches a button and his window slides down. "An eyedropper for the road?"

After they enter SCP's parking garage and Abe and Tash have walked off to their cars, Sandy gestures Jim back to him. Scratching his head sleepily, he says, "Jim, have you seen much of Arthur lately?"

"Oh, a little. Once since we got back, I guess."

Sandy considers what line of questioning would be best. "Do you know if he's involved in anything, you know, anything more serious than those posters he puts up?"

Jim blushes. "Well, you know. I'm not really sure. . . ."

So Arthur is involved. And Jim knows about it. Meaning that Jim may be involved, too. Possibly. Probably. It's hard for Sandy to imagine Jim taking part in sabotage actions against local industrial plants, but who can say? He is one to follow an idea.

And now it's Sandy's turn to consider how much he can say. Jim is one of his best friends, no doubt about it, but Bob Tompkins is a major business partner, and by extension he has to be careful of Raymond's interests too. It's a delicate question, and he's tired. There doesn't seem to be any pressing hurry in the matter; and it would be better, actually, if he had more of substance to tell Jim, if he decides to speak to him. He's certain now that Arthur Bastanchury is working for Raymond, and pretty sure that Jim is working with Arthur. The question is, does Raymond work for anyone? That's the important thing, and until he learns more about it there's no use in upsetting Jim, he judges. Truth is, he's too tired to think about it much right now.

He pats Jim's arm. "Arthur should be careful," he says wearily, and turns to go to the elevator. "And you too," he says over his shoulder, catching a surprised look on Jim's face. He gets in the elevator. Three A.M. If he gets up at seven, he can reach his dad before lunch in Miami.

54

Jim gets several days in a row at the office of First American Title Insurance and Real Estate Company, which is good for his bank account if not for his disposition. On one of these days Humphrey comes in grinning triumphantly. "We're doing it, Jimbo. We're building the Pourva Tower. Ambank approved the loan package, and the last papers were signed today. All we have to do is reconfirm the other financiers within the next few days, so it's just a matter of doing the computer work quickly, before anyone cools off."

"Humphrey, you still don't have any occupants for this building."

"Well, we've got all those interested parties. Besides, it doesn't matter! We'll get them when the building is there!"

"Humphrey! What's the occupancy rate for new office buildings in OC? Twenty percent?"

"I don't know, something like that. But it's bound to change, so much business is moving in here."

"I don't see why you say that. The place is saturated."

"No way, Jim. There's no such thing."

"Aggh . . ." Nothing he can say to that. "I still think it's stupid."

"Listen, Jim, the rule is, when you have the money and you have the land, you build! It's not easy getting the two together at the same time. As you know from how this one's gone. But we've done it! Besides, this one will do well—we'll even be able to advertise that it has a filtered view of the ocean."

"Filtered by the whole bulk of the Santa Ana Mountains, eh Hump?''

"No! You can see down over Robinson Rancho, a little bit of it anyway.''

"Yeah, yeah. Build another empty tower.''

"Don't worry about that, Jim. Our only problem is to make sure everything moves along as fast as possible.''

Jim goes home from his clerking in a foul mood. The phone rings and he grabs it up. "What!''

"Hello, Jim?''

"Ah, Hana! Hey, how are you?''

"Something wrong?''

"No, no, I always answer the phone like that after a day at the office. Sorry.''

She laughs. "You'd better come up here for dinner then.''

"You bet! What should I bring?''

And so an hour later he's tracking into the hills, out the Garden Grove Freeway, across to Irvine Park and the Santiago Freeway, and then up narrow, deep Modjeska Canyon. Hana lives beyond the Tucker Bird Sanctuary, up a narrow side canyon, in a converted garage at the end of a gravel drive, in a grove of big old eucalyptus trees. The main house is a small whitewashed colonial-style cottage; its general modesty doesn't hide the fact of the secluded, wooded yard, the exclusiveness of it all. Hana's landlord is rich. And Hana?

Her garage has been turned into a painter's studio, mostly. The main room fills most of the place, and it's stacked with canvases and materials like her studio at Trabuco J.C. Kitchen and bathroom have been partitioned off in one corner, and a bedroom not much bigger than the bathroom is in the other corner. "I like it," Jim says. "It reminds me of my place, only nicer." Hana laughs. "You don't have any of your paintings up.''

"God no. I like to be able to relax. I mean, imagine sitting around looking at your mistakes all the time.''

"Hmm. They all have mistakes?''

"Sure.''

She's staring past him at the floor, throwing her sentences out casually. Attack of shyness, it seems. Jim follows her into the kitchen, and helps her take hamburgers out to a hibachi on the gravel drive.

They barbecue the meat and eat the hamburgers out on the driveway, sitting in low lawn chairs. They talk about the coming semester and their classes. About Hana's painting. Jim's work at the office. It's very relaxed, though Hana's eyes look anywhere but at Jim.

After dinner they sit and look up at the sky. There are even some stars. The eucalyptus leaves click together like plastic coins. It's a warm evening, there's a touch of Santa Ana wind blowing, even.

Hana suggests a walk up the canyon. They take the dinner materials inside, and then walk up the narrow, dark road.

"Do you know much about the Modjeskas?" Hana asks as they walk.

"A little. Helen Modjeska was a Polish actress. Her real name was something longer, and very Polish. She married a count, and their salon in Warsaw was very fashionable. The salon members got the idea of starting a utopia in southern California. This was in the 1870s. And they did it! The colony was down near Anaheim, which was also a utopian project started by a group of Germans. The Modjeskas' thing fell apart when none of them wanted to do farm work, and the Modjeskas moved to San Francisco, where she took up acting again. She became very famous there, and the count was her business manager, and they did well. Then in the late 1880s they returned, and bought the place up here. They called it Arden."

"*As You Like It.* What a nice idea."

"Yeah. This time it was a life of leisure—no farming. They had vineyards and orange groves and flower gardens, and a big shady lawn, and a pond out front with swans in it. During the days they rode horses around their land, and in the evenings Helen gave readings from her various roles."

"Very idyllic."

"True. It seems unreal, now. Although it's funny, up here I can imagine it happening. There's this feeling of being completely cut off from the world."

"I know. That's one of the things I like best about living up here."

"I believe it. It's amazing you can get that feeling anywhere in OC."

"Yeah, well, you should see Santiago Freeway at rush hour. Bumper to bumper."

"Of course. But here, and now . . ."

She nods, touches his upper arm. "Here, follow this trail. This little side canyon is pretty long and deep, and there's a way up to a lookout point over Riverside."

They hike through trees, up a steep-sided narrow canyon, one without a road at its bottom. Hana leads the way. Jim can hardly believe it; they're out in the bush! No condos! Can it be real?

The canyon's sandstone walls steepen until they're in a sort of roofless hallway, moving single file up a steep trail through the brush and trees. There's a stale, damp smell in the air, as if the sun seldom reaches the canyon's bottom. Then the walls lay back, and the canyon opens up into a small amphitheater filled with live oak. They turn back and up, and climb the walls they had previously been under, until they're on a ridge; there's a view back down to the scattered lights in Modjeska Canyon. And off to the east, as Hana said, there is a long fuzzy band of light, just visible: the Highway 15 corridor, in Riverside County.

"Whoah. You can really see a long way. Do you come up here often?"

He thinks he sees a small smile, but in the dark he can't be sure. "No. Not often. Look here." She walks to a big oak. "This tree's called the Swing Tree. Someone's tied a rope on that big upper branch, out away from the trunk. You take it"—she grabs the thick rope with both hands, just above a knot at the end of it —"and walk back uphill with it—and then—"

She runs down the hill, swings off into the space above the canyon, makes a slow turn, flies back in and runs to a halt.

"Whoah! Let me try that!"

"Sure. There are two ways to go—you can run straight out and come straight back in, or you can take off angling out away from the tree, and that'll put you in a circle and land you on the other side of the trunk. You have to be sure to go hard that way, though, to get around the trunk all the way. "

"I see. Believe I'll go straight out, this time."

"Good idea."

He seizes the rope, runs outward, flies off into space. It's slow, dark. Air hoots in his ears. He feels a little point of something like weightlessness, or weight coming back, at the outer limit of his ride—hung out there for a moment—then it's around and back in, whoah, got to run quick on touchdown. "Great! Fantastic! I want to do it again."

"Well then we'll just have to take turns. My turn now." She takes off with a quick sprint. Dark shape floating out there, hair flying wild against the stars—creak of rope against branch, up above—flying woman coming in from deep space, right at him—"Whoah!" He catches her up and they collide into a hug.

"Oops. Sorry. Took off at an angle, I guess."

He flies again. It's funny how simple all the real pleasures are (did he think that?). It's a long rope, the flights last a long time. Don't try to figure out how long, Jim thinks. It doesn't matter. Avoid timing, distance records, etcetera. . . .

After a few straight in-and-out runs, Hana takes the rope and runs out to the left, swings free of the ground, curves out, then left to right across the sky, spinning slowly, until she comes back in to the right side of the trunk. Round the horn. It looks lovely. "Let me try that!"

"Okay. Take off hard."

He does, but leaves the ground before he gets that last push-off step in. Oh well. Flying, here, spinning in a great circle, long seconds of a deep dream-flying calm. Coming back in he turns to face landward and notes that the tree trunk is going to—oops—

He just manages to turn sideways as he crashes into the tree. He tumbles to the ground, stunned.

He's lying in leaves. Hana has rushed over and is crouched over him. "Jim! Are you okay?"

He pulls her down and kisses her, surprising them both.

"Well, I guess you are."

"Not sure, though. Here—" He kisses her again. Actually, about half his body is sore indeed. Right ear, shoulder, ribs, butt, thigh, all of them are pounding. He ignores them all, pulls Hana onto him. The kiss extends off into a long sequence. Her hands are running over him very gently, making sure he's still all there. He reciprocates, and their kisses get a lot more passionate. Time out to breathe.

They're in a great drift of leaves, between two big roots that run over the hard ground. Leaves, whatnot—it's probably better not to investigate too closely. The leaves are dusty, dry, crunchy under them. They're lying side by side now, and clothes are giving way. In the dark Jim can just barely see her face against his, nothing more. The lack of visual stimulation, of the image, is disorienting. But that look on her face—all shyness gone, that small inward smile . . . his heart thumps, his skin is flushed or somehow made more sensitive, he can feel better, the rough uneven ground under his good side, his bad side throbbing in the cool air, crackling leaves, her hands on him, their mouths, whoah—when has a mere kiss ever felt like this? And it's Hana Steentoft, his friend, here; the distance gone, the inwardness turned out onto him, the friendship suddenly blooming like a Japanese paper flower hitting a bowl of water. It's exciting! They make love, and that's more exciting yet. Jim's body goes into a kind of shell-shocked mode: such a sequence of intense sensation! He mentions it to her at a certain still interval and she laughs. "Better watch it, you're going to be wanting to crash every time before you make it."

"Kinky indeed. Can you imagine it? Getting intimate—oh, excuse me—"

"Stand up and run straight into the wall—"

"There, okay, I'm ready now. . . ."

When their giggling subsides, Jim says, "I'll only do it with you. You'll understand."

"You'll only do it with me?" Quick grin, mischievous movement against him—"Yes"—and they are back in the world of sex, a duet collaborating in the most fascinating variations on a theme: the kinetic melody with its intense blisses, accompanied by crackling leaves and the odd squeak, hum, moan, grunt, whoah, exhalation, endearment, giggle, and a whole lot of heavy breathing. It's incredible fun.

55

They sleep together cuddled like spoons. In the morning Jim wakes
to find Hana already at work, painting at a table in the main room.
She's put on a bulky sweater and army fatigues. He watches her,
noticing the brusque concentration, the tangled hair, the tree-trunk
legs. The indirection that is not really shyness, but some unnamed
cousin to shyness. She gets up and walks into the kitchen, passes
a mirror without even noticing it. He gets up to run give her a
hug. She laughs at him.

"So," she says after breakfast. "When do I get to read something of yours?"

"Oh, well." He panics. "I really don't have anything ready
right now."

And he cringes a little to see the quick grimace on her face.
She thinks he's being stupid. Wonders if he isn't just lying about
his poetry, a bogus artist trying to impress her, with nothing behind
it. He can see all that in the quick flow of expression in her face,
which is just as quickly suppressed. No, no! But he really is scared;
his poetry is so trivial, and there is so little of it, he's sure her
estimation of him will drop radically when she reads it. So he
doesn't want her to. But that desire in itself gives it all away. She
might even be imagining it's worse than it really is. Jim sighs,
confused. Hana lets the matter slide.

He fills in as he so often does, by telling tall tales of his
friends' exploits. Tashi and the night surfing. Humphrey's empty
tower. That kind of thing.

After a while Hana looks at the floor. "And when am I going
to meet these amazing friends of yours?"

Jim gulps. It's the same question, isn't it: do I get to be part of your life? And by God, he wants her to be; he's forgotten whatever reservations he might have had about her. What were they about, her clothes, her *look*? Absurd. "There's a party at Abe's house tonight. His parents are going on vacation and he has the house to himself. Want to come?"

"Yes." She smiles, looks up at him.

Jim smiles too. Although he's remembering that Virginia will probably be there. As well as two dozen other perfect examples of the Modern California Woman. But he doesn't care, he tells himself. He doesn't care at all.

However, when he tracks by that evening to pick her up, she's wearing the very same army surplus pants, with their Jackson Pollock paint spray all over them. And yet another bulky brown-on-brown wool sweater. Jim winces. Then he notices that she has washed and brushed her hair, and it's drying still, curling in a way he thinks stunning. Anyway who cares about this stuff? He doesn't care about it. He doesn't care at all. He shakes it off, they get in his battered old car and drive.

Abe lives in an annex of his parents' house up on Saddleback Mountain, on the Santiago Peak side, just below the peak, over-looking all of OC and beyond. It's the most exclusive neighborhood of all, in accordance with Humphrey's law, height = money. Switchbacking up the steep residential road they pass mansion after mansion, most hidden from the road by a botanical garden's variety of trees and lawns, all as exotic and glossy as houseplants. But some are right out there for people to see:

Mirrored boxes that resemble the industrial complexes in
    Irvine,
Pagodas, chateaux,
Complicated wooden-box structures à la Frank Lloyd
    Wright,
Or the Greene brothers' Gamble house in Pasadena,
(Cardboard shacks in a field of mud!)
Mission-style monsters of whitewash and orange tile
    roofs,
Circus tent shapes of glass and steel that imitate
The dominant mall designs down on the floodplain. . . .
You live here, sure. There's no doubt of it.

They track slowly and enjoy eyeballing the passing parade of architectural extravagance, making fun of most of the homes, ogling lustfully the few that strike them as tasteful, livable places. And marveling always that these are single-family dwellings, and not disguised duplexes, triplexes, aps or condos. It's really hard to believe. "Like seeing an extinct animal," Jim says.

"Dinosaurs, grazing in your backyard."

Abe's parents, the Bernards, live on the outside of one of the hairpin turns near the top of the road, on a little deck of land all their own. The home is a multilevel sprawl, made entirely of wood; a Japanese garden out front has bonsai pines overhanging moss lawns, big odd-shaped boulders, and a small pool with a bridge over it. They've arrived early, so there's still parking on the street in front of the house. They get out, walk up and over the pool. "Just like the Modjeskas," Hana says softly. "All they need are swans."

As they approach the massive oak front doors, Abe and his father open them and walk out. Dr. Francis Bernard is a well-known logician who holds patents on some important computer software; he's also been a diplomat and social activist. He is one of the calmest people Jim has ever met; very quiet, and not much like Abe, except for the sharp dark face, the black hair. Jim introduces Hana to them. Mrs. Bernard left for Maui a couple weeks before, and Abe and his father have been living together alone since that time; now Dr. Bernard is off to the airport, headed for Maui himself. The two of them shake hands. Abe says, "Well, brother . . ."

"Brother," scoffs Dr. Bernard, obviously pleased. "See you in a month." And with a quiet good-bye he's off, into the garage.

"Come on in," Abe says, glancing at Hana curiously.

They enter the house and follow Abe through a succession of rooms, to a kind of enclosed porch or pavilion, overlooking the terraced yard that stands high above OC. Below them spreads the whole lightshow, just sparking up to full power in the hazy dusk. A plain of light.

Hana notices the view and goes out on the terrace to have a look. Abe and Jim retire to the porch kitchen and work up a chili con queso dip in a big crockpot. Jim tells Abe about the things that impressed him during the trip to Europe, making each event into something profoundly significant, as he so often does with Abe. Abe responds with his sharp, interested questions, attentive to moods and significances himself. And then there is his sudden laugh, transforming something Jim has been solemn about to high comedy; supplying the wit but acting as if it were Jim's. At times like this it's hard to imagine Abe as the unresponsive and scornful friend that Jim often feels him to be; now Jim too is a "brother." Is this a matter of mood, or is it just that whomever Abe fixes his full attention on becomes "brother" for that period of attention—which can be distracted, or missing from the start?

No way of knowing. Abe is the most inscrutable of Jim's friends, that's all there is to it. Visiting him up in this mansion Jim is reminded of Shelley's visits to Byron. It's gross flattery to compare himself to Shelley, he knows that, but there is something in the thought of the poor and idealistic poet visiting his rich, worldly, complex and powerful friend that reminds him of this feeling, up here on the very roof of OC.

So when Hana comes back inside and sits on a stool beside him, Jim watches with as much pleasure as apprehension the process of these two friends getting acquainted. Hana is plopped on a stool, the wind has pushed her hair into its usual disorder, and as Dennis would say, she looks like something the cat dragged in. But Abe clearly enjoys talking to her; she's got a quick wit and can keep up with him. In that realm they're both far beyond Jim, who only laughs and cuts chilis for the dip. Abe, curious as always about people's work and their livelihoods, questions Hana closely about how the art business is carried on, and Jim learns things he didn't know before.

"And you?" Hana says. "Jim says you're a paramedic?"

Abruptly Abe laughs, elbows Jim. "Telling her about us, eh?"

Jim grins. "All lies, too."

Abe nods at Hana. "Yeah, I work for the OC Freeway Rescue squads."

"That must be hard work sometimes."

Jim winces a little inside; when he says things along these

lines Abe tends to scowl at him or ignore him. But now he says, "Sure, sometimes. It's up and down. You get callused to the bad parts, though, and the good parts stay good always."

Hana nods. She's eyeing Abe closely, and he is inspecting the chili con queso; and she says, "So you two were on the wrestling team, hey? How long have you known each other?" Abe grins at Jim. "From the beginning."

Then Sandy and Angela come in from the yard entrance, and it's time for more introductions. With Sandy there the tempo jumps and pretty quickly they're jabbering away like they're old friends who haven't seen each other in a year. Hana chatters as much as any of them, chiefly to Abe but increasingly with Sandy and Angela. Angela, bless her heart, couldn't be friendlier. And then the crowd begins to arrive, Humphrey and his sometime ally Melina, Rose and Gabriela, Arthur, Tashi and Erica, Inez, John and Vikki, and so on; the party begins in earnest, people swirl in the slow ocean current patterns of parties everywhere. Hana stays on her stool and forms a sort of island around which one current swells; people stop in this eddy to talk to her. She asks a lot of questions, tries to sort out who's who, laughs. She's a hit. Jim, coming back to her after many small forays out into the currents, is pleased to see Hana and Abe engage in a long conversation, and Sandy join it; then Hana and Angela have a talk that leaves them laughing a lot, and even though Jim suspects that he is the subject of the laughter, he is pleased. All going so well.

Then Virginia arrives. When Jim sees her, blond mane breaking light in the hallway, his heart races. He moves to Hana and Angela and disrupts their conversation with some false heartiness, feeling nervous indeed. Virginia is quick to spot them, and she hurries over, smiling a bright smile full of malice. "Well hello, James. I haven't seen you in a while!"

"No."

"Aren't you going to introduce me to your new friend?"

"Oh, yeah. Virginia Novello, this is Hana Steentoft."

"Hello, Hana." Virginia extends a hand, and in her direct gaze there is a smiling, straightforward contempt. She's judged this dowdy newcomer in a single glance, and wants Jim to know it. Angrily, fearfully, Jim looks sideways at Hana; she is gazing past Virginia, at the floor, indifferent to her, waiting for her to go. Virginia has been dismissed. Virginia smiles at Jim with open hostility, walks off without saying anything more.

Afterward, on the way home, Hana refuses to go to Jim's place. "Let's go to mine."

So they do. As they track she says, "That's one expensively dressed crowd of women you hang out with."

"Ah, yeah." Jim isn't listening, he's pleased at the whole evening, and at a final small gathering with Abe and Sandy and Angela. "They really go overboard into the whole thing. I'm so glad you don't care about any of that."

"Don't be stupid, Jim."

"Huh?"

"I said, don't be stupid."

"Huh?"

"Of course I care! What do you think I am?"

She's angry with him, he's just heard it. "Ah."

And suddenly he gets it: no one can escape. You can pretend not to care about the image, but that's as far as the culture will let you get. Inside you have to feel it; you can fight it but it'll always be there, the contemptuous dismissal of you by the Virginia Novellos of the world. . . . No doubt Hana saw that look and was perfectly aware of it, all the rest of the evening. And she did look different from the rest of the women there; how could anyone forget that in such a crowd of them? And now he had implied that she was so far out of the norm that she wouldn't have the common human response, wouldn't even notice, wouldn't even care.

He's a fool, he thinks. Such a fool. . . . What to say? "Sorry, Hana. I think you're beau—"

"Quiet, Jim. Just shut up about it, okay?"

"Okay."

He drives her to her home in an awkward, ominous silence.

56

The time comes for Judge Andrew H. Tobiason of the Fourth Court of Appeals of the District of Columbia to make his judgment in the case of Laguna Space Research versus the United States Air Force. Dennis McPherson is there in the courtroom with Louis Goldman, seated just behind the plaintiff's bench that is occupied by three of Goldman's colleagues from his firm. On the other side are the Air Force lawyers, and McPherson is unpleasantly surprised to see behind them Major Tom Feldkirk, the man who got him into this in the first place. Feldkirk sits at attention and stares straight ahead at nothing.

Behind the parties in the case, the rather formal and imposing neoclassical room is filled with reporters. McPherson recognizes one of the main feature writers from *Aviation Week*, in a big crowd of others from the aerospace press. It's hard for McPherson to remember that much of this is taking place in public; it seems to him a very private thing. And yet here they are in front of everybody, part of tomorrow's business page without a doubt, if not the front pages. Newsheets and magazines everywhere, filled with LSR vs. USAF! It's too strange.

And it's too fast. McPherson has barely gotten seated, and used to the room and the seashell roar of its muttering crowd, when the judge comes in his side door and everyone stands. He's barely down again when the sergeant-at-arms or some official of the court like that declares, "Laguna Space Research versus United States Air Force, Case 2294875, blah blah blah blah . . ." McPherson stops listening to the announcement and stares curiously at Feldkirk, whose gaze never leaves the judge. If only he could stand up and say across the room, "What about the time you gave us this program as our own project, Feldkirk? Why don't you tell the judge about that?"

Well. No use getting angry. The judge no doubt knows about that anyway. And now he's saying something—McPherson bears down, focuses his attention, tries to ignore the feeling that he's caught in a trap he doesn't understand.

Judge Tobiason is saying, in a quick, clipped voice, "So in the interests of national security, I am letting the contract stand as awarded."

Goldman makes a quick tick with his teeth. The gavel falls. Case closed, court dismissed. The seashell mutters rise to a loud chatter, filling the room like the real sound of the ocean. McPherson stands with Goldman, they walk down the crowded central aisle.

By chance McPherson comes face to face with Tom Feldkirk. Feldkirk stares right through him, without even a blink, and marches out with the other Air Force people there. No looking back.

He's sitting in a car with Goldman. Goldman, he realizes, is angry; he's saying, "That bastard, that bastard. The case was clear." McPherson remembers the feeling he had at the ceremony where the contract was awarded; this is nothing like that for him, but for Goldman . . .

"We can pursue this," Goldman says, looking at McPherson and striking the steering switch. "The GAO's report has got the House Appropriations Committee interested, and several aides to members of the House Armed Services Committee are up in arms about it. We can make a formal request for a congressional investigation, and if some representatives are open to the idea then they could sic the Procurements Branch of the Office of Technology Assessment on them, as well as light a fire under the GAO. It could work."

McPherson, momentarily exhausted at the complexity of it all, only says "I'm sure we'll want to try it." Then he takes a deep breath, lets it out. "Let's go get a drink."

"Good idea."

They go up to a restaurant in Georgetown and sit at a tiny table placed under the street window. Window shoppers check them out to see if they are mannequins. They down one drink in silence. Goldman describes again the plan to influence the committees in Congress, and it sounds good.

After a while Goldman changes the subject. "I can tell you what went on behind the scenes at the Air Force. We finally got the whole story."

Curious despite his lassitude, McPherson nods. "Tell me."

Goldman settles back in his seat, closes his eyes briefly. He is getting over his anger at the judge's contempt for the rule of law, he's convinced they can win in Congress, and he's seduced by the gossip value of the story he's ferreted out: McPherson can read all that clearly. He's getting to know this man. "Okay, it started as far as you knew when Major Feldkirk came to you with a superblack program."

"Right." The cold bastard.

"But the truth is, that was part of a story that has been going on for years. Your Major Feldkirk works for Colonel T. D. Eaton, head of the Electrical Systems Division at the Pentagon—and Eaton works for General George Stanwyck, a three-star general also based in the Pentagon, and responsible for much of the ballistic missile defense. Now, your superblack program was presented to the Secretary of the Air Force as part of a campaign to pull the power of weapons procurement a little closer to the chest, so to speak—back completely in the Pentagon's power. Official reasoning for that was that procurement is in terrific disarray, because so many ballistic missile defense programs are getting into serious cost overruns, or deep technical trouble."

"I'm aware of that," McPherson says bleakly.

"The fact is, the whole procurement system is so badly screwed up that Congress is about to intervene again, which is one reason we have a very good chance there."

"That's the official reason, you said? And the unofficial?"

"That's where it gets interesting. Stanwyck, okay, he's in the Pentagon. Three-star general. And General Jack James, out at Air Force Systems Command at Andrews Air Force Base, is a four-star general. And they know each other."

Goldman looks at the palm of one hand, shakes his head. "It's curious how these things last. They went to the Air Force Academy together, you see. They started the same year, they were classmates. And you know how the officers are graduated from the military academies in ranked order? Well, those two were the competition for number one. In the last year it got pretty intense.''

"You're kidding me,'' McPherson exclaims. ''In *school*?''

"I know. It's sort of unbelievable what's behind these kind of conflicts, but several sources have confirmed this. I guess the whole thing was well-known in Boulder at the time. No one knows exactly how the rivalry started—some talk about a practical joke, others a disagreement over a woman cadet, but no one really knows—it's just one of those things that got rolling and kept going. I personally think it was probably just the number one thing, the competition for that. And James ended up first in the class, with Stanwyck second.

"Ever since then James has always done just that little bit better in terms of promotion. But recently Stanwyck got assigned to the Pentagon. And since then he's been a big force in the development of remotely piloted vehicles for combat missions. As you probably know, most of the Air Force brass has a strong bias against unpiloted vehicles, no matter how much sense they make in terms of current weapons technology.''

"Sure. If all combat planes become remotely piloted, it'll be cheaper and fewer people will be killed, but where's the glory?''

"Exactly. If it happens, the whole Air Force becomes nothing but air traffic controllers, and they can't stand it. No more flying aces, no more right stuff, the whole tradition down the tubes. So it's obvious why they're so opposed to it. James among them, since he was a big flyer, one of the so-called flying colonels when they were choosing the design for the second generation ATF. But Stanwyck, now, he's been on the ground for a long time. And he'd like nothing more than to ground the flyboys too, and have James know it was all his doing. Thus all James's fault.

"Not only that, but Stanwyck is part of the Pentagon group that is trying to centralize all the armed forces, which would weaken the autonomy of the Air Force, and indirectly strip Air Force Systems Command, out at Andrews, of any real independent power at all.''

McPherson shakes his head. ''So we were pawns in a battle between two parts of the Air Force? It wasn't even interservice?''

Goldman pauses to consider it. ''Basically true. But it was

the program that was the pawn, though. And from what we now know, I suspect it was a pawn that Stanwyck intended to sacrifice all along. Because"—he stops to sip at his drink—"it was Stanwyck himself who told James of the existence of the Stormbee program. This was after you had been working on your superblack proposal for some time, see, *after* Stanwyck had made sure, by the use of in-house spies, or inquiries from Feldkirk or whatever, that you had a good, workable system. Only at that point, when the superblack mechanism was already rolling to award LSR the contract, did Stanwyck tell James about it, supposedly in the course of answering a request for information. But I think it was planned. I think that that was the shoving of the pawn out into an exposed position, to set up the sacrifice."

"You mean Stanwyck wanted the program taken away and turned white?"

"Well, think about what had to happen as a result. James gets mad as hell, and because he's a four-star general he has the authority to make it a white program, and take over the administration of the bidding process. At that point, you people at LSR are doomed, because no matter what the various other bids look like, James is bound and determined that LSR is not going to win this contract, because you are the company that Stanwyck chose. At the same time, as Stanwyck well knows, LSR has a damn good system worked up. So . . . do you see?"

"He set James up to initiate cheating in the evaluation process," McPherson says. He feels a certain theoretical pleasure in understanding at the same time that disgust is twisting his stomach again. "If it happened, and we protested successfully, then James loses power."

"He might even lose his job! They might force him to retire, no doubt about it. At this point James has his back to the wall, and that's a fact."

"So Stanwyck's gambit worked. The pawn was taken, but the king is in trouble."

"Yes." Goldman nods precisely. "And as you might guess, it's people in Stanwyck's command at the Pentagon who have leaked a fair amount of the material used by us and the GAO. Now, Judge Tobiason is either on James's side, or he isn't aware of the conflict and is only protecting the Air Force. Or else he disapproves of the fight and only wants to stop it. Impossible to tell. We don't really know. It doesn't really matter, now that that stage of the battle is over.''

''And where did you get this information about Stanwyck and James?''

''From James's subordinates. He isn't much liked, and the story is widespread at Andrews. And from Stanwyck's people, who want it known.''

''Hmph.''

They order another round, then talk about tactics in the campaign to get Congress to act. Goldman is enthusiastic about this in a way McPherson hasn't seen before; apparently Goldman wrote off their chances in court ever since Tobiason was appointed judge in the case, so that this is the point where he can really work with some hope of success.

But McPherson finds himself very tired of the matter. The truth is, the day has seen the end of one of their last chances. Once a pawn has been sacrificed successfully and taken off the board, what real chance is there for it to petition its way back on, to protest the way it was used, to redress its grievances?

Well, Goldman thinks their chances are pretty good. It isn't exactly chess, after all. Much more ambiguous and uncertain. But McPherson goes back to the Crystal City Hyatt Regency feeling depressed, and more than a little drunk.

Out one of the great mirror-windowed walls of the Hyatt stands the Pentagon Annex, a massive concrete bunker defended against all the world. Impenetrable. Who could really believe it could be defeated?

He gets lost on the way to his room, has to consult three bad maps and walk half a mile of halls to find it. When he does there's nothing there but the bed, the video, a window facing the inky Potomac. Can he stand to turn the video on?

No. He sits on the bed. Tomorrow he can fly home. Be back with Lucy. Only fourteen hours to get through till then.

Some two hours later, just as he is falling asleep watching the dead video screen, the phone rings. He leaps up as if shot. Answers it.

''Dennis? Tom Feldkirk here. I—I just wanted to tell you that I'm sorry about what's happened in this case. I didn't have any part in it and didn't have any way to change things. And I want you to know I don't like what's happened one bit.'' The man's voice is strained to the point of shaking. ''I'm damned sorry, Dennis. It isn't how I meant it to happen.''

McPherson sits dully with phone to ear. He thinks of the stories Goldman told him that evening. It's possible, even likely, that Feldkirk wasn't aware of how the superblack program would be used by Stanwyck. He probably found out after it was too late to do anything about it. Another pawn in the game. Otherwise why even call?

''Dennis?''

''That's all right, Tom. It wasn't your fault. Maybe next time it'll go better.''

''I hope so. I hope so.''

Awkward good-bye. McPherson hangs up, looks at his watch. Only twelve hours to go.

57

In 1940 the population was 130,000. By 1980 it was 2,000,000.

At that point the northwestern half of the county was saturated. La Habra, Brea, Yorba Linda, Placentia, Fullerton, Buena Park, La Mirada, Cerritos, La Palma, Cypress, Stanton, Anaheim, Orange, Villa Park, El Modena, Santa Ana, Garden Grove, Westminster, Fountain Valley, Los Alamitos, Seal Beach, Huntington Beach, Newport Beach, Costa Mesa, Corona del Mar, Irvine, Tustin: all of these cities had grown, merged, melted together, until the idea that twenty-seven cities existed on the land was just a fiction of administration, a collection of unnoticed street signs, announcing borders that only the maps knew. It was one city.

This new megacity, "Orange County North," had as its transport system the freeways. The private car was the only way; the little train system of the early days had been pulled out, like the more extensive electric rail network in Los Angeles, to make more room for cars. In the end there were no trains, no buses, no trams, no subways. People had to drive cars to work, to get food, to do all the chores, to play—to do anything.

So after the completion of the Santa Ana Freeway in the late 1950s, the others quickly followed. The Newport and Riverside freeways bisected the county into its northwest and southeast halves; the San Diego Freeway followed the coast, extended the Santa Ana Freeway south to San Diego; the Garden Grove, Orange, and San Gabriel freeways added ribbing to the system, so that one could get to within a few miles of anywhere in Orange County North that one wanted to go, all on the freeways.

Soon the northwestern half was saturated, every acre of land bought, covered with concrete, built on, filled up. Nothing left but the dry bed of the Santa Ana River, and even that was banked and paved.

Then the Irvine Ranch was bought by a development company. For years the county government had taxed the ranch as hard as it could, trying to force it out of agriculture, into more tract housing. Now they got their wish. The new owners made a general plan that was (at first) unusually slow and thoughtful by Orange County standards; the University of California was given ten thousand acres, a town was built around it, a development schedule was worked up for the rest of the land. But the wedge was knocked into the southeast half of the county, and the pressure for growth drove it ever harder.

Meanwhile, in the northwest half the congestion grew with an intensity that the spread to the southeast couldn't help; in fact, given the thousands of new users that the southward expansion gave to the freeway system, it only made things worse. The old Santa Ana Freeway, three lanes in each direction, was clogged every day; the same was true of the Newport Freeway, and to a lesser extent of all the freeways. And yet there was no room left to widen them. What to do?

In the 1980s a plan was put forth to build an elevated second story for the Santa Ana Freeway, between Buena Park and Tustin; and in the 1990s, with the prospect of the county's population doubling again in ten years, the Board of Supervisors acted on it. Eight new lanes were put up on an elevated viaduct, set on massive pylons thirty-seven feet above the old freeway; they were opened to southbound traffic in 1998. Three years later the same was done for the Newport and Garden Grove freeways, and in the triangle of the elevated freeways, three miles on each side, the elevated lanes were joined by elevated gas stations and convenience stops and restaurants and movie theaters and all the rest. It was the beginning of the "second story" of the city.

The next generation of freeways were the Foothill, Eastern, and San Joaquin, all designed to ease the access to the southern half of the county. When those were in it made sense to connect the ends of the Garden Grove and Foothill freeways, which were only a few miles from each other; and so they were spliced by a great viaduct above Cowan and Lemon Heights, leaving the homes below devalued but intact. Then the new Santiago and Cleveland freeways were built in the same way, flying through the sky on great pylons, above the new condos springing up everywhere in the back hills, in what used to be Irvine Ranch, Mission Viejo Ranch, O'Neill Ranch—now the new towns of Santiago, Silverado, Trabuco, Seaview Terrace, San Juan Springs, Los Pinos, O'Neill, Ortega, Saddleback, Alicia, and so on and so on. And as the land was subdivided, platted, developed, covered with concrete, built up, the freeway system grew with it. When the national push for the electromagnetic road track system began, the freeways of Orange County were in place and ready for it; it only took five years to make the change, and work created by this transformation helped head off the recession of the Boring Twenties before it plunged into outright worldwide depression. A new transport system, a new boom; always the case in Orange County, as in all the American West.

So the southeast half of Orange County, when the flood burst over the Irvine Ranch and the development began, grew even faster than the northwest half had, fifty years before. In thirty quick years it became indistinguishable from the rest of the megacity. The only land left was the Cleveland National Forest. The real estate companies hungrily eyed this empty, dry, hilly land; what condos could be put up there, what luxury homes, on the high slopes of old Saddleback Mountain! And it only took a sympathetic administration in Washington to begin the dismemberment of this insignificant little national forest. Not even any forest there! Why worry about it! The county was crowded, they needed that 66,000 acres for more homes, more jobs, more profits, more cars, more money, more weapons, more drugs, more real estate, more freeways! And so that land was sold too.

And none of that ever went away.

58

Abe and Xavier have been sitting around headquarters for a good half of their shift, a rare event indeed. They've been playing video football, pumping weights, napping, and playing more football. Xavier is killer at the game, he plays for money at the Boathouse, and he hits the keys of his control board like a typist going at two hundred words a minute, so that all eleven of his men play like inspired all-stars. On offense Abe is constantly being tackled for a loss, sacked, intercepted, or having his punts blocked, and once on defense he gets steamrolled every way possible. In the latest game the stat board shows him with minus 389 yards rushing, in a game he is losing 98–7. And he got the seven by screaming, *"Look out!"* just after beginning a play, actually fooling Xavier into glancing around while he tossed a successful bomb.

So Abe quits.

"No, Abe, no! I'll play with my eyes shut, I swear!"

"No way."

And Abe is napping again when the alarm goes, a high, not-so-loud ringing that squeezes every adrenal gland in his body. He's up and out and fastening his seat belt before he's even awake, and only as they zip out onto Edinger and into traffic does his heart rate sink back to a halfway reasonable patter. Another year off his life, no doubt; firemen and paramedics have a really high heart attack rate, as a result of the damage caused by these sudden leaps of adrenal acceleration. "Where'm I going?"

"Proceed northward on the Newport until encountering the Garbage Grove Freeway, west to the Orange Freeway, north to Nutwood and over to State. We have been called to render assistance at a car crash."

"You're kidding."

Abe notices that Xavier's hand is clamped on the radio microphone so tight that the yellowy palm is almost completely white. And the joky rapid-fire patter has an edge in it, it always did of course, but now it burrs X's voice to the point where the dispatcher asks him to repeat things sometimes. Xavier needs a long vacation, no doubt about it. Or a change of work. He's burning out, Abe can see it happening shift by shift. But with his own family, and the dependency of what sounds like a good chunk of Santa Ana's populace, he can't afford to quit or to take a long break. Pretty obviously he won't stop until it's him that breaks.

Abe concentrates on driving. Traffic is bad where the Garden Grove Freeway bleeds into the Orange and Santa Ana, in the giant multilevel concrete ramp pretzel, every ramp stopped up entirely, it's offtrack time again, the song of the sirens howling up and down, power sensation as the truck leaps under his foot, the tracked cars on his right flying by in a blur of color, one long rainbow bar of neon metal flowing by, whoops there's a car offtrack right in their path blocking it entirely, heavy brakes. "Shit! What's that doing there!"

"Get back ontrack."

"I'm trying, man, can't just drive over these civilians you know." Abe puts on flasher, blinkers, the truck is strobing light at a score of frequencies, should hypnotize the car drivers if nothing else. No break in the traffic appears.

"They think we a Christmas tree," X says angrily, and leans far out of his window to wave futilely at the passing stream. "Just edge over into them, man."

Abe takes a deep breath, eases in the clutch, steers right. Xavier shouts abuse at the cars in the fast lane, and finally says to Abe, "Go for it," and blindly Abe floors it and steers over into the lane, expecting a crunch from the side any second. As soon as he gets past the stalled car on the shoulder he veers back onto the concrete shoulder and guns it, fishtailing almost into the rail. Xavier is waving thanks to the driver who gave them the gap. They're up to speed again. "We got a dangerous job," Xavier says heavily as he settles back into his seat. "Opportunities for impaction while attempting to reach our designated destination are numerous indeed."

Abe sings the last line of their "Ode to Fred Spaulding":

And he never, exceeded, the speed, limit—againnnn!

Xavier joins in and they cackle wildly as they trundle at eighty miles an hour up the freeway shoulder. Abe's hands clamp the steering wheel, Xavier's palm is white-person white on the mike.

X says, "Have you heard the latest Fred Spaulding joke? Fred sees the overpass pylon coming at them, he shouts back into the ambulance compartment, 'Tell the victim we'll have him there in a second!' "

Abe laughs. "That's like the one where he asks the victim what's the definition of bad luck."

"Ha! Yeah. Or where he asks him to explain double-indemnity insurance."

"Ha! ha! Or the one where he says, 'Have you got insurance?' and the victim says, 'No!' and Fred says, 'Don't worry about it!' "

Xavier is helpless at this, he puts his forehead on the dash and giggles away. When he's done he says, "Wish I didn't believe in insurance. You wouldn't believe how much I pay every month."

"It's a good bet, remember that."

"That's right. You die young, the insurance company says, 'You win!' " He laughs again, and Abe is cheered to see it. Abe adds:

"And if you lose the bet, you're still alive."

"Exactly."

They reach Nutwood, turn off the freeway and head west to College Avenue, shooting through the shops and restaurants and laundromats and bookstores that serve Cal State Fullerton. Crowds watch them pass, cars skitter over to the slow track or slide into empty parking slots, giving Abe little scares each time they hesitate and almost scatter into his path. Familiar surge of power as they part traffic likes Moses at the Red Sea. Up ahead traffic is dense, stopped, the brake lights go off in his brain, Chippie car lights rolling red and blue in the intersection. "We need the cutters," Xavier reports from the radio. "Code six."

Abe sucks down air, he's breathing rapidly. He drives onto a sidewalk to make half a block, thumps back over the curb and crawls by cars to the *sota*.

They're there. Three-car job. Sits, something in the silicon. Or maybe this was a combination of silicon breakdown and human error. College had a green light, cars were pouring through, apparently; a truck fired through its red light on Nutwood and broadsided a left-lane car that was caught against the car in the right lane, the three of them skidding over into a traffic light and a power pole, knocking the poles flat over. Both the cars are crunched, especially the middle one, which is a pancake. And the truck driver isn't too well off either, no seat belt natch.

Abe is out of the truck and on the move, dragging his cutters over to the cars, where Chippies are gesturing violently for him. Someone's caught in the middle car, and with all the sparks from the power lines, they fear electrocution for those inside.

There are two people in the front seat of the sandwiched car. Abe ignores the driver as she appears dots, sets to work on the roof of the car to get to the passenger. Again he's at work, cutting with a delicate touch as the snips shear the steel with great creaks and crunches, metallic shrieks covering repeated moans from the girl in the passenger seat. Xavier slithers in from above and is quickly at work, giving a rapid sequence of very exact commands to Abe above, "Cut another foot and a half back on the midline and pull it up. Farther. Okay, take that sidewall out of the rear door, we can get her out here." Stretcher set, for a teenager in yellow blouse and pants, all stained blood red in an alarmingly bright pattern. Xavier and the Chippies run her to the truck and Abe works his way into the smashed car to check on getting the driver out. In the right rear door, lean over the blood-soaked seatback—

It's Lillian Keilbacher. Face white, lips cut, blond hair thrown back. It's definitely her. Her chest—crushed. She's dead. Dots, no doubt about it. That's Lillian, right there. Her body.

Abe backs out of the car. He notes that the car was a new

Toyota Banshee, a little sport model popular among kids. Seems he's gone deaf; he sees the turmoil of spectators and cars around them, but can't hear a thing. He remembers Xavier, sweating, talking in a near hysteria about the time he turned over a dead kid in a car and saw, just for a moment, his son's face. He makes a move toward the car, thinking to check the girl's ID. But no, it's her. It's her. Carefully he walks to the curb and sits on it.

"Abe! Where—Abe! What are you doing, man?" Xavier is crouched at his side, hand on his shoulder. "What's wrong?"

Abe looks at him, croaks, "I know her. The driver. Friend of the family. Lillian, Lillian Keilbacher."

"Oh, man. . . ." Xavier's face scowls with distress; Abe can't stand to look at him. "We got to go anyway, the other one's still alive. Come on, bro. I'll drive, you can work in back."

Abe is qualified to do the medic work, but when they reach the truck he can't face it. He balks at the rear door. "No, man. I'll drive."

"You sure you can?"

"I'll drive!"

"Okay. Be careful. Let's go to Anaheim Hospital."

Abe gets in. Seat belt on. He drives. He's a blank; he finds himself at the freeway exit leading to Anaheim Memorial and he can't remember a single thought from the drive, or the drive itself. Xavier pops his head through the window. "This one looks like she'll pull through. Here, make a left here, man, ER is at the side."

"I know."

Xavier falls silent. Wordlessly they sit as Abe drives them to the ER ramp. He sits and listens while Xavier and the nurses get Lillian's friend inside. Memory brings up to him the image of Lillian's dead face rolling toward him, looking through him. His diaphragm's all knotted, he's not breathing well. He blanks again.

Xavier opens the driver's door. "Come on, Abe, slide over. I'll drive for a while."

Abe slides over. Xavier puts them on the track to the street. He glances at Abe, starts to say something, stops.

Abe swallows. He thinks of Mrs. Keilbacher, his favorite among all his mother's friends. Suddenly he realizes she'll have to be told. He imagines the phone call from a stranger, this is the

Fullerton police, is this Mrs. Martin Keilbacher? At the thought his jaw clamps until he can feel all his teeth. No one should ever have to get a call like that. Better to hear it from—well, anybody. Any other way has to be better. He takes a deep breath. "Listen, X, drive me up onto Red Hill. I got to tell her folks, I guess." As he says this he begins to tremble.

"Oh, man—"

"Someone's got to tell them, and I think this would be better. Don't you?"

"I don't know. —We're still on duty, you know."

"I know. But they're almost on the route back to the station."

Xavier sighs. "Tell me the way."

As they turn up the tree-lined, steep street that the Keilbachers live on, Abe begins shaking in earnest. "This one on the left."

Xavier stops the truck. Abe looks past the white fence and the tiny yard, to their window of the duplex. A light is on. He gets out, closes the truck door quietly. Walks around the hood. Come on, he thinks, open the door and come out, ask me what's wrong, don't make me come knock on your door like this!

He knocks on the door, hard. Rings the bell. Stands there.

No answer.

No one's home.

"Shit." He's upset; he knows he should feel relieved, but he doesn't, not at all. He walks around the duplex, looks in the kitchen window. Dark. Light left on in the living room while they're out, SOP. Xavier is leaning his head out the window. Abe returns to the truck. "No one's home!"

"It's all right, Abe. You did what you could. Get back in here."

Abe stands, irresolute. Can't leave a note in the door about this! And the two of them are still on duty. But still, still . . . he can't rid himself of the idea that he should tell them. He climbs back in the truck, and as he sits he has an idea. "Jim's folks live up here too, and his mom is a good friend of theirs. Drive me by there and I'll tell her and she can take over here, we can get back to the station. They go to church together and everything."

Xavier nods patiently, starts up the truck. He follows Abe's directions and drives them past house after house. Then they are at Jim's parents' duplex, well remembered by Abe from years past, looking just the same to him. Drapes are closed, but lights are on inside.

Abe jumps out and walks to the kitchen door, which is the one the family always uses. Rings the bell.

The door opens on a chain, and Lucy McPherson looks out suspiciously. "Abe! What are you doing here?"

At the question Abe loses the feeling that it made sense to come to her. Lucy closes the door to undo the chain, opens it fully. She looks at him curiously, not getting it. "It's good to see you! Here, come in—"

Abe waves a hand quickly. Lucy squints at him. She's nice, Abe thinks, he can remember a hundred kindnesses from her when he was the new kid in Jim's group. But in recent years he's noticed a distance in her, a certain reserve behind her cheery politeness that seems to indicate disapproval . . . as if she perhaps thought Abe was responsible for whatever changes in Jim she doesn't like. It has irked him, and a couple times he found himself wanting to say, Yes, yes, I personally have corrupted your innocent son, sure.

Random thoughts, flashing through Abe's confusion as he sees that tiny squint of suspicion or distrust. "I—I'm sorry, Mrs. McPherson." Say it. "I've got bad news," and he sees her eyes open wide with fear, he puts a hand forward quickly: "No, not about Jim—it's about Lillian Keilbacher. I just came from their house, and there's no one home to tell! You know, you know I'm a paramedic."

Lucy nods, eyes shining.

"Well," Abe says helplessly, "I just found Lillian in a car crash we were called to. And she was dead, she'd been killed."

Lucy's hand flies to her mouth, she turns to one side as if bracing for a blow. It's as bad as Mrs. Keilbacher. No, it's not.

"My Lord. . . ." She reaches out hesitantly, touches Abe's arm. "How awful. Do you want to come in and sit down?"

That's almost too much. Abe can't take it, and he backs up a step, shakes his head. "No, no," he says, choking up. "I'm still on call, got to go back to work. But I thought . . . someone they knew should tell them."

She nods, looking at him with a worried expression. "I agree. I'll go get the Reverend Strong, and we'll try to find them."

Abe nods dumbly. He looks up into her eyes, shrugs. For a

moment they share something, some closeness he can't define.
"I'm sorry," he says.

"I'm glad you came here," she says firmly. And she walks
him back to the truck. Something in the kindness of those words,
and in the fact that his task is done, breaks the restraints in Abe,
he can feel the shock of it again; and he shakes hard all the way
back to the station, while X drives grimly, muttering "Oh, man
. . . oh, man . . ."

Back at the station they collapse on the couch. The football
game mocks them.

After a while Xavier says slowly, "You know, Abe, I don't
think we're cut out for this job."

Abe drinks his coffee as if it were whiskey. "No one is."

"But some more than others. And not us. You've got to be
stupid to do this job right. No, not stupid exactly. It takes smarts
to do it right. But . . ." He shakes his head.

"You've got to be a robot," Abe says dully. "But I'll be
damned if I'll become a robot for the sake of some job." He drinks
again.

"Well . . ." X can only shake his head. "That was bad luck,
tonight. Damned bad luck."

"A new definition." But neither of them even cracks a smile.

For a long time they just sit there on the couch, side by side,
staring at the floor.

Xavier nudges him. "More coffee?"

59

Lucy returns to the duplex and wanders the rooms aimlessly. Dennis is due back from Washington late that night. Jim's got class.
Briefly she cries. "Oh, Lillian—"

Then she goes to put on her shoes. "Got to get organized,

here.'' She calls the Keilbachers. No answer. She's got her sweater on, ready to go—but where? She calls the church. Reverend's out on call, she gets his answering machine. Everyone's gone! What is this? Vicar Sebastian, ineffectual as always, answers his phone and is reduced to speechlessness by Lucy's news. He and Lillian were good friends, it may be he even had a crush on her. So he's no help. Lucy finally says she'll come pick him up. He agrees. Then she calls Helena, who thank the Lord is home, and tells her the bad news. Helena can't believe it. She agrees to meet Lucy at the church.

Lucy drives to the church without seeing a thing. She just had lunch with Emma Keilbacher that day, and Emma didn't mention any plans to go out that evening, did she? So hard to remember at a time like this. And she just worked with Lillian yesterday—

She forbids herself to think along those lines, and collects herself before going in to the church offices. Helena is already there, bless her. The vicar, pale and red-eyed, slows them for a prayer that Lucy has no patience for. They've got to find Emma and Martin.

So they get into Lucy's car, and she drives to the Keilbachers' house. Still no one home.

"I suppose they could have gone out to eat when Martin came home. . . ."

"They usually just go to Marie Callendar's during the week."

"Yeah, that's right." Between them Lucy and Helena know every restaurant that Emma and Martin might frequent. So Lucy drives them to Marie Callendar's, but they're not there.

"Where next?"

They try the El Torito on Chapman. No luck there. They track to Three Crowns, and then Charlie's; the Keilbachers are nowhere to be seen.

They return to the house. No luck. It's really very frustrating.

After that it's a matter of friends they might be visiting. Vicar Sebastian feels telephoning around is a bad idea, so there follows a nightmarish interval of visits to all the friends of the Keilbachers they know: finding they aren't there, pausing to give the friends the news, driving on.

Lucy begins to feel more and more strongly that they should *find* them, it strikes her as terrible, somehow, that so many people should know and Emma and Martin still be unaware. They're all getting frustrated, vexed, upset; it's hard to agree on what to try next.

"Do you suppose they already heard from the police?" Sebastian asks.

Lucy shakes her head. "Abe came straight to me, there wouldn't have been time, I don't think."

They track all the way to Seal Beach where the Jansens moved, then into Irvine, back to the house, over to the church, then to the Cinema 12 theaters down in Tustin. . . . No luck, they just aren't to be found.

"Where *are* they?" Lucy demands angrily. Helena and the vicar, cowed by Lucy's determination to find them, are out of ideas.

Defeated, Lucy can only drive back to their house, frustrated and mystified. Where in the world are they?

She parks on the street in front of the Keilbachers' duplex. The three of them sit in the car and wait.

There isn't much to say. The whole neighborhood is still. The streetlight overhead flickers. Street, gutter, curb, grass, sidewalk, grass, driveways, houses, they're all flickering too, leeched of color by the mercury vapor's blue glow: a gray world, flickering a little. It's strange: like holding watch for some mysterious organization, or performing a new ritual that they don't fully understand. So strange, Lucy thinks, the things life leads you into doing.

Headlights appear at the bottom of the street, and Lucy's heart jumps in her, like a small child trapped inside, trying to escape. The car approaches slowly. Turns into the Keilbachers' driveway.

"Oh, my God," says Helena, and begins to cry.

The vicar begins to cry.

"Now wait a minute," Lucy says harshly as she opens the door and begins to get out of the car. "We're doing God's work here—we're his messengers, and it's God speaking now, not us," and sure enough it must be true, because here's Lucy McPherson crossing the lawn toward the surprised Keilbachers, Lucy who gets teary if she's told the story of someone's suffering or sacrifice, Lucy who waters up if you look at her sideways—here she is just as calm as can be, as she stands before Emma and Martin and gives them the news—as steady as a doctor, as they help Emma off the lawn and inside. And all through that long horrible night, as Emma is racked with hysterical grief, and Martin sits on the back porch staring at little handprints in the concrete, at nothing, it's Lucy that they turn to to make coffee, to fix soup, to hold Emma, to deal with the police, and with the mortuary, and with all the business that the others cannot face, shaken as they are; it's Lucy they turn to.

60

When Dennis arrives home from Washington, very late that night, exhausted and depressed, he finds an empty house. And no note. At first he's angry, then worried; and he can't think what to do about it. It's completely unlike Lucy, he can't think of a possible explanation where she could be at three in the morning. Has she left him, like Dan Houston's wife? A moment of panic spikes into him at the thought; then he shakes his head, clearing it of such nonsense. Lucy wouldn't do it.

Has something happened to her? An hour passes and the fear grows in him, then almost two hours pass, and it's just occurred to him that he could call the reverend, rather than the police, when she pulls into the driveway. He hurries out to greet her, relieved and angry.

"Where have you been!"

She tells him.

"Ah," he says stiffly, and puts his arms around her. Holds her.

He's too tired for this, he thinks. Too tired.

They stand there. He's awfully tired. He remembers a game he played with his brother when they were boys, during the marathon driving tours his parents took them on. At night in the motel rooms they took a deck of cards and divided it, and made card houses on the floor, in opposite corners of the room. Card fortresses would be a better name for them. Then they took a plastic spoon from McDonald's, and used it as a projectile—bent it back like a catapult arm with their thumbs and fingers, and let fly. The spoon took the most hilarious knuckleball flights across the room, and mostly missed. They laughed. . . .

And when the spoon hit the card houses, it was so *interesting*; it didn't matter whose was hit, it was just fun to see what happened. They noted that the card houses acted in one of two ways when struck by a direct hit. *Thwap!* They either collapsed instantly, the cards scattering, or else they resisted, settled down a little, and somehow in the hunkering down lost little or none of their structural integrity, their ability to hold up. Perhaps curiosity about that made Dennis an engineer.

Random images, in the exhausted mind. Where did that come from, he thinks. Ah. We're the card house now. There's never a situation where one card is threatened, the others left in peace; they're all threatened together and at once. All in a permanent crisis. How long has it been going on? Spoons flying from every direction. And the house of cards either holds or flies apart.

He's too tired for this, too depressed; there's no comfort in him to give. Lucy begins to sob in earnest. He tries to remember the Keilbacher girl; he only saw her a few times, flitting in and out. Blond hair. A lively kid. Nice. Easier to imagine Martin and Emma. Ach. Bad luck. Terrible luck. Worse by far than having Judge Andrew Tobiason turn down a protest despite the evidence; worse than anything possible in all that world of corruption and graft. Ach, it's bad everywhere. Spoons from every direction. He'll have to check out Jim's car, make sure it's all right. He doesn't know what to say. Lucy always wants something said, words, words, but he doesn't have any. Are there any words for this? No. Some strange stubbornness, of an interlocking placement, holds certain card houses up, under a fluky barrage of blows. . . . He hugs her harder, holds them up.

61

Jim hears about it the next day, from Lucy. "It was Abe who was the paramedic called to the accident."

"Oh, no. You're kidding."

"No, and he drove by to tell the Keilbachers, but they weren't home, so he came by to tell me. He looked bad."

"I bet."

Jim tries to get Abe on the phone, but Abe's parents are still on vacation and there's no answer up at the house; the answering machine is off.

He goes to the funeral the next morning, and stands at the back of the chapel at Fairhaven Cemetery. Watches the ceremony dully. He knew Lillian Keilbacher mostly in churches, he thinks. There was a time in high school when he was volunteered by Lucy to help build the Bible school on the back of the church lot; the church was too poor to hire a real construction crew, and the work was all volunteer, led by two churchgoing carpenters who seemed to get a kick out of it all, though it went awfully slowly. Every day that Jim was there he saw a skinny blond girl with braces who had the biggest, most enthusiastic hammer swing you could imagine. The carpenters used to go pale as they watched, but she was surprisingly accurate. That was Lillian. Jim can see perfectly the delighted brace-bright grin of the girl as she knocked a nail all the way in to the wood with one immense swing, Don the head carpenter clutching his heart and spluttering with laughter. . . .

They move outside into a shaft of sun. The cemetery is under the upper level of the Freeway Triangle, a concrete sky like low threatening clouds, but there is a big skylight gap overhead to let a little sunlight down. They walk slowly behind a hearse as it navigates the complex street plan of the city of the dead. Population over 200,000. Again Jim walks behind, watching the little crowd of people around the Keilbachers, the way they hold together. There is a feeling in their church community, standing on its little island of belief in the flood of twenty-first-century America, a feeling of solidarity that Jim has never experienced again since he stopped going. The camaraderie, the joy they shared, building that little Bible school! And it turned out solid, too, it's still there. Yes, there's no doubt Lucy is on to something with her involvement in the church. . . . But his faith. He has no faith. And it can't be faked. And without faith . . . .

Beyond the last row of graves is an orange grove, standing under a big skylight. The procession is in shade now, under the concrete underside of the Triangle, and the wide shaft of light falling on the green-and-orange trees is thick with dust, very bright. The trees are almost spheres, sitting on the ground: green spheres, dotted with many bright orange spheres. It's the last orange grove in all of Orange County. It belongs to the cemetery, and is slowly being taken out to make room for the dead.

The ceremony at graveside is short. No sign of Abe, Jim notes. He excuses himself to a disapproving Lucy, and slips off; the idea of a wake is too much.

He tracks up Saddleback Mountain, listening to Beethoven's *Hammerklavier Sonata.* There's no one home at Abe's place.

He follows the road up to the lookout parking lot on Santiago Peak, the easternmost of Saddleback's two. The western one, Modjeska Peak, is a few feet lower. He gets out of the car, walks to the stone wall on the parking lot's edge, looks down at Orange County.

There spread below him is his hometown. During the daytime it's a hazy jumble of buildings and flying freeway viaducts, no pattern visible. Even the upper level in the Freeway Triangle, which dominates the central plain, is hard to pick out. It's as if they brought cement trucks with their big cylindrical barrels up to this peak, and let loose a flood of concrete lava that covered the entire plain. Western civilization's last city.

Jim recalls the view from the hilltop in Itanos.

His thoughts are scattered, he can't make them cohere. Things are changing in him, the old channels of thought are breaking up and disappearing, with nothing new to take their place. He feels incoherent.

Depressed, he drives back down the mountain. He feels he should locate Abe, so he goes to Sandy's. Abe is not there, and neither is Sandy. Angela has heard of the accident, and she takes Jim out to the balcony, talks to him about other things. Jim sits there dully, touched by Angela's concern. She really is a wonderful person, one of his best friends, the sister his family didn't provide.

Now she stares at the palms of her hands, looking troubled. "Everything seems to be going wrong," she says. "Have you heard that Erica has broken off the alliance with Tashi?"

"No—what?"

"Yeah. She did it at last. She's stopped coming by here, too. I guess she decided on a total change." Angela isn't bitter, but she does sound sad. They sit on the balcony, looking at each other. The hum of the freeway wafts over them.

"It's no big surprise," Angela says. "Erica's been unhappy now for a long time."

"I know. . . . I wonder how Tash is taking it."

"It's so hard to tell with Tash. I'm sure he's upset, but he doesn't say much."

He does to Jim, though. Sometimes. "I should go see him. My God, everyone! . . ."

"I know."

The doorbell rings, and through the houseplants comes Virginia. "Hello, Jim." Quick kiss on the cheek. "I heard about your friend. I'm really sorry."

Jim nods, touched by her concern. Seems everyone pulls together at times like these.

Virginia looks lovely in the hazy afternoon light, hair banded white gold, flashing with an almost painful brightness. It's all part of the pattern, Jim sees. This is what it means to have friends, to be part of a functioning community. And that's what they are; another island poking out of the concrete. . . .

"Let me take you out to dinner," Virginia says, and gratefully Jim agrees. Angela sees them off with determined cheerfulness. They take Jim's car and track down to the Hungry Crab in Newport Beach.

Since they haven't talked in a while, there is a fair amount to say; and as they work their way through two bottles of wine and a crab feast, they get more and more festive. Jim can even describe the various comedies of the European jaunt; their fighting is past, they're beyond that, into a more mature stage of their relationship. Jim watches Virginia laugh, and the sight of her is more intoxicating than the wine: perfect glossy hair like a cap of jewels, deep beach tan, snub nose, freckles, wide white smile, a perfect match for the decor, perfect, perfect, perfect.

So he is quite drunk, both with wine and with his proximity to this beautiful animal, when they pay the bill and leave. Out into the salt cool of a Newport Beach evening, lurching together, holding hands, laughing at a pair of goggle-eyed sunburnt tourists—thoroughly enjoying themselves as they approach a group of students walking their way.

Then Jim sees Hana Steentoft in the group, head down in characteristic pose. As the group passes them she looks up at him, looks down again. The group walks by and into the Crab.

Jim has stopped, and at some point jerked his hand free of Virginia's. Now as he looks back at the restaurant the old sardonic smile is on her face. She says, "Ashamed to be seen with me, eh?"

"No, no."

"Sure."

Jim doesn't know what to say, he can't concentrate on Virginia right now, he doesn't care what Virginia thinks or feels. All he wants to do is rush into the Crab and try to explain things to Hana. It's like a nightmare: somehow trapped in an old disaster alliance, which poisons the new relationship—he's had nightmares just like this! How could it be happening?

But it is happening, and here he is, standing on the sidewalk with a furious Virginia Novello. Abandoning her in Newport Beach and running in to throw himself at Hana's feet in a group of friends is just too melodramatic for Jim, too extreme, he can't see himself doing it.

So he stays to face Virginia's wrath.

"You really are rude, you know that, Jim?"

"Come on, Virginia. Give me a break."

How easily they fall back into it. All the variations on a theme:

It's all your fault. No it's not; I'm not conceding a thing to you;
it's all your fault. Back and forth, back and forth. You're a bad
person. No I'm not, I'm a good person. You're a bad person.
There are a lot of ways to say these things, and Jim and Virginia
rehearse the whole repertory on the way home, the little moment
of camaraderie completely and utterly forgotten.

Their favorite coda, as Jim tracks into South Coast Plaza and
stops the car: "I don't want to ever see you again!" Virginia
shouts.

"Good!" Jim shouts back. "You won't!"

And Virginia slams the door and runs off.

Jim takes a deep sigh, puts his forehead down on the steering
switch. How many people can he hurt at once? This day . . .

He sits for several minutes, head miserably on the dash, worrying about Hana. He's got to do something, or he'll . . . he doesn't
know what. Abe. Can't find Abe. Tashi! Man, it's hitting everywhere at once, as if the whole island is threatened by flood. All
falling apart! He tracks down Bristol, heading toward Tashi's place.

62

Up on Tashi's roof it's quiet and dark. The tent is lit on one side
by the dull glow of a lamp inside. On the other side of the roof,
among the vegetable trays, there's a dim glow of hibachi coals.
Tashi, a big bulk in the darkness, sits in a little folding beach chair
beside the fire. A sweet soy smell of teriyaki sauce rises from the
meat on the fire. "Hey, Jim."

"Hey, Tash." Jim picks up a folded beach chair from beside
the tent wall and unfolds it. Sits.

Tash leans forward to flip over one of his infamous turkey
burgers, and the grease flares on the coals for a moment, lighting
Tashi's face. He looks as impassive as ever, picking up a water

bottle, spraying out the flames. In the renewed dark he squeezes a little of his homemade teriyaki on the turkey burgers, and they hiss and steam aromatically.

"I heard about Erica."

"Hmm."

"She just left?"

". . . It was a little more complicated than that. But that's what it comes down to." Tash leans forward again, slides the spatula under the burger and checks it out. Puts it into a sandwich already prepared. Eats.

"Damn." Jim finds himself furious with Erica. "She just . . . did it?"

"Umph."

"Unbelievable." To leave someone like Tash! "Stupid woman. Man, it's such a dumb thing to do!"

Tash swallows. "Erica doesn't think so."

Jim clicks his tongue, irritated. Tash seems so even-headed about the whole thing, as if he has judged the matter and found he is perhaps in agreement with Erica. . . .

Tash finishes eating. "Let's get stoned."

They get out a full container of California Mello, and lid the whole thing, back and forth, back and forth, until the tears are running down Jim's face, and his corneas feel like thick slabs of glass. White-orange clouds, heavily underlit by the city, roll slowly inland. Slowly, very slowly, Jim's anger subsides. It's still there, but it's been muted, banked like the coals in the hibachi to a small, melancholy feeling of betrayal. That's life. People betray you, betray your friends. He recalls the look on Debbie Riggs's face as she yelled at him. He himself has betrayed more people than have ever betrayed him, and the realization dampens his anger even more. He was shifting onto Erica what he felt toward himself. . . .

"Angela called," Tash says. "She said you went to dinner with Virginia?"

"Yeah. Damn it."

Tash chuckles. "How is she?"

"Feeling enormous amounts of righteous indignation, I would guess, this very moment."

"Virginia nirvana, eh?"

Jim laughs. They can insult each other's ex-allies, and cheer each other up. Very sensible. The Mello continues to kick in and he sees how silly his thoughts are. He's blasted into a calm almost beyond speech.

"Whoah."

"No lie."

"Heavy."

"Untold."

They chuckle, but only in a very mellow way.

Much cloud gazing later, Jim says, "So what will you do?"

"Who knows." After a long silence: "I don't think I can go on living this way, though. It's too much work. I've been thinking about moving." And suddenly Jim can hear pain in Tashi's voice, he understands that the stoic mask is a mask and nothing more. Of course the man is hurt. Emotions punch their way through the fog of the Mello, and Jim regrets the anesthetizing. He feels, all of a sudden, overwhelmingly helpless. There's nothing he can do to help, not a thing.

"Where to?"

"Don't know. Far away."

"Oh, man."

They sit together in silence, and watch a whole lot of orange clouds float inland.

63

When Jim tracks home later that night, he is feeling about as low as he can remember feeling. He's below music, he doesn't even try it. Just the sounds of the freeway as he types in the program for home and tracks along, slumped back in his seat. Even in the middle of the night the lightshow is pinballing all over the basin, a clutch of silent helicopters hovering over the Marine Station like flying saucers, jets booming down onto John Wayne, the flying freeways almost at capacity. . . .

Again home strikes him as an empty shell, a dirty little studio under a freeway, filled with futile paper and plastic attempts to stave off reality. Which isn't such a bad idea. He goes to the videotapes, sees the stack of them that Virginia and he made on their bedroom systems, when they were first going out. Perversely he feels a strong desire to look at one. Virginia undressing, in the casual routine of taking off clothes, with the thoughtlessness of untying shoelaces. Standing naked before a tall complex of mirrors, brushing her hair and watching the infinity of images of herself. . . .

"No!" The repugnance at his desire rises faster than the desire itself, a new feeling in Jim. If he becomes captive to her video image tonight, just hours after their last fight, how much easier will it be in the weeks and months to come? It'll be so easy just to concentrate on the image . . . and he'll be in thrall to it, having an affair with a video lady, like so many other men in America.

Fearfully he grabs up the stack of cassettes. "I'm pulling out for good," he shouts at the video, and laughs crazily. He pulls an eyedropper of Buzz from his bookshelf and lids drops until he's blind. Instant hum in all his nervous system, replacing lust. Like the buzz in the telephone wires, or the freeway magnetic tracks, a sort of drunkenness of the nerves, which makes him want to get really drunk. He goes to the fridge, pops a Bud, downs it. Downs another one.

Back to the cassettes. "I live a life of symbolic gestures, and not much more," he tells the room. "But when it's all you've got . . ."

There are nine cassettes of Virginia and him, the labels penciled over, sometimes in Virginia's hand: US, *IN BED*. Should he save just one? "No, no, no." He throws them all in his daypack, goes outside.

It's a warm night. Overhead the freeway hums, right in phase with Jim's nerves. He can see the sides of the cars in the fast lane zoom by, one headlight each. One of the freeway's great concrete pylons thrusts out of the sidewalk just three houses down. The maintenance men's ladder starts ten feet up, but the neighborhood kids have tied a nylon rope ladder to it. With some difficulty, aware of his buzz, his drunkenness, Jim gets the daypack on his back and ascends the ladder. When his head is at the level of the freeway he stops. Buzz of cars passing, lightshow of headlights strobing by, zoom zoom zoom zoom. Funny to think that only the little units extending down from the front axle, not quite touching the shiny strip of the track, are guiding the cars, and keeping them from running into each other, or over the rail above Jim's head, down onto the houses below. Magnetism, what is it, anyway? Jim shakes his head, confused. Concentrates on the task at hand. Left arm wrapped over a step of the ladder, he frees the daypack from his right arm and twists it around to unzip it. Out comes a cassette. All the cars' tires run over approximately the same part of the freeway; they've made two black bands on the freeway's white concrete, a couple feet to left and right of the track, and almost two feet wide themselves. He's not too far from the nearer one.

He slides a cassette over the concrete, and it stops right in the black band. The next car to pass crunches it to smithereens. Loops of tape blow off to the side.

''Yeah! Good shot!'' Jim continues to cheer himself on as cassette after cassette skids onto the tire track of the fast lane, and is reduced to plastic fragments and streamers of tape.

The last one, however, goes too far, landing between the tire marks and the guidance track. Without pausing to think about it Jim climbs onto the freeway, catching the daypack on the rail and practically pulling himself off into space. Oops. During one of the rare gaps in traffic he runs out into the fast lane, recovers the cassette, trips and staggers, puts the cassette on the tire marks, scrambles desperately back to the ladder.

A big car crunches the cassette under its wheels.

Carefully, awkwardly, Jim descends. Safe on the ground again, he sucks in a deep breath. ''Probably should have kept just one.'' He laughs. ''No backsliding now, boy! You're free whether you like it or not.'' Overhead, long tangles of videotape float across the sky.

64

No sooner has Jim returned to his ap, which, to tell the truth, looks just as dreary and lifeless as before, than there's a sharp knock at the door. He opens it.

"Abe! What are you doing here?"

Abe smiles lopsidedly.

Stupid question. Abe's eyes have a drawn, tired, defiant look, and Jim understands: he's here for the company. For help. Jim can hardly believe it. Abe's never come to Jim's place before, except once or twice to pick him up. Given their homes it makes sense to go up Saddleback and hang out there, on the roof of OC, if hanging out is what they're going to do.

"I'm here to get wasted," Abe says harshly, and laughs.

"What, Sandy's not home?"

"That's right." Again the abrupt laugh. But then Abe's direct gaze catches Jim's eye, admitting that there's more to it than that. Abe steps in, looks around. Jim sees it through Abe's eyes.

"Let's go outside," he says, "and sit on the curb. I'm sick of this place."

Seated on the curb, next to the fire hydrant at the corner, feet crossed in the gutter, they can look up at the freeway overhead and see the roofs of the cars in the fast lane, see the fans of light from the headlights, sweeping by. Two men sitting on a curb.

Abe pulls out one of Sandy's monster spliffs and lights it. They pass it back and forth, expelling great clouds of smoke into the empty street. A passing car tracks through the cloud and scatters it. "Quit passing so quickly," Abe says at one point. "Take two hits, then pass it. Don't you even know how to smoke a joint?"

"No."

They sit silently. Nothing to say? Not exactly. Jim supposes that his value in times like these is his willingness to start conversations, to talk about things that matter.

"So," he says, coughing on a deep hit. "You were the paramedics called to Lillian's crash, huh?"

"Yeah."

"You and Xavier?"

"Yeah."

Long pause.

"How's he doing?"

A shrug. "I don't know. Same as ever. Falling apart, hanging on. I guess it's a permanent condition for X."

"Sounds tough."

Abe purses his mouth. "Impossible. I can't do it, anyway."

He starts fidgeting in typical Abe fashion, finally getting up to squat on his hams, balancing over his feet with armpits on knees, in the aboriginal crouch that is a favorite with him, because then even sitting takes nervous energy. "Have I changed much this last year, that you can tell?"

"Everyone changes."

Abe gives him a sidelong glance, laughs sharply. "Even you?"

"Maybe," Jim says, thinking of the last month. "Maybe, at last."

Abe accepts that. "Yeah. Well, I'm wondering. I mean, I've been getting like X, all this last year. I'm wondering if I can keep going. You know . . ."

His voice tightens, he's looking down in the gutter now. "X told me that once when he was losing it bad he couldn't stand any of the crashes with kids in them. Because once he looked in this backseat and found a body and said to himself, What the hell is this black kid doing with these white folks, and he turned it over and it had one of his kids' faces. And he sort of fainted on his feet, and when he came to it was some white kid he'd never seen."

"My God."

"I know. You can see why X worries me. But—but"—Abe is still resolutely looking in the gutter—"when I saw it was Lillian, I stepped away and all of a sudden remembered X's story and I thought I had gone crazy, that it wasn't her and I had hallucinated it. And then when I was sure it was Lillian, I mean really sure . . . I was almost glad!''

''I understand.''

''No you don't!''

Abe jumps up, paces back and forth in front of Jim, out in the street. He hands Jim the forgotten spliff: ''You don't understand! You think you do because you read so fucking much, but you never really do any of it so you don't really know!''

Jim looks at Abe calmly. ''That's probably true.''

Abe grimaces, shakes his head a few times. ''Ah, no. That's bullshit. Everyone knows, as long as they're not sleepwalkers. But shit. I would rather have had Lillian Keilbacher dead than have gone crazy for even one minute!''

''Just at that moment, you mean. It's a natural reaction, you were shocked out of your mind. You can think anything at times like that.''

''Uhn.'' Abe isn't satisfied by that. But he sits down on the curb again, takes the spliff.

''Most people would have just freaked on the spot.''

Abe shakes his head, taking a hit. ''Not so.''

''Well, not many would try to go tell the family like you did.''

''Uhn.''

They smoke a while in silence.

Jim takes a deep breath; he's used to the Bernards' Saddleback house becoming a brooding, Byronic place, overhanging the world; but it appears Abe can confer the atmosphere wherever he goes, if his immense nervous energy is spinning him in the right way, in the right mode . . . so that Jim's streetcorner curb under its sodium vapor light now swirls with heraldic significance, it looks like an Edward Hopper painting, the bungalow aps lined out side by side, the minilawns, empty sidewalks, fire hydrant, orange glare of light, giant pylons and the great strip of freeway banding the white-orange sky—all external signs of a dark, deep moodiness.

Abe holds the spliff between thumb and forefinger, speaks to it softly. ''It's getting so that anytime I can hear that *sound*''—glancing up briefly at the freeway—''or, or anytime I see a stream of headlights flowing red white, I hear the snips ripping through the metal. I hear the cutting hidden in the rest of the sound, sometimes I even hear some poor torn-up bastard moaning—just in the freeway sounds!''

He's squishing the spliff flat, and suddenly he hands it back to Jim.

''And following taillights is like blood over exposed bone, red on white, you know the headlights, so bright coming at you . . . I mean I really see that.''

His voice is going away, Jim can barely hear his words. ''The way the cars crumple and shear, and the blood—there's a lot of it in a body. And their faces always look so—like Lillian's face, it was so . . .'' He's shaking now, his whole body is racked with shaking, his face is contorted in the mask that faces go to when crying is stopped short no matter the cost to the muscles. Abruptly he stands again.

As if on a string Jim stands too. Tentatively he puts a hand to his friend's shoulder. ''It's your work, Abe. It's hard work, but it's good work, I mean we need it. It's what you want to do—''

''It's *not* what I want to do! I don't want to do it anymore! Man, haven't you been listening?'' He jerks away from Jim, turns and paces around him like a predatory animal. ''Pay attention, will you?'' he almost shouts. ''I'm going crazy out there, I tell you, I can't even do my job anymore!''

''Yes you can—''

''I cannot! How do you know? Don't tell me what I can or can't do out there—so fucking glib—'' He reaches up and takes a wild swing at Jim's upraised hand, hits it away, swings again and backhands Jim on the chest, for an instant he looks like he's going to beat Jim up, and appalled Jim holds his arms up across his chest to take the blows—

Abe stops himself, shudders, twists away, takes off rapidly down the street; turns, wavers indecisively, plops down on the curb and leans over the gutter, face between his knees, buried in his hands. And there he rocks back and forth, back and forth.

Jim, frightened, his throat crimped tight at the sudden exposure to so much pain, stands there helplessly. He doesn't know what to do, doesn't have any idea what Abe might *want* him to do.

After a long while he walks down the street, and sits down next to Abe, whose rocking gets slower and slower as his shaking subsides. They both just sit there.

The forgotten roach, black with oil, is still pressed between Jim's thumb and forefinger; he pulls a lighter from his shirt pocket, torches the roach's ashy end, sucks on it till it blooms smoke. He takes a hit so big that he can't contain it, and coughs hard. Abe has his elbows on his knees now, and he's staring silently out at the street. His face is all streaked. Jim offers him the roach. He takes it, puffs on it, passes it back, all without a word. A final paroxysm shudders through his flesh, and then he's still.

After a while he looks at Jim with a wry grimace. "See what I mean?"

Jim nods. He's at a loss for words. Without premeditation he says, "Yeah, man. You're fucking nuts."

Abe laughs shortly. Sniffs.

They finish the roach in silence. They sit on the curb and watch the traffic hum by overhead.

Abe sighs. "I never thought it would get this hard."

65

Abe leaves. Shaken to the core, Jim finds himself prowling his ap restlessly. Nothing in it offers the slightest consolation. What a day it's been. . . .

The longer he stays in the ap, the more intense becomes his helpless, miserable nervousness. He can't think what to do. What time is it, anyway? Three A.M. The dead hour. Nothing to do, no one to turn to—the friends he might have looked to for help are looking to him, and he isn't up to it.

There isn't a chance of sleeping. The malignancy of thought, vision and memory, all drugged, speeded up, spiked by fear, makes sleep out of the question. The day keeps recurring in his mental theater in a scramble of images, each worse than the last, the sum making him sick with a synergistic toxicity. He recalls Hana's face, as she saw him and Virginia stagger out of the Hungry Crab together. No great scowl of anguish or despair, no nothing that melodramatic; just a quick snap of shock, of surprise, and then an instantly averted gaze, a disengagement, a refusal to look at him. Goddamn it!

He gives up on any attempt to get hold of himself, and calls Hana's number, without a thought in his head as to what he's going to say. At the sound of the ring he panics, his pulse shoots up, he'd hang up if he weren't sure that Hana would know it was him waking her and then failing to hold together the nerve to speak to her, and with that prospect before him he holds on, through ring after ring . . . .

Nobody home.

66

Nobody home.

How did it happen?

At first it was a result of the tracts, the freeways, the cars. If you lived in a new suburb, then you had to drive to do your shopping. How much easier to park in one place, and do all your shopping in one location!

So the malls began. At first they were just shopping centers. A big asphalt parking lot, surrounded on two or three sides by stores; there were scores of them, as in most of the rest of America.

Then they became complexes of parking lots mixed with islands of stores, as in Fashion Square, the oldest shopping center in the county. They were popular. They did great at Christmastime. In effect they became the functional equivalent of villages, places where you could walk to everything you needed—villages tucked like islands into the multilayered texture of autopia. Once you parked at a shopping center, you could return to a life on foot. And at that idea the body, the brainstem, said Yeah.

South Coast Plaza was one of the first to go beyond this idea, to complete the square of stores and roof it, putting the parking lot on the outside. Call it a mall. An air-conditioned island village—except, of course, that all the villagers were visitors.

When South Coast Plaza opened in 1967 it was a giant success, and the Segerstrom family, heirs to the lima bean king C. J. Segerstrom, kept building on their land until they had the mall of malls, the equivalent of several fifty-story buildings spread out over a thousand acres, all of it enclosed. A sort of spaceship village grounded on the border between Santa Ana and Costa Mesa.

They made a lot of money.

Other malls sprang up, like daughter mushrooms in a ring around SCP. They all grew, enclosing more space, allowing more consumers to spend their time indoors. Westminster Mall, Huntington Center, Fashion Island, the Orange Mall, Buena Park Center, the City, Anaheim Plaza, Brea Mall, Laguna Hills Mall, Orange Fair Center, Cerritos Center, Honer Plaza, La Habra Fashion Square, Tustin Mall, Mission Viejo Fair, Trabuco Marketplace, the Mission Mall, Canyon Center, all were in place and flourishing by the end of the century, growing by accretion, taking up the surrounding neighborhoods, adding stores, restaurants, banks, gyms, boutiques, hairdressers, aps, condos. Yes, you could live in a mall if you wanted to. A lot of people did.

By 2020 their number had doubled again, and many square miles of Orange County were roofed and air-conditioned. When the Cleveland National Forest was developed there was room for a big one; Silverado Mall rivaled SCP for floorspace, and in 2027 it became the biggest mall of all—a sign that the back country had arrived at last.

The malls merged perfectly with the new elevated freeway system, and midcounty it was often possible to take an offramp directly into a parking garage, from which one could take an escalator through the maze of a mall's outer perimeter, and return to your ap, or go to dinner, or continue your shopping, without ever coming within thirty feet of the buried ground. Everything you needed to do, you could do in a mall.

You could live your life indoors.

And none of that, of course, ever went away.

67

Dennis gets a call from Washington, D.C. "Dennis? It's Louis Goldman. I wanted to tell you about the latest developments in the Stormbee case. It's looking very hopeful, I think."

"Yeah?"

"We've been pursuing several avenues here, and a couple are really moving for us. We've been in contact with Elisha Francisco, the aide to Senator George Forrester. Forrester is head of the Senate Budget Committee, and he's on the Armed Services Committee, and he's been in a kind of a feud with the Air Force for about four years. So his office is always receptive to ammunition for this feud, and when I gave Francisco the facts of our case he jumped on the matter instantly."

"And what can they do?" McPherson asks cautiously.

"They can do a lot! Essentially the GAO, the Congress's watchdog, was steamrolled in our case, and Congress is touchy about being ignored like that. Senator Forrester has already asked the Procurements Branch of the Office of Technology Assessment for an independent report on the matter. That should be really interesting, because the OTA is as far out of the pressure points as you can be in this town. Procurements Branch at OTA has the reputation of being the most impartial assessment group that you can bring to bear on the military. Anyone in Congress can ask them for a report, and no one else has any leverage on them at all, so they pride themselves on giving a completely unbiased spread of the pros and cons, on *anything*. Nerve gas, biological warfare, persuasion technology, you name it, they'll give you a report on it that sticks to technological efficiency and only that.''

"So we might see the report that the GAO should have made?''

"That's right. And Forrester will hammer the Air Force with it, too, you can bet on that.''

"Can he get the Stormbee decision thrown out, then?''

"Well, not all by himself. There's no mechanism for it, see. The best that could happen is that the Secretary of the Air Force would knuckle under to Congress's prodding, but that isn't too likely, no matter how much Forrester hammers them. However, if there were another appeal by LSR moving forward at the same time as this—if we appeal the decision to a higher court, and all this other stuff is breaking in Congress, then a new judge will almost certainly overturn Tobiason's decision, and you'll be back in business.''

"You think so?''

"I'm sure of it. So we're sending a letter to you and to Argo/Blessman advising you to authorize us to initiate an appeal, but I wanted to tell you about it since you're the liaison, so you can do what needs to be done at your end.''

"Yeah, sure. I'll get right on it. So—so, you think we have a chance with this?''

"It's better than that, Dennis. Senator Forrester is one of the most powerful people in Washington, and he's a good man, as straight as they come. He doesn't like what he's heard about this, and he's not one to forget. I think it's our turn at last.''

"Great.''

McPherson writes a memo to Lemon immediately after the phone call, outlining what he has learned and suggesting immediate approval of the appeal.

As he writes down the facts, his hopes come flooding back. It seems to him, all of the sudden, that the system might really work after all. The network of checks and balances is almost suffocating in its intricacy—it is perhaps too intricate; but what that means in the end is that power is spread out everywhere, and no one part of the network can cheat another, without the balance of the whole being upset. When that happens the other parts of the network will step in, because their own power is threatened if any other part gains too much; they'll fly in with a check like a hockey defenseman's, and the balance will be restored. The Air Force tried to assert that it was above the system, outside the network; now the rest of the network is going to drag them back into it. It's the American way, stumbling forward in its usual clumsy, inefficient style—maddening to watch, but ultimately fair.

So, feeling better about that, he spends the rest of the day working on the Ball Lightning program. And here too he sees signs of some progress, signs that they might possibly reach the deadline with a workable system. The programmers have come to him chattering with excitement about a program that will successfully latch the beams from several lasers to a missile, in a phased array; this vastly increases the intensity of the beam, so that the shock pulse will work again. They also believe they can track the missiles past the boost phase, by extrapolating their courses very precisely. Combine that with the shorter dwell time offered by the phased array and . . . they might just be able to knock down the percentage specified by the Air Force. It could happen. Even though it may take them into the post–boost phase a bit.

Spurred by the possibility, McPherson wheedles, coaxes, and bullies Dan Houston into reactivating his brain and doing his share of the work; it will take a push effort by everyone to get the job done in time, a sort of phased array of effort. And Houston is a mess. He's never mentioned to Dennis the evening at El Torito when Dennis had to help him down to his car; but now it's clear to Dennis that that was not a particularly unusual evening. Dan is drinking heavily every day; he needs a haircut, sometimes he needs a shave, his clothes look slept in; really, he's the stereotype of the man whose ally has left him, whose life is falling apart. Sometimes Dennis wants to snap at him, say, "Come off it, Dan, you're living a video script!"

But then it occurs to him that Houston's pain is real enough, and that this is the only way he knows how to express it, if he is consciously living the role. And if not, it's just what happens when you don't care anymore, when you've lost hope, when you've started drinking hard.

So McPherson takes him out to lunch, and listens to his whole sad story, which he is now willing to talk about openly—"The truth is, Mac, Dawn has moved up to her folks'." "Oh, really?"

—and Dennis gives him a pep talk, and talks to him in intense detail about what needs to be done by Houston and Houston's part of the team, and he even refuses to allow Houston to order another pitcher of margaritas, though that only gets him a look of dull resentment. "Do it after work if you have to, Dan," McPherson snaps, irritated with him. Stewart Lemon tactics? Well, whatever it takes; they don't have much time left.

And the fact is, Houston puts in a better afternoon's effort than he has in weeks and weeks. By God, McPherson thinks, looking over his list of Things To Do before he goes home—we might pull it off after all.

68

Jim sleeps on his living room couch through the day, curled on his side around a tensely knotted stomach. He wakes often, each time more exhausted than the last. Every time he gains enough autonomy to pull himself upright, he calls Hana. No answer, no answering machine. More uneasy, unrestful sleep. His dreams are sickening, the problems in them more outlandishly insoluble than ever before. In the last of them he dreams he and all his friends have been captured by the Russians and held in the Kremlin. He tries to escape through a pinball machine, but the glass top slides back too quickly and cuts off his head. He has to climb back out and go through the ordeal of finding his head without the help of his eyes, then place the head back on his neck and balance it there very carefully. No one will believe he is walking around with his head chopped off. Premier Kerens, in a uniform with lots of medals, is flanked by Debbie and Angela and Gabriela, all wearing nothing but underwear bottoms. "Okay," the premier says, holding up a device like an artificial hand that will cut out hearts. "You choose which one goes first."

He wakes up sweating, his stomach clenched as if by cramp. About two P.M. he tries Hana again, and she answers.

"Hello?"

"Ah? Oh! Hana! It's Jim. I've . . . been trying to get hold of you."

"Have you."

"Yeah, but you weren't home. Listen, ah, Hana—"

"Jim, I don't feel like talking to you right now."

"No, Hana, no—I'm sorry!"

But she's hung up.

"Shit!" He slams down the phone so hard it almost cracks. After a moment he dials the number again. Busy signal, hateful sound. She's left the phone off the cradle. No chance for contact. It's so stupid! "Oh, man."

He wants to go up there, beg her forgiveness. Then he gets angry at the unfairness of it, he wants her to beg his forgiveness, for being so unreasonable. "Come on! I was just having dinner with a friend! After the funeral of another friend!" But that isn't exactly true. He pulls his big Mexican cookbook from the shelf and furiously slams it to the floor, kicks it across the kitchen. Very satisfying, until the moment he stops.

An hour later, angrier than ever, he calls up Arthur. "Arthur, have you got anything ready to go?"

"Well—come on over and we'll talk about it."

Jim tracks over to Arthur's place in Fountain Valley. Arthur's face is flushed, he is in a strong field of excitement, he takes Jim's upper arm in a tight grip and grins. "Okay, Jim, we're on for another strike, but this one's a little different. The target is Laguna Space Research." His straightforward blue gaze asks the obvious question.

Jim says, "What about the night watchmen they made the announcement about?"

"They've been taken out of the plants and are out on the perimeter."

"Why?" Jim doesn't understand.

Arthur shrugs. "We're not sure. Someone bombed a computer company's plant up in Silicon Valley, and a janitor inside was killed. Not our doing, but LSR doesn't know that. So they're going to automatic defenses and a perimeter watch. It's going to be a little more dangerous. We've got them all running scared. But this time—well, I wasn't going to call you, because it was LSR.''

Jim nods. ''I appreciate it. But it's the ballistic missile defense system we're going after, right?''

''Right. LSR has the lion's share of the boost-phase defense, Ball Lightning as they call it. A successful strike against it could be devastating.'' Arthur's excitement is evident in the tightness of his grip on Jim's arm.

''I want to do it,'' Jim says.

It's the only avenue of action left to him, and he can't stand not to act; the tension in him would drive him mad. ''My father's in another program, this won't have anything to do with him. Besides, it has to be done. It has to be done if anything is ever going to change!''

Arthur nods, still looking at him closely. ''Good man. It'll be easier with your help, I'll admit that.''

Gently Jim shifts his arm out of Arthur's grip. Arthur looks at his hand, surprised. ''I'm wired,'' he confesses. ''It's tomorrow night, see. Tomorrow night, and I thought I was doing it on my own.''

''Same procedure?''

''Yeah, everything'll go just the same. Should be simple, as long as we keep a good distance away and under cover, and . . .''

Jim listens to Arthur absently, distracted by his own anger, by everything else. He thought the commitment to action would release some of the tension in him; instead he is more tense than ever, he almost needs to bend over, give in to the contraction of the stomach muscles. Laguna Space Research . . . Well, do it! None of these companies should be exempt! Something has to be done!

It's time to act, at last.

69

Sandy hears about the planned attack on LSR from Bob Tompkins, who gives him a call that afternoon. "Good news, Sandy. Raymond is going to give us a hand in the matter of the lost laundry. Our guardian angel is going to have some trouble tomorrow night, at about midnight. One of those accidents that have been happening lately, you know."

"One of Arthur's ventures?" Sandy asks.

Brief silence at the other end. "Yeah, but let's not talk about it in too much detail now. The point is, when the accident happens our guardian angels will have their hands full, and it'll be on the side opposite our little aquatic problem, so we think surveillance there will be temporarily abandoned. If you're ready out there, you'll be able to rescue the laundry you had to put on hold."

"I don't know, Bob." Sandy is frowning to himself. "I don't like the sound of it, to tell you the truth."

"We need that laundry, Sandy. And since you put it there, you'll have the easiest time finding it again."

"I still don't like it."

"Come on, Sandy. We didn't make the mess. In fact, we're the ones making you the opportunity to get out of it gracefully. Solvently. Just go for a little night boating, cruise in to your beach, collect the laundry, and return. There won't be a problem tomorrow night, and all will be well."

Sandy recognizes the threat behind the pleasantry, and in some ways it does sound like a very easy out of a sticky dilemma, which up to this point has only offered him the choice of either big debt, or the permanent loss of his Blacks Cliffs friends (at best). And it does sound like it will go. . . .

"Okay," he says unwillingly. "I'll do it. I'll need some help, though. My assistant from last time probably won't be interested."

"We'll send someone, along with the keys to a motorboat based in Dana Point. In fact I may come myself."

"That would be good. What time does this happen?"

"Tomorrow, midnight."

"All right. And you'll show when?"

"I'll give you a call tomorrow morning. Me or a friend will meet you in Dana Point in the evening."

"All right."

"Tubular, man. See you then."

Sandy calls Tash and asks for his help, but as he expected, Tash refuses to have anything to do with it. "It's stupid, Sandy. You should pass on the whole thing."

"Can't afford to."

This gives Tashi pause, but in the end he still refuses.

Sandy hangs up, sighs, checks his watch. He's already late for half a dozen appointments, and he's still got twenty calls to make. In fact he's going to have to pinball around all day and tomorrow morning to get ready for this rescue operation. No rest for the weary. He lids some Buzz and Pattern Perception, starts tapping out a phone number.

As the line rings he thinks about it.

Now he knows that Jim is working with Arthur, and Arthur is working for Raymond, and that Raymond is pursuing a private vendetta for private purposes—and perhaps making a profit on the side, or so it appears. The shape of the whole setup is clear to him.

But now—now he's in a situation where he can't do anything with what he knows. All his detective work was done with the idea that he could tell Jim something Jim didn't know, help him out, perhaps warn him away from trouble. Tell him what was really going on, so that he wouldn't continue thinking he was part of some idealistic resistance to the war machine, or whatever he is thinking—so he could get out of it before something went wrong.

Now Sandy can't do anything of the kind. In fact he has to hope that Jim does a good job of it. "Come through for me, Jimbo. . . ."

70

Lemon gets a call from Donald Hereford in New York. It looks like a sunny evening in Manhattan.

Hereford gets right to the point: "Have you gotten all of the night watchmen out of the plant out there?"

"Yes, we did that right after you visited. But listen, the Ball Lightning team reports some significant breakthroughs, and I thought I should tell you about them—"

Hereford is shaking his head. "Just keep the situation in the plant stable, especially in the next few days."

Lemon nods stiffly, frustration tugging at the corners of his mouth. "Do you know . . ."

Hereford frowns. "We've found the source of the difficulty. He's doing it for hire."

"And he's been hired by?"

But that's going too far. Hereford looks out at New York's big harbor, says, "Let's not talk about this anymore now. Later we might be able to discuss it more fully."

"Okay."

He'll never find out anything more about this, Lemon realizes; it's happening on a level he isn't on, it's above him. Part of him is galled by the realization; part of him is happy not to know, not to be involved. Leave this sort of thing to others!

Hereford is about to switch off when Lemon remembers something else. "Oh, listen, we've gotten a request from our legal representative in Washington, to file an appeal in the Stormbee decision." He describes the situation in detail. "So, it sounds like another appeal and we'll really have a good chance of success."

331

Hereford frowns. "Let me get back to you on that," he says, and the screen goes blank.

71

The next day, after a productive morning and a busy lunch conferring with Dan Houston, Dennis gets a call from Lemon's secretary Ramona, instructing him to come up for a conference with the boss. McPherson needs to talk to him anyway, so he ignores his usual irritation at the peremptory summons and goes on up.

Lemon is standing in front of his window as usual, looking out at the sea. He seems on edge, ill at ease—at least to a certain minute extent. It's hard to tell, but McPherson has had to become an expert in reading the tiny signals that mark his boss's mercurial mood swings, and now, as he sits down on the hot seat and watches Lemon pacing, he senses something unusual, a tension beyond the usual manic energy.

At first he speaks only of the Ball Lightning program. He really grills McPherson about it, a cross-examination as intense as any Lemon has ever subjected him to, something reminiscent of an SSEB questioning back in Dayton. Lemon hasn't discussed technical matters in such detail as this in years; he's really done his homework.

But why? McPherson can't figure it out.

"What it comes down to," Lemon says heavily when he is done, "is that you've got a great idea for a phased array attack, which takes us far into the post–boost phase. But we can't meet the specs that we supposedly proved we could meet, in the initial proposal that won us the program."

"That's right," McPherson says. "It isn't physically possible."

"Not for you, you mean."

McPherson shrugs. He's so tired of Lemon he doesn't even

care about hiding it anymore. "Not for me, right. I can't change the laws of physics. Maybe you can. But if you fake tests to try to bend the laws of physics, you always get caught at this point, don't you."

Lemon's eyes are just barely narrowed, a dangerous sign. "You're saying Houston faked the tests on the proposal?"

"We've just gone over all the data, right? We've known this ever since you put me on the program. What's the point of all this? Someone either concocted a good-looking test, with real but irrelevant results—and if that's faking the Air Force has been doing it for years—or else someone made a stupid mistake, and assumed the test proved the system would work in the real world, when it didn't."

Lemon nods slowly, as if satisfied with something. For a long time he stands staring out the window.

McPherson watches him; he's lost the drift of the meeting, he still doesn't know what Lemon wanted him here for. Confirmation that the Ball Lightning program is really and truly sunk? It isn't, if you stretch the definition of the boost phase, give the defense more time; but Lemon doesn't seem interested in that, he seems to think that the Air Force will reject the system if any spec is unfulfilled. And he may be right about that, but they have to try.

McPherson brings up the matter of Goldman's phone call and the Stormbee appeal.

Lemon nods. "I got your memo yesterday."

"We only need to give them an okay to initiate the appeal, and we're in business. It looks really promising, from Goldman's account."

Lemon turns his head to look at him. Face blank. No expression at all. Sunlight makes his left eye look like crystal.

Slowly he shakes his head. "We've gotten other instructions from Hereford. No appeal."

"What?"

"No appeal."

Even through his shock, McPherson can see that Lemon is not rubbing this one in in his usual style, taunting McPherson with it. In fact, he looks uncomfortable, depressed. But all this is just his continuous Lemon-watch, going on automatically under the shock of the news.

McPherson stands. "Just what the hell is going on? We've

worked on this for a year now, and put some twenty million dollars into it, and we're right on the edge of winning the contract!"

Lemon puts a hand up. "I know," he says wearily. "Sit down, Mac."

When McPherson remains standing, Lemon sits himself, on the edge of his desk.

"It's a victory we can't afford to win."

"What?"

"That's Hereford's decision. And I suppose he's right, though I don't like it. Do you know what a Pyrrhic victory is, Mac?"

"Yes."

Lemon sighs heavily. "Sometimes it seems like all the victories are Pyrrhic, these days."

He gathers himself, looks at McPherson sharply. "It's like this. If we win this one—force the Air Force to take back their award, and win the contract ourselves—then we've got the Stormbee system, sure. But we've also embarrassed the Air Force in front of the whole industry, the whole country. And if we do that, then Stormbee is the last program we can ever expect to get from the Air Force again. Because they'll remember. They'll do their best to bankrupt us. Already they've got our balls in a vise with this Ball Lightning program going bad on us. That's bad enough, but beyond that—no more black programs, no more superblack programs, no more early warnings on RFPs, no more awards in close bidding competitions, consistent screwings on the MPCs—my God, they can do it to us! It's a buyer's market! There's only one buyer for space defense systems, and that's the United States Air Force. They've got the power."

Lemon's face twists bitterly as he acknowledges this. "I hate it, but that's the case. We've got to be agreeable, and stand up for our rights when we have to, but without really beating them, see. So Hereford is right, even though I hate to say it. We can't afford to win this one. So we're giving up. The law firm will be called off."

McPherson can barely think. But he remembers something: "What about the investigation in Congress?"

"That's their doing. We won't cooperate any further. It's belly-up time—bare the throat to the top dog, goddamn it." Lemon gets up, goes to the window. "I'm sorry, Mac. Go home, why don't you. Take the rest of the day off."

McPherson finds he is already standing. When did that happen? He's at the door when Lemon says, perhaps to himself, "That's the way the system works."

And then he's out in the hall. In the elevator. In his mouth is a coppery taste, as if he had thrown up, though he feels no nausea. The body's reaction to defeat is a bitterness at the back of the throat. The idea of being "bitter" is another concept taken directly from sensory experience. He knows he is bitter because his throat gags on a coppery taste roiling at the back of his mouth. He's in his office. The whole operation, so neat, so efficient, so *real* looking, is all a sham, a fake. The work done in this office might as well be replaced by the scripts of a video screenplay; it would all come to the same in the end. Engineering, he thinks, isn't real at all. Only the power struggles of certain people in Washington are real, and those battles are based on whims, personal ambitions, personal jealousies. And those battles make the rest of the world unreal. The walls around him might as well be cardboard (thwack! thwack!), the computers empty plastic shells —all parts of a video set, a backdrop to the great battles of the stars in the foreground. He's an extra in those battles, his little scene has been filmed—then the script rewritten, the scene tossed out. His work, tossed out.

He goes home.

72

About the time Dennis is called into Lemon's office to hear the bad news, Jim gets a call from Lucy. "Are you coming up to dinner tonight like you said?"

Oh, man— "Did I say *tonight*?"

"I've made enough for three already. You said you would, and we haven't seen you in weeks."

Uh-oh. That tone in her voice, the ultimate Lucy danger signal. . . .

Very reluctantly Jim says, "Okay."

"And did you visit Uncle Tom like you said you would?"

"Oh, man. No. I forgot."

Now she really is upset. There's something wrong there, up at the folks'. "I didn't go this week because of the funeral," she says, voice strained, "and you didn't go last week when I thought you did—no one's been down there for almost three weeks. Oh, Jim, you get down there today and then you come to dinner, you hear me?"

"Yeah! I hear you." He doesn't want to cross her when she's in this temper, when her voice sounds like that. "I'm on my way. Sorry, I just forgot."

"You don't just forget things like that!"

"All right. I know. I'll see you for dinner."

"Okay."

So he's off to Seizure World, which in his mood is the last place in the world he wants to be, but there he is and in a black mood indeed he slams his car door and goes to the reception desk of the nursing home complex. "Here to see Tom Barnard."

He's sent along. In the hall outside Tom's room a nurse stops him. "Are you here to see Tom?" Accusation in her eyes. "I'm glad someone finally came. He's been having a hard time."

"What's this?" Jim says, alarmed.

Hard glance. "His respiration has gotten a lot worse. I thought he was going into a coma last week."

"What? Why wasn't his family told about it?"

The nurse shrugs, the gaze still hard. "They were."

"The hell they were! I'm his family, and I wasn't told."

Another shrug. "The front desk makes the calls. Don't you have an answering machine?"

"Yes, I do," Jim says sharply, and moves by her to Tom's door. He knocks, gets no answer, hesitates, enters.

Inside it's stuffy, the bedsheets are rumpled. Tom is flat on his back, his breath harsh and labored, his skin gray, his freckled bald pate yellowish.

His eyes slide over in his motionless head to look at Jim. At first there's no recognition, and this sends a stab of fear so far down into Jim that nothing else in the past miserable week bears any comparison to it. Then Tom blinks, he shifts awkwardly on his bed, says, "Jim. Hello." His voice is a dry rasp. "Here. Help me up."

"Oh, man, Tom, are you sure? I mean wouldn't it be better for you if you stayed flat, maybe?" Desperate fear that Tom will overexert himself somehow, die right here in front of him. . . .

"Help me up. I'm not a Q yet, no matter, evidence to the contrary." Tom tries pulling up onto his pillow himself, fails. "Help me, boy."

Jim holds his breath, helps Tom up so that his shoulders are on the pillow and his head leaning against the wall behind the bed. "Let me get the pillow behind your head."

"No. Bends my neck too far forward. Need all the airspace I can get."

"Ah. Okay."

They sit there and look at each other.

"I'm sorry I haven't been by in a while," Jim says. "I—well, I've been busy, Mom's been busy too. I was supposed to come last week but I forgot. I'm really sorry. The nurse says you haven't been feeling well."

"Got a cold. Almost killed me."

"I'm sorry."

"Not your fault. Stupid to die from a cold. So I didn't." Tom chuckles and it makes him cough, all of a sudden he's hacking for breath and Jim, heart pulsing right there in his fingertips, helps him back down onto the bed and turns up his oxygen flow to maximum. Slowly, painfully, Tom regains control of his breathing. He stares up at Jim and again his eyes don't register any recognition.

"It's Jim, Tom."

"How are you, Jim?"

"I'm fine, Tom, fine."

"Little trouble breathing. I'm okay now. The nurses never come when you ring. Once I was dreaming. I flailed out at something. And knocked this oxygen out of my nose. Pain woke me up, my nose was bleeding. Suffocating in here, regular air now and I suffocate. Can you imagine that? So I rang the bell. And they never came. Managed to pick the tube up. Stuck it in my mouth 'cause my nose. Bleeding. Stayed that way ringing the bell. Nurse came at seven when the new shift started. Graveyard shift sleeping. I did that myself, working at the Mobil station. Around three all the work done, no one awake. Whole town quiet and foggy, streetlights blinking red. I'd sleep by the heater under the cash register. Or walk around picking up cigarette butts off the asphalt.''

"When was this, Tom?''

"But when I wake up it's only this room. Do you think they put me in prison for something? I do. Public defender for too long. I've seen too many jails. They all look like this. People are cruel, Jim. How can they do it? How?''

Tom stops, unable to catch his breath anymore, and for a while he only breathes, sucking the air in over and over. Jim holds on to his clammy palm. It seems he has a fever. He rocks his head back and forth restlessly, and when he talks again it's to other people, a whispered outrush of words punctuated by indrawn gasps, incoherent muttering that Jim can't make sense of. Jim can only hold his hand, and rock in the chair with him, feeling like a black iron weight will expand out of his stomach and fill him and topple him over.

The old man looks up at him with a wild expression. "Who are you?''

Jim swallows, looks at the ceiling, back at Tom. "Your great-nephew, Jim. Jim McPherson. Lucy's son.''

"I remember. Sorry. They say the oxygen loss kills brain cells. According to my calculations, my brain is ten times gone.'' He wheezes once to indicate a laugh. "But I may be off by a magnitude.'' Wheezes again. He looks out the window. "It's hard to stay sane, alone with your thoughts.''

"Or in any other situation, these days.''

"That so? Sorry to hear you say that. Me—I try not to think too much anymore. Save what's left. Live in, I don't know. Memory. It's quite a power. What can explain it?''

Jim doesn't know what to say. Nothing explains the memory, as far as he knows. Nothing explains how a mind can cast back through the years, live there, get lost there. . . .

"Tell me another story, Tom. Another story about Orange County.''

Tom squeezes his eyes shut. Face a map of raw red wrinkles in gray skin.

"Ah, what haven't I told you, boy. It's all confused. When I first came to Orange County. The groves were still everywhere. I've told you that." He breathes in and out, in and out, in and out.

"Our first Christmas here there was a Santa Ana wind. And there was a row of big eucalyptus trees behind our house. Our street stuck right into a grove, the first thrust. And the trees squeaked when the Santa Ana blew. And leaves spinning down. Smelled of eucalyptus. And—ah. Oh. It was the night we were supposed to go Christmas caroling. My mom organized it. My mom was a lot like yours, Jim McPherson. Working for people. And mine was a music teacher. So all the kids were gathered, and a few of the parents, and we went around the neighborhood. Singing. Only half the houses in the development were finished. That wax is hot when it drips on your hand. And the wind kept blowing the candles out. It was all we could do to light them. Made shells of aluminum foil. And we sang at every house. Even the house of a Jewish family. My mom had some secular Christmas carol ready, I forget what it was. Funny idea. Where she found these things! But everyone came out and thanked us, and we had cookies and punch afterwards. Because everyone there had just moved out from the Midwest, you see? This was the way it was done. This is what you did to make a place a home. A neighborhood, by God. Because they didn't know! They thought they lived in a neighborhood still. They didn't know everyone would move, people be in and out and in and out—they didn't know they had just moved into a big motel. They thought they were in a neighborhood still. And so they tried. We all tried. My mother tried all her life."

"Mine too."

But Tom doesn't hear, he's off in a dark Santa Ana wind, muttering to himself, to his childhood friends, trying to recall the name of that carol, trying to keep the candles lit.

So they hold hands and look at the wall. And the old man falls asleep.

Jim frees his hand, stands, checks to see that the oxygen line is clear and the tank over half-full. He straightens the sheets the best he can. He looks at Tom's face and then finds he can't look anymore. In fact he has to sit down. He holds his head, squeezes hard, waits for the fit to pass. When it does he hurries out of the place and drives home to dinner.

73

So Jim gets to his parents' home not long after Dennis does.

Dennis is out under their little carport, working on the motor of his car. "Hi, Dad." No answer. Jim's feeling too low for this sort of thing, and he goes into their portion of the house without another word.

Lucy asks about Tom.

"He's had a cold. He's not so well."

Hiss of breath, indrawn. Then she says, "Go out and talk to your father. He needs something to take his mind off work."

"I just said hello and he didn't say a thing."

"Get out there and talk to him!" Fiercely: "He needs to talk to you!"

"All right, all right." Jim sighs, feeling aggrieved, and goes back outside.

His father stands crouched over the motor compartment, head down under the hood, steadfastly ignoring Jim. Ignoring Jim and everything else, Jim thinks. A retreat into his own private world.

Jim approaches him. "What are you working on?"

"The car."

"I know that," Jim snaps.

Dennis glances up briefly at him, turns back to his task.

"Want some help?"

"No."

Jim grits his teeth. Too much has happened; he's lost all tolerance for this sort of treatment. "So what are you working on?" he insists, an edge in his voice.

Dennis doesn't look up this time. "Cleaning the switcher points."

Jim looks into the motor compartment, at Dennis's methodically working hands. "They're already clean."

Dennis doesn't reply.

"You're wasting your time."

Dennis looks at him balefully. "Maybe I ought to work on your car. I don't suppose that would be wasting my time."

"My car doesn't need work."

"Have you done any maintenance on it since I last looked at it?"

"No. I've been too busy."

"Too busy."

"That's right! I've been busy! It isn't just in the defense industry that people get busy, you know."

Dennis purses his mouth. "A lot of night classes, I suppose."

"That's right!" Angrily Jim walks up to the side of the car, so that only the motor compartment and the hood separate him from Dennis. "I've been busy going to the funerals of people we know, and trying to help my friends, and working in a real estate office, and teaching a night class. Teaching, that's right! It's the best thing I do—I teach people what they need to know to get by in the world! It's good work!"

Dennis's swift, smoldering glance shows he understands very clearly the implication of Jim's words. He looks back down at the motor, at his hands and their intensely controlled maneuvers. A minute passes as he finishes cleaning the points.

"So you don't think I do good work, is that it?" he says slowly.

"Dad, people are starving! Half the world is starving!" Jim is almost shaking now, the words burst out of him: "We don't need more bombs!"

Dennis picks up the point casing, places it over the points, takes up a wrench and begins to tighten one of the nuts that holds it to the sidewall.

"Is that all you think I do?" he asks quietly. "Make bombs?"

"Isn't that what you do?"

"No, it isn't. Mostly I make guidance systems."

"It's the same thing!"

"No. It isn't."

"Oh come on, Dad. It's all part of the same thing. Defense! Weapons systems!"

Dennis's jaw is bunched hard. He threads the second nut, begins to tighten it, all very methodically.

"You think we don't need such systems?"

"No, we don't!" Jim has lost all composure, all restraint. "We don't have the slightest need for them!"

"Do you watch the news?"

"Of course I watch the news. We're in several wars, there's a body count every day. And we provide the weapons for those wars. And for a lot of others too."

"So we need some weapons systems."

"To make wars!" Jim cries furiously.

"We don't start the wars by ourselves. We don't make all the weapons, and we don't start all the wars."

"I'm not so sure of that—it's great business!"

"Do you really think that's it?" Surely that nut is tight by now. "That there are people that cynical?"

"I suppose I do, yes. There are a lot of people who only really care about money, about profits."

Abruptly Dennis pulls the wrench off the nut.

"It's not that simple," he says down at the motor, almost as if to himself. "You want it to be that simple, but it isn't. A lot of the world would love to see this country go up in smoke. They work every day to make weapons better than ours. If we stopped—"

"If we stopped they would stop! But what would happen to profits then? The economy would be in terrible trouble. And so it goes on, new weapon after new weapon, for a hundred years!"

"A hundred years without another world war."

"All the little wars add up to a world war. And if they go nuclear it's the end, we'll all be killed! And you're a part of that!"

"Wrong!" *Bang* the wrench hits the underside of the hood as Dennis swings it up, points it at Jim. Behind the wrench Dennis's face is red with anger, he's leaning over the motor compartment, staring at Jim, his face an inch from the hood; and the wrench is shaking. "*You listen to what I do,* boy. I help to make systems

for use in precision electronic warfare. And don't you look at me like they're all the same! If you can't tell the difference between electronic war and the mass nuclear destruction of the world, then you're too stupid to talk to!'' *Bang* he hits the underside of the hood with the wrench. There's a hoarse edge in his voice that Jim has never heard before, and it cuts into Jim so sharply that he takes a step back.

"I can't do a thing about nuclear war, it's out of my hands. Hopefully one will never be fought. But conventional wars will be. And some of those wars could kick off a nuclear one. Easily! So it comes to this—if you can make conventional wars *too difficult to fight*, just on technical grounds alone, then by God you put an end to them! And that lessens the nuclear threat, the main way that we might fall into a nuclear war, in a really significant way!''

"But that's what they've always said, Dad!'' Appalled by this argument, Jim's face twists: "Generation after generation—machine guns, tanks, planes, atomic bombs, now this—they were all supposed to make war impossible, but they don't! They just keep the cycle going!''

"Not impossible. You can't make war impossible, I didn't say that. Nothing can do that. But you can make it *damned* impractical. We're getting to the point where any invasion force can be electronically detected and electronically opposed, so quickly and accurately that the chances of a successful invasion are nil. Nil! So why ever try? *Can't you see?* It could come to a point where no one would try!''

"Maybe they'll just try with nuclear weapons, then! Be sure of it!''

Dennis waves the wrench dismissively, looks at it as if surprised at its presence, puts it down carefully on the top of the sidewall. "That would be crazy. It may happen, sure, but it would be crazy. Nuclear weapons are crazy, I don't have anything to do with them. The only work I do in that regard is to try and stop them. I wish they were gone, and maybe someday they will be, who knows. But to get rid of them we're going to have to have some other sort of deterrent, a less dangerous one. And that's what I work at—making the precise electronic weapons that are the only replacement for the nuclear deterrent. They're our only way out of that.''

"There's no way out," Jim says, despair filling him.

"Maybe not. But I do what I can."

He looks away from Jim, down at the concrete of the driveway.

"But I can only do what I can," he says hoarsely. The corners of his mouth tighten bitterly. "I can't change the way the world is, and neither can you."

"But we can try! If everyone tried—"

"If pigs had wings, they'd fly. Be realistic."

"I *am* being realistic. It's a business, it's using up an immense amount of resources to no purpose. It's corrupt!"

Dennis looks down into the motor compartment, picks up the wrench, turns it over. Inspects it closely. His jaw muscles are bunching rhythmically, he looks like he's having trouble swallowing. Something Jim has said . . .

"Don't you try to tell me about corruption," he says in a low voice. "I know more than you'll ever imagine about that. But that's not the system."

"It is the system, precisely the system!"

Dennis only shakes his head, still staring at the wrench. "The system is there to be used for good or bad. And it's not all that bad. Not by itself."

"But it *is*!" Jim has the sinking feeling you get when you are losing an argument, the feeling that your opponent is using rational arguments while you are relying on the force of emotion; and as people usually do in that situation, Jim ups the emotional gain, goes right to the heart of his case: "Dad, the world is *starving*."

"I *know* that," Dennis says very slowly, very patiently. "The world is on the brink of a catastrophic breakdown. You think I haven't *noticed*?"

He sighs, looks at the motor. "But I've become convinced . . . I think, now, that one of the strongest deterrents to that breakdown is the power of the United States. We can scare a lot of wars away. But up till now most of our scare power has been nuclear, see, and using it would end us all. So little wars keep breaking out because the people who start them know that we won't destroy the whole world to stop them. So if . . . if we could make the deterrent more precise, see—a kind of unstoppable surgical strike that could focus all its destructiveness on invading armies, and only on them—then we could dismantle the nuclear threat. We wouldn't need it because we'd have the deterrent in another form, a safer form.

"So"—he looks up at Jim, looks him right in the eye—"so as far as I'm concerned, I'm doing the work that is most likely to free people from the threat of nuclear war. Now *what*"—voice straining—"what better work could there be?"

He looks away.

"It was a good program."

Jim doesn't know what to say to that. He can see the logic of the argument. And that fearful strain in his father's voice . . . His anger drains out of him, and he's amazed, even frightened, at what he has been saying. They've gone so far beyond the boundaries of their ordinary discourse, there doesn't seem any way back.

And suddenly he recalls his plans for the night: rendezvous with Arthur, assault on Laguna Space Research. He can't stand across from Dennis with that in his mind, it makes him sick with trembling.

Dennis leans against the car, face down, the averted expression as still as stone. He's lost in his own thoughts. His hands are methodically working with the wrench, loosening a nut on the next point casing. Jim tries to say something, and the words catch in his throat. What was it? He can't remember. The silence stretches out, and really there's nothing he can say. Nothing he can say.

"I—I'll go in and tell Mom you're about ready to eat?"

Dennis nods.

Unsteadily Jim walks inside. Lucy is chopping vegetables for the salad, over by the sink, in front of the kitchen window that has the view of the carport. Jim walks over and stands next to her. Through the window he can see Dennis's side and back.

Lucy sniffs, and Jim sees she is red-eyed. "So did he tell you what happened down at work?" she asks, chopping hard and erratically.

"No! What happened?"

"I saw you talking out there. You shouldn't argue with him on a day like today!" She goes to blow her nose.

"Why, what happened?"

"You know they lost that big proposal Dad was working on."

"Sort of, I guess. Weren't they appealing it?"

"Yes. And they were doing pretty well with that, too, until today." And Lucy tells him as much as she knows of it all, pieced together from Dennis's curt, bitter remarks.

"No!" Jim says more than once during the story. "No!"

"Yes. That's what he said." She puts a fist to her mouth. "I don't think I've ever seen him as down as this in my whole life."

"But—but he just stood out there . . . he just stood out there and defended the whole thing! All of it!"

Lucy nods, sniffs, starts chopping vegetables.

Stunned, Jim stares out the window at his father, who is meticulously tightening a nut, as if tamping down the last pieces of a puzzle.

"Mom, I've gotta go."

"What?"

He's already to the front door. Got to get away.

"Jim!"

But he's gone, out the door, almost running. For a moment he can't find his car key. Then he's found it, he's off and away. Tracking away at full speed.

Dennis will think he's left because of their argument. "No!" Jim can barely see the streets, he doesn't know what he's doing, he just tracks for home. Halfway there he goes to manual and tracks to the Newport Freeway. Southbound, under the great concrete ramp of the northbound lanes, in the murky light of the groundlevel world, in the thickets of halogen light. . . . He punches the dashboard, gets off at Edinger to turn back north, then returns to the southbound lanes. Where to go? Where can he go? What can he do? Can he go back up there to dinner with his parents? Eat a meal and then go blow up his father's company? For God's sake!—how could he have gotten to this point?

On he drives. He knows the defense industry is a malignancy making money in the service of death, in the face of suffering, he knows it has to be opposed in every way possible, he knows he is right. And yet still, still, still, still, still. That look on Dennis's face, as he stared down at the immaculate motor of his car. Lucy, looking out the window about to cut her thumb off. "It was a good program." His voice.

Mindlessly Jim tracks north on the San Diego Freeway. But what in the world is there for him in L.A.? He could drive all night, escape. . . . No. He turns east on the Garden Grove Free-way, south on the Newport. Back in the loop, going in circles. Triangles, actually. Furious at that he tracks south into Newport Beach, past the Hungry Crab which makes him feel sick, physically sick. He has fucked up every single aspect of his life, and he's still at it. Going for an utterly clean sweep.

At the very end of the Newport peninsula he gets out of his car, walks out to the jetty. The Wedge isn't breaking tonight, the waves slosh up and down the sand as if the Pacific were a lake.

Someone's got a fire going in a barbecue pit, and yellow light and shadows dance over the dark figures standing around it as the wind whips the flames here and there. It's too dark to walk very far over the giant boulders of the jetty. A part of him wonders why he would want to, anyway. The jetty ends, he would have to return to the world eventually, face up to it.

He returns to his car. For a long time he just sits in it, head on the steering switch. Familiar smell, familiar sight of the dusty cracked dash . . . sometimes it feels like this car is his only home. He's moved a dozen times in the last six years, trying to get more room, better sun, less rent, whatever. Only the car remains con-stant, and the hours spent in it each day. The real home, in autopia; so true. Too true.

Except for his parents' home. Helplessly Jim thinks of it. They moved into the little duplex when Jim was seven. He and his dad played catch in the driveway. One time Jim missed an easy throw and caught it in the eye. They threw balls onto the carport roof and Jim caught them as they rolled off. Dad set up a backboard. He painted an old bike he bought for Jim, painted it red and white. They all went for a trip together, to see the historical museum and the last acres of real orange grove (part of Fairview Cemetery, yes).

The junk of the past, the memory's strange detritus. Why should he remember what he does? And does any of it matter? In a world where the majority of all the people born will starve or be killed in wars, after living degraded lives in cardboard shacks, like animals, like rats struggling hour to hour, meal to meal—do his middle-class suburban Orange County memories matter at all? Should they matter?

It's ten P.M.; Jim has an appointment soon. He clicks the car on, puts it on the track to Arthur Bastanchury's ap.

74

So Jim turns around and tracks back up the freeway. Somewhere over Costa Mesa he decides what to do. "Oh, man." He picks up his car's phone, calls Arthur. His heart stutters at the same frequency as the ringing phone: Br-r-r-r-r-r-ring! Br-r-r-r-r-r-ring!

"Hello?"

"Arthur. It's Jim. I can't make it to your house in time to leave for the rendezvous. I'll meet you there at the parking lot where we get the boxes."

Silence. Curtly Arthur says, "Okay. You know the time."

"Yeah. I'll be there then."

Back onto Newport Freeway, north to Garden Grove Freeway (typing instructions into his carbrain), out west and off at Haster, under the City Mall's upper level.

Dim world of old streets, gutters matted with trash.
Dead trees. Garbage Grove.
Old suburban houses, boarding a family per room.
The streetlights not broken are old halogen: orange gloom,
An orange glaze on it all.
A roofed world. The basement of California.
You've never lived here, have you.

Hyperventilating, Jim looks around him for once. Parking lots, laundromats, thrift shops: "You had to go to Cairo to see this!" he shouts, and for a moment his resolve is confused; he feels like invisible giants are aiming invisible giant firehoses at him, battering him this way and that in a game he knows nothing of; he can only hold to his plan, try not to think anymore. Stop thinking, stop thinking! It's time to act! Still his stomach twists, his heart stutters as he is buffeted about by contrary ideas, contrary certainties about what is right. . . .

Lewis Street is the same as always, a kind of tunnel alley behind the west side of the City Mall, both sides floor to ceiling with warehouses, truck-sized metal doors shut and padlocked for the night.

He reaches Greentree, which dead-ends into Lewis like one sewer pouring into another. The concrete roof overhead holds a few halogen bulbs, a few mercury vapor bulbs. No plan to it. Jim tracks forward slowly, enters the small parking lot set between warehouses, twenty slots set around two massive concrete pylons that support the upper levels of the mall. There's the same car as always, a blue station wagon, on a parking track at the back of the lot.

Jim turns into the lot, flicks his headlights on and off three times. He stops his car beside the station wagon, gets out.

Four men surround him, pinning him against his car. He's seen all of the faces before, and they recognize him too. "Where's Arthur?" the tallest black guy says.

"He'll be here in a few minutes," Jim says. "Meanwhile let's get the equipment into my car. We can't use Arthur's tonight, and as soon as he shows up he wants us out of here."

The man nods, and Jim swallows. No turning back.

He follows the four men to the back of the station wagon, and the hatchback is pulled up with an airy hiss. In the dark orange shadows Jim can just make out the six plastic boxes. He picks up one in his turn; it's heavier than he remembered. Steps awkwardly to his car. "Backseat," he says, and onto the shabby cracking vinyl they go, five in the backseat, one on the passenger seat.

Jim shuts the door of his car, checks his watch. It's ten till eleven. Arthur will be here soon. He leans in the driver's window and pushes the button that activates the program he typed in on the way up the freeway. The four men don't notice. Jim returns to the station wagon.

"Big load tonight," says the man who spoke before.

"Big job to do."

"Yeah?"

"You'll see it in the papers."

"I'm sure."

Jim paces around the two cars nervously. Twice he walks out to Lewis and looks up and down the long tunnel street. Several warehouses down, in a gap between buildings, there is an infrequently used entrance to the mall; Jim noticed it on one of their earlier runs. It looks almost like a service entrance, but it's not.

The four men are standing around the station wagon, watching him with boredom, amusement, whatever. Jim is thankful it makes sense to act nervously, because he's not sure he could stop it. In fact he feels like throwing up, his whole body is hammering with his pulse, he can't even breathe without a great effort. Still time to—

Headlights, approaching. Jim looks at his watch. It's time, it's time, adrenaline spikes up through him: "Hey!" he calls to the men. "Police coming!"

And his car jerks forward on its own, out of the parking lot and down Lewis to the south, accelerating as fast as it can. Jim takes off running north, toward the little back entrance to the mall.

Up the entrance steps, almost tripping; he's scared out of his mind! Into the mall maze, up to concourse level, then up a broad, gentle staircase to mezzanine; once there there are ten directions he can run in, and he takes off with only a single glance back.

Two of the men are chasing him.

Jim runs full speed through the crowd of shoppers, skipping and dodging desperately to avoid knots of people, open airshafts, planters, fountains, hall displays and food stands. Up a short escalator three steps at a time, around the big open space filled by the laser fountain. Looking down and across he can see his pursuers, already lost. Then one spots him and they're off running again. They're in a tough position, trying to chase someone in a mall; if Jim had more mall experience he'd lose them in a second. As it is he's lost himself. Floors and half floors, escalators and staircases extending everywhere in the broken, refracted space . . . shops are going out of business every day because shoppers can't ever find the same place twice; what chance for two men pursuing a panic-stricken, very mobile individual? It's a three-D maze, and

Jim has only to run a random pattern, trending westward, and he's lost them.

Or so Jim thinks, fearfully, as he runs. But when he reaches the east side of the mall and flies through the entryway doors, damned if the two men aren't coming up an escalator back there, at full speed!

Outside, however, on the street bordering the parking lot, he sees his car, which has made it there on its own. Good programming. He runs out to where it sits by the curb, noticing only at the last second the three policemen approaching to inspect it.

Panic on top of panic; Jim's systems almost blow out at the sight, but his pursuers are in the parking lot now and there's no time to lose. Without thinking he runs up to the car and shouts at the policemen, "It's mine! They're robbing me, they dragged me out of the car and now they're chasing me!"

The three policemen regard him carefully, then look as he points at the two men, running across the parking lot. "That's them!"

The two men see what's happening, and quickly turn and run back inside. Perfect.

But there's Arthur and the other two suppliers, tracking up in Arthur's car, stuck in the traffic on the street. Jim says quickly, "There's the rest of them in that car there! Quick, right there! Yeah!"

And he points. And Arthur sees him pointing.

Arthur ignores the policemen flagging him down and shifts to the fast track. This gets the cops' attention, and two of them hustle off to their truck, parked behind Jim's car. The third appears to be staying behind, and he's looking into Jim's car curiously.

Jim says, "There's the others again, Officer!" and points at the east doors of the mall. While the policeman peers in that direction Jim yanks open his car's door, leaps in and jams the accelerator to the floor. The car jerks away over the right track, leaving the policeman shouting behind him.

Jim makes a sharp right on Chapman, because ahead of him on the City Avenue, the police truck is in hot pursuit of Arthur and his two companions. Arthur . . . .

Jim tracks onto the Santa Ana Freeway south. He's free of

all pursuit, as far as he can tell. His reaction is to feel acutely sick to his stomach. He might even throw up in his car. And that look on Arthur's face, as he saw Jim pointing him out to the police . . . "No, no! That isn't what I meant! . . . ."

Nothing for it now. Arthur will very likely be picked up, with the two suppliers. But will the police have any reason for holding them? Jim has no idea. He only knows he's in a car with six boxes of felony-level weaponry, and the police likely have his license plate number. And he's just betrayed a friend to the police, for no reason. No reason? My God, he can't tell! He has the feeling that he has, in fact, betrayed everyone he knows, in one way or another.

He checks the rearview mirror nervously, looking for CHP, local police, sheriffs, state troopers—who knows what they'll send after industrial saboteurs? He catches sight of his unshaven face, the expression of sick fear on it. And suddenly he's furious, he slams his fist against the dash, filled with disgust for himself. "Coward. Traitor. Fucking idiot!" Unleashed at last, all the directionless angers pour out at once, in fists flailing the dash, in incoherent, sobbing curses. "You know—you know—what should—be done—and you—can't—*do it!*"

All control gone, he remembers the cargo he has and tracks like a madman to South Coast Plaza. He jams to a halt in an open-air parking lot across from SCP's administrative tower, jumps out of his car, tears open the box on the passenger seat, pulls out a Harris Mosquito missile with its Styx-90 payload. There among scattered parked cars he glues the little missile base to the concrete and aims it at the dark windows of the tower. He sets the firing mechanism, clicks it on. The missile suddenly gives out a loud *whoosh* of flame and disappears. Up in the administrative tower a window breaks, and there's a tinkle of glass, a tinny little alarm sounding. Jim hoots, drives away.

Up into Santa Ana, to the office of First American Title Insurance and Real Estate. It's dark, no one is there. Another missile set in the parking lot, aimed at the main doors; it'll melt every computer in there, every file. He'll be out of a job! He laughs hysterically as he sets the mechanism and turns it on. This time the missile breaks a big plate-glass window, and the alarms are howlers.

In the distance there are sirens. What else can he knock out?

The Orange County Board of Supervisors, yeah, the crowd that has systematically helped real estate developers to cut OC up, in over a hundred years of mismanagement and graft. Down under the Triangle to the old Santa Ana Civic Center. It's dark there too, he can set up his Mosquito without any danger. Click the firing mechanism over and the little skyrocketlike thing will fly in there and knock the whole corrupt administration of the county apart. So he does it and laughs like mad.

Who else? He can't think. Something has snapped in him, and he can't seem to think at all.

There's a closed Fluffy Donuts; why not?

Another real estate office; why not?

One of the Irvine military microchip factories; why not?

In fact, he's close to Laguna Space Research. And he's crazy enough with anger now to want to punish them for his betrayals, made for their sake. They deserve a warning shot, they should know how close they came to destruction. Give them a scare.

And then they'll know to look out, to be on guard.

As confused in his action as in his thinking, Jim gets lost in a Muddy Canyon condomundo, but when he comes out of it he's at an elementary school on the edge of a canyon, and across the canyon is LSR. He unboxes two Mosquitos and carries them out to a soccer field overlooking the canyon. Sets them up, aims them both for the big LAGUNA SPACE RESEARCH signs at the entrance to the plant. He clicks over the firing mechanism and hustles back to the car.

Just a couple left. He blasts two more dark real estate offices in Tustin.

Only the boxes left, now; he throws them out on the Santa Ana Freeway, watches traffic back up behind him. Back onto the streets in Tustin, his breath catching in his throat, in ragged, hysterical sobs. Redhill Mall mocks all his efforts, even when he gets out and throws stones at its windows. They're shatterproof and the stones bounce away. He can't make OC go away, not with his idiot vandalism, not even by going crazy. It's everywhere, it fills all realities, even the insane ones. Especially those. He can't escape.

He drives home, still mindless with rage and disgust. His ap maddens him, he rushes to the bookcase and pulls it over, watches it crunch the CD system under it. He kicks the books around, but they're too indestructible and he moves on to his computer. A hard left and the screen is cracked, maybe a knuckle too. "Stupid asshole." He goes and gets a frying pan to complete the job. Crack! Crack! Crack! On to the disks. Each one crunched is a couple thousand pages of his utterly useless writing gone for good—thank God! Drawers of printed copy, not that much of it, and it's easy to rip in fourths and scatter around like confetti. What else? CDs, he can frypan all his mix-and-match symphonies to plastic smithereens, reassemble the scattered pieces and finally get the random mishmash the method deserves. What else? A sketch of Hana's, ripped in half. Orange crate labels, smashed and torn apart. The room's beginning to look pretty good. What else?

Into the bedroom. First the video system, he can bring those cameras down and smash them to pieces. And the maps! He leaps up, catches the upper edge of one of the big Thomas Brothers maps, rips it down. It tears with a long, dry sound. The other maps come down as well, he ends up sitting in a pile of ripped map sections, tearing them into ever-smaller fragments, blinded by tears.

Suddenly he hears a car pull up and stop on the street out front. Right in front of his ap. Police? Arthur and his friends? Panic surges into Jim's mindless rage again, and he wiggles out the little bedroom window, across the yard filled with dumpsters. It occurs to him that Arthur and his friends might want to trash his ap in revenge for his betrayal, and at the thought he doubles over laughing. Won't they get a surprise? Meanwhile he continues through the applex, staggering, giggling madly, bent over the hard knot of his stomach. . . .

No problem losing pursuit in such a warren. The boxes we live in! he thinks. The boxes! Okay, he's out on Prospect, they'll never find him. Police cars are cruising, heading down toward Tustin and the scene of his attacks. Busy night, hey Officer? Jim feels an urge to run out into the street and shout "I did it! I did it!" He actually finds his feet on the track when fear jumps him and he hauls ass back into the dark between streetlights, shivering uncontrollably. Are those people on foot, back there? That's not normal, he has to run again. Can't go back for his car, no public transport, can't reach anywhere on foot. He laughs hard, tries hitchhiking. Turn right down Hewes. He gives up hitchhiking, no one ever picks up hitchhikers, and besides where is he going? He jogs down Hewes to 17th, gasping. Over into Tustin, onto Newport, then Redhill. A couple of times he stops to pick up good stones, and then throws them through the windows of real estate offices that he passes. He almost tries a bank but remembers all the alarms. By now he must have tripped off a score of lesser alarms, are the computers tracking his course this very moment, predicting the moves that he is helplessly jerking through?

People passing in cars stare at him: pedestrians are suspicious. He needs a car. Cut off from his car he is immobilized, helpless. Where can he go? Can he really be here, doing this? Is he really in this situation? He seizes an abandoned hubcap, frisbees it into the window of a Jack-in-the-Box. A beautiful flight, although the window only cracks. But it's like hitting a beehive; employees and customers pour out and in a second are after him. He takes off running into the applex behind him, threads his way silently through it. He stumbles over a bicycle, picks it up with every intention of stealing it and pedaling off, gives up and drops it when he sees the Mickey Mouse face, staring at him from between the handlebars.

Back on Redhill, farther south, he sees a bus. Incredible! He jumps on it, pays, and off they go. Only one other passenger, an old woman.

He stays on all the way to Fashion Island, trying vainly to catch proper hold of his breathing. The more time he has to think, the angrier he gets at himself. So that I'll go out and do something even stupider! he thinks. Which will make me angrier, which will make me do something even more stupid! . . . Hopping out at Fashion Island he goes immediately to a Japanese plastic bonsai garden with some real, and truly fine, rocks in it. Rocks like shot puts. After pulling some of the plastic trees apart he picks up these rocks, and has one big one in each hand as he approaches the Bullock's and I. Magnin's. Huge display windows, showing off rooms that could house a hundred poor people for five hundred years. All there to display rack after chrome rack of rainbow-colored clothes. He takes aim and is about to let fly with both of them at once, when there is a grunt of surprise from behind him, and he is grabbed up and lifted into the air.

He struggles like a berserker, swings the rocks back viciously, where they clack together and fall out of his hands; he kicks, wriggles, hisses—

"Hey, Jim, lay off! Relax!"

It's Tashi.

75

Jim relaxes. In fact, when Tashi lets him down and lets go of him, he almost falls. When he recovers from the little blackout he tries to pick up one of the rocks and heave it at the I. Magnin's, but Tashi stops him. Tash takes the two rocks, underhands them back into the shredded garden. "For Christ's sake, Jim! What in the world is wrong?"

Jim sits down and starts to shake. Tash crouches beside him. He can't seem to breathe right anymore. He's hurt something inside, every breath spikes pain through him. "I—I—" He can't talk.

Tash puts a hand on his shoulder. "Just relax. It's okay now."

"It's not! It's not!" The hysteria floods back. . . . "It's not!"

"Okay, okay. Relax. Are you in trouble?"

Jim nods.

"Okay. Let's go up to my place, then, and get you out of sight. Come on." He helps him up.

They walk uphill, along the lit sidewalks through the dark of Newport Heights, and reach Tashi's tower. A police car hums by, and Jim cowers. Tash shakes his head: "What in the hell has happened?"

Up on Tashi's roof Jim manages to stutter out part of the story.

"Your breathing is all fucked up," Tash observes. "Here, lid some of this." He gets him to lid some California Mello. Then Tash stands in front of his big tent and thinks it over.

"Well," he says, "I was planning on taking a farewell trip anyway. And it sounds like you should get out of town for a while. Here, just sit down, Jim. Sit down! Now, I'm going to stuff another sleeping bag, and get you a pack packed. We'll have to buy more food in Lone Pine in the morning. You just sit there."

Jim sits there. It's possible he couldn't do anything else.

An hour later Tash has them packed. He puts one compact backpack over Jim's shoulders, picks up another for himself, and they're off. They descend to Tashi's little car, get onto the freeway.

Jim, in the passenger seat, stares at the lightflood of red/white, white/red. Autopia courses by. Slowly, millimeter by millimeter, his stomach begins to unknot. His breathing gets better. Somewhere north of L.A. he jerks convulsively, shudders.

"My God, you won't believe what I did tonight."

"No lie."

Jim tries to tell it. Over and over Tashi exclaims "Why? But why?"

And over and over Jim says, "I don't know! I don't know."

When he finishes they are on an empty dark road, up on the high desert northeast of L.A. Jim, shivering lightly, jerking upright from time to time, falls into a restless sleep.

76

(And meanwhile, out at sea, a small boat is drifting onshore, rising and falling on a small swell, coming ever closer to the short bluff at Reef Point. Then as it nears the reefs searchlights burst into being, their glare blinds everyone around, the black water sparkles, the heavy boom of a shot blasts the air, reverberates—

A warning shot only. But the two men obey the voice hammering over the loudspeakers, they stand hands overhead, eyes terrified, looking like the figures in the Goya sketch of insurgents executed by soldiers under a tree—)

77

When Jim wakes they are tracking through the Alabama Hills in the Owens Valley. The oldest rocks in North America look strange in this hour before dawn, rounded boulders piled on each other in weird, impossible formations. Beyond them the eastern escarpment of the Sierra Nevada rises like a black wall under the indigo sky. Tashi sits in the driver's seat listening to Japanese space music, a flute wandering over Oriental harp twanging; he looks awake, but lost in some inner realm.

In the roadside town of Independence, which looks like a museum of the previous century, Tashi rouses. "We need more food." They stop at an all-night place and buy some ramen, cheese, candy. Outside Tash goes to a phone box and closes himself in for a call. It really is like a museum. When he comes out he is nodding thoughtfully, a little smile on his face. "Let's go."

They turn west, up a road that heads straight into the mountains. "Here comes the tricky part," Tash says. "We only have a wilderness permit for one, so we'll have to take evasive action on the way in."

"You have to get a permit to go into the mountains?"

"Oh yeah. You can get them at Ticketron." Tash laughs at Jim's expression. "It's not a bad idea, actually. But sometimes it's not practical."

So they track up the immense slope of the range's eastern face, following a crease made over eons by a lively stream. Tashi's car slows on the steep road. They leave behind the shrubs and flowers of the Owens Valley, track up among pines. Their ears pop. They follow a series of bends in the road, lose sight of the valley below. The air rushing in Tashi's window gets cooler.

They come to a dirt road that forks down to the stream on their left. Tashi stops, drives the car off the track, hums down the dirt road on battery power. "Fishing spot," he says. "And still outside the park boundary."

They put the extra food in the backpacks, put the packs on, and walk up the asphalt road. It's getting light, the sky is sky blue and soon the sun will rise. The road flattens and Jim sees a parking lot and some buildings, surrounded on three sides by steep mountain slopes. "Where do we go?"

"That's the ranger station. We're supposed to check in there, and real soon a couple of rangers will be out on the trails to make sure we have. There's another one stationed in Kearsarge Pass, which is the main pass here, right up on top." He points west. "So we're going north, and we'll get over the crest of the range on a cross-country pass I know."

"Okay." It sounds good to Jim; he doesn't know what a cross-country pass is.

They hike around the parking lot and into a forest of pines and firs. The ground is layered with fragrant brown needles. The sun is shining on the slopes above them, though they are still in shadow. They reach a fork in the trail and head up a canyon to the north.

They hike beside a stream that chuckles down drop after drop. "L.A.'s water," Tashi says with a laugh. Scrub jays and finches flit around the junipers and the little scraps of meadow bordering the stream. Each turn of the trail brings a new prospect, a waterfall garden or jagged granite cliff. The sun rises over a shoulder to the east, and the air warms. Despite the rubbing of his boots against his heels, Jim feels a small trickle of calmness begin to pour into him and pool. The cool air is piney, the stream exquisite, the bare rock above grand.

They ascend into a small bowl where the stream becomes a little lake. Jim stands admiring it openmouthed. "It's beautiful. Are we staying here?"

"It's seven A.M., Jim!"

"Oh yeah."

They hike on, up a rocky trail that rises steeply to the east.
It's hard work. Eventually they reach the rock-and-moss shore of
another surrealistically perfect pond.

"Golden Trout Lake. Elevation ten thousand eight hundred
feet."

Suddenly Jim understands that they're at the end of the trail,
at the bottom of a bowl that has only one exit, which is the
streambed they have just ascended. "So we're staying here?"

"Nope." Tash points above, to the west, where the crest of
the Sierra Nevada looms over them. "Dragon Pass is up there.
We go over that."

"But where's the trail?"

"It's a cross-country pass."

It all comes clear to Jim. "You mean this so-called pass of
yours has no trail over it?"

"Right."

"Whoah. Oh, man. . . ."

They put on their packs, begin hiking up the slope. In the
morning sun it gets hot. Jim suspects the tweaks from each heel
indicate blisters. The straps of his pack cut into his shoulders. He
follows Tashi up a twisting trough that Tash explains was once a
glacier's bed. They are in the realm of rock now, rock shattered
and shattered again, in places almost to gravel. Occasionally they
stop to rest and look around. Back to the east they can see the
Owens Valley, and the White Mountains beyond.

Then it's up again. Jim steps in Tashi's elongated footprints
and avoids sliding back as far as Tash does. He concentrates on
the work. How obvious that this endless upward struggle is the
perfect analogy for life. Two steps up, one step back. Finding a
best path, up through loose broken granite, stained in places by
lichen of many colors, light green, yellow, red, black. The goal
above seems close but never gets closer. Yes, it is a very pure,
very stripped-down model of life—life reduced to stark, expansive
significance. Higher and higher. The sky overhead is dark blue,
the sun a blinding chip in it.

They keep climbing. The repetition of steps up, each with its
small tweak from the heels, reduces Jim's mind to a little point,
receiving only visual input and the kinetics of feeling. His thighs
feel like rubber bands. Once it occurs to him that for the last half

hour he has thought of nothing at all, except the rock under him. He grins; then he has to concentrate on a slippery section. Sweat gets in his eye. There's no wind, no sound except their shoes on the rock, their breaths in their throats.

"We're almost there," Tashi says. Jim looks up, surprised, and sees they are on the last slope below the ridge, the edge of the range with all its towers extending left to right above them, for as far as they can see. They're headed for a flat section between towers. "How do you feel?"

"Great," says Jim.

"Good man. The altitude bothers some people."

"I love it."

On they climb. Jim gets summit fever and hurries after Tashi until his breaths rasp in his throat. Tashi must have it too. Then they're on top of the ridge, on a very rough, broad saddle, made of big shards of pinkish granite. The ridge is a kind of road running north–south, punctuated frequently by big towers, serrated knife-edge sections, spur ridges running down to east, out to west. . . . To the west it's mountains for as far as they can see.

"My God," Jim says.

"Let's have lunch here." Tashi drops his pack, pulls off his shirt to dry the sweaty back of it in the sun. There is still no wind, not a cloud in the sky. "Perfect Sierra day."

They sit and eat. Under them the world turns. Sun warms them like lizards on rock. Jim cuts his thumb trying to slice cheese, and sucks the cut till it stops bleeding.

When they're done they put on the packs and start down the western side of the ridge. This side is steeper, but Tashi finds a steep chute of broken rock—talus, he teaches Jim to call it—and very slowly they descend, holding on to the rock wall on the side of the chute, stepping on chunks that threaten to slide out from under them. In fact Jim sends one past the disgusted Tashi and sits down hard, bruising his butt. His toes blister in the descent. The chute opens up and the talus fans down a lessened slope to a small glacial pond, entirely rockbound: aquamarine around its perimeter, cobalt in its center.

They drink deeply from this lake when they finally reach it. It's mid- or late afternoon already. "Next lake down is a beauty," says Tash. "Bigger than this one, and surrounded by rock walls, except there's a couple of little lawns tucked right on the water. Great campsite.''

"Good.'' Jim's tired.

The west side of the range has a great magic to it. On the east side they looked down into Owens Valley, and so back to the world Jim knows. Now that link is gone and he's in a new world, without connection to the one Tashi yanked him from. He can't characterize this landscape yet, it's too new, but there's something in its complexity, the anarchic profusion of forms, that is mesmerizing to watch. Nothing has been planned. Nevertheless it is all very complex. No two things are the same. And yet everything has an intense coherence.

Clouds loft over the great eastern range. They descend, crossing a very rough field of lichen-splotched boulders. Mosses fill cracks, mosses and then tiny shrubs. Cloud shadows rush over them. Jim wanders off parallel to Tashi so he can find his own route. For a long time they navigate the immensity of broken granite, each in his own world of thought and movement. Already it seems like they have been doing this for a long time. Nothing but this, for as long as the rock has rested here.

Late in the afternoon they come to the next lake, already deep in the shadow of the spur ridge circling it. Its smooth surface reflects the rock like a blue mirror.

"Whoah. Beautiful.''

Tashi's eyes are narrowed.

"Uh-oh. We can't camp here—there's *people* over there!''

"Where?''

Tashi points. Jim sees two tiny red dots, all the way on the other side of the lake. Slightly larger dot of an orange tent. "So what? We'll never hear them, they won't bother us.''

Tashi stares at Jim as if he has just proposed eating shit. "No way! Come on, let's follow the exit stream down toward Dragon Lake. There's bound to be a good campsite before that, and if not it's a fine lake.''

Wearily Jim humps his pack and follows Tashi down the crease in the rib that holds the lake in, where water gurgles over flat yellow granite and carves a ravine in the slope falling off into a big basin.

They hike until sunset. The sky is still light, but the ground and the air around them are dim and shadowed. Alpine flowers gleam hallucinogenically from the black moss on the stream's flat banks. Gnarled junipers contort out of cracks in the rock. Each bend in the little stream reveals a miniature work of landscaping that makes Jim shake his head: above the velvet blue sky, below the dark rock world, with the stream a sky-colored band of lightness cutting through it. He's tired, footsore, he stumbles from time to time; but Tash is walking slowly, and it seems a shame to stop and end this endless display of mountain grandeur.

Finally Tash finds a flat sandy dip in a granite bench beside the stream, and he declares it camp. They drop their packs.

Four or five junipers.
To the west they can see a long way;
A fin of granite, poking up out of shadows.
"Fin Dome," Tashi says.
To the east the great crest of the ridge they crossed is
    glowing,
Vibrant apricot in the late sunset light.
Each rock picked out, illuminated.
Each moment, long and quiet.
The stream's small voice talks on and on.
Light blue water in the massy shadows.
Two tiny figures, walking aimlessly:
"Whoah. Whoah. Whoah."
Slowly the light leaks out of the air.
And you have always lived here.

"How about dinner?" says Tashi. And he sits by his pack.

"Sure. Are we going to build a fire? There's dead wood under these junipers."

"Let's just use the stove. There really isn't enough wood in the Sierras to justify making fires, at least at this altitude."

They cook Japanese noodles over a small gas stove. Somehow Jim manages to knock the pot over when cooking his, and when he grabs the pot to save his noodles from spilling, he burns the palm and fingers of his left hand. "Ah!" Sucks on them. "Oh well."

Tashi has brought a tent along, but it's such a fine night they decide to forgo it, and they lay their sleeping bags on groundpads spread in the sandy patches. They get in the bags and—ah!—lie down.

The moon, hidden by the ridge to the east, still lights the wild array of peaks surrounding them, providing a monochrome sense of distance, and an infinity of shadows. The stream is noisy. Stars are dumped all across the sky; Jim has never seen so many, didn't know so many existed. They outnumber the satellites and mirrors by a good deal.

Soon Tashi is asleep, breathing peacefully.

But Jim can't sleep.

He abandons the attempt, sits up with his bag pulled around his shoulders, and . . . watches. For a moment his past life, his life below, occurs to him; but his mind shies away from it. Up here his mind refuses to enter the mad realm of OC. He can't think of it.

Rocks. The dark masses of the junipers, black needles spiking against the stars. Moonlight on steep serrated slopes, revealing their shapes. Ah, Jim—Jim doesn't know what to think. His body is aching, stinging, and throbbing in a dozen places. All that seems part of mountains, one component of the scene. His senses hum, he's almost dizzy with the attempt to really take it in all at once: the music of falling water and wind in pine needles, the vast and amazingly complex vision of the stippled white granite in the foreground, the moonlit peaks at every distance. . . . He doesn't know what to think. There's no way he can take it all in, he only shivers at the attempt. There's too much.

But he has all night; he can watch, and listen, and watch some more. . . . He realizes with a flush in his nerve endings, with a strange, physical rapture, that this will be the longest night of his life. Each moment, long and quiet, spent discovering a world he never knew existed—a home. He had thought it a lost dream; but this is California too, just as real as the rock underneath his sore butt. He raps the granite with scraped knuckles. Soon the moon will rise over the range.

78

Stewart Lemon is visited by Donald Hereford, out from New York early on the morning after Jim's rampage. Hereford steps out of the helicopter that has brought him over from John Wayne, and walks out from under the spinning blades without even the suggestion of a stoop or a run. He looks over at the physical plant that he and Lemon inspected together not more than two weeks before.

"What happened?" he says to Lemon.

Lemon clears his throat. "An assault was made, I guess, but something went wrong with it. No one knows why. They got the sign at the entrance to the parking garage. And—and we caught a pair in a boat offshore, but they didn't have anything on them, so . . . ."

Feeling silly, Lemon walks Hereford from the helipad around the physical plant to the car entrance to the complex. There six round metal poles stick out of two hardened puddles of blue plastic. They're the signs that used to announce LAGUNA SPACE RESEARCH to the cars passing by. Ludicrous.

Two FBI analysts are at work at the site, and they pause to speak briefly with Hereford and Lemon. "Appears it was a couple of the Mosquitoes that they've been using around here. Made by Harris, and carrying a load of Styx-ninety."

Hereford makes a *tkh* sound with tongue and roof of mouth, kneels to touch the deformed plastic. He leads Lemon away from the FBI agents, around the building and out in the open ground near the helipad.

"So." His mouth is a tight, grim line. "That's that."

"Maybe they'll try again?"

Brusque shake of the head.

Lemon feels his fear as a kind of tingling in his fingers.

"Couldn't we somehow . . . stimulate another attack?"

Hereford stares. "Stimulate? Or simulate?" He laughs shortly. "No. The point is, we've been warned. So now it's our responsibility to see it doesn't happen again. If it does, it will look like we let it. So."

Lemon swallows. "So what happens now?"

"It's already happening. I've given instructions for the Ball Lightning program to be moved to our Florida plant and given to a new team. The Air Force is going to descend on us next month no matter what we do, but hopefully we can indicate to them that we have already acknowledged the problem in the production schedule and taken steps to rectify it."

Lemon hopes that his face doesn't look as hot as it feels. "It's not just a problem in the production schedule—"

"I know that."

"The Air Force will know it too."

"I'm aware of that." Hereford's glance is very, very cold. "At this point I don't have a whole lot of options left, do I? Your team has given me a program that could very easily do a Big Hacksaw on us. In fact I would bet now that that's what will happen, no matter what I do. But I still have to take all the last twists I can. It's possible that the ballistic missile defense problems that everyone else is having will camouflage us. You never know."

"So what do I do with my team here?" Lemon demands.

"Fire them." Calmly Hereford looks at him. "Lay off the production unit. Shift the best engineers somewhere else, if there's room for them."

"And the executive team?"

Hereford's gaze never wavers. "Fire them. We're clearing house, remember? We have to make sure the Air Force sees that we're serious. Do the usual things, forced retirements, layoffs, whatever it takes. But do it."

"All right. All right." Lemon thinks fast. "McPherson's gone—he's been in charge of the technical side of Ball Lightning for the last few months, and anyway, after the Stormbee fiasco our Andrews friends will be happy to see him go, no doubt. But Dan Houston, now . . . Houston's a useful fellow. . . .''

In the face of Hereford's baleful stare Lemon can't continue. He begins to understand how Hereford got so high so fast. There's a ruthlessness there that Lemon has never even come close to. . . .

Finally Hereford says, ''Houston too. All of them. And do it fast.''

And then, as he turns to go back to the waiting helicopter: ''You're lucky you aren't going with them.''

79

Early that afternoon Dennis McPherson finds out that he is forcibly retired. Dismissed. Fired. The news comes in a freshly printed and stiffly worded letter from Lemon. He's given two months' notice, of course, but given his accumulated vacation time and sick leave—and since there's nothing left to work on, as someone else is overseeing the transfer of the Ball Lightning program to the Florida plant—which is a meaningless and in fact stupid maneuver, as far as McPherson can tell—well . . . Nothing to keep him here. Nothing at all.

He makes sure with a quick calculation of his vacation days on the desk calculator. Nope. In fact they owe him a few days. But after twenty-seven years of work here, what does it matter?

Numbly he orders up a box and packs his few personal possessions from the office into it. He gives the box to his secretary Karen to mail to him. She's been crying. He smiles briefly at her, too distracted by his own thoughts to respond adequately. She tells him that Dan Houston has been dismissed too. ''Ach,'' he says. That on top of everything else; bad for Dan. ''I think I'll go home now,'' he says to the office wall.

The quick, shocked automatism of his actions gives him one moment of satisfaction; he's on his way out when Lemon steps out of the elevator and says, "Dennis, let me talk to you," with that automatic boss-assumption in his hoarse voice, the assumption that people will always do as he says. And without a glance back McPherson keeps on walking, out the door and down the stairs to the parking garage.

Driving out he doesn't even notice the melted company sign at the entrance.

Automatic pilot home, as on so many other days of his life. It's impossible to believe this is the last one. Traffic is a lot better this time of day. The only real clog is at the Laguna Freeway-Santa Ana Freeway interchange. On the way up Redhill the streets look empty and wrongly lit, like a bad movie set of the city. Same with Morningside, and his house.

Lucy is out. At the church. Dennis sits down at the kitchen table. Funny how not once during the struggle for the Stormbee program did it occur to him that he was fighting for his job. He thought he was only fighting for the program. . . .

He sits at the kitchen table and looks dully at the salt and pepper shakers. He's numb; he even knows he's numb. But that's how he feels. Just go with your feelings, Lucy always says. Fine. Time to get behind some deep shock, here. Dive full into numbness.

It was nice the way he was able to walk out on Lemon at last. Just like he always wanted to. What could they possibly have in mind moving the Ball Lightning program to Florida? It'll just screw up the work they were doing on the phased array; and if they had gotten that working right—

But no. He laughs shortly. A habit of mind. Working on the problems at home, in reveries around this table.

What will he think about now?

He solves the problem by not thinking anything.

Lucy comes home. He tells her about it. She sits down abruptly.

He glances up from the table, gives her a look: well? That's that—nothing to be done. She reaches across the table and puts her hand on his. Amazing how extensive the private language of an old married couple can be.

"You'll get another job."

"Uhn." That hadn't occurred to him, but now he doubts it.

It's not a track record that is likely to impress the defense industry too much.

Lucy hears the negative in his grunt and goes to the sink. Blows her nose. She's upset.

She comes back, says brightly, "We should go up to our land by Eureka. It would do you good to get away. And we haven't seen that land since the year it burned. Maybe it's time to build that cabin you talk about."

"The church?"

"I can get Helena to fill in for me. It would be fun to have a vacation." She is sincere about this; she loves to travel. "We might as well make what good we can out of the opportunity. Things will work out."

"I'll think about it." Meaning, don't pester me about it right now.

And so she doesn't. She begins making dinner. Dennis watches her work. Things will work out. Well, he's still got Lucy. That's not going to change. Poor Dan Houston. She's all sniffly. He almost grins; she hates the idea of that cabin on the coast of northern California, away from all her friends. It's always been his idea. Build a cabin all by himself, do it right. There must be churches up there, she'd have new friends inside a week. And he—well, it doesn't matter. He doesn't have any friends down here, does he? None to speak of, anyway—a colleague or two, most of them long gone to different companies, out of his life. "I should call Dan Houston." So it wouldn't make any difference, being up near Eureka. He loved that tree-covered sweep of rocky coastline, its bare empty salt reaches.

"We could visit, anyway," he says. "It's too late in the year to start building. But we could pick the site, and look around a bit."

"That's right," Lucy says, looking steadfastly into the refrigerator. "We could make a real vacation of it. Drive up the coast all the way."

"Stop at Carmel, first night."

"I like that place."

"I know."

Fondness wells up in him like some sort of . . . like a spasm of grief. As he comes out of the numbness his feelings are jumbled.

He doesn't know exactly what he feels. But there is this woman here, his wife, whom he can count on to always, always, always put the best face on things. No matter the effort it costs her. Always. He doesn't deserve her, he thinks. But there she is. He almost laughs.

She glances at him cautiously, smiles briefly. Maybe she can sense what he's feeling. She goes to work at the counter by the stove. A sort of artificial industriousness there, it reminds him of LSR. Ach, forget it. Forget it. Twenty-seven years.

As Lucy is serving the hot casserole, the phone rings.

She answers it, says hesitantly, "Yes, he's here."

She gives the phone to Dennis with a frightened look.

"Hello?"

"Dennis, this is Ernie Klusinski." One of Dennis's long-lost colleague friends, now working for Aerojet in La Habra.

"Oh hi, Ernie. How are you?" Unnatural heartiness to his voice, he can tell.

"Fine. Listen, Dennis, we've heard over here about what happened at LSR today, and I was wondering if you wanted to come up and have lunch with me and my boss Sonja Adding, to sort of talk things over. Look into possibilities, you know, and see if you're at all interested in what we're doing here." Pause. "If you're interested, of course."

"Oh I'm interested," Dennis says, thinking fast. "Yeah, that's real nice of you, Ernie, I appreciate it. Uh, one thing though"—he pauses, decides—"Lucy and I were thinking of taking a vacation up the coast. Given the opportunity, you know." Ernie laughs at this feeble jest. "So maybe we can do it when I get back?"

"Oh sure, sure! No problem with that. Just give me a ring when you get back, and we'll set it up. I've told Sonja about you, and she wants to meet you."

"Yeah. That'd be nice. Thanks, Ernie."

They hang up.

Still thinking hard, Dennis returns to the table. Stares at his plate, the casserole steaming gently.

"That was Ernie Klusinski?"

"Yeah, it was." It's been a strange day.

"And what did he want?"

Dennis gives her a lopsided grin. "He was head-hunting. Word has gotten around I was let go, and Ernie's boss is interested in talking to me. Maybe hiring me."

"But that's wonderful!"

"Maybe. Aerojet has got those ground-based lasers, phase six of the BMD—I'd hate to get mixed up in that again."

"Me too."

"It's a goddamned waste of time!" He shakes his head, returns to the topic at hand. "But they're big, they have a lot of things going. If I could get into the right department . . ."

"You can find that out when you talk to them."

"Yeah. But . . ." How to say it? He doesn't understand it himself. "I don't know . . . I don't know if I want to get back into it! It'll just be more of the same. More of the same."

He doesn't know what he feels. It's nice to be wanted, real nice. But at the same time he feels a kind of despair, he feels trapped—this is his life, his work, he'll never escape it. It'll never end.

"You can figure that out after you talk to them."

"Yeah. Oh. I told him we'd be off on vacation for a while."

"I heard that." Lucy smiles.

Dennis shrugs. "It would be good to see our property." He eats for a while, stops. Taps his fork on the table. "It's been a strange day."

That night they pack their suitcases and prepare the house, in a pre-trip ritual thirty years old. Dennis's thoughts are scattered and confused, his feelings slide about from disbelief to hurt to fury to numbness to bitter humor to a kind of breathless anticipation, a feeling of freedom. He doesn't have to take the job at Aerojet, if it comes to that. On the other hand he can. Nothing's certain anymore. Anything can happen. And he'll never have to deal with Ball Lightning again; he never has to listen to Stewart Lemon boss him around, ever again. Hard to believe.

"Well, I should call Dan Houston."

Reluctantly he does it, and is more relieved than anything else to get an answering machine. He leaves a short message suggesting that they get together when he returns, and hangs up thoughtfully. Poor Dan, where is he tonight?

Lucy calls up Jim. No answer. And his answering machine

isn't turned on. "I'm worried about him," she says, nervously packing a suitcase.

"Leave a note on the kitchen screen. He'll see it when he comes over."

"Okay." She closes the suitcase. "I wish I knew . . . what was wrong with him."

"*He* doesn't even know what's wrong with him," Dennis says. He's still annoyed with Jim for leaving before dinner, the previous night. It hurt Lucy's feelings. And it was a stupid argument; Dennis is surprised he ever let himself say as much as he did, especially to someone who doesn't know enough to understand. Although he *should* understand! He should. Well—his son is a problem. A mystery. "Let's not worry about him tonight."

"All right."

Dennis loads the car trunk. As they go to bed Lucy says, "Do you think you'll take this other job?"

"We'll see when we get back."

And the next morning, at 5:00 A.M., their traditional hour of departure, they back out of the driveway and track down to the Santa Ana Freeway, and they turn north, and they leave Orange County.

80

By the time Tashi and Jim return to Tashi's car, three days later, Jim is a wreck. He has several big blisters, three badly burned fingertips, a cut thumb, a bruised butt, a badly scratched leg, a knee locked stiff by some unfelt twist, a torn arch muscle in his left foot, deeply sun-cracked lips, and a radically sunburnt nose. He has also stabbed himself in the face with a tent pole, almost poking out his eye; and he tried to change the stove canister by candlelight, thereby briefly blowing himself up and melting off his eyelashes, his beard stubble, and the hair on his wrists.

So, Jim is no Boy Scout. But he is happy. Body a wreck, mind at ease. At least temporarily. He's discovered a new country, and it will always be there for him. Both physically, just up the freeway, and mentally, in a country in his mind, a place that he has discovered along with the mountains themselves. It will always be back there somewhere.

He moans as they reach the car and throw their packs in the back, he moans as Tashi drives the car up the dirt road to the track, and heads down; he moans as he sits in the passenger seat. But in truth, he feels fine. Even the prospect of returning to OC can't subdue him; he has new resources to deal with OC, and a new resolve.

"We should get Sandy to come up here with us," he says to Tashi. "I'm sure he'd love it too."

"He used to come up with me," Tash says. "Too busy now. And . . ." He makes a funny moue with his mouth. "We'll have to see how Sandy is doing when he gets back. He should be out on bail, I guess."

"What?"

"Well, see . . ." And Tashi tells him about the aphrodisiac run, the stashing of the goods at the bottom of the bluff below LSR. "So with LSR's security tightened, the drugs were stuck there, see. So, apparently the attack you guys were going to make on Laguna Space was supposed to serve as a distraction that would cover Sandy while he snuck in by sea and recovered the stash."

"*What?* Oh my God—"

"Calm down, calm down. He's all right. I called Angela the next morning when we stopped for food, to find out what had happened. Sandy was caught by LSR's security forces, and turned over to the police. No problem."

"No problem! Jesus!"

"No problem. Being nabbed by cops isn't the worst thing that could happen. I was worried that he might have gotten hurt. He easily could have been shot, you know."

That idea is enough to stun Jim into complete silence.

"It's okay," Tash says after a while.

"Jesus," says Jim. "I didn't know! I mean, why didn't Sandy tell me!"

"I don't know. But then what would you have done, anyway?" Jim gulps, speechless.

"Since Sandy's okay, it's probably better you didn't know."

"Oh, man. . . . First Arthur, and now Sandy. . . ."

"Yeah." Tash laughs. "You changed a lot of people's plans, that night. But that's okay."

And they track on south. Jim's mind is filled again with OC problems, he can't escape them. That's what it means to go back; it'll be damned hard to keep even a shred of the calm he felt in the Sierras. He could lose that new country he discovered, and he knows it.

Tash, too, gets quieter as they approach home. On they drive, in silence.

In the evening they track over Cajon Pass and down through the condomundo hills to the great urban basin. L.A., City of Light. The great interchange where 5 meets 101, 210 and 10 looks utterly unreal to them, a vision from another planet, one entirely covered by a city millions of years old.

Soon they're back in OC, where the vision at least has familiarity to temper their new astonishment. They know this alien landscape, it's their home. The home of their exile from the world they have so briefly visited.

Tashi drops Jim off at his ap.

"Thanks," Jim says. "That was . . ."

"That's okay." Tash rouses from the reverie he has been in throughout southern California. "It was fun." He sticks out a hand, unusual gesture for him, and Jim shakes it. "Come and see me."

"Of course!"

"Good-bye, then." Off he goes.

Jim's alone, on his street. He goes into his ap. It's a wreck too; he and his home are of a piece. Same as always. He observes the detritus of his hysteria, his madness, with a certain equanimity, tinged with . . . remorse, nostalgia; he can't tell. It's not a happy sight.

Over piles of junk, the trashed bookcase and the broken CDs and disks, to the bathroom. He strips. His dirty body is surely dinged up. He steps in the shower, turns it on hot. Pleasure and stinging pain mix in equal proportions, and he hops about singing:

Swimming in the amniotic fluid of love
Swimming like a finger to the end of the glove
When I reach the end I'm going to dive right in
I'm the sperm in the egg: did I lose? did I win?

Gingerly he dries off, gingerly he crawls into bed. Sheets are such a luxury. He's home again. He doesn't know what that means exactly, anymore. But here he is.

He spends the next day down at Trabuco Junior College, arranging next semester's classes, and then back home, cleaning up. A lot of his stuff has been wrecked beyond saving. He'll have to build up the music collection again from scratch. Same with the computer files. Well, he didn't lose much of value in the files anyway.

The wall maps, now; that's a real shame. He can't really afford to replace them. Carefully he takes the tatters off the walls, lays each map in turn facedown on the floor, tapes up all the rips, flattens them as best he can. Puts them back up.

Well, they look a little strange: rumpled, with tear marks evident. As if some paper earthquake has devastated the paper landscape, three times over no less, a recurrent disaster patched up again and again. Well . . . that sounds about right, actually. A map is the representation of a landscape, after all, and many landscapes, like OC's, are principally psychic. Besides, there isn't anything else he can do about it.

He then wanders the living room gathering the torn paper scattered around the desk. This heap of scraps represents the sum total of his writing efforts. Seeing them ripped apart, he feels bad. The stuff on OC's history didn't really deserve this. Well . . . it's all still here, in the pile somewhere. He begins to inspect each piece of paper, spreading them over the couch in a new order, until all the fragments have been reunited. He tapes the pages together as he did the maps. After that he reads them, throws away everything except the historical pieces. Other than those, he will start from scratch.

When he's done with that job he gets out the vacuum cleaner and sucks the dust up from everywhere the thing can reach. Sponge and cleanser, dust rag, paper towels and window cleaner, laundry whitener for spots on the walls . . . he goes at it furiously, as if he were on a hallucinogen and had conceived a distaste for clutter and dirt, seeing it in smaller and smaller quantities. Music from his little kitchen radio, luckily overlooked in the purge, helps to power him; the latest by Three Spoons and a Stupid Fork:

> You are a carbrain
> You're firmly on track
> You're given your directions
> And you don't talk back
> You're very simply programmed
> And you don't have much to say
> And you're gonna have a breakdown
> It'll happen some day.

"Well fuck you!" Jim sings at the radio, and continues the song on his own: "And after the breakdown, the carbrain can see, cleaning all his programs, so he can be free. . . ."

Yes, there must be an *order* established; nothing fetishistic, but just a certain pattern, symbolic of an internal coherence that is as yet undefined. He's struggling to find a new pattern, working with the same old materials. . . .

All his poor abused books are on the couch. Stupid to attack them like that. Luckily most were just thrown around. He props up the bookcase of bricks and boards, starts to reshelve them. Is the alphabet really a significant principle for ordering books? Let's try putting them back arbitrarily, and see what comes of it. Make a new order.

Finally he's done. The late afternoon sun ducks under the freeway, slants in the open window. Door open, shoo out all the dust motes with a cross breeze. The place actually looks neat! Jim carries the accumulated trash out to the dumpster, comes back. He carries out the busted-up bedroom video system, throws it away too. "Enough of the image." He comes back in and finds himself surprised. It's not a bad ap, at least at this time of the day, of the year.

He makes himself a dinner of scrambled eggs. Then he calls Hana. No answer, no answering machine. Damn. He calls his parents. Their answering machine is on, which surprises him. It's not a Friday evening; where are they? They usually only turn on the machine when they leave town.

There's nothing to do at home, so after a while he drives over to check it out.

No one home, that's right. A note from Lucy is on the kitchen screen.

"Jim—Dad's been laid off at work—we've gone up to Eureka to visit our place—please water plants in family room etc.—we'll be back in two weeks."

Laid off! But there's no lack of work at LSR!

Confused, Jim wanders his childhood home aimlessly. What could have happened?

It's odd, seeing the place this empty. As if all of them have gone for good.

Why did they fire him? "Bastards! I should have let them melt you down! I should have helped them do it!"

But if he had, then his father just as certainly would have been fired, wouldn't he? Jim can't see how the destruction of the plant in Laguna Hills would have made it any likelier that LSR would have kept his father on; in fact, the reverse seems more likely. He doesn't really know.

Jim stands in the hallway, where he can see every room of the little duplex, the rooms where so much of his life has been acted out. Now just empty little rooms, mocking him with their silence and stillness. "What happened?" He recalls Dennis's face as he looked over the opened motor compartment of the car, Dennis holding to his beliefs with a dogged tenacity. . . .

Jim leaves, feeling aimless and empty. I'm back, he thinks, I'm ready to start up in a new way. Begin a new life. But how?

It's just the same old materials at hand. . . . How do you start a
new life when everything else is the same?

81

He tracks down to Sandy's, refusing even to look at South Coast
Plaza.

Sandy's door opens and it's quiet inside. Angela's there. "Oh
hi, Jim."

"Hi Angela. Is Sandy—is Sandy okay?"

"Oh yeah." Angela leads him into the kitchen, which seems
odd, so quiet and empty. "He's fine. He's gone down to Miami
to visit his father."

"I just heard from Tashi what happened the other night.
We've been up in the mountains since then or I would've been by
sooner. I'm really, really sorry—"

Angela puts a hand on his arm to stop him. "Don't worry
about it, Jim. It wasn't your fault. Tash told me what you did,
and to tell you the truth, I'm glad you did it. In fact I'm proud of
you. Sandy's all right, after all. And he'll be back in a few days
and everything will be back to normal."

"But I heard he got arrested?"

"It doesn't matter. They can't make any of the charges stick.
Arrests by security cops don't mean much to the courts. Sandy
and Bob said they were just boating out there, and there was nothing
to indicate they weren't. Really, don't worry about it."

"Well . . ."

Angela sits him down, comforts him in typical Angela style:
"Sandy wasn't even to shore when they caught him. It was pretty
scary, he said, because they fired a warning shot to stop him, and
then they had submachine guns aimed at him and all. And he spent
a couple days in jail. But nothing's going to come of it, we hope.

Sandy may have to quit dealing for a while. Maybe for good. That's my opinion." She smiles a little.

Jim asks about Arthur.

"He's disappeared. No one knows where he's gone or what's happened to him. I'm not sure I care, either." Apparently she blames Arthur for getting all of them involved with the sabotage/drug rescue attempt at LSR; although, Jim thinks, that's not exactly right. For a moment she looks bleak, and all of a sudden Jim sees that her cheerfulness is forced. Optimism is not a biochemical accident, he thinks; it's a policy, you have to work at it. "That was damned stupid, what he was doing," she says, "and he was using you, too. You should have known better."

"I guess." They were being used to cover a drug run, after all; what can he say? And in the earlier attacks . . . was that all there was to it? "But . . . no, I think Arthur believed in what we were doing. I don't think he was doing it for money or whatever—he really wanted to make a change. I mean, we have to resist somehow! We can't just give in to the way things are, can we?"

"I don't know." Angela shrugs. "I mean we should try to change things, sure. But there must be ways that are less dangerous, less harmful."

Jim isn't so sure. And after they sit in silence for a while, thinking about it, he leaves.

On the freeway, feeling low. How could he have guessed that sabotaging the sabotage would get Sandy in such trouble? Not to mention Arthur! And what, in the end, did he and Arthur accomplish? Were they resisting the system, or only part of it?

He wonders if anything can ever be done purely or simply. Apparently not. Every action takes place in such a network of circumstances. . . . How to decide what to do? How to know how to act?

He drives by Arthur's ap in Fountain Valley. Into the complex, up black wood stairs with their beige stucco sidewalls, along the narrow corridor past ap after ap. Number 344 is Arthur's. No one answers his knock: it's empty. Jim stands before the window and looks at the sun-bleached drapes. That visionary tension in Arthur, the excitement of action . . . he had believed in what he was doing. No matter what the connection with Raymond was. Jim is certain of it. And he finds he is still in agreement with Arthur; something has to be done, there are forces in the country that have to be resisted. It's only a question of method. "I'm sorry, Arthur," he says aloud. "I hope you're okay. I hope you keep working at it. And I'll do the same."

Walking back to his car he adds, "Somehow." And realizes that keeping this promise will be one of the most difficult projects he will ever give himself. Since both Arthur and his father are "right"—and at one and the same time!—he is going to have to find his own way, somewhere between or outside them—find some way that cannot be co-opted into the great war machine, some way that will actually help to change the thinking of America.

It's late, but he decides to drive down to Tashi's place, to discuss things. He needs to talk.

He takes the elevator up the tower, steps out onto the roof. It's empty. The tent is gone.

"What the hell?"

What is *happening*? he thinks. Where is everyone *going*? He walks around the rooftop as if its empty concrete can give a clue to Tashi's whereabouts. Even the vegetable tubs are gone.

Below him sparkle the lights of Newport Beach and Corona del Mar. Somewhere someone's playing a sax, or maybe it's just a recording. Sad hoarse sax notes, bending down through minor thirds. Jim stands on the edge of the roof, looking out over the freeways and condos to the black sea. Catalina looks like an overlit sea liner, cruising off on the black horizon. Tashi. . . .

*   *   *

After an insomniac night on the living room couch, Jim calls Abe. "Hey, Abe, what happened to Tashi?"

"He left for Alaska yesterday." Long puase. "Didn't he say good-bye to you?"

"No!" Jim remembers their parting after the drive back. "I suppose he thinks so. Damn."

"Maybe you were out when he called."

"Maybe."

"So how did you like the mountains?"

"They were great. I want to tell you about it—you going to be home today?"

"No, I'm going to work soon."

"Ah."

Long silence. Jim says, "How's Xavier?"

"Hanging in there." Another silence.

But maybe Abe hears something in it. "Tell you what, Jim, I'll call you tomorrow, see if you're still up for getting together. We've got to plan a celebration for when Sandy comes back, anyway. As long as nothing happens to his dad."

"Yeah, okay. Good. You do that. And good luck today."

"Thanks."

Jim tracks by First American Title Insurance and Real Estate Company, just because he can't think of anything to do and old habits are leading him around.

Humphrey is out front, looking morosely at the construction crew that is cleaning up the inside of the building. It's a mess in there—it resembles fire damage, although it isn't black. They've got most of it cleaned.

"They blew it away," Humphrey tells him. "Someone blasted it with a bomb filled with a solvent that dissolved everything in there. They got a whole bunch of real estate companies, the same night."

"Oh," Jim says awkwardly. "I hadn't heard. I was up in the mountains with Tashi."

"Yeah. They got all my files and everything else." He shakes his head bleakly. "Ambank has already pulled out of the Pourva Tower project because of the delays, they said. I just think they're scared, but whatever. It doesn't matter. The project is a goner."

"I'm sorry, Humph," Jim says. "Real sorry." And the part of him that would have been pleased at this unexpected turn—something good coming out of his madness, after all—has gone away. Seeing the expression on Humphrey's face it has vanished, at least for the moment, from existence. "I'm sorry."

"That's all right," Humphrey says, looking puzzled. "It wasn't your fault."

"Uh-huh. Still, you know. I'm sorry."

All these apologies. And he's going to have to give Sheila Mayer a call sometime, and apologize to her too. He groans at the thought. But he's going to have to do it.

So Jim spends the afternoon pacing his little living room. He stares at his books. He's much too restless to read. To be on his own, by himself—not today, though! Not today. He calls Hana again. No answer, no answering machine. "Come on, Hana, answer your phone!" But he can't even tell her that.

Okay. Here he is. He's alone, on his own, in his own home. What should he do? He thinks aloud: "When you change your life, when you're a carbrain suddenly free of the car, off the track, what do you do? You don't have the slightest idea. What do you do if you don't have a plan? You make a plan. You make the best plan you can."

Okay. He's wandering the living room, making a plan. He walks around aimlessly. He's lonely. He wants to be with his friends—the shields between him and his self, perhaps. But they're all gone now, scattered by some force that Jim feels, obscurely, that he initiated; his bad faith started it all. . . . But no, no. That's magical thinking. In reality he has had hardly any effect on anything. Or so it seems. But which is right? Did he really do it, did he really somehow scatter everyone away?

He doesn't know.

Okay. Enough agonizing over the past. Here he is. He's free, he and he only chooses what he will do. What will he do?

He will pace. And mourn Tashi's departure. And rail bitterly against . . . himself. He can't escape the magical thinking, he knows that it has somehow been all his fault. He's lonely. Will he be able to adapt to this kind of solitude, does he have the self-reliance necessary?

But think of Tom's solitude. My God! Uncle Tom!

He should go see Tom.

He runs out to the car and tracks down to Seizure World.

On the way he feels foolish, he is sure it's obvious to everyone else on the freeway that he is doing something utterly bizarre in order to prove to himself that he is changing his life, when in reality it's all the same as before. But what else can he do? How else do it?

Then as he drives through the gates he becomes worried; Tom was awfully sick when he last dropped by, anything can happen when you're that old, and sick like he was. He runs from the parking lot to the front desk.

But Tom is still alive, and in fact he is doing much better, thanks. He's sitting up in his bed, looking out the window and reading a big book.

"How are you, boy?" He sounds much better, too.

"Fine, Tom. And you?"

"Much better, thanks. Healthier than in a long time."

"Good, good. Hey Tom, I went to the mountains!"

"Did you! The Sierras? Aren't they beautiful? Where'd you go?"

Jim tells him, and it turns out Tom has been in that region. They talk about it for half an hour.

"Tom," Jim says at last, "why didn't you tell me? Why didn't you tell me about it and make me go up there?"

"I did! Wait just a minute here! I told you all the time! But you thought it was stupid. Bucolic reactionary pastoral escapism, you called it. Mushrooms on the dead log of Nature, you said."

That was something Jim read once. "Damn my reading!"

Tom squints. "Actually, I'm reading a great book here. On early Orange County, the ranchero days. Like listen to this—when the rancheros wanted to get their cowhides from San Juan Capistrano to the Yankee trading ships off Dana Point, they took them to the top of Dana Point bluff, at low tide when the beach was really wide, and just tossed them over the side! Big cowhides thrown off a cliff like frisbees, flapping down through the air to land out there on the beach. Nice, eh?"

"Yes," Jim says. "It's a a lovely image."

They talk a while longer about the book. Then a nurse comes by to shoo Jim away—visiting hours are over for a while.

"Jail's closed, boy. Come back when you can."

"I will, Tom. Soon."

Okay. That's one stop, one step. That's something that will become part of the new life. All his moaning about the death of community, when the materials for it lay all around him, available anytime he wanted to put the necessary work into it. . . . Ah, well.

Okay. What else? Restlessly Jim tracks home, starts pacing again. He tries calling Hana, gets no answer. And no machine. Damn it, she's got to be home sometime!

What to do. No question of sleep, it's early evening and again this isn't a night for it, he can tell. His head is too full. As a seasoned insomniac he knows there isn't a chance.

He stops by his desk. Everything neatly in place, the torn-up and taped-together OC pages on top at one corner. He picks them up, starts to read through them.

As he does, the actual words on the page disappear, and he sees not OC's past but the last few weeks. His own past. Each painful step on the path that got him here. Then he reads again, and the anguish of his own experience infuses the sentences, fills the county's short and depressing history of exploitation and loss. Dreams have ended before, here.

Okay. He's a poet, a writer. Therefore he writes. Therefore he sits down, takes up a sheet of paper, a ballpoint pen.

There's a moment in OC's past that he's avoided writing about, he never noticed it before and at first he thinks it's just a coincidence; but then, as he considers it, it seems to him that it has been more than that. It is, in fact, the central moment, the hinge point in the story when it changed for good. He's been afraid to write it down.

He chews the end of the pen to white plastic shards. Puts it to paper and writes. Time passes.

82

This is the chapter I have not been able to write.

Through the 1950s and 1960s the groves were torn down at the rate of several acres every day. The orchard keepers and their trees had fought off a variety of blights in previous years— the cottony cushion scale, the black scale, the red scale, the "quick decline"—but they had never faced this sort of blight before, and the decline this time was quicker than ever. In these years they harvested not the fruit, but the trees.

This is how they did it.

Gangs of men came in with trucks and equipment. First they cut the trees down with chain saws. This was the simple part, the work of a minute. Thirty seconds, actually: one quick downward bite, the chain saw pulled out, one quick upward bit.

The trees fall.

Chains and ropes are tossed over the fallen branches, and electric reels haul them over to big dumpsters. Men with smaller chain saws cut the fallen trees into parts, and the parts are fed into an automatic shredder that hums constantly, whines and shrieks when branches are fed into it. Wood chips are all that come out.

Leaves and broken oranges are scattered over the torn ground. There is a tangy, dusty citrus smell in the air; the dust that is part of the bark of these trees has been scattered to the sky.

The stumps are harder. A backhoelike tractor is brought to the stump. The ground around the stump is spaded, churned up, softened. Chains are secured around the trunk, right at ground level, or even beneath it, around the biggest root exposed. Then the tractor backs off, jerks. Gears grind, the diesel engine grunts and hums, black fumes shoot out the exhaust pipe at the sky. In jerks the stump heaves out of the ground. The root systems are not very big, nor do they extend very deeply. Still, when the whole thing is hauled away to the waiting dumpsters, there is a considerable crater left behind.

The eucalyptus trees are harder. Bringing the trees down is still relatively easy; several strokes of a giant chain saw, with ropes tied around the tree to bring it down in the desired direction. But then the trunk has to be sawed into big sections, like loggers' work, and the immense cylinders are lifted by bulldozers and small cranes onto the backs of waiting trucks. And the stumps are more stubborn; roots have to be cut away, some digging done, before the tractors can succeed in yanking them up. The eucalyptus have been planted so close together that the roots have intertwined, and it's safest to bring down only every third tree, then start on the ones left. The pungent dusty smell of the eucalyptus tends to overpower the citrus scent of the orange trees. The sap gums up the chain saws. It's hard work.

Across the grove, where the trees are already gone, and the craters bulldozed away, surveyors have set out stakes with red strips of plastic tied in bows around their tops. These guide the men at the cement mixers, the big trucks whose contents grumble as their barrels spin. They will be pouring foundations for the new tract houses before the last trees are pulled out.

Now it's the end of a short November day. Early 1960s. The sun is low, and the shadows of the remaining eucalyptus in the west wall—one in every three—fall across the remains of the grove. There are nothing but craters left, today; craters, and stacks of wood by the dumpsters. The backhoes and tractors and bulldozers are all in a yellow row, still as dinosaurs. Cars pass by. The men whose work is done for the day have congregated by the canteen truck, open on one side, displaying evening snacks of burritos and triangular sandwiches in clear plastic boxes. Some of the men have gotten bottles of beer out of their pickups, and the *click pop hiss* of bottles opening mingles with their quiet talk. Cars pass by. The distant hum of the Newport Freeway washes over them with the wind. Eucalyptus leaves fall from the trees still standing.

Out in the craters, far from the men at the canteen truck, some children are playing. Young boys, using the craters as fox-holes to play some simple war game. The craters are new, they're exciting, they show what orange roots look like, something the boys have always been curious about. Cars pass by. The shadows lengthen. One of the boys wanders off alone. Tire tracks in the torn dirt lead his gaze to one of the cement mixers, still emitting its slushy grumble. He sits down to look at it, openmouthed. Cars pass by. The other boys tire of their game and go home to dinner, each to his own house. The men around the trucks finish their beers and their stories, and they get into their pickup trucks—thunk! thunk!—and drive off. A couple of supervisors walk around the dirt lot, planning the next day's work. They stop by a stack of wood next to the shredder. It's quiet, you can hear the freeway in the distance. A single boy sits on a crater's edge, staring off at the distance. Cars pass by. Eucalyptus leaves spin-nerdrift to the ground. The sun disappears. The day is done, and shadows are falling

across our empty field.

83

When Jim is done, he types a fair copy into the computer. Prints it up. He sticks it in with the taped-up pages. No, those poor tape-up jobs won't do. He types them all into the computer again, filling them out, revising them. Then he prints up new copies of each. There we go. Orange County. He never was much of a one for titles. Call it *Torn Maps*, why not.

Much of the night has passed. Jim gets up stiffly, hobbles

out to look around. Four A.M.; the freeways at its quietest. After a bit he goes back inside, and holds the newly printed pages in his hands. It's not a big book, nor a great one; but it's his. His, and the land's. And the people who lived here through all the years; it's theirs too, in a way. They all did their best to make a home of the place—those of them who weren't actively doing their best to parcel and sell it off, anyway. And even them . . . Jim laughs. Clearly he'll never be able to resolve his ambivalence regarding his hometown, and the generations who made it. Impossible to separate out the good from the bad, the heroic from the tawdry.

Okay, what next? Light-headed, Jim wanders his home again, the pages clutched in his hand. What should he do? He isn't sure. It's awful, having one's habits shattered, having to make one's life up from scratch; you have to invent it all moment to moment, and it's hard!

He eats some potato chips, cleans up the kitchen. He sits down at his little Formica kitchen table; and briefly, head down on his pages, he naps.

While he's asleep, crouched uncomfortably over the table, he dreams. There's an elevated freeway on the cliff by the edge of the sea, and in the cars tracking slowly along are all his friends and family. They have a map of Orange County, and they're tearing it into pieces. His father, Hana, Tom, Tashi, Abe, his mom, Sandy and Angela . . . Jim, down on the beach, cries out at them to stop tearing the map; no one hears him. And the pieces of the map are jigsaw puzzle pieces, big as family-sized pizzas, pale pastel in color, and all his family take these pieces and spin them out into the air like frisbees, till they stall and tumble down onto a beach as wide as the world. And Jim runs to gather them up, hard work in the loose sand, which sparkles with gems; and then he's on the beach, trying to put together this big puzzle before the tide comes in—

He starts awake.

He gets up; he has a plan. He'll track up the Santiago Freeway to Modjeska Canyon and Hana's house, with his pages, and he'll sit down under the eucalyptus trees on the lawn outside her white garage, and he'll wait there till she comes out or comes home. And then he'll make her read the pages, make her see . . . whatever she'll see. And from there . . . well, whatever. That's as far as he can plan. That's his plan.

He goes to the bathroom, quick brushes his teeth and hair, pees, goes out to the car. It's still dark! Four-thirty A.M., oh well. No time like the present. And he gets in his car and tracks onto the freeway, in his haste punching the wrong program and getting on in the wrong direction. It takes a while to get turned around. The freeway is almost empty: tracks gleaming under the moon, the lightshow at its absolute minimum, a coolness to the humming air. He gets off the freeway onto Chapman Avenue, down the empty street under flashing yellow stoplights, past the dark parking lots and shopping centers and the dark Fluffy Donuts place that stands over the ruins of El Modena Elementary School, past the Quaker church and up into the dark hills. Then onto the Santiago Freeway, under the blue mercury vapor lights, the blue-white concrete flowing under him, the dark hillsides spangled with streetlights like stars, a smell of sage in the air rushing by the window. And he comes to Hana's exit and takes the offramp, down in a big concrete curve, down and down to the embrace of the hills, the touch of the earth. Any minute he'll be there.

ACKNOWLEDGMENTS

Some of my friends and family gave me a lot of help with various aspects of this book. I'd like to thank Terry Baier, Daryl Bonin, Brian Carlisle, Donald and Nancy Crosby, Patrick Delahunt, Robert Franko, Charles R. Ill, Beth Meacham, Lisa Nowell, Linda Rogas, and Victor Salerno.

A special thanks to Steve Bixler and Larry Huhn; and to my parents.